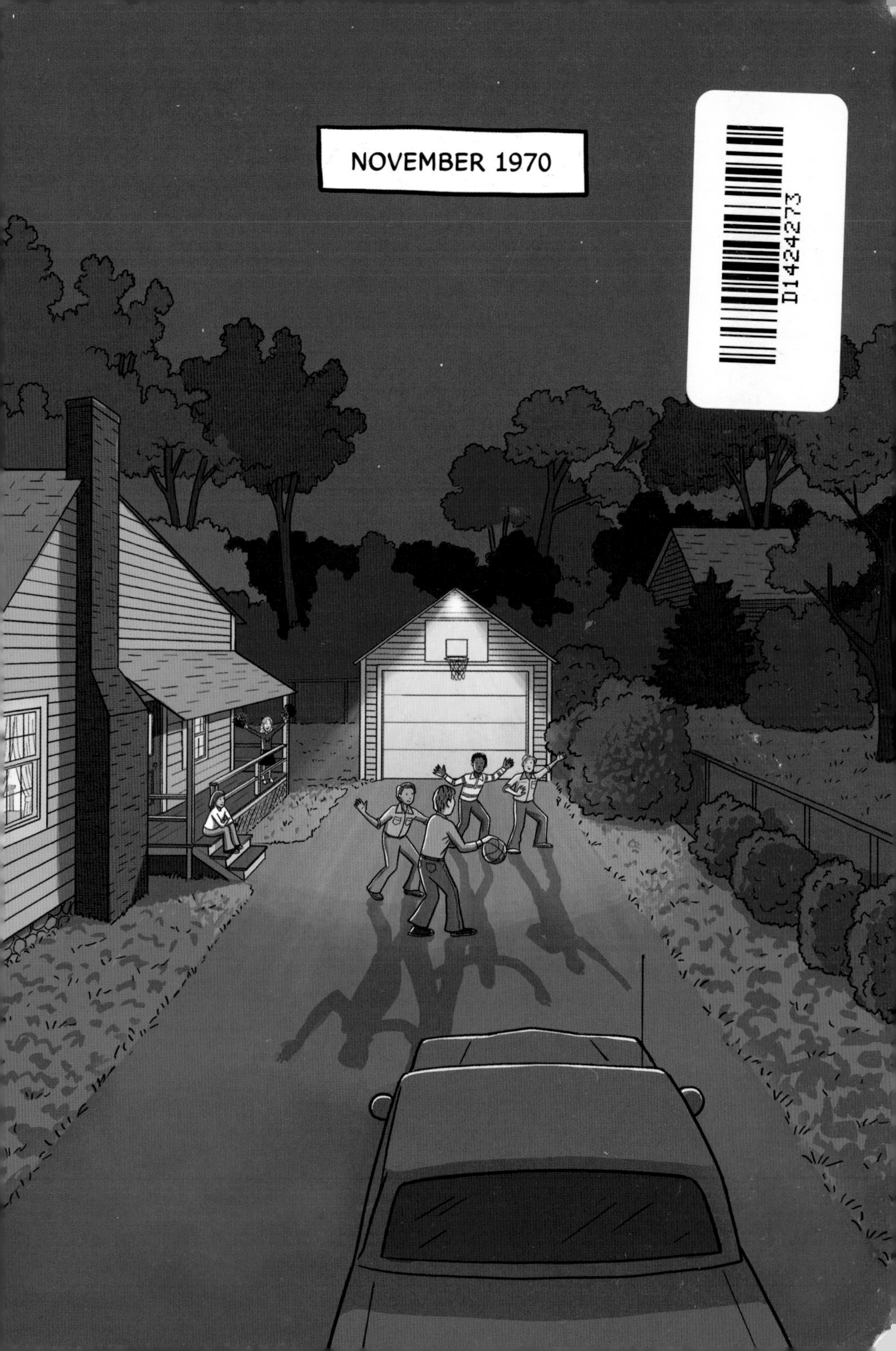
NOVEMBER 1970

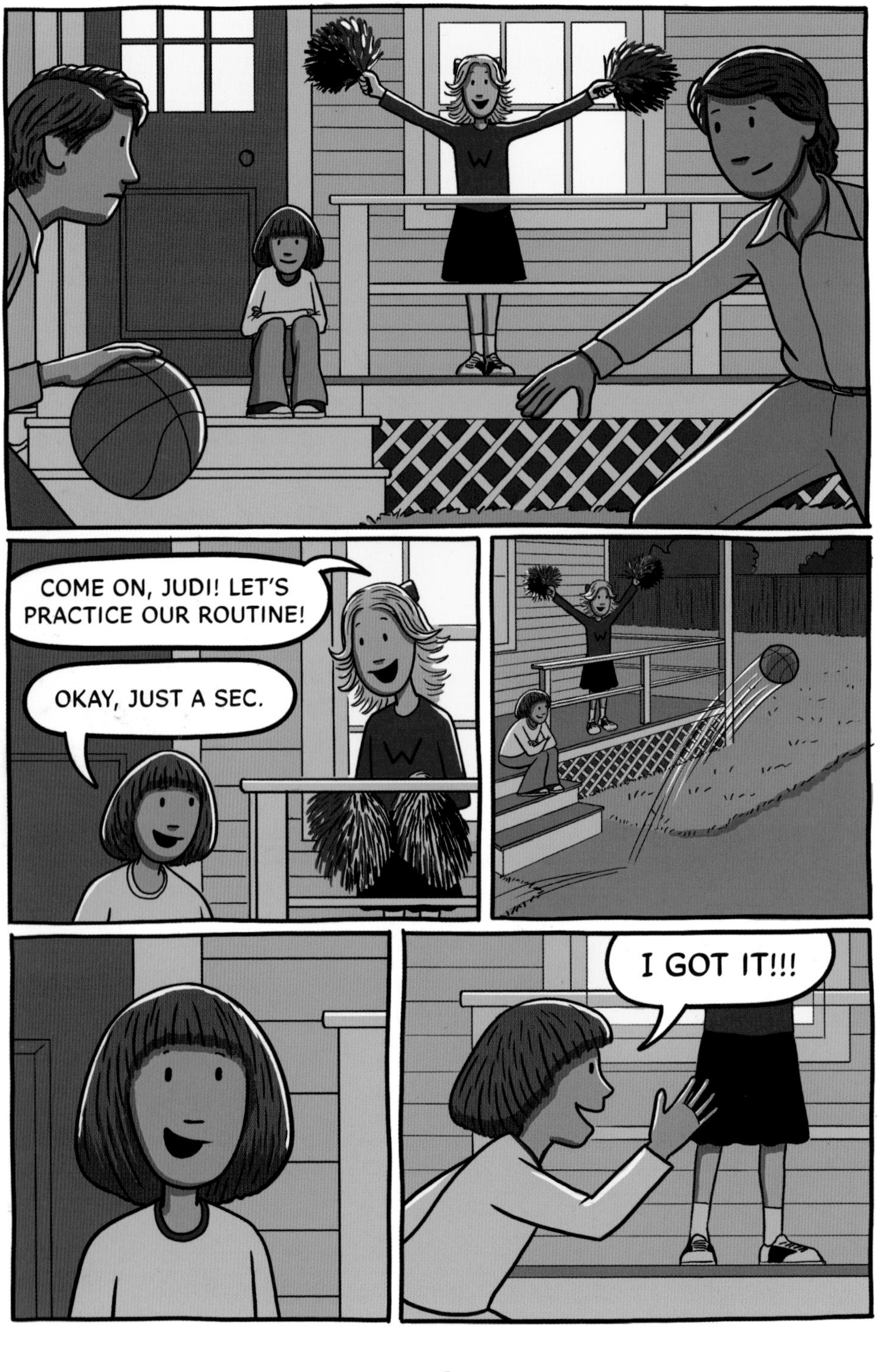
COME ON, JUDI! LET'S PRACTICE OUR ROUTINE!
OKAY, JUST A SEC.
I GOT IT!!!

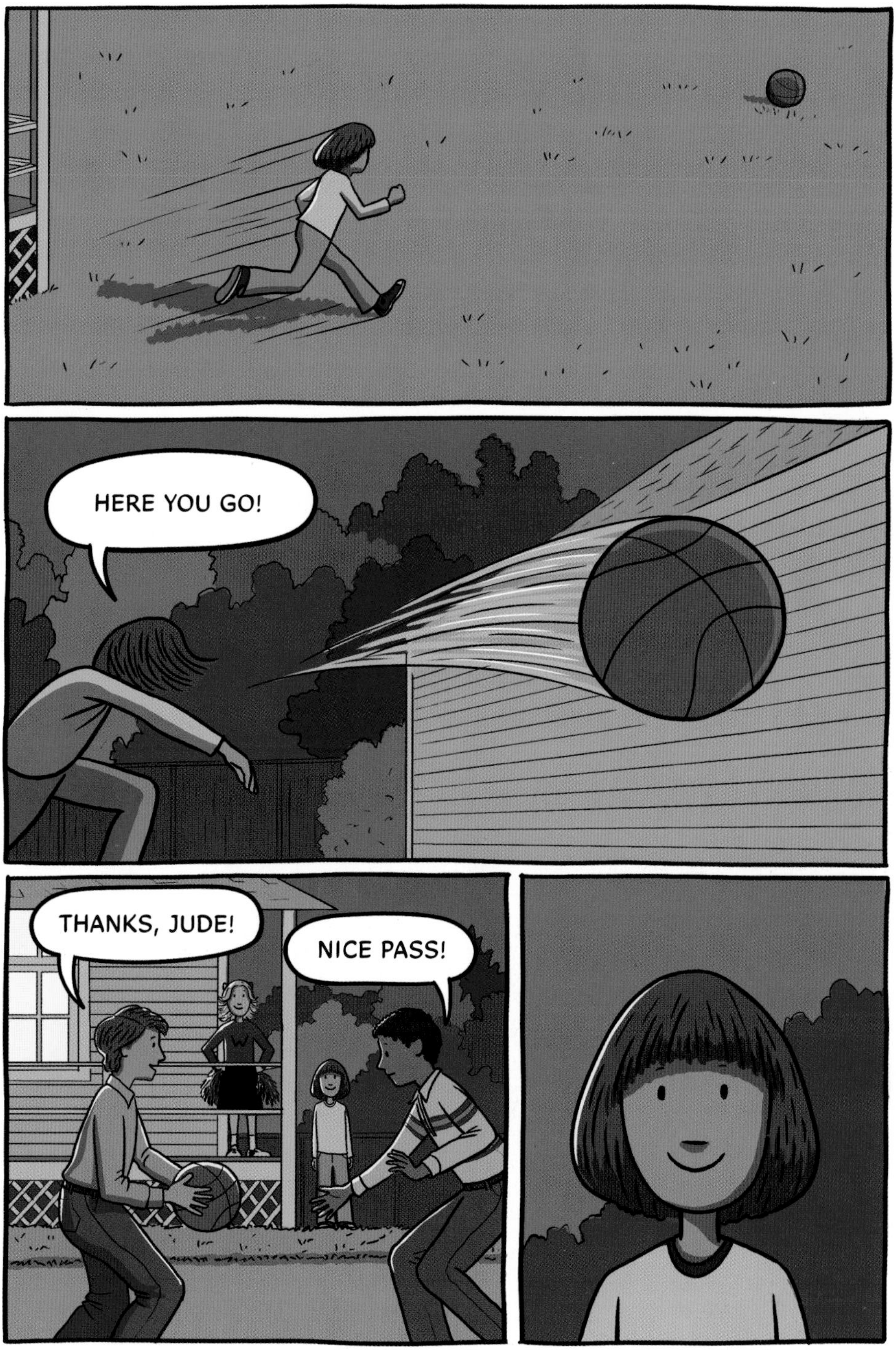
HERE YOU GO!
THANKS, JUDE!
NICE PASS!

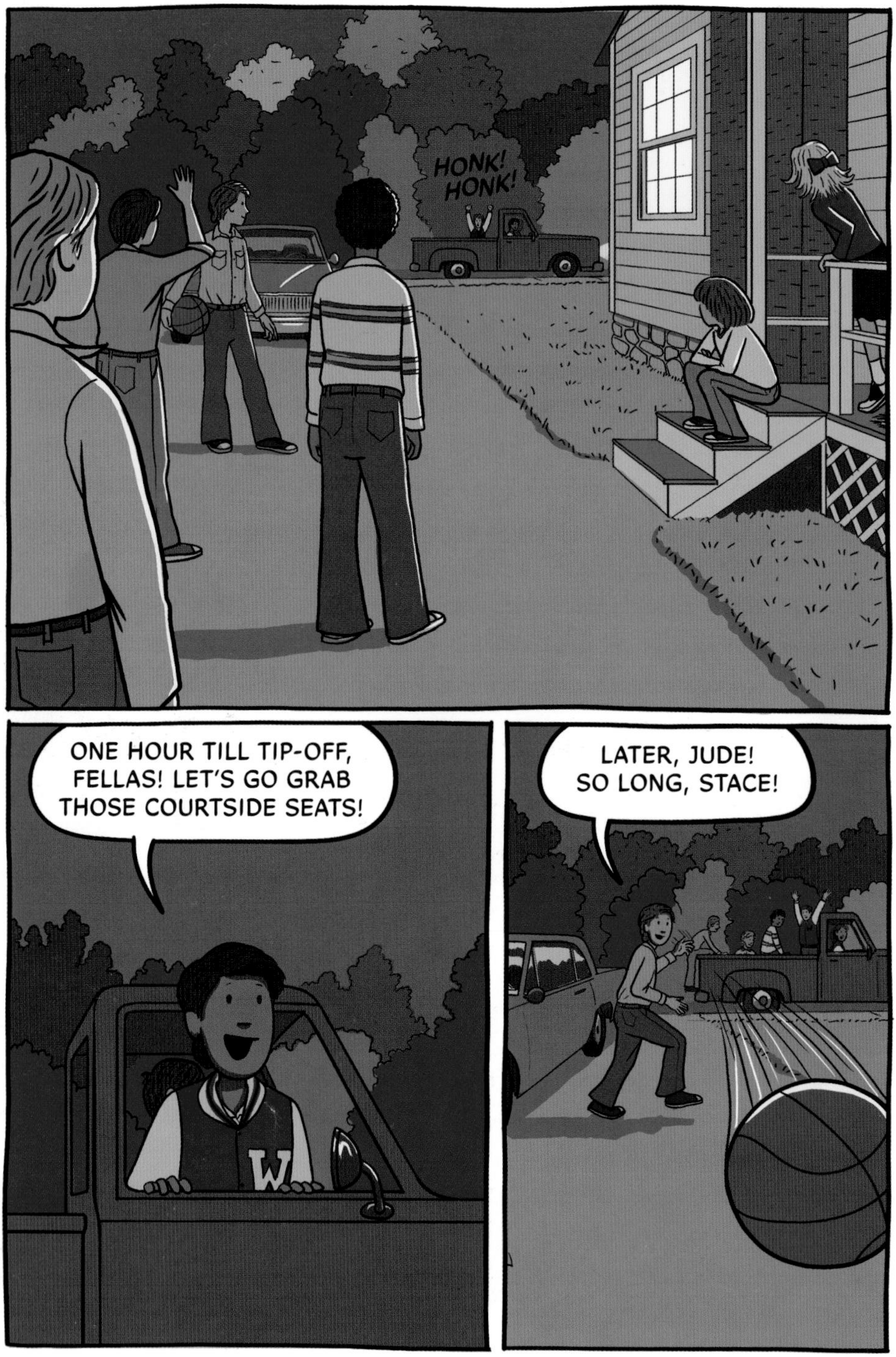
HONK! HONK!
ONE HOUR TILL TIP-OFF, FELLAS! LET'S GO GRAB THOSE COURTSIDE SEATS!
LATER, JUDE! SO LONG, STACE!

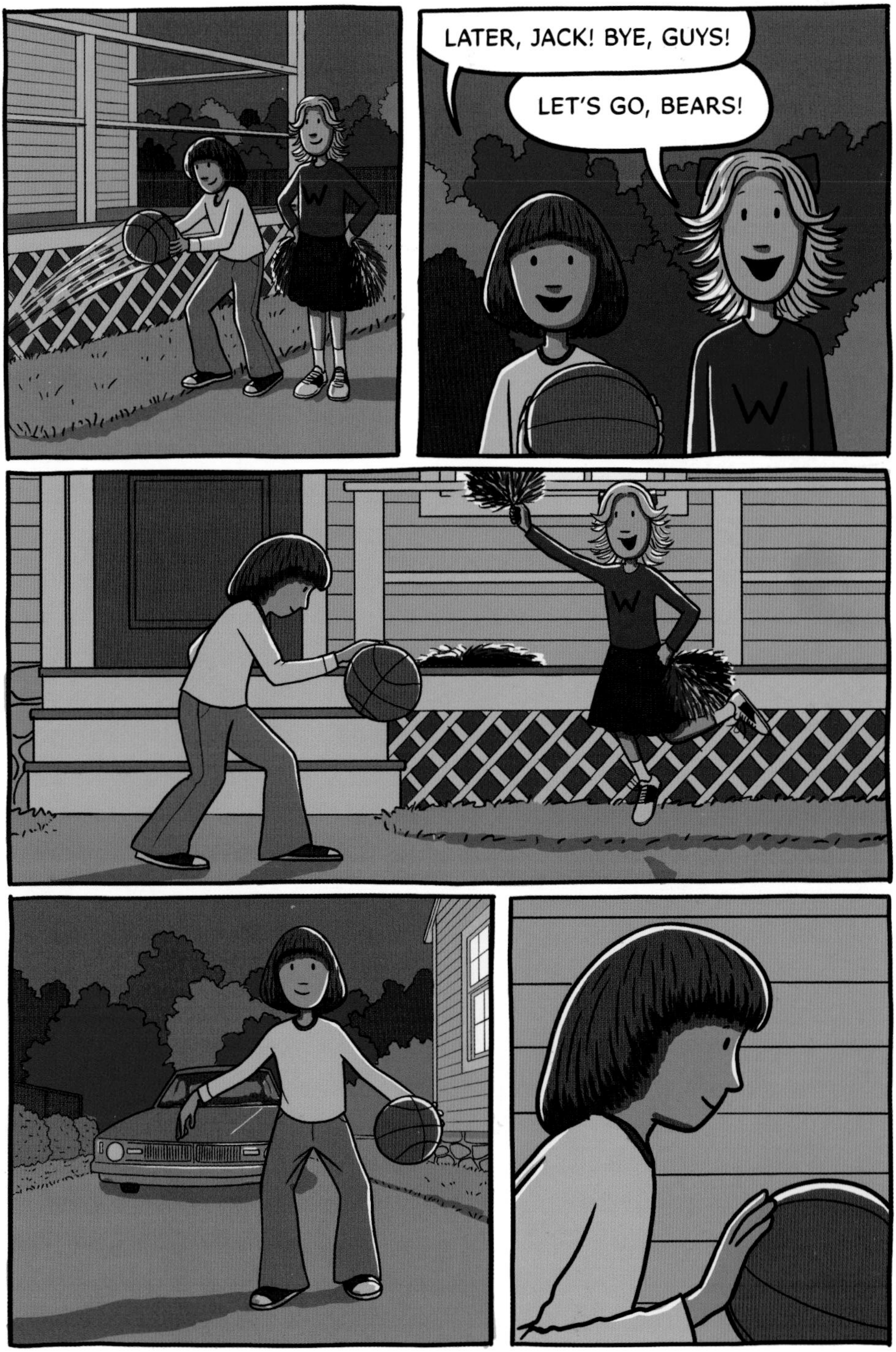
LATER, JACK! BYE, GUYS!
LET'S GO, BEARS!
W
W
W

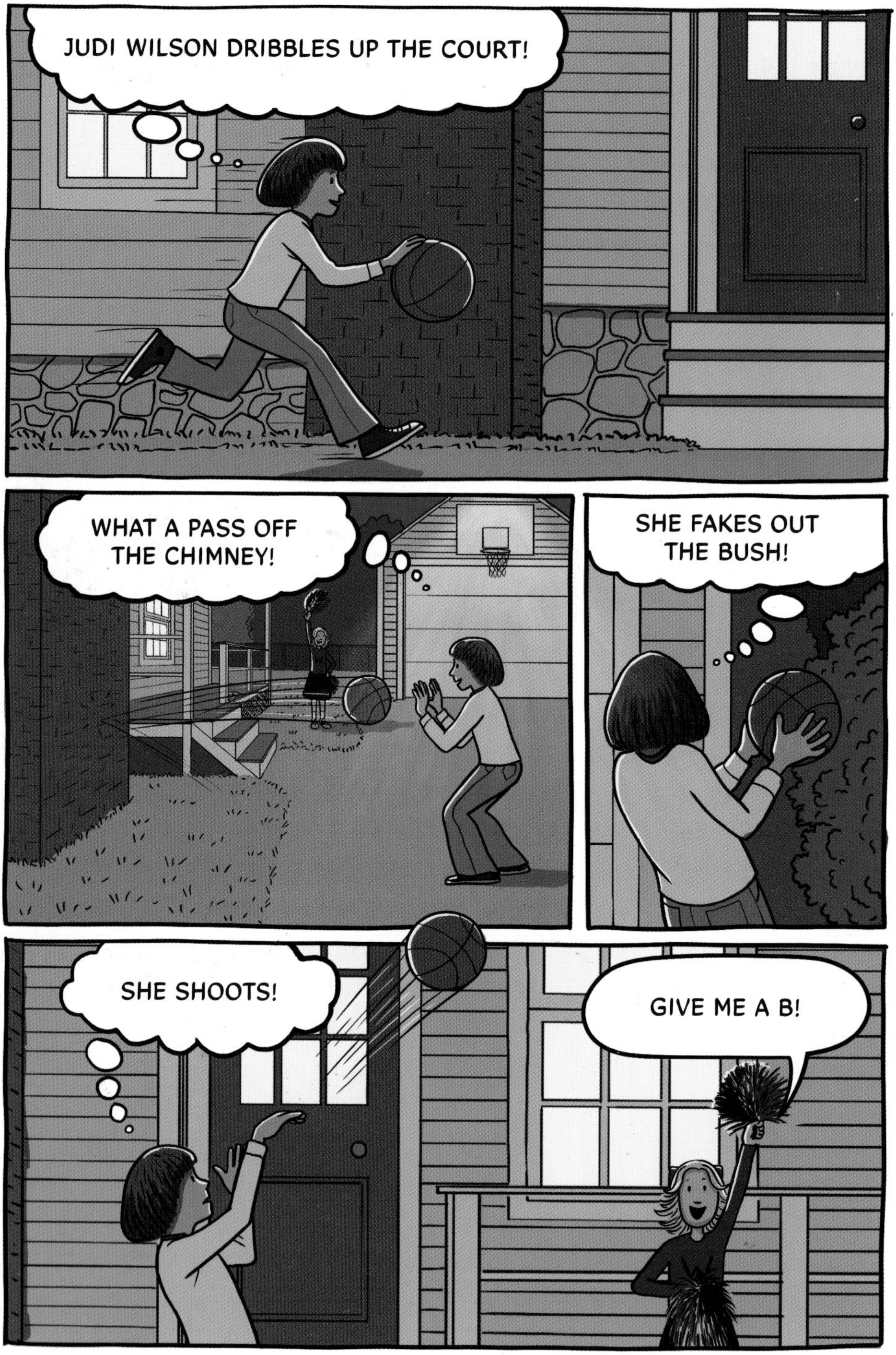
JUDI WILSON DRIBBLES UP THE COURT!
WHAT A PASS OFF THE CHIMNEY!
SHE FAKES OUT THE BUSH!
SHE SHOOTS!
GIVE ME A B!

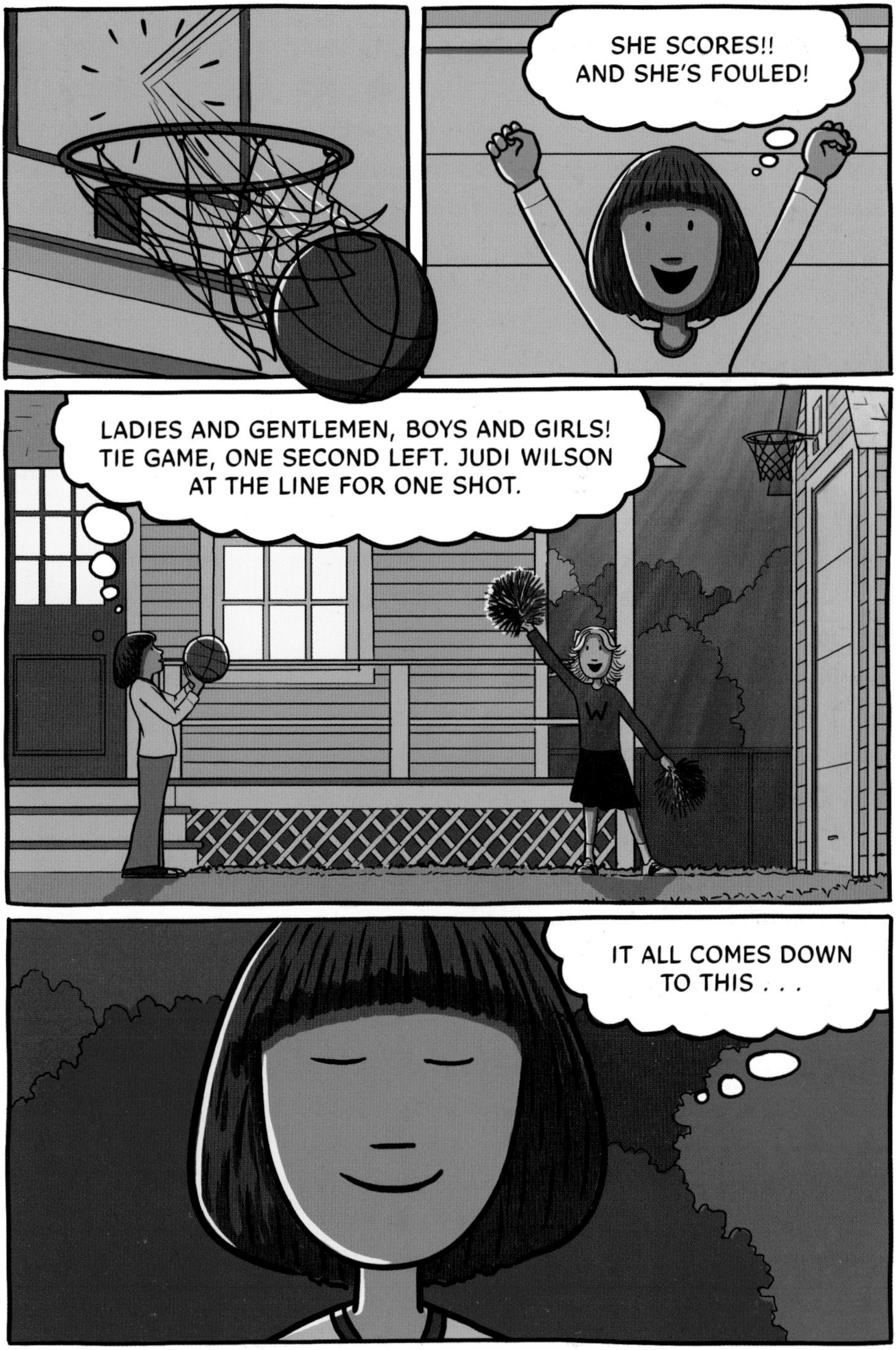
SHE SCORES!! AND SHE'S FOULED!
LADIES AND GENTLEMEN, BOYS AND GIRLS! TIE GAME, ONE SECOND LEFT. JUDI WILSON AT THE LINE FOR ONE SHOT.
W
IT ALL COMES DOWN TO THIS . . .

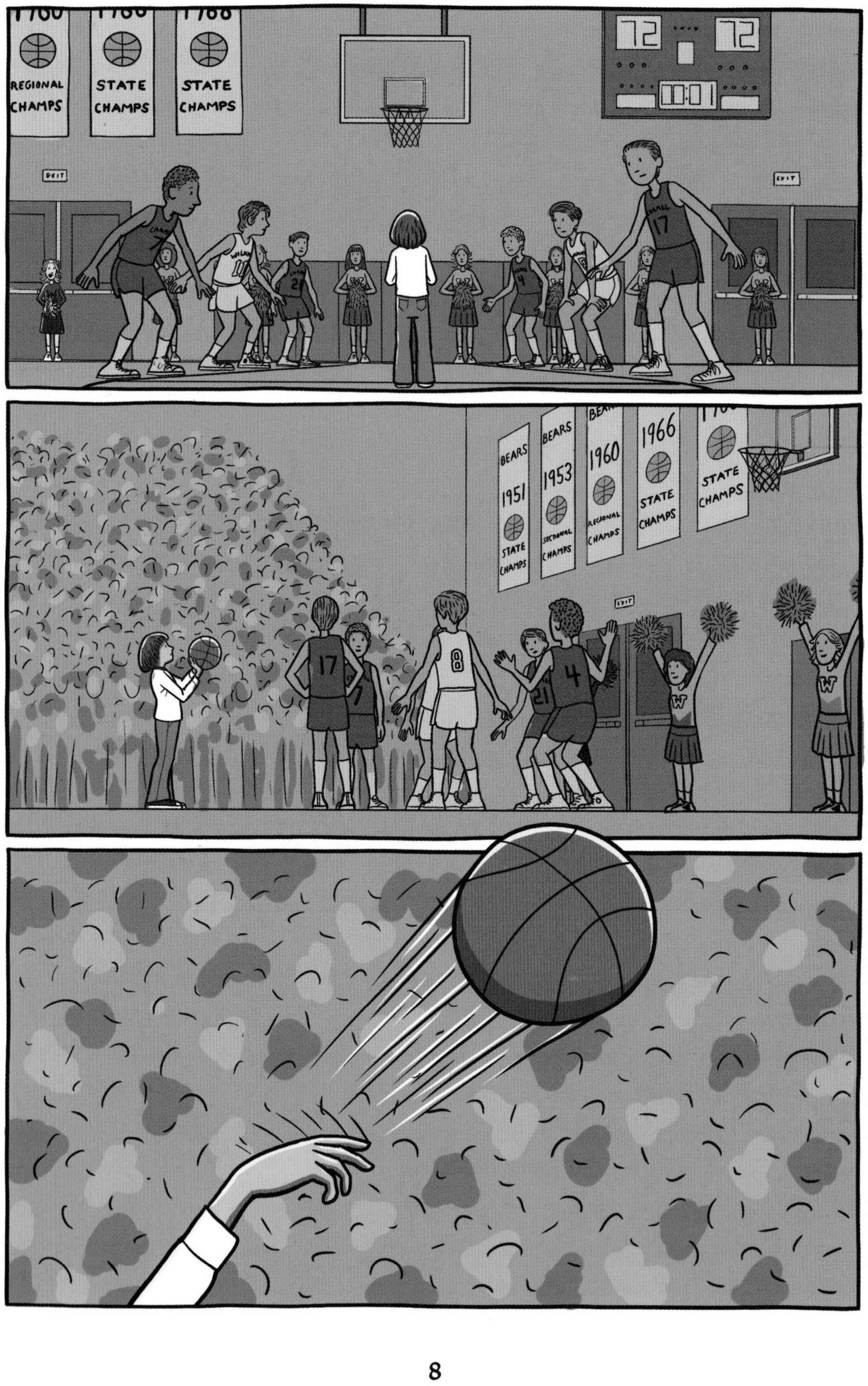
REGIONAL CHAMPS
STATE CHAMPS
STATE CHAMPS
72
72
00:01
EXIT
EXIT
BEARS 1951 STATE CHAMPS
BEARS 1953 SECTIONAL CHAMPS
BEARS 1960 REGIONAL CHAMPS
1966 STATE CHAMPS
STATE CHAMPS
EXIT

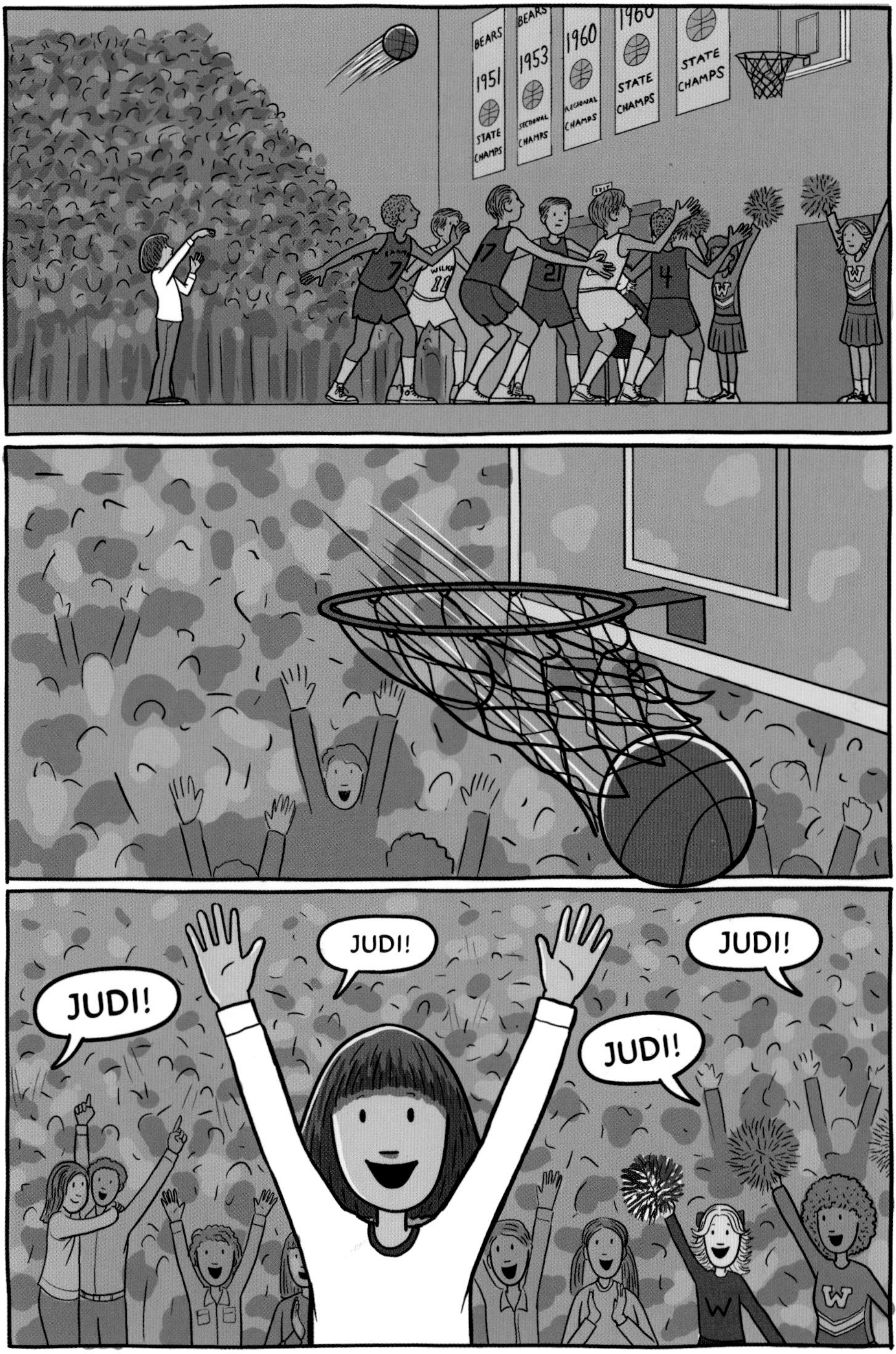
BEARS 1951 STATE CHAMPS
BEARS 1953 SECTIONAL CHAMPS
1960 REGIONAL CHAMPS
1960 STATE CHAMPS
STATE CHAMPS
JUDI!
JUDI!
JUDI!
JUDI!

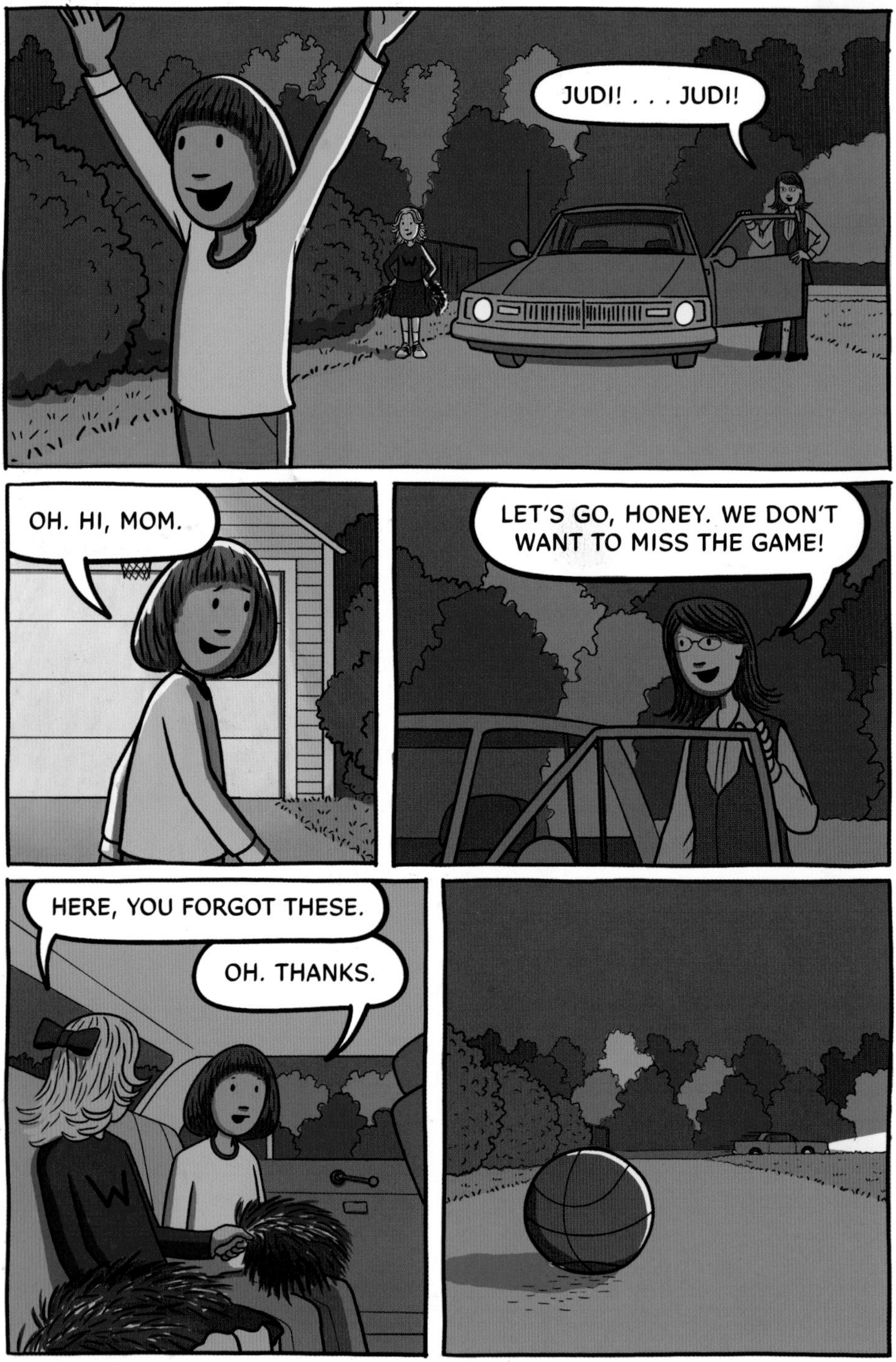
JUDI! . . . JUDI!
OH. HI, MOM.
LET'S GO, HONEY. WE DON'T WANT TO MISS THE GAME!
HERE, YOU FORGOT THESE.
OH. THANKS.

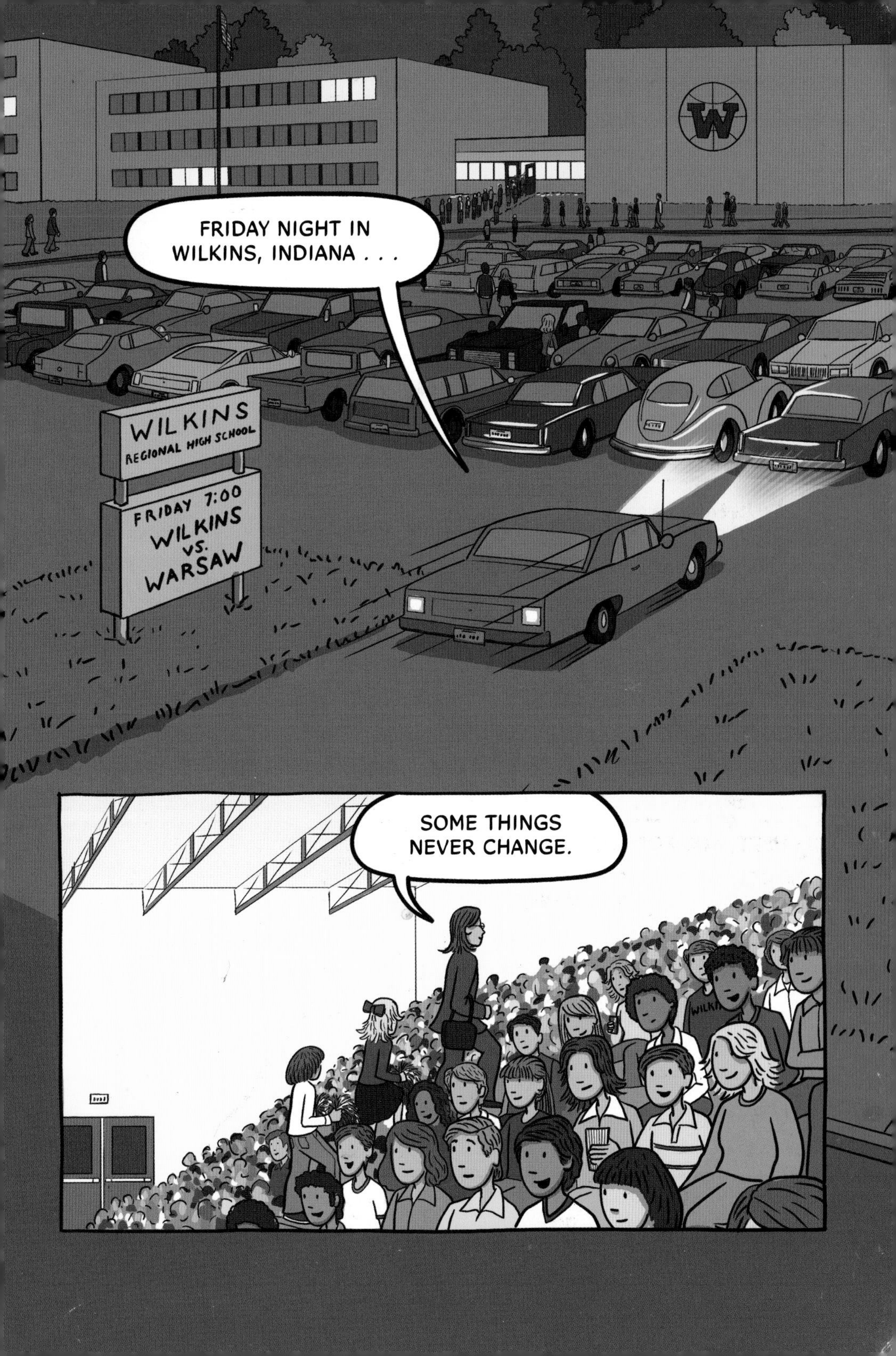
FRIDAY NIGHT IN WILKINS, INDIANA . . .
WILKINS REGIONAL HIGH SCHOOL
FRIDAY 7:00 WILKINS VS. WARSAW
SOME THINGS NEVER CHANGE.

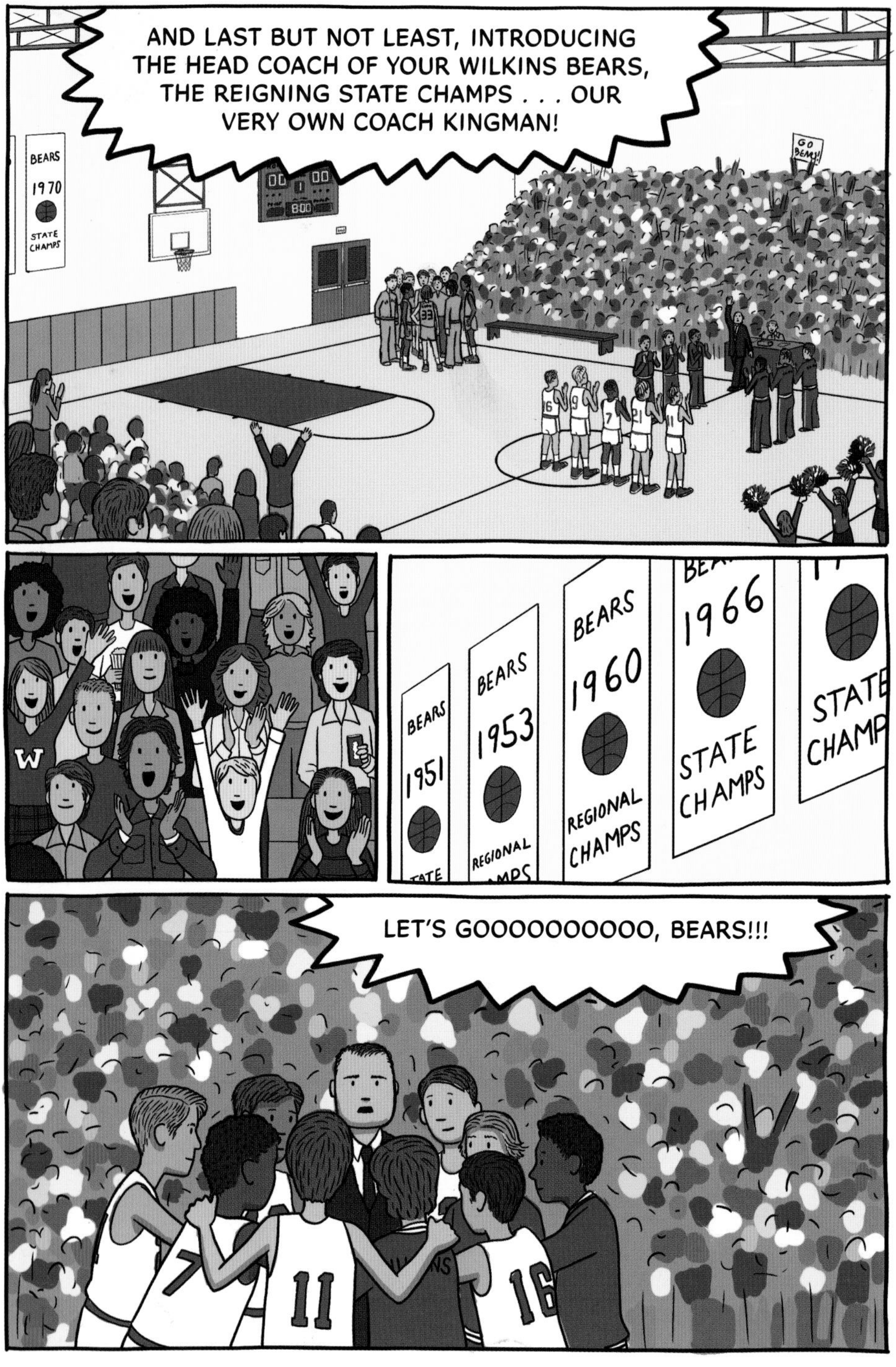
AND LAST BUT NOT LEAST, INTRODUCING THE HEAD COACH OF YOUR WILKINS BEARS, THE REIGNING STATE CHAMPS . . . OUR VERY OWN COACH KINGMAN!
BEARS
1970
STATE CHAMPS
BEARS
1951
BEARS
1953
REGIONAL
BEARS
1960
REGIONAL CHAMPS
1966
STATE CHAMPS
LET'S GOOOOOOOOOO, BEARS!!!

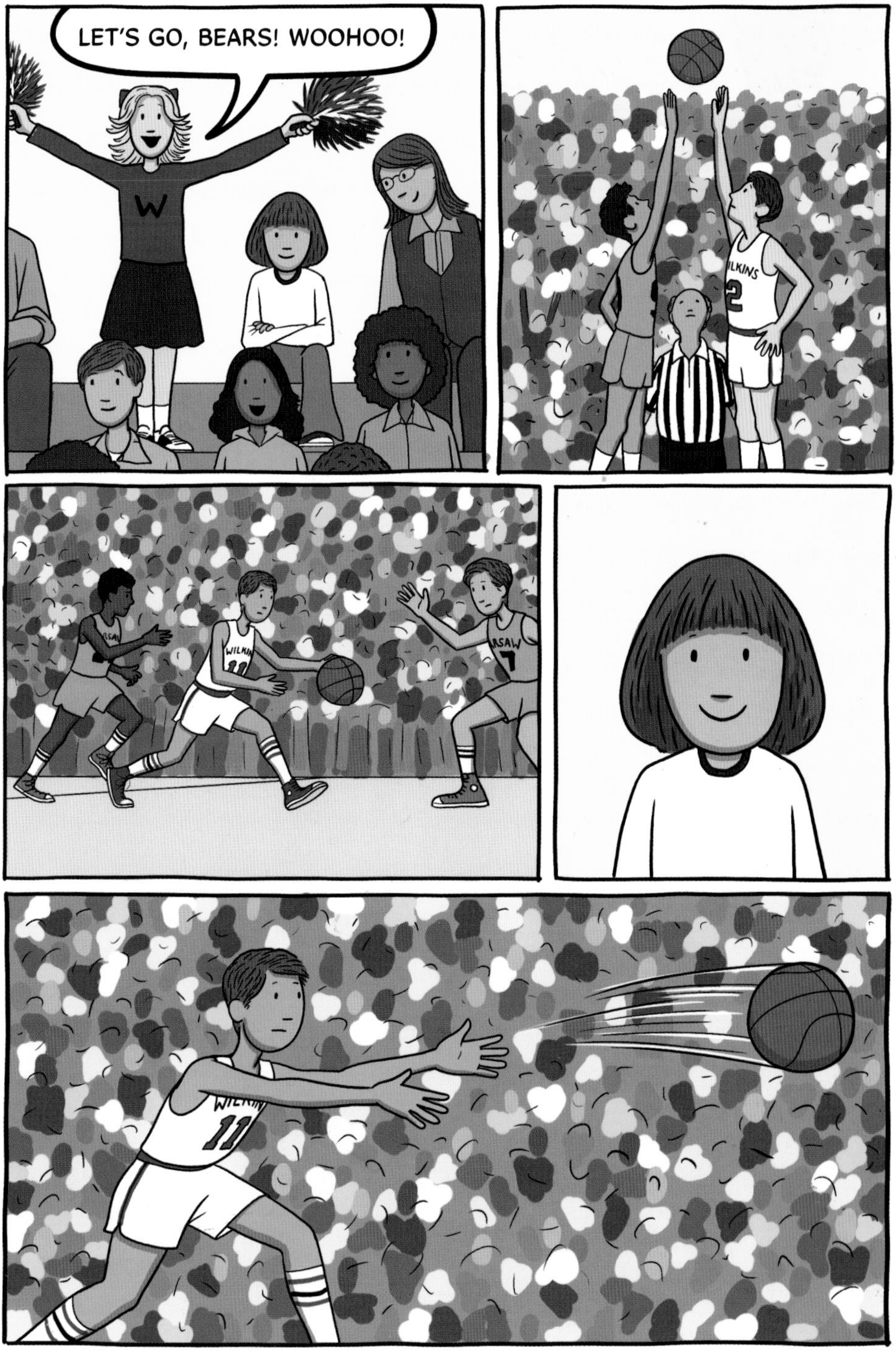
LET'S GO, BEARS! WOOHOO!
W
WILKINS
WILKINS
11

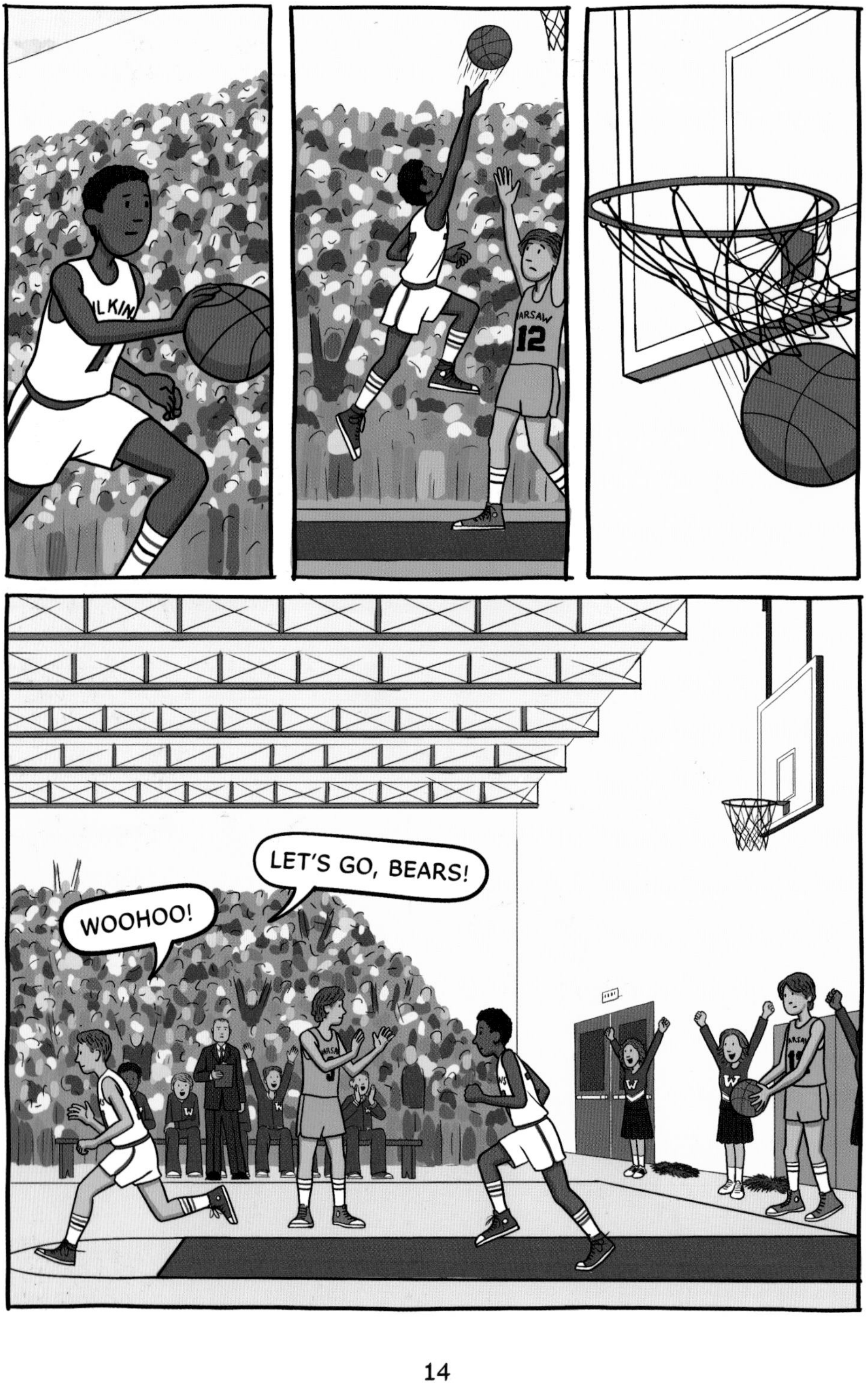
LET'S GO, BEARS!
WOOHOO!

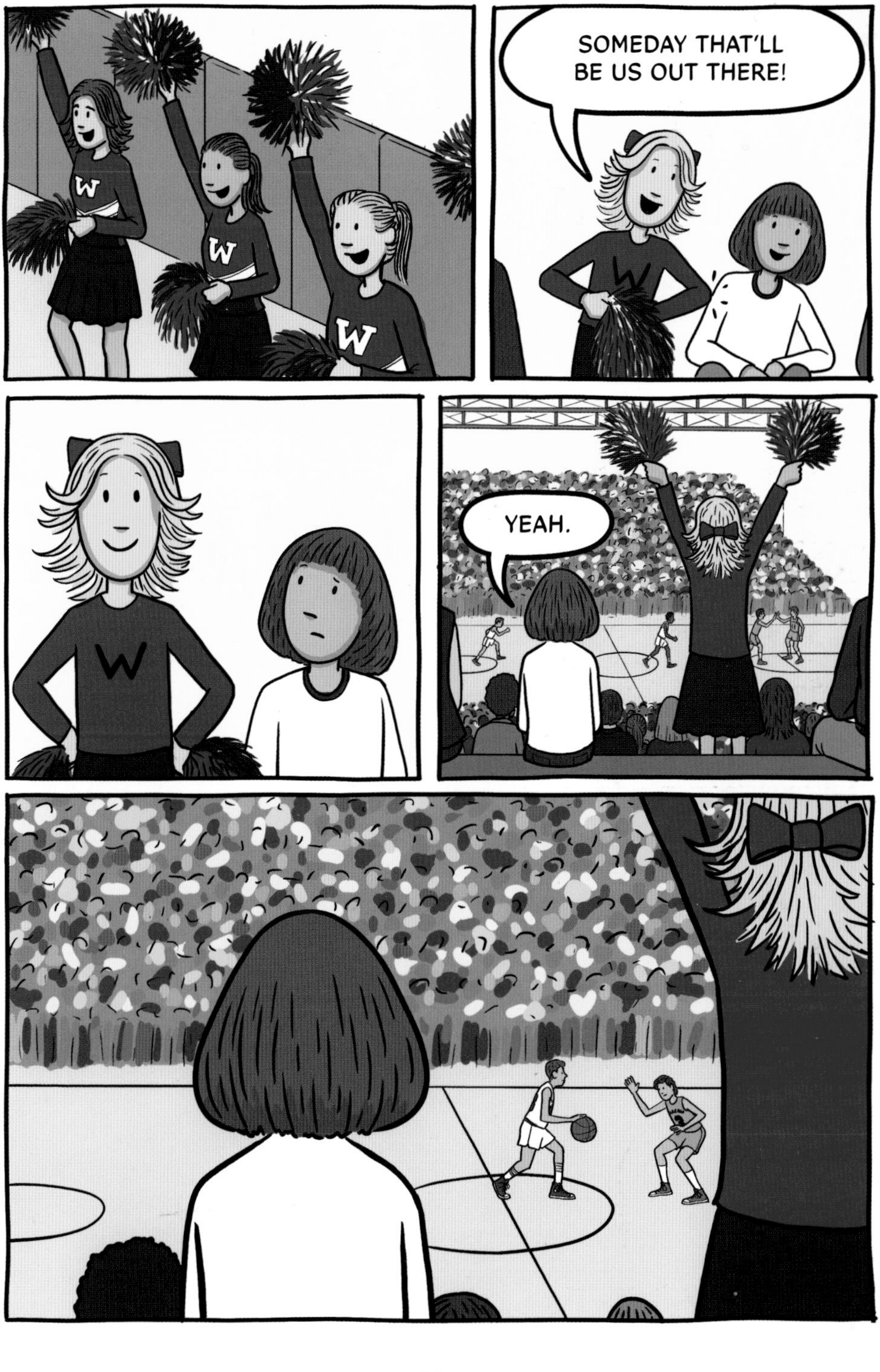
SOMEDAY THAT'LL BE US OUT THERE!
YEAH.

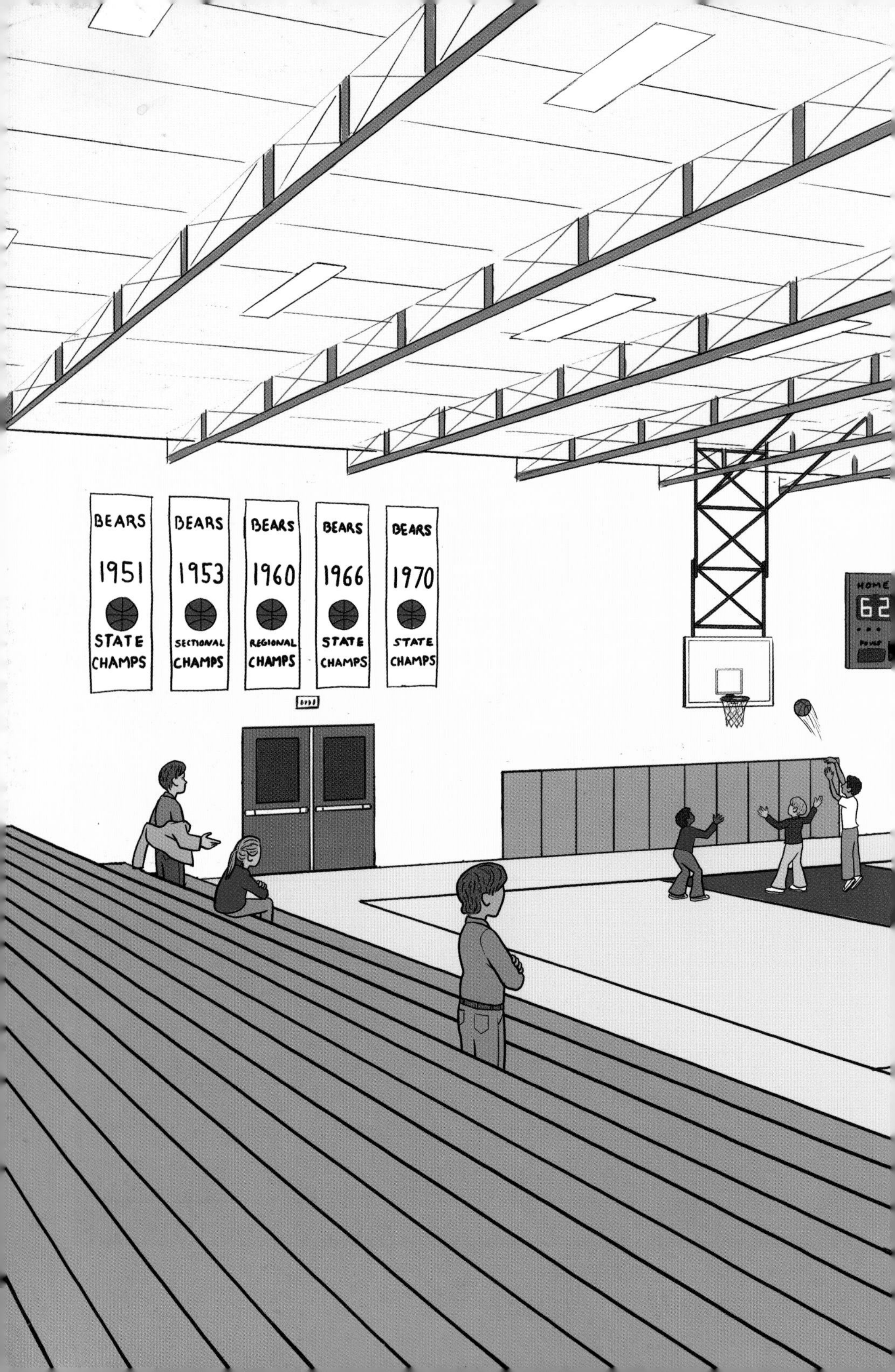
BEARS 1951 STATE CHAMPS
BEARS 1953 SECTIONAL CHAMPS
BEARS 1960 REGIONAL CHAMPS
BEARS 1966 STATE CHAMPS
BEARS 1970 STATE CHAMPS
HOME
62

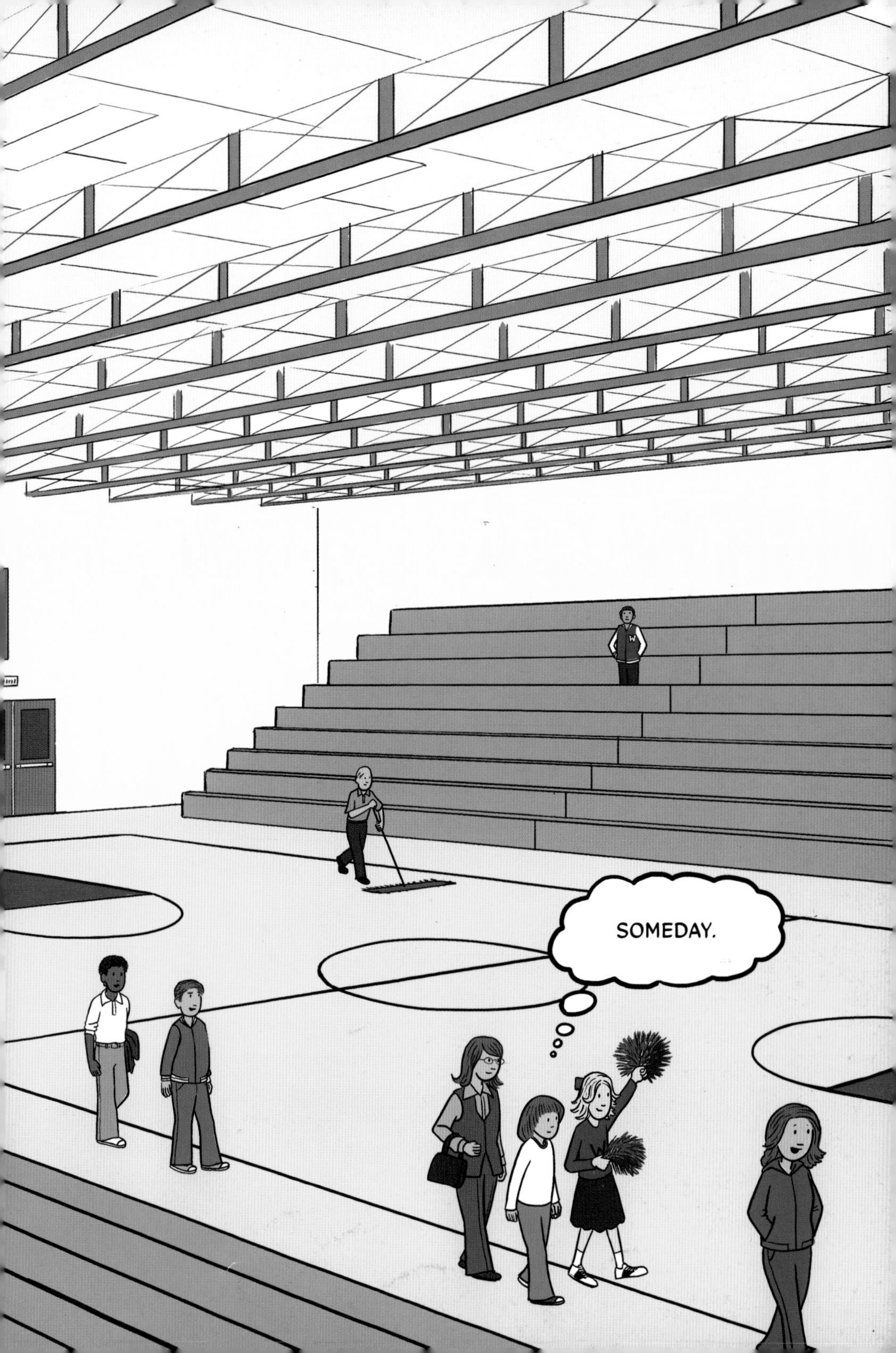
SOMEDAY.

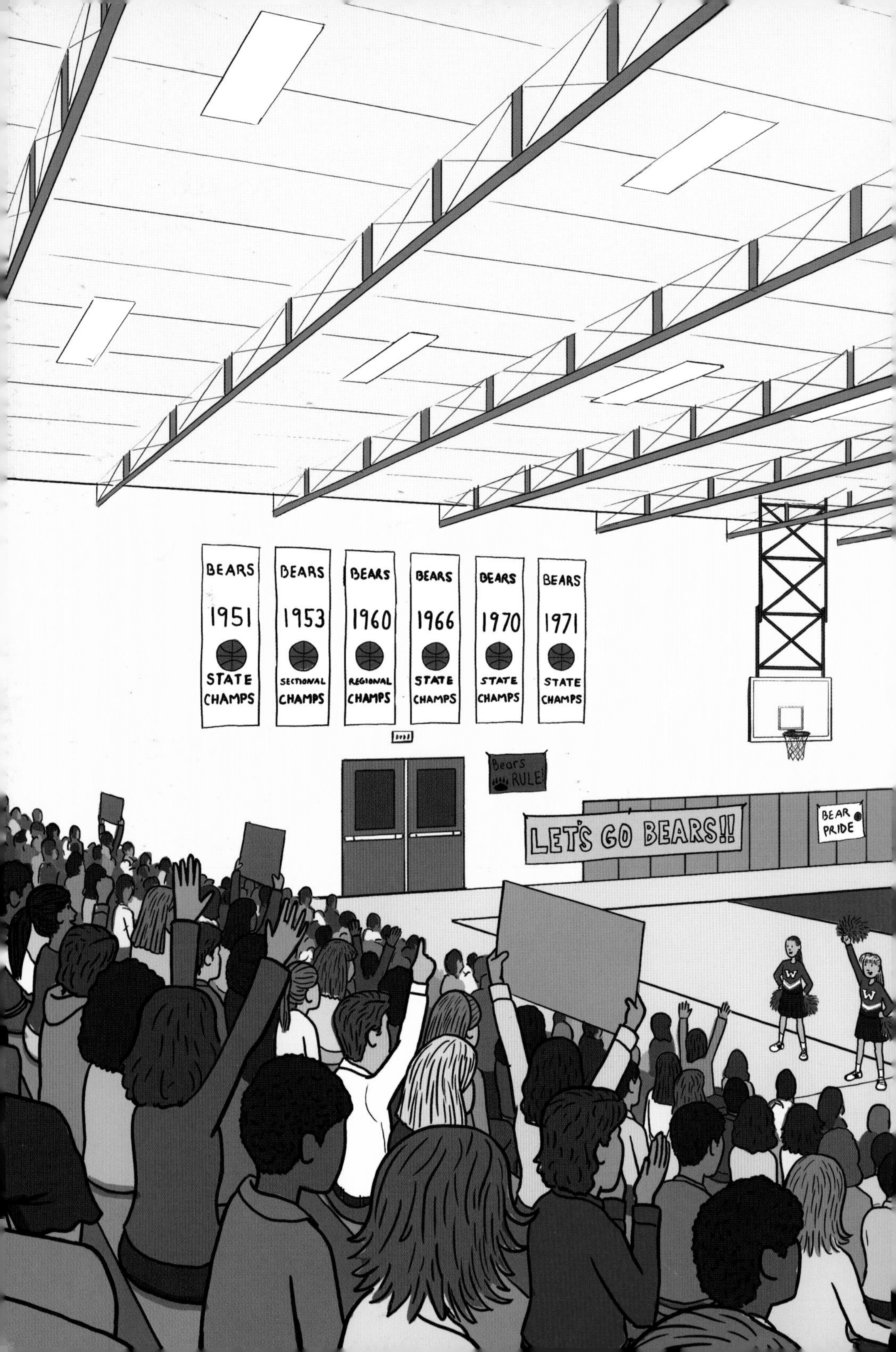
BEARS 1951 STATE CHAMPS
BEARS 1953 SECTIONAL CHAMPS
BEARS 1960 REGIONAL CHAMPS
BEARS 1966 STATE CHAMPS
BEARS 1970 STATE CHAMPS
BEARS 1971 STATE CHAMPS
Bears RULE!
LET'S GO BEARS!!
BEAR PRIDE

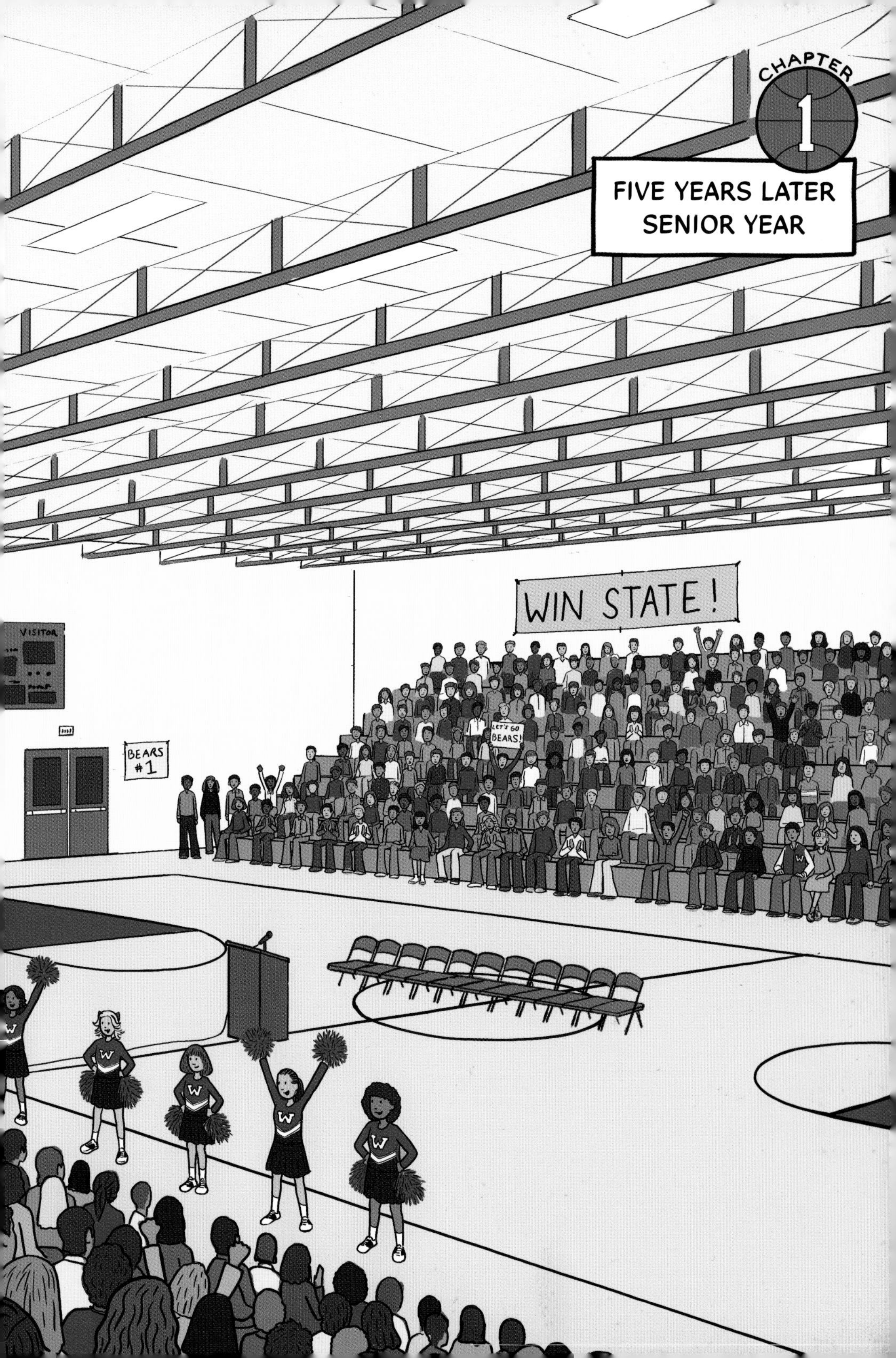
CHAPTER
1
FIVE YEARS LATER
SENIOR YEAR
WIN STATE!
VISITOR
BEARS
#1
LET'S GO
BEARS!

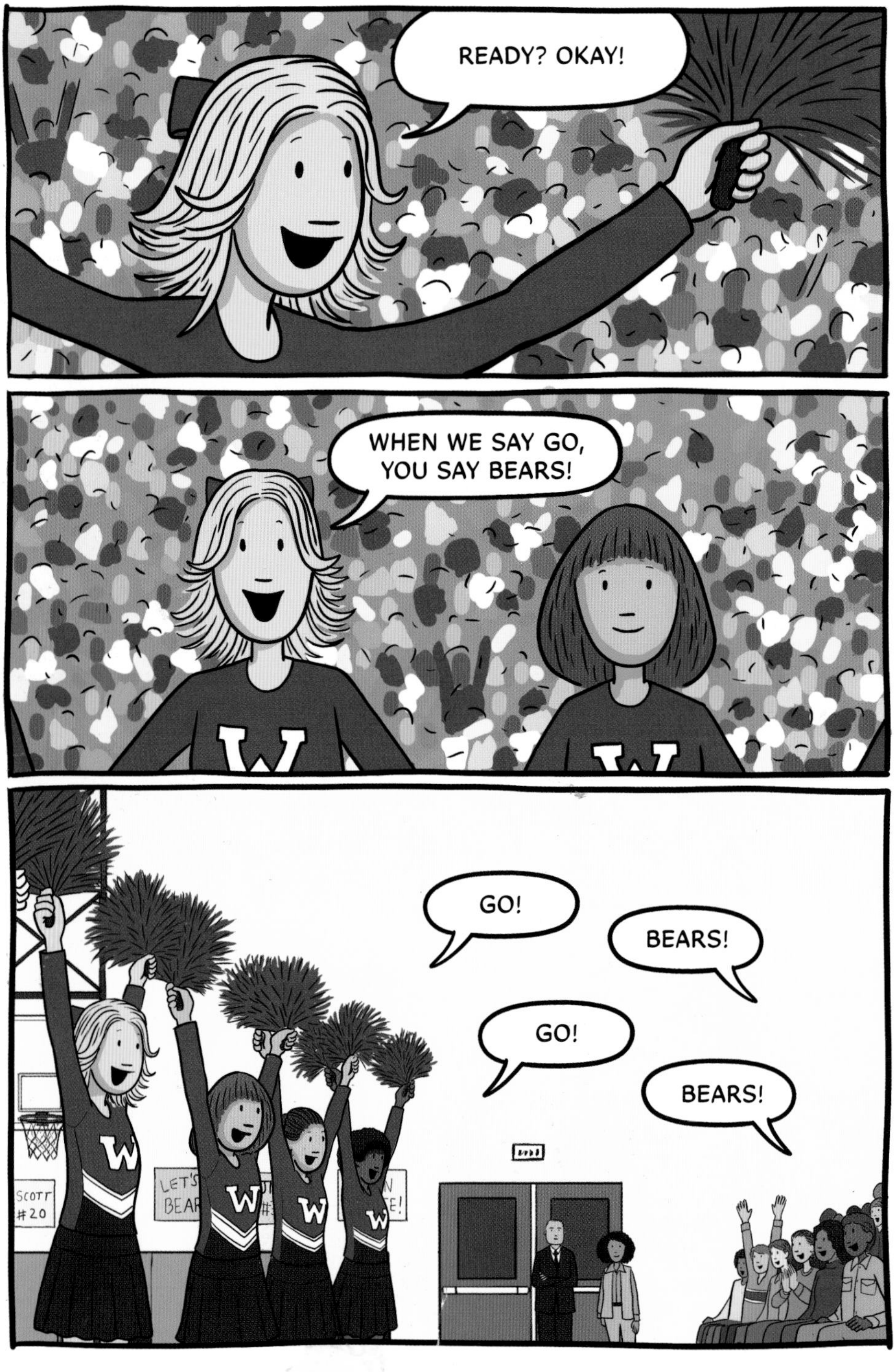
READY? OKAY!
WHEN WE SAY GO, YOU SAY BEARS!
GO!
BEARS!
GO!
BEARS!
SCOTT #20

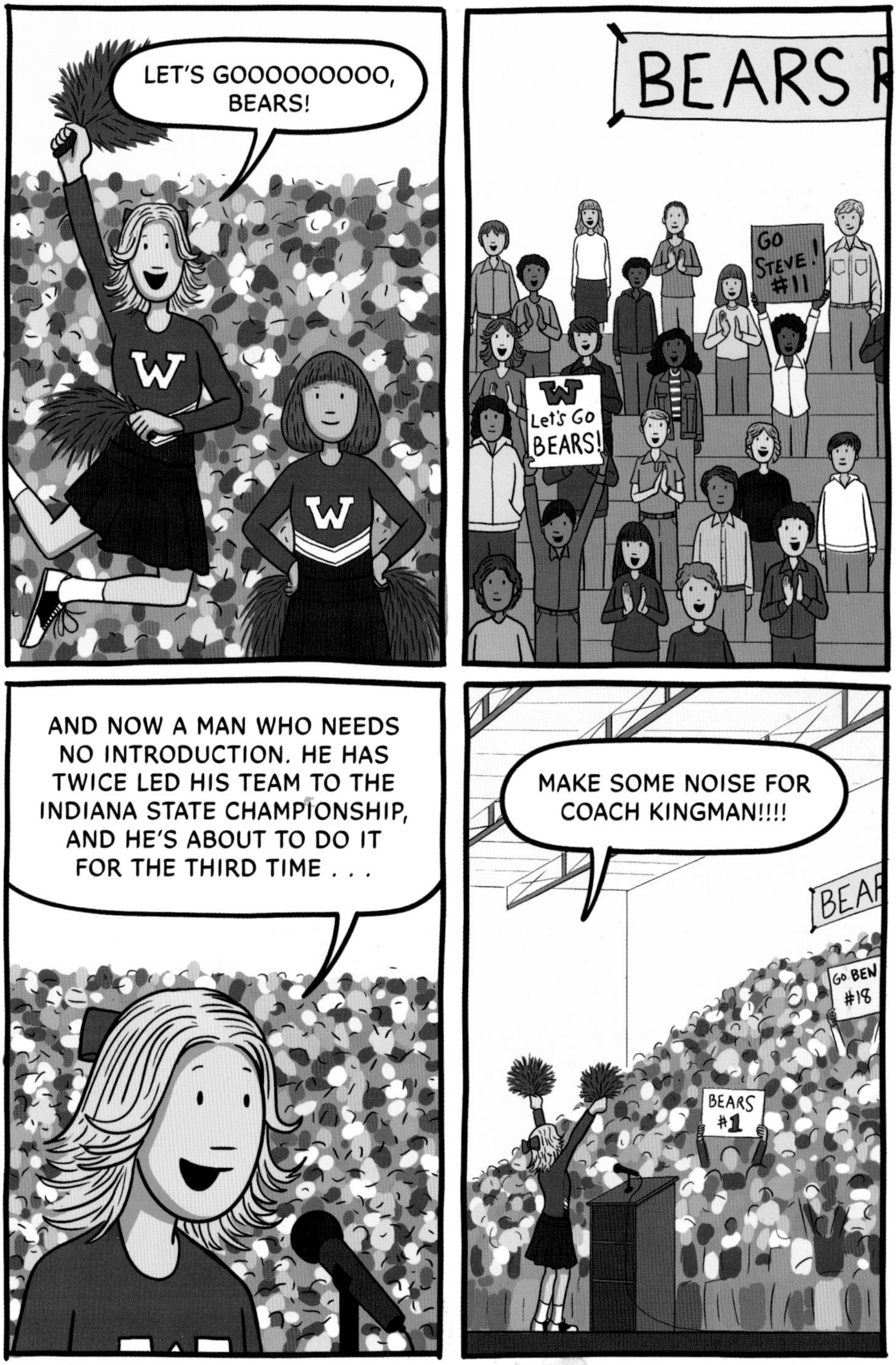
LET'S GOOOOOOOOO, BEARS!
BEARS
GO STEVE! #11
Let's Go BEARS!
AND NOW A MAN WHO NEEDS NO INTRODUCTION. HE HAS TWICE LED HIS TEAM TO THE INDIANA STATE CHAMPIONSHIP, AND HE'S ABOUT TO DO IT FOR THE THIRD TIME . . .
MAKE SOME NOISE FOR COACH KINGMAN!!!!
GO BEN #18
BEARS #1

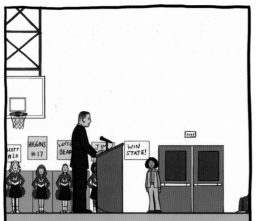

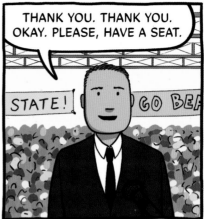

HIGGINS #17
WIN STATE!
THANK YOU. THANK YOU. OKAY. PLEASE, HAVE A SEAT.
STATE!
BEFORE WE GET THIS PEP RALLY UNDERWAY, ONE OF YOUR . . . TEACHERS . . . WOULD LIKE TO MAKE A QUICK ANNOUNCEMENT.
BOOOO!
COME ON!
GO, BEARS!
HI, EVERYONE.
HI. MY NAME IS MISS MONTEZ. I HAVE SOME EXCITING NEWS TO SHARE.
#20

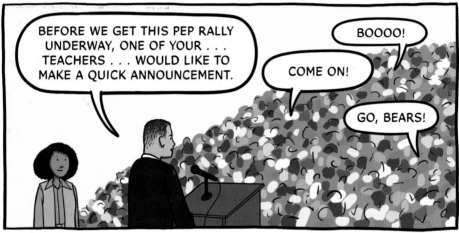

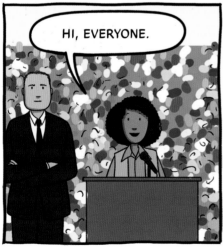

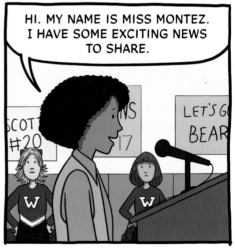

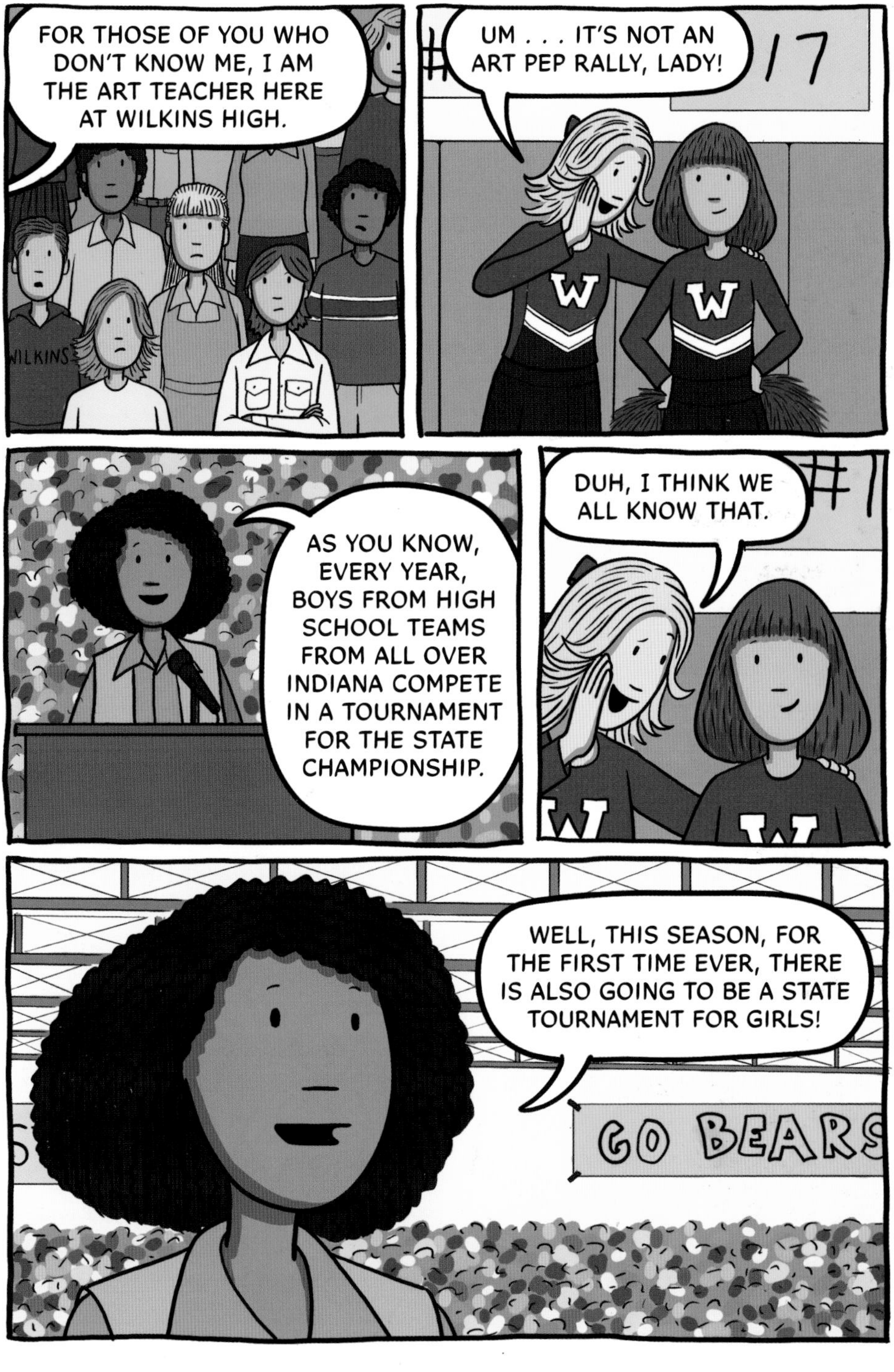
FOR THOSE OF YOU WHO DON'T KNOW ME, I AM THE ART TEACHER HERE AT WILKINS HIGH.
WILKINS
UM . . . IT'S NOT AN ART PEP RALLY, LADY!
17
W
W
AS YOU KNOW, EVERY YEAR, BOYS FROM HIGH SCHOOL TEAMS FROM ALL OVER INDIANA COMPETE IN A TOURNAMENT FOR THE STATE CHAMPIONSHIP.
DUH, I THINK WE ALL KNOW THAT.
WELL, THIS SEASON, FOR THE FIRST TIME EVER, THERE IS ALSO GOING TO BE A STATE TOURNAMENT FOR GIRLS!
GO BEARS

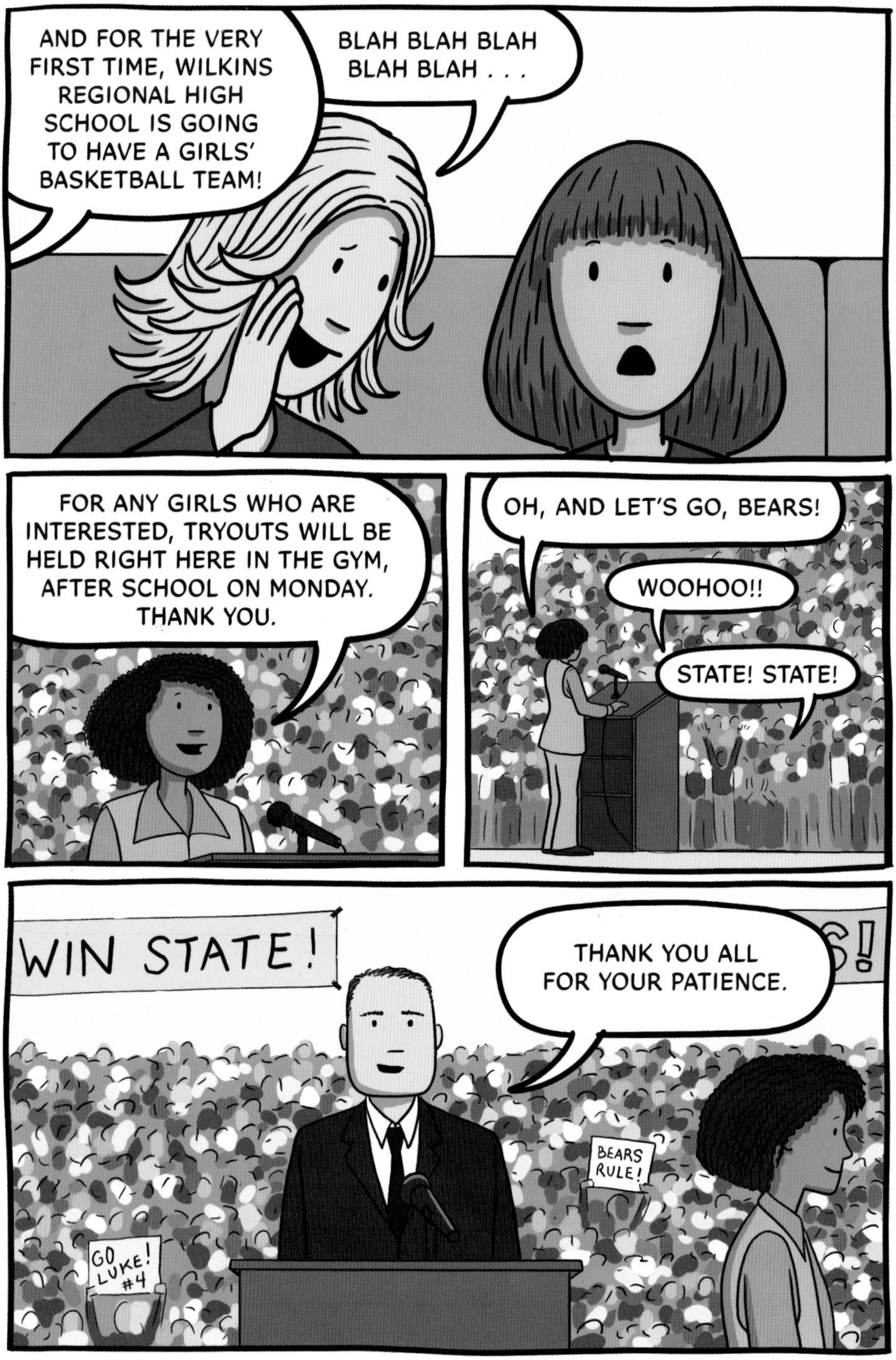
AND FOR THE VERY FIRST TIME, WILKINS REGIONAL HIGH SCHOOL IS GOING TO HAVE A GIRLS' BASKETBALL TEAM!
BLAH BLAH BLAH BLAH BLAH . . .
FOR ANY GIRLS WHO ARE INTERESTED, TRYOUTS WILL BE HELD RIGHT HERE IN THE GYM, AFTER SCHOOL ON MONDAY. THANK YOU.
OH, AND LET'S GO, BEARS!
WOOHOO!!
STATE! STATE!
WIN STATE!
THANK YOU ALL FOR YOUR PATIENCE.
BEARS RULE!
GO LUKE! #4

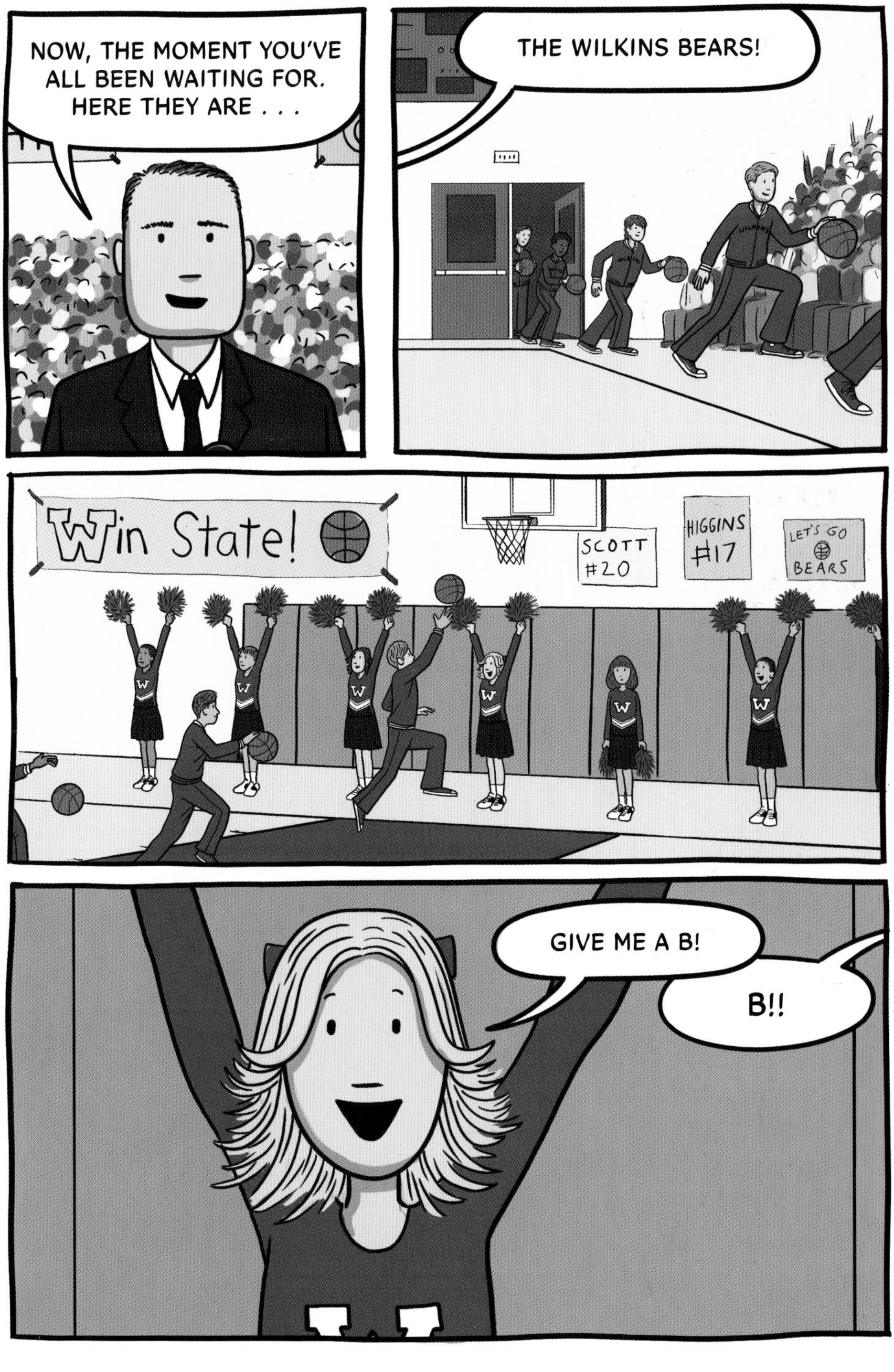
NOW, THE MOMENT YOU'VE ALL BEEN WAITING FOR. HERE THEY ARE . . .
THE WILKINS BEARS!
Win State!
SCOTT #20
HIGGINS #17
LET'S GO BEARS
GIVE ME A B!
B!!

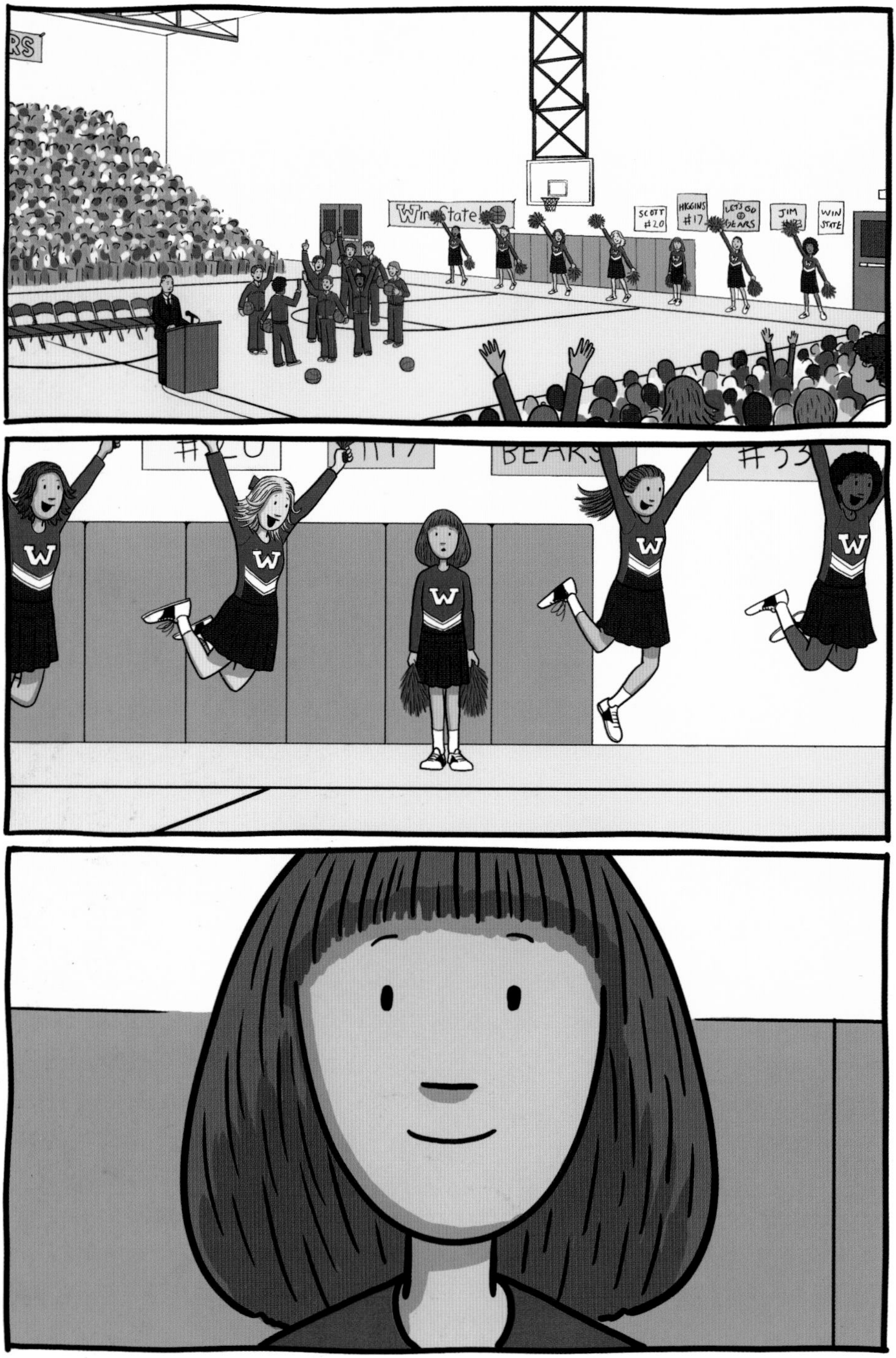
SCOTT #20
HIGGINS #17
JIM
WIN STATE

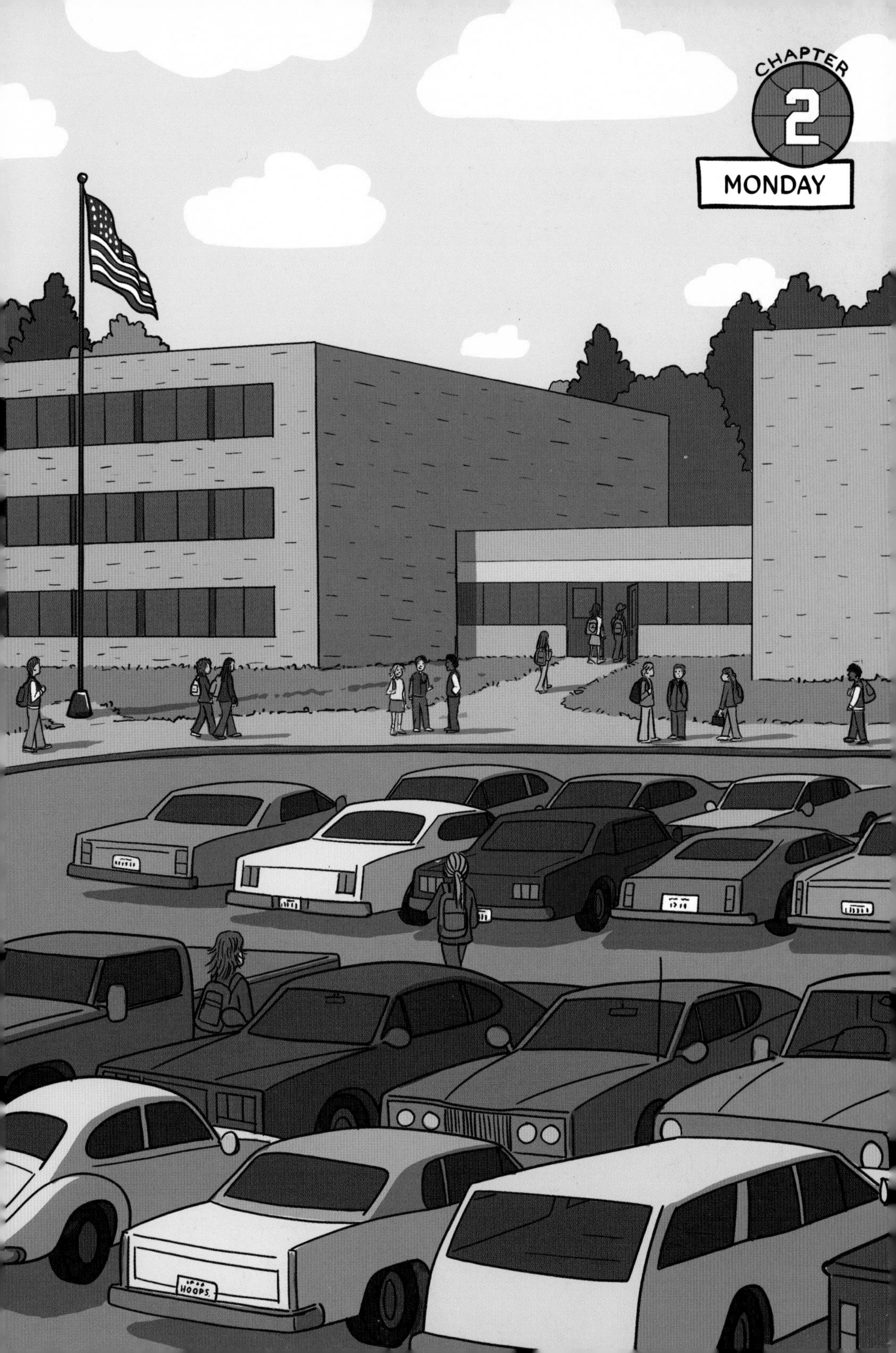
CHAPTER
2
MONDAY
HOOPS

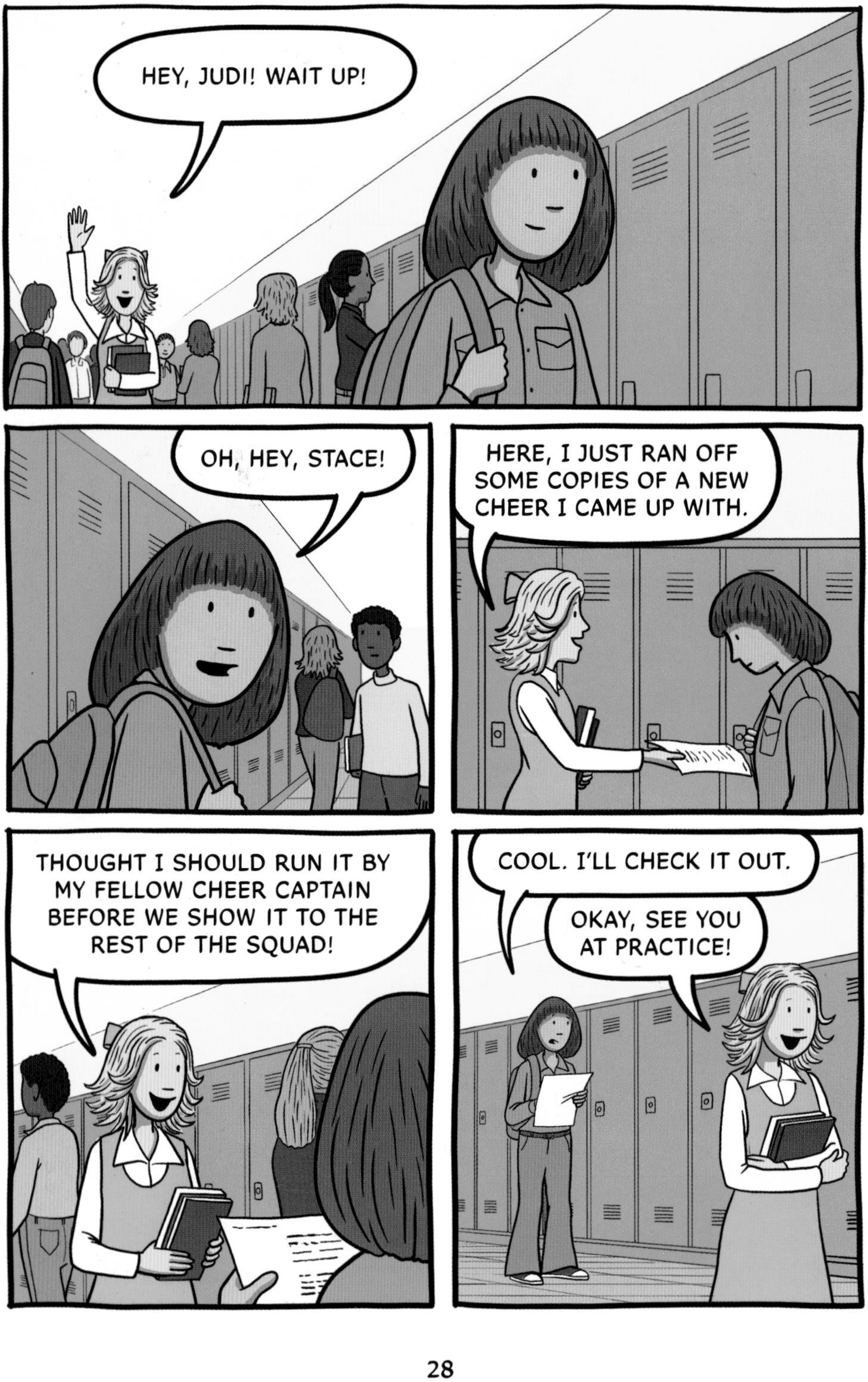
HEY, JUDI! WAIT UP!
OH, HEY, STACE!
HERE, I JUST RAN OFF SOME COPIES OF A NEW CHEER I CAME UP WITH.
THOUGHT I SHOULD RUN IT BY MY FELLOW CHEER CAPTAIN BEFORE WE SHOW IT TO THE REST OF THE SQUAD!
COOL. I'LL CHECK IT OUT.
OKAY, SEE YOU AT PRACTICE!

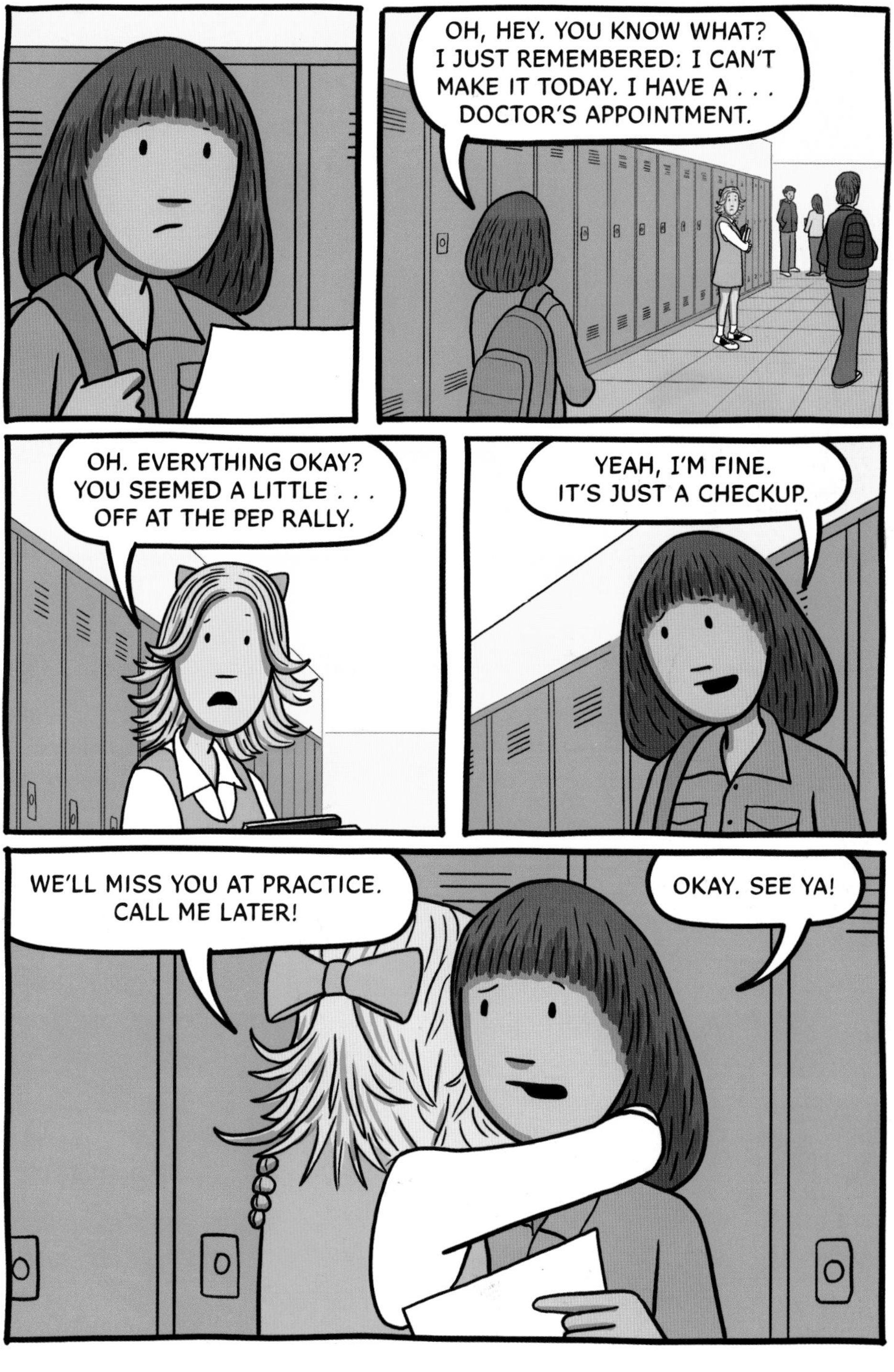
OH, HEY. YOU KNOW WHAT? I JUST REMEMBERED: I CAN'T MAKE IT TODAY. I HAVE A . . . DOCTOR'S APPOINTMENT.
OH. EVERYTHING OKAY? YOU SEEMED A LITTLE . . . OFF AT THE PEP RALLY.
YEAH, I'M FINE. IT'S JUST A CHECKUP.
WE'LL MISS YOU AT PRACTICE. CALL ME LATER!
OKAY. SEE YA!

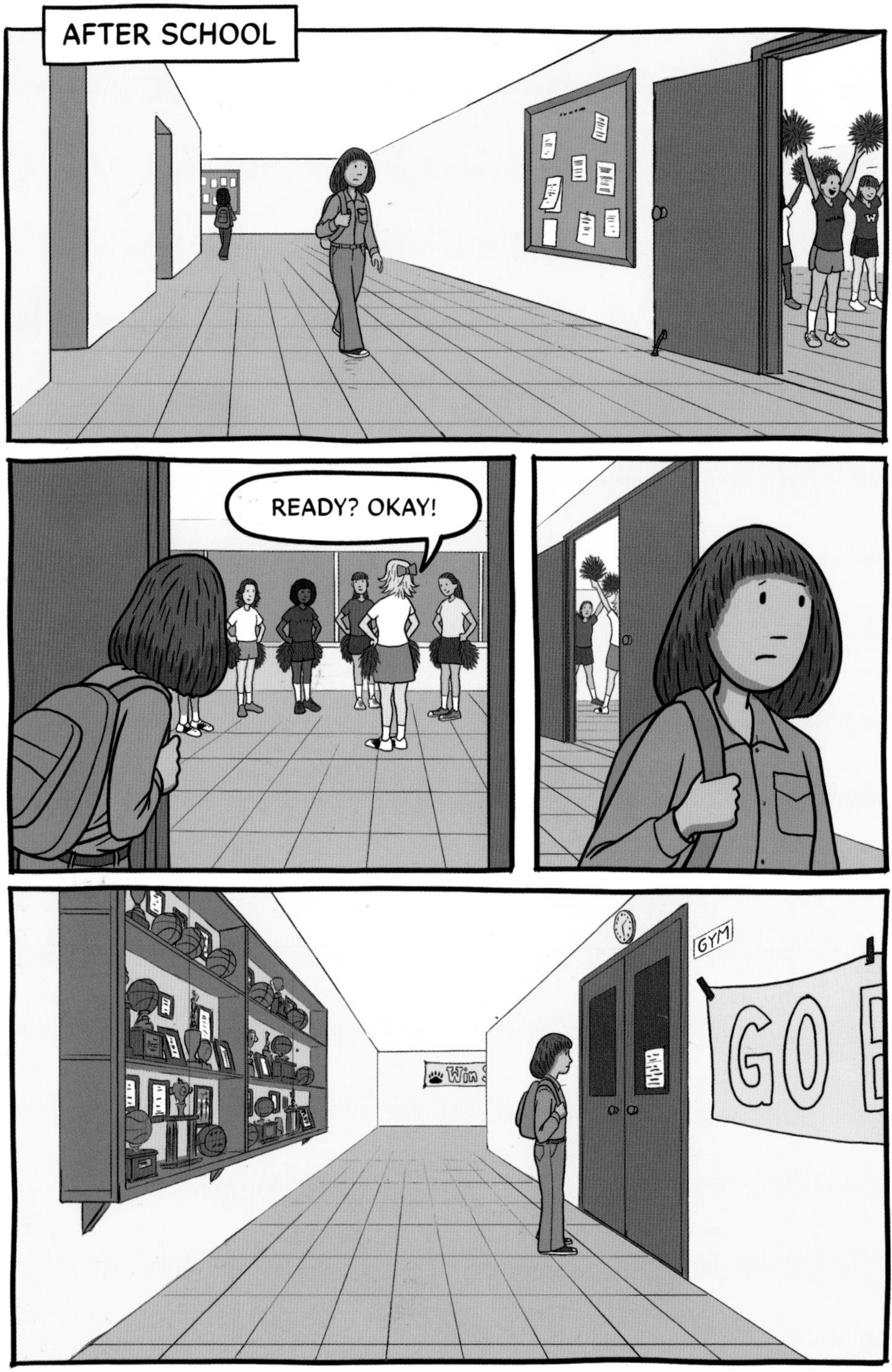
AFTER SCHOOL
READY? OKAY!
Win
GYM
GO

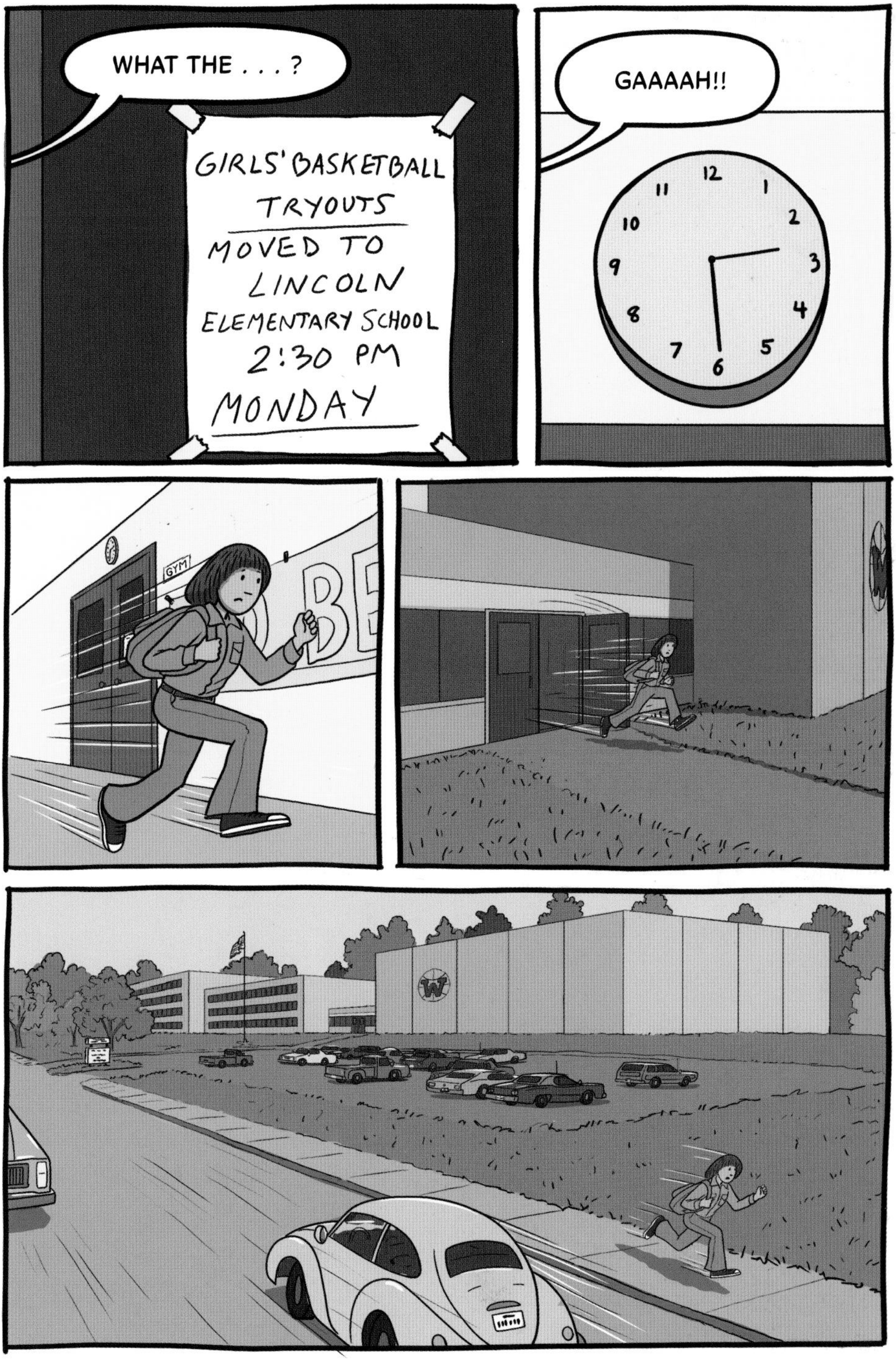
WHAT THE . . . ?
GIRLS' BASKETBALL TRYOUTS
MOVED TO LINCOLN ELEMENTARY SCHOOL
2:30 PM
MONDAY
GAAAAH!!
GYM

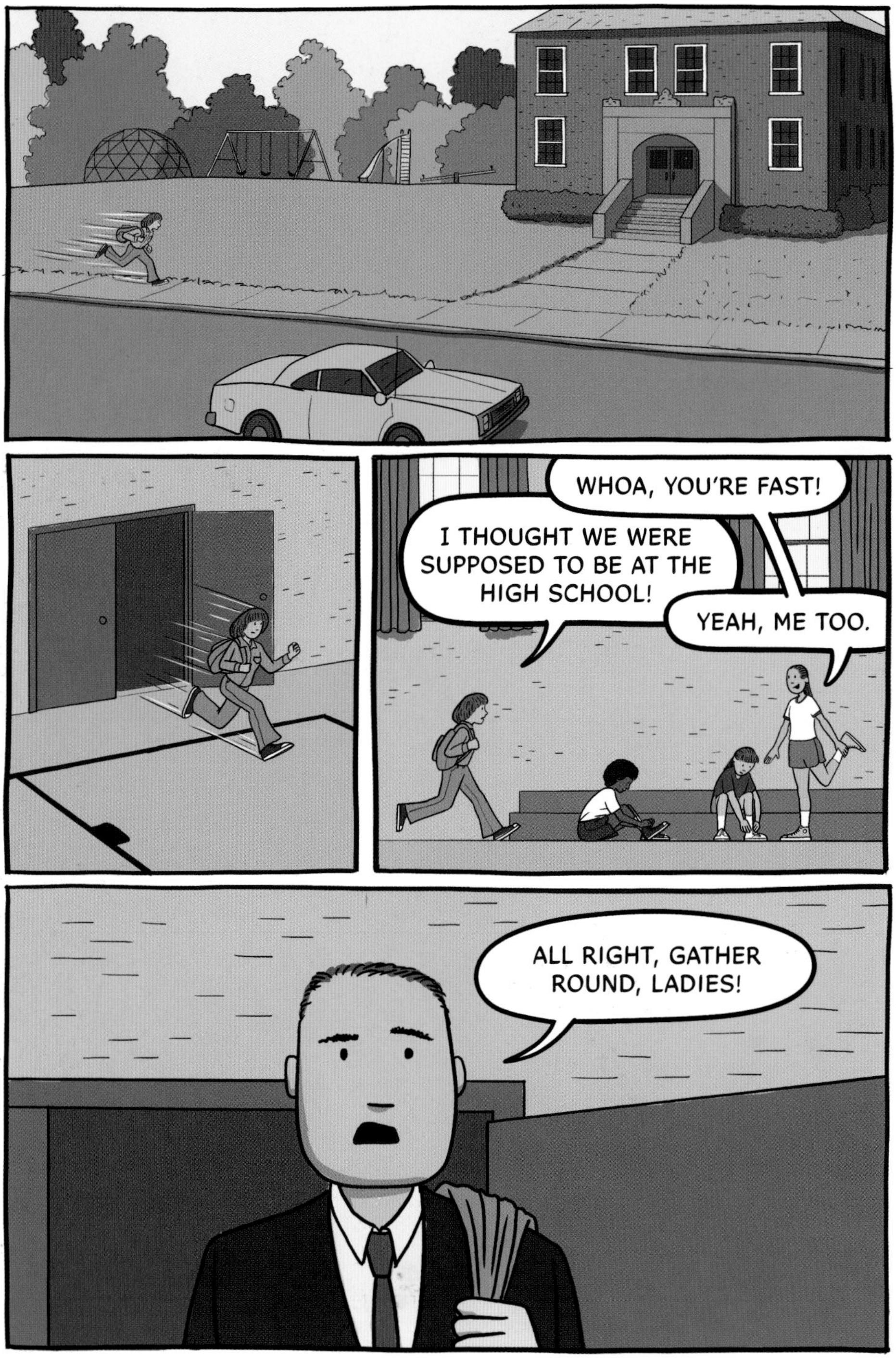
WHOA, YOU'RE FAST!
I THOUGHT WE WERE SUPPOSED TO BE AT THE HIGH SCHOOL!
YEAH, ME TOO.
ALL RIGHT, GATHER ROUND, LADIES!

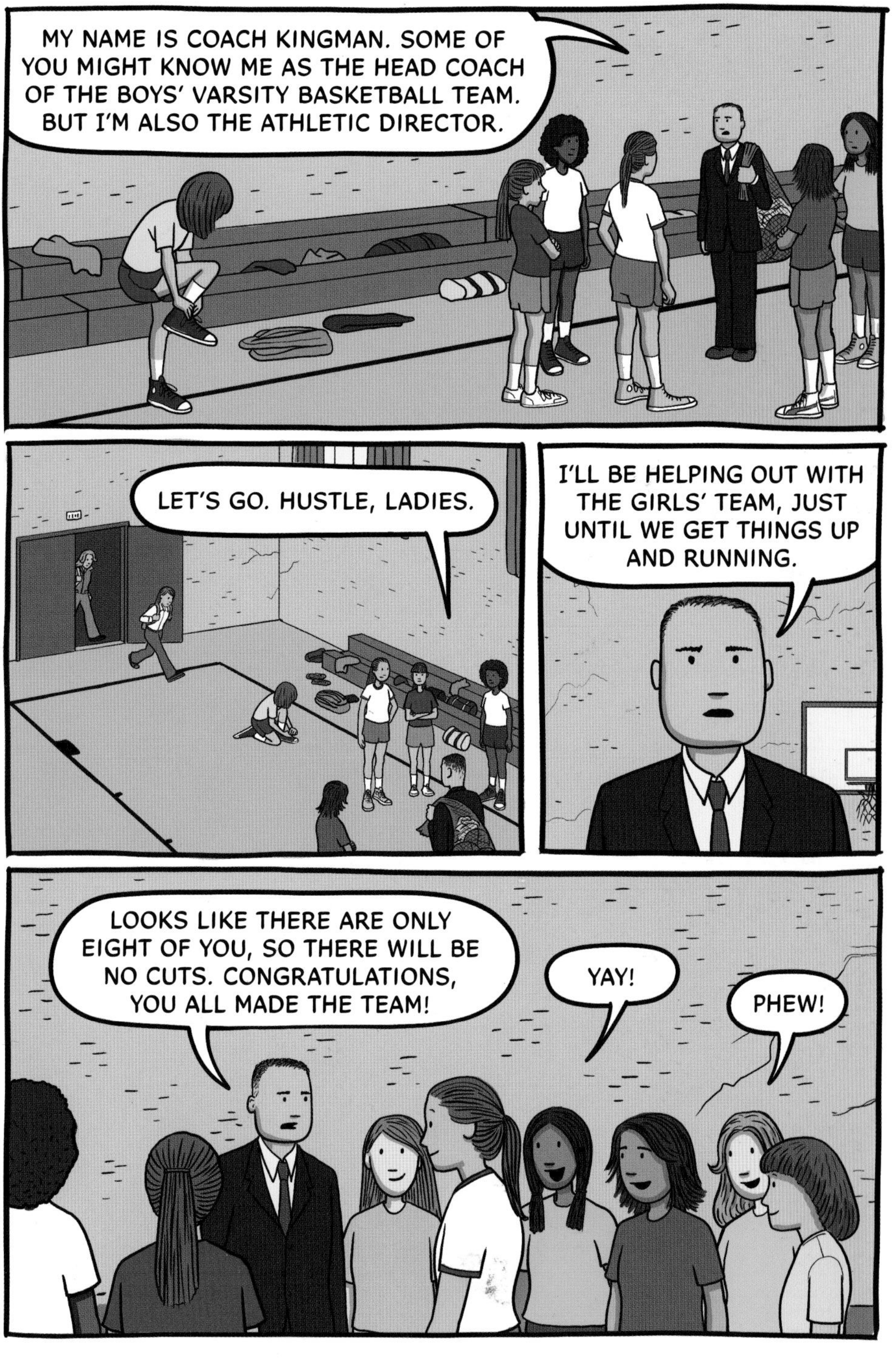
MY NAME IS COACH KINGMAN. SOME OF YOU MIGHT KNOW ME AS THE HEAD COACH OF THE BOYS' VARSITY BASKETBALL TEAM. BUT I'M ALSO THE ATHLETIC DIRECTOR.
LET'S GO. HUSTLE, LADIES.
I'LL BE HELPING OUT WITH THE GIRLS' TEAM, JUST UNTIL WE GET THINGS UP AND RUNNING.
LOOKS LIKE THERE ARE ONLY EIGHT OF YOU, SO THERE WILL BE NO CUTS. CONGRATULATIONS, YOU ALL MADE THE TEAM!
YAY!
PHEW!

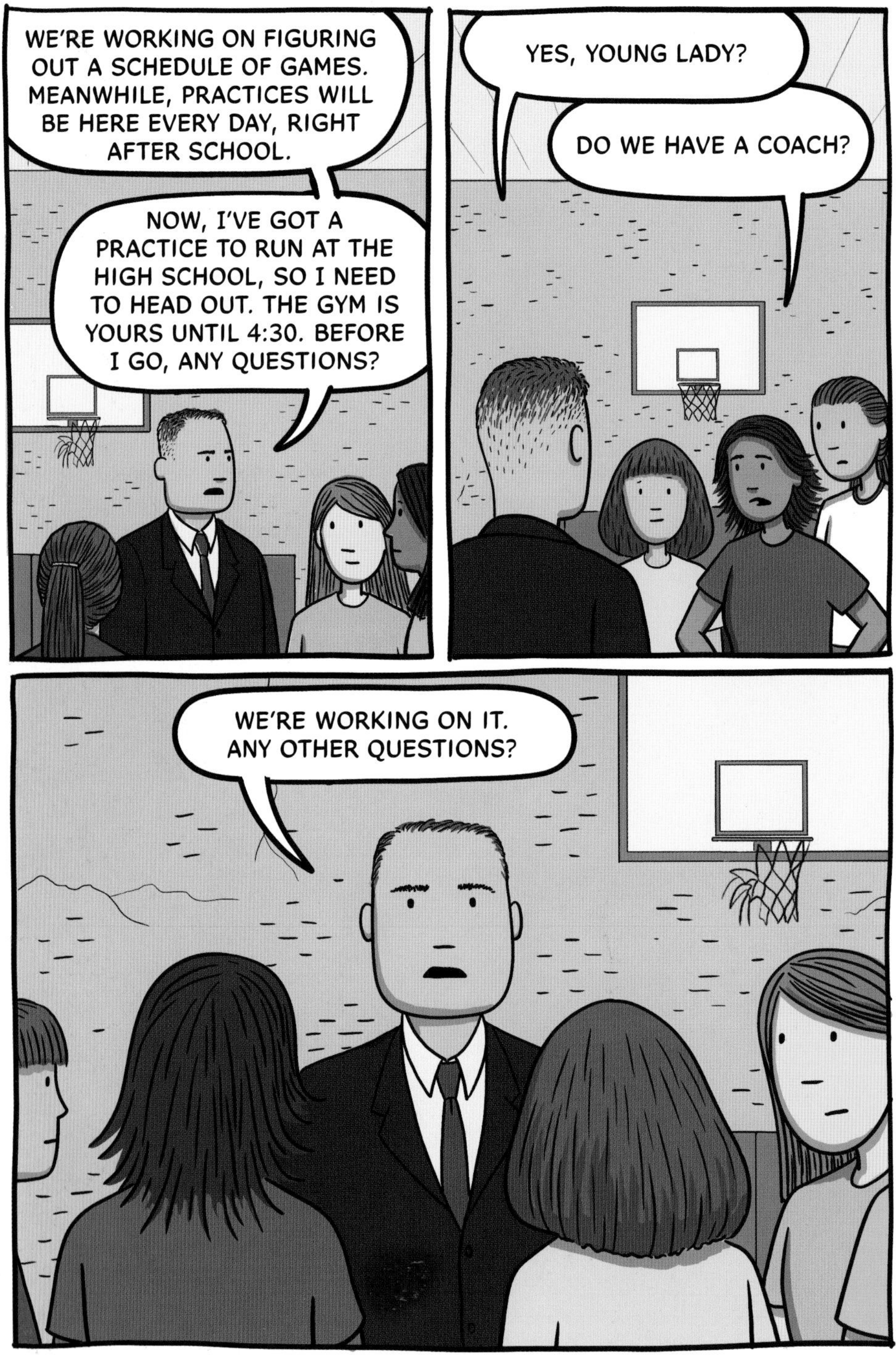
WE'RE WORKING ON FIGURING OUT A SCHEDULE OF GAMES. MEANWHILE, PRACTICES WILL BE HERE EVERY DAY, RIGHT AFTER SCHOOL.
NOW, I'VE GOT A PRACTICE TO RUN AT THE HIGH SCHOOL, SO I NEED TO HEAD OUT. THE GYM IS YOURS UNTIL 4:30. BEFORE I GO, ANY QUESTIONS?
YES, YOUNG LADY?
DO WE HAVE A COACH?
WE'RE WORKING ON IT. ANY OTHER QUESTIONS?

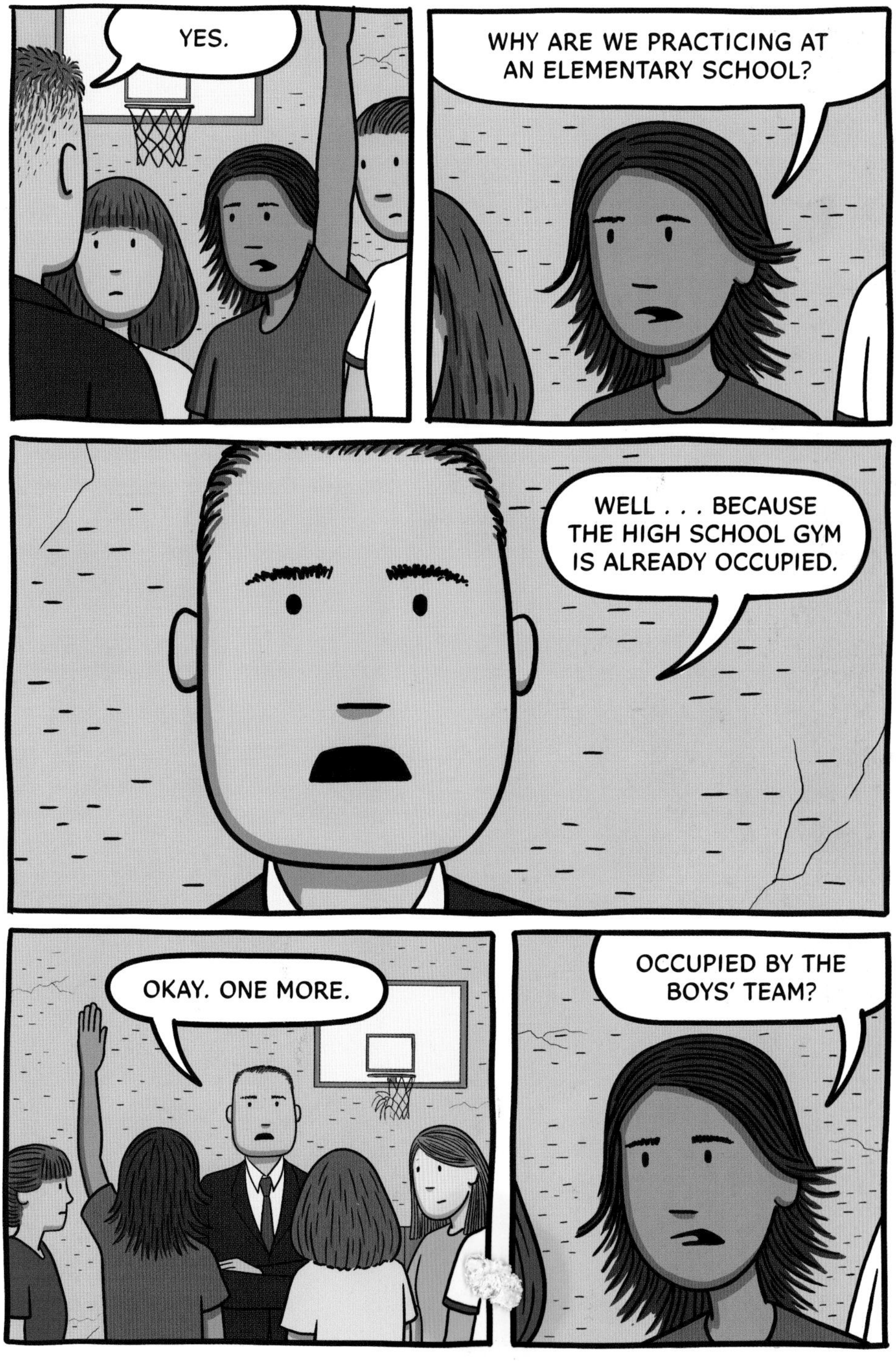
YES.
WHY ARE WE PRACTICING AT AN ELEMENTARY SCHOOL?
WELL . . . BECAUSE THE HIGH SCHOOL GYM IS ALREADY OCCUPIED.
OKAY. ONE MORE.
OCCUPIED BY THE BOYS' TEAM?

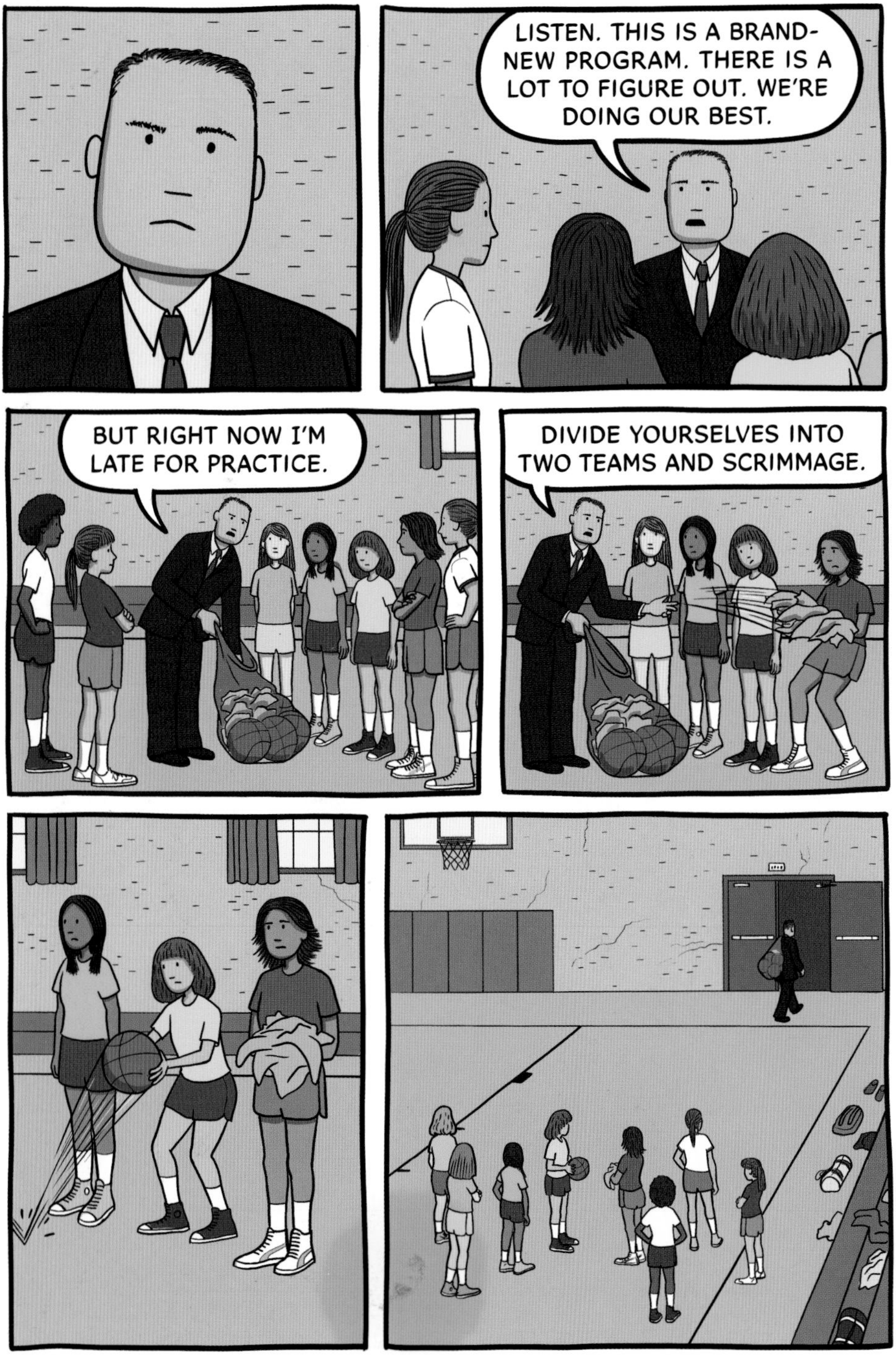
LISTEN. THIS IS A BRAND-NEW PROGRAM. THERE IS A LOT TO FIGURE OUT. WE'RE DOING OUR BEST.
BUT RIGHT NOW I'M LATE FOR PRACTICE.
DIVIDE YOURSELVES INTO TWO TEAMS AND SCRIMMAGE.

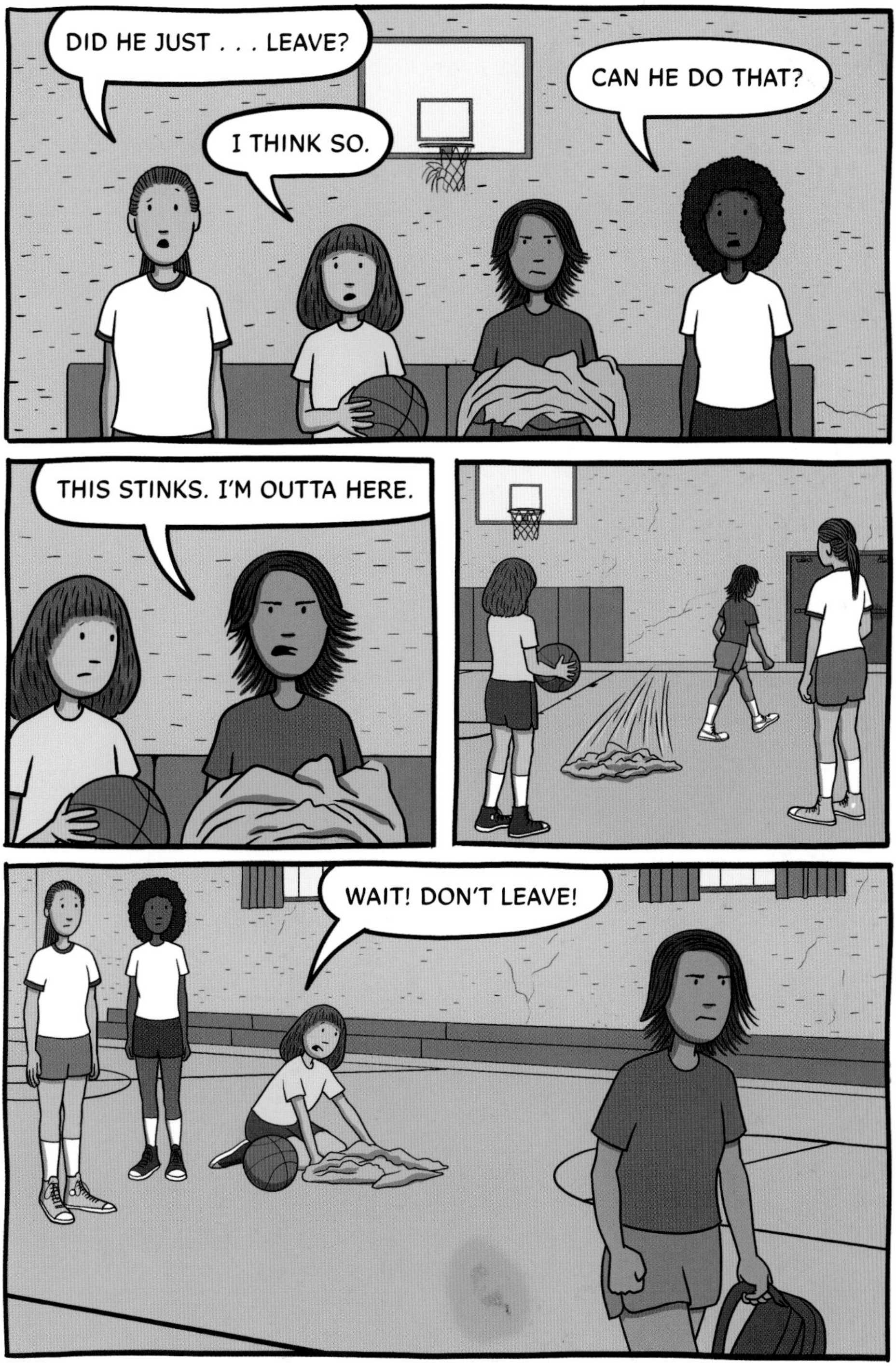
DID HE JUST . . . LEAVE?
I THINK SO.
CAN HE DO THAT?
THIS STINKS. I'M OUTTA HERE.
WAIT! DON'T LEAVE!

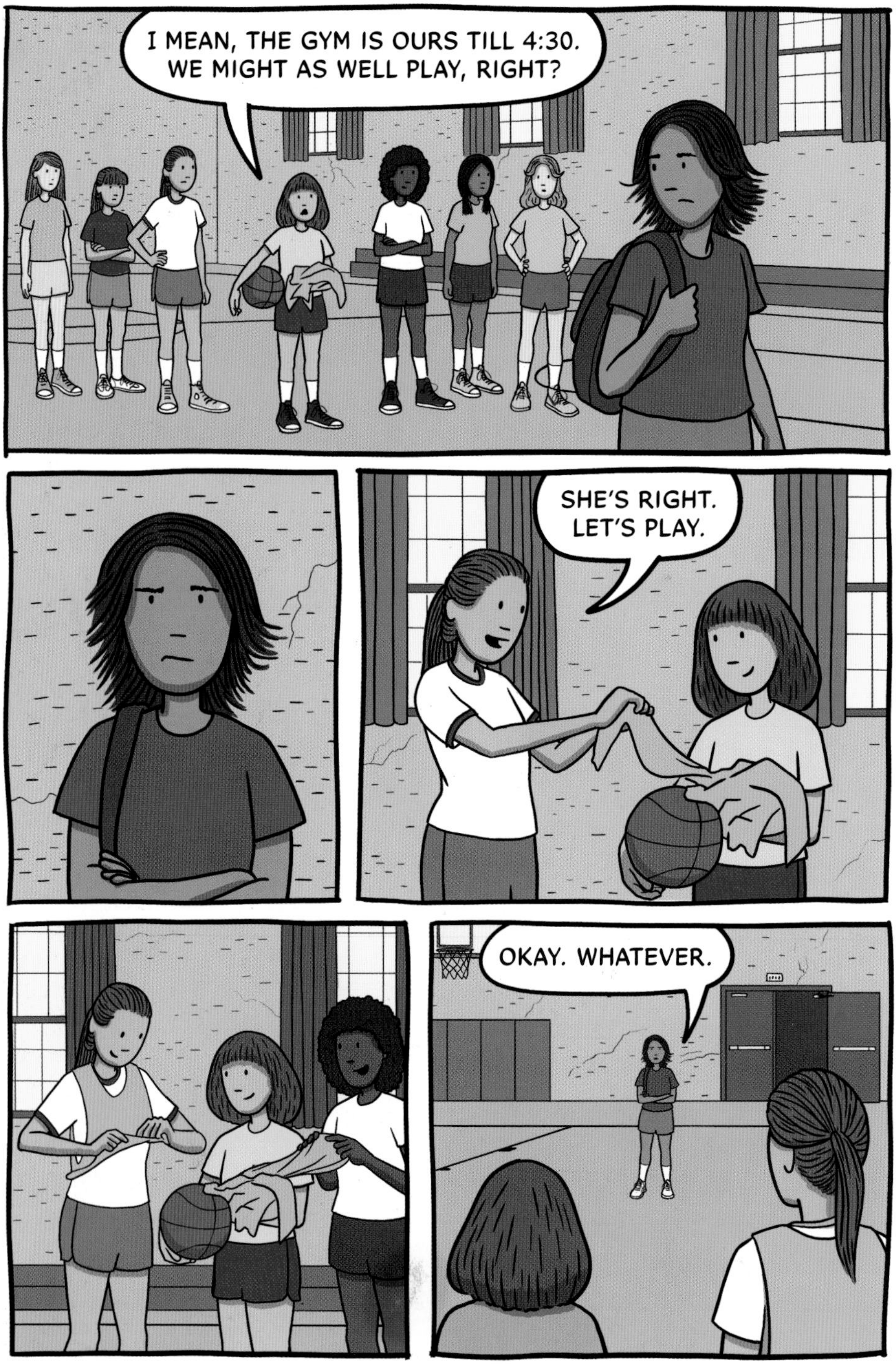
I MEAN, THE GYM IS OURS TILL 4:30. WE MIGHT AS WELL PLAY, RIGHT?
SHE'S RIGHT. LET'S PLAY.
OKAY. WHATEVER.

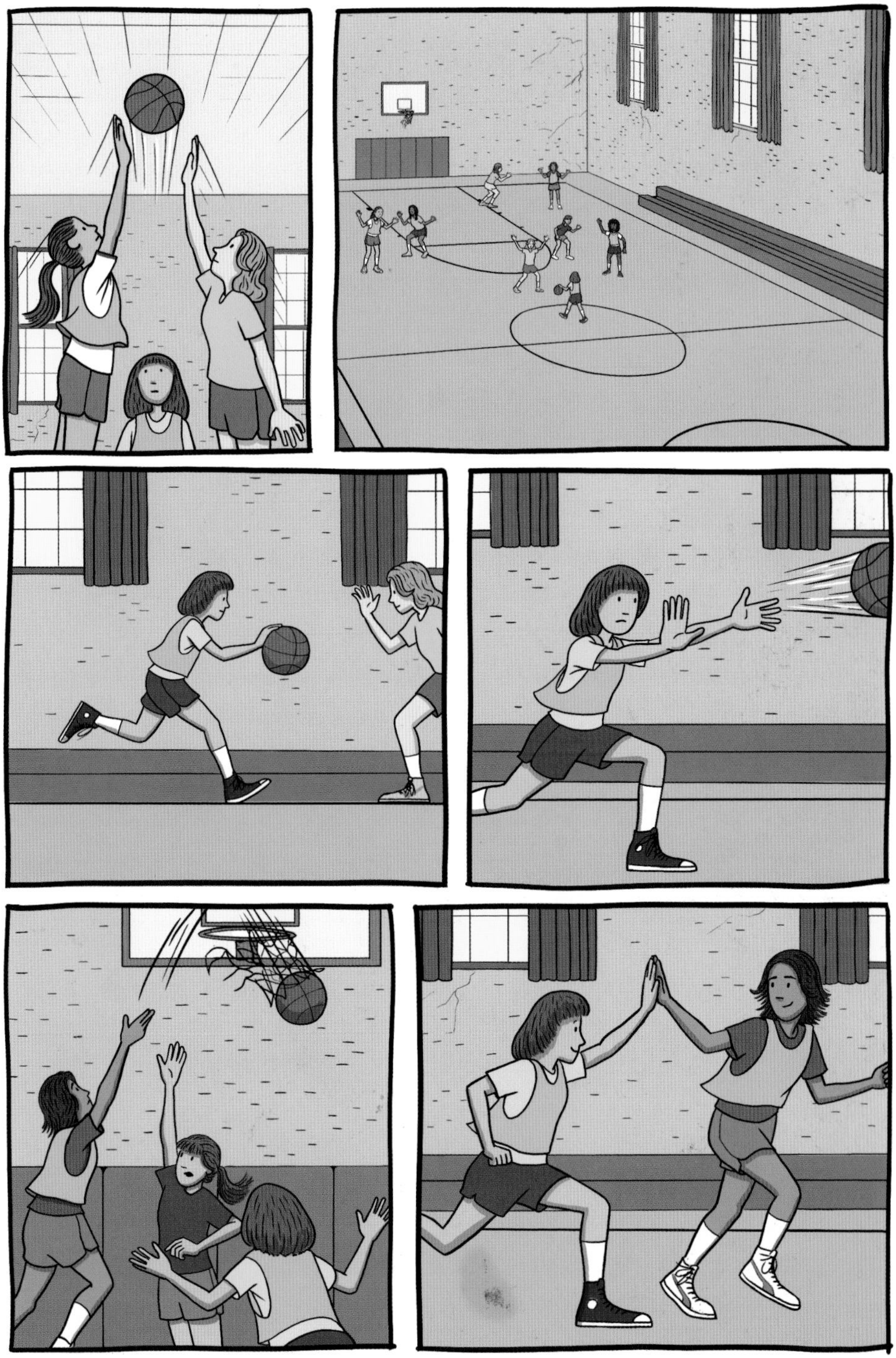

LATER THAT NIGHT

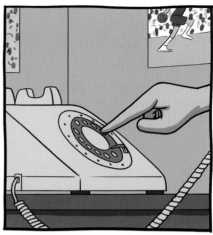

HELLO?

40

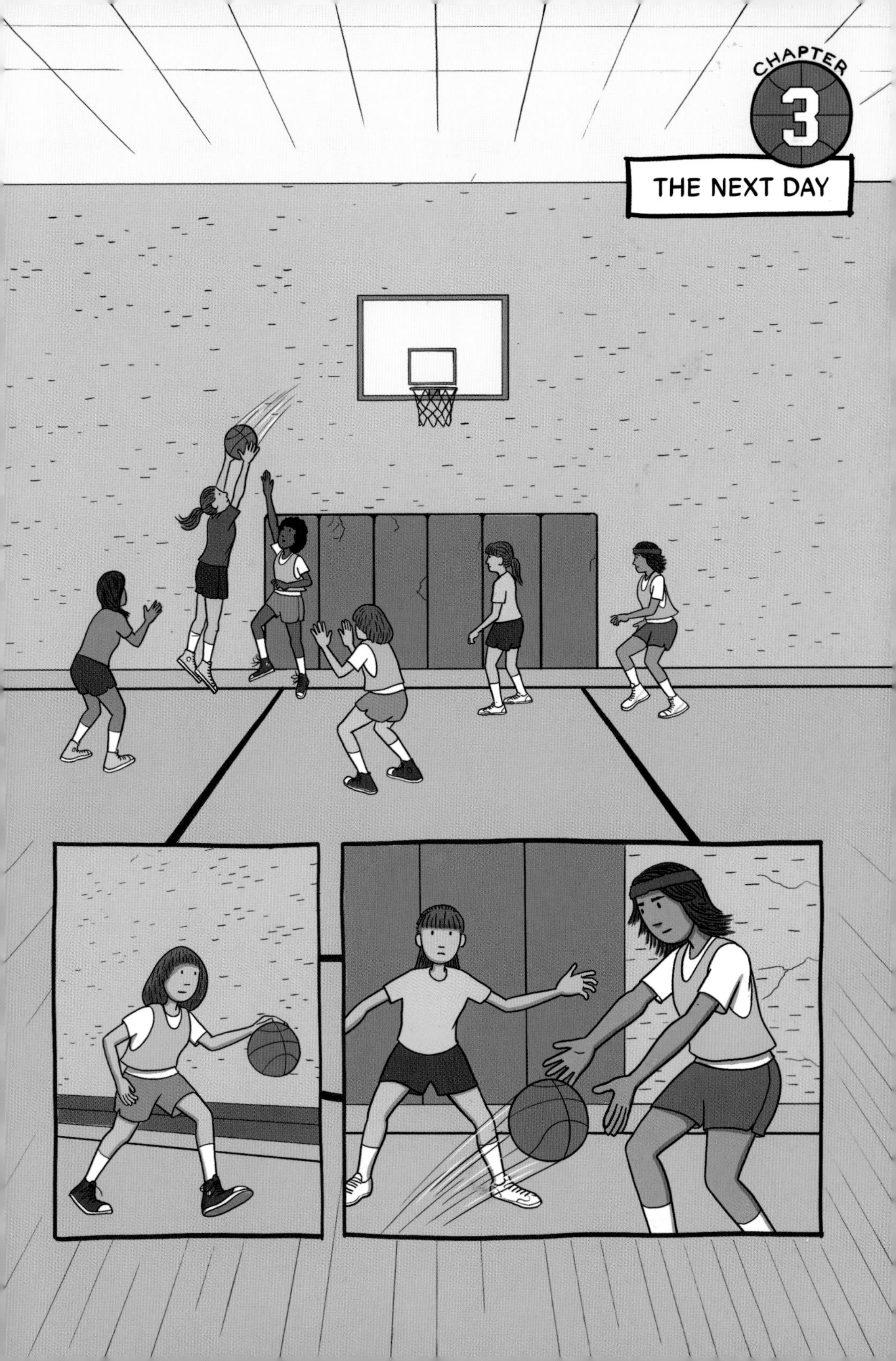
CHAPTER
3
THE NEXT DAY

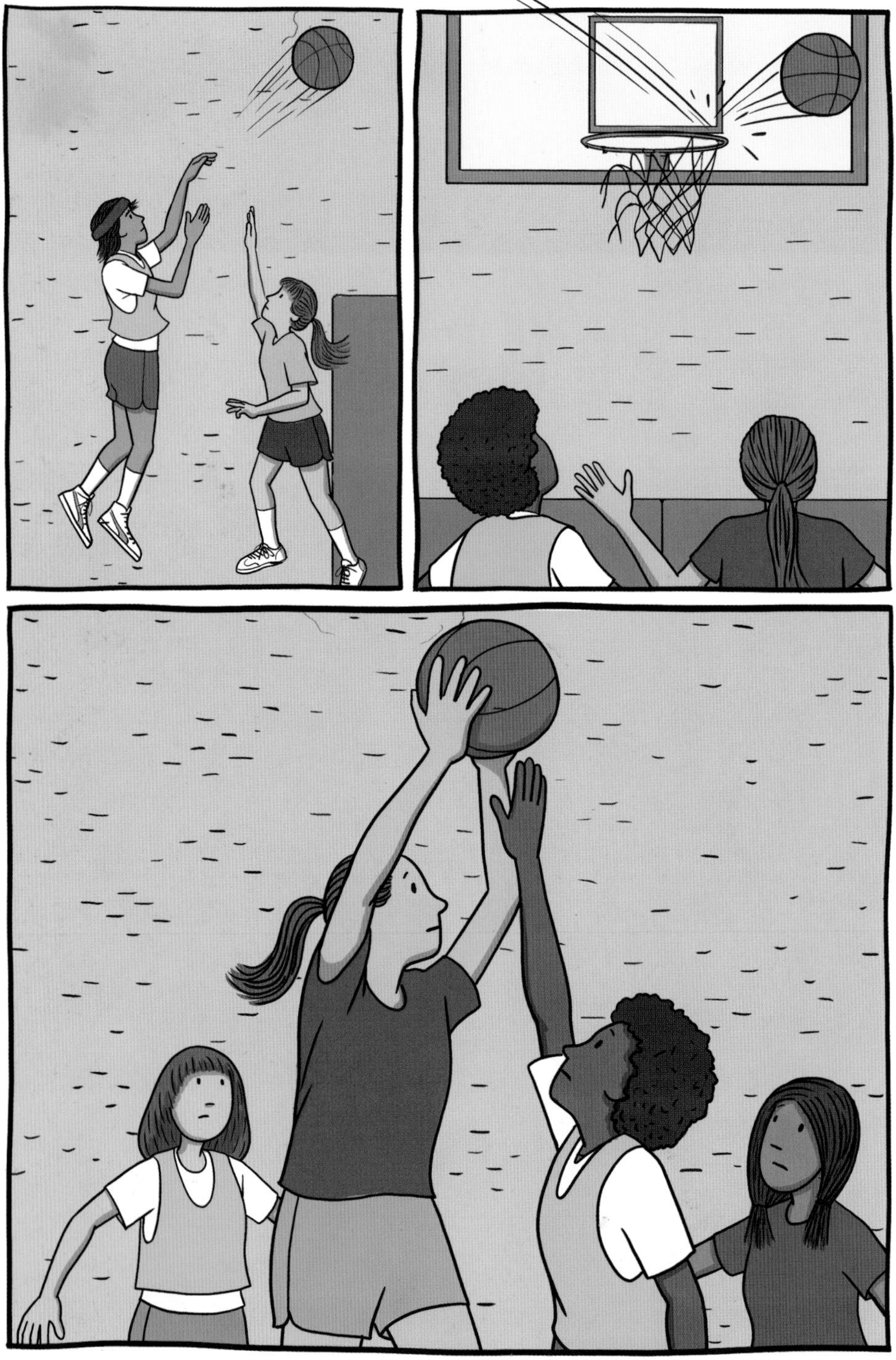

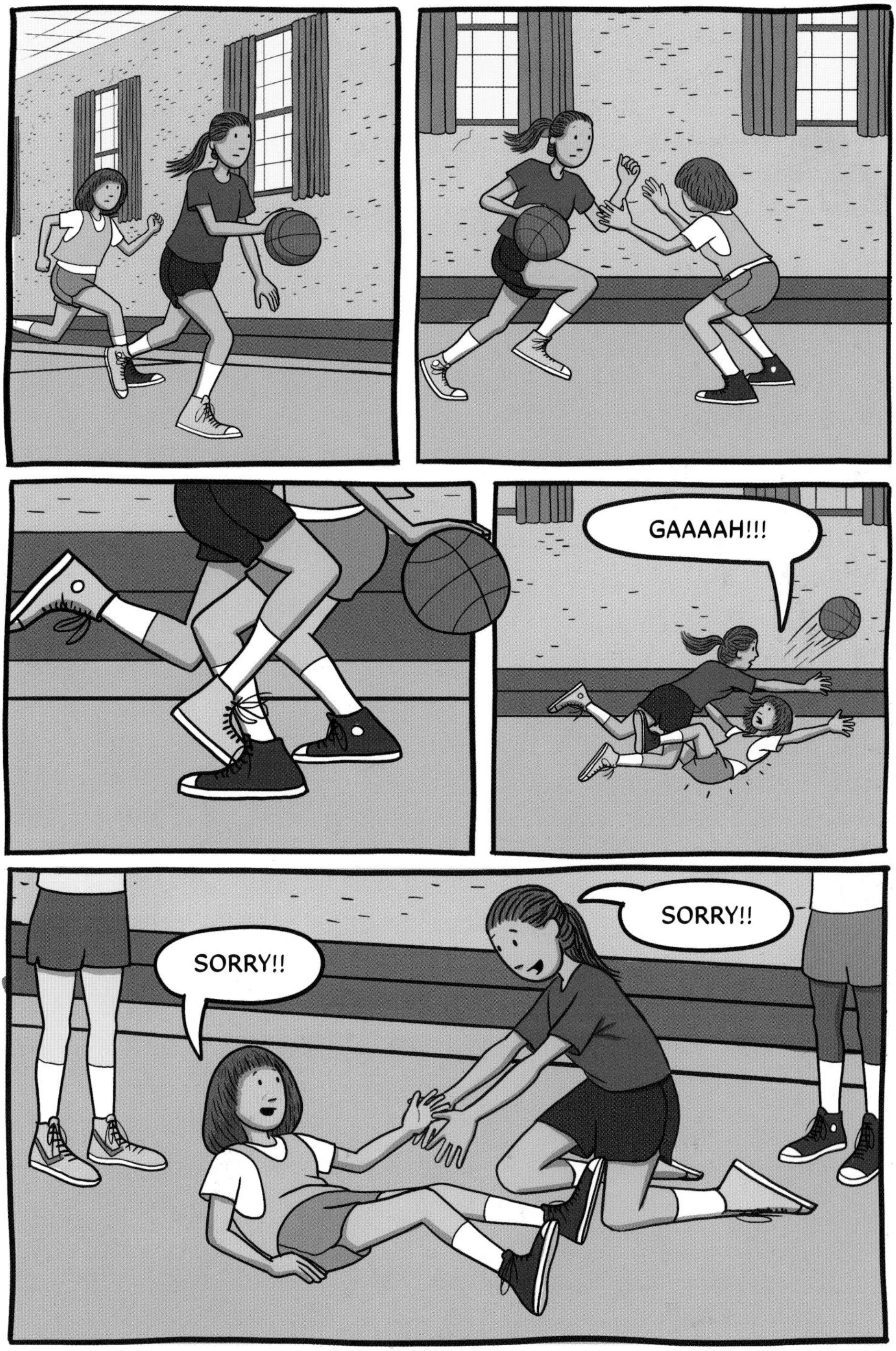
GAAAAH!!!
SORRY!!
SORRY!!

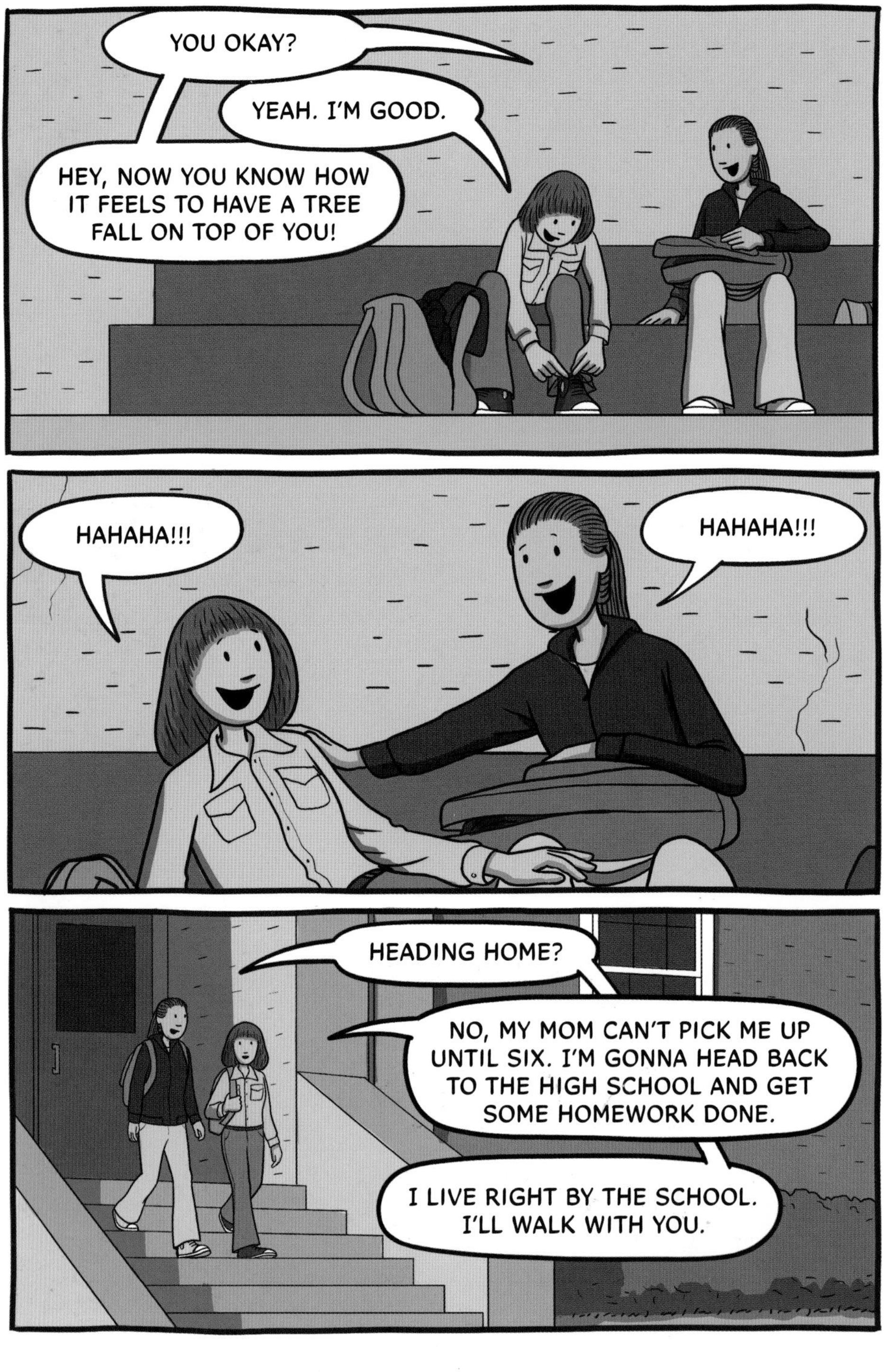
YOU OKAY?
YEAH. I'M GOOD.
HEY, NOW YOU KNOW HOW IT FEELS TO HAVE A TREE FALL ON TOP OF YOU!
HAHAHA!!!
HAHAHA!!!
HEADING HOME?
NO, MY MOM CAN'T PICK ME UP UNTIL SIX. I'M GONNA HEAD BACK TO THE HIGH SCHOOL AND GET SOME HOMEWORK DONE.
I LIVE RIGHT BY THE SCHOOL. I'LL WALK WITH YOU.

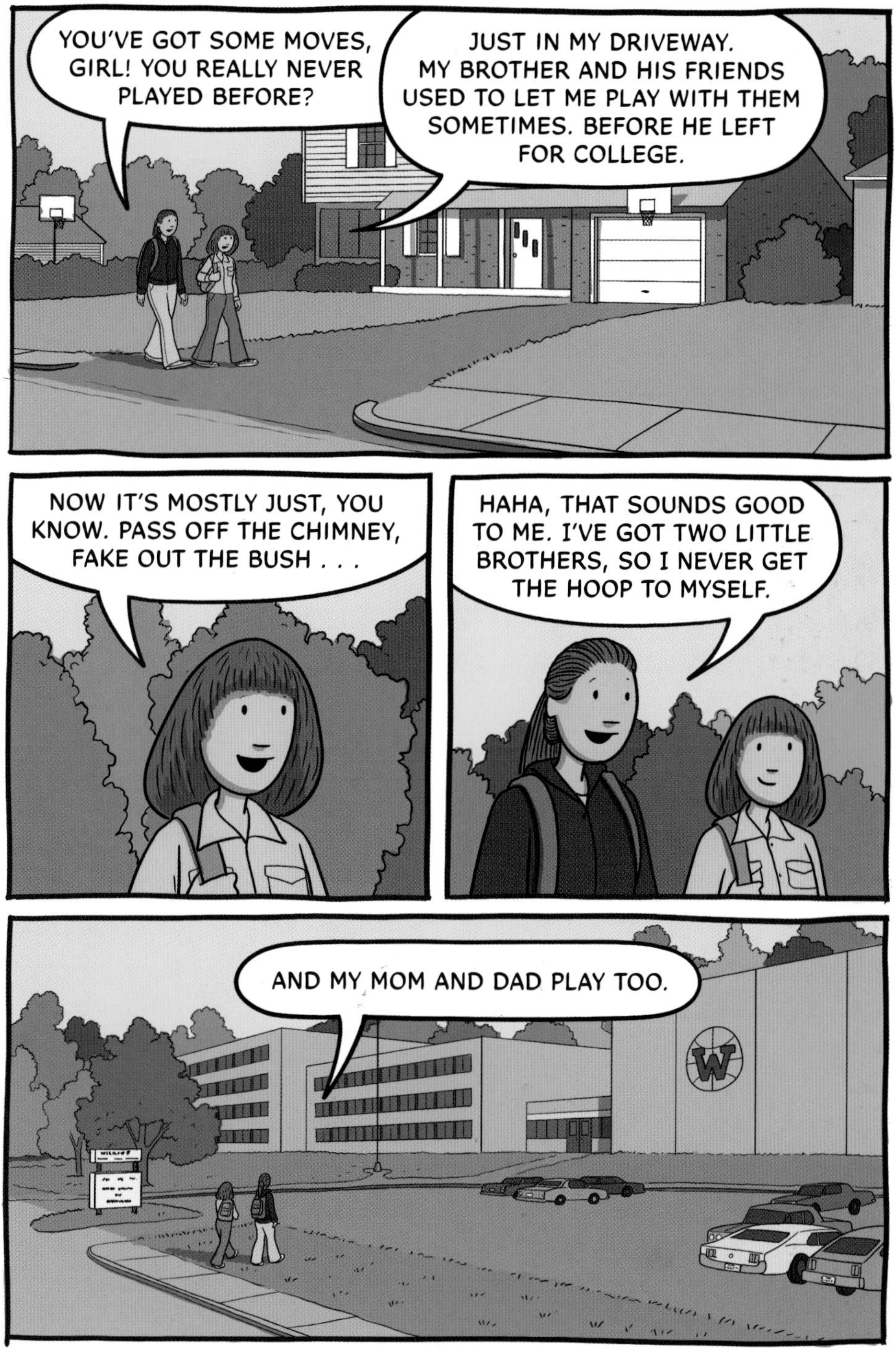
YOU'VE GOT SOME MOVES, GIRL! YOU REALLY NEVER PLAYED BEFORE?
JUST IN MY DRIVEWAY. MY BROTHER AND HIS FRIENDS USED TO LET ME PLAY WITH THEM SOMETIMES. BEFORE HE LEFT FOR COLLEGE.
NOW IT'S MOSTLY JUST, YOU KNOW. PASS OFF THE CHIMNEY, FAKE OUT THE BUSH . . .
HAHA, THAT SOUNDS GOOD TO ME. I'VE GOT TWO LITTLE BROTHERS, SO I NEVER GET THE HOOP TO MYSELF.
AND MY MOM AND DAD PLAY TOO.
W

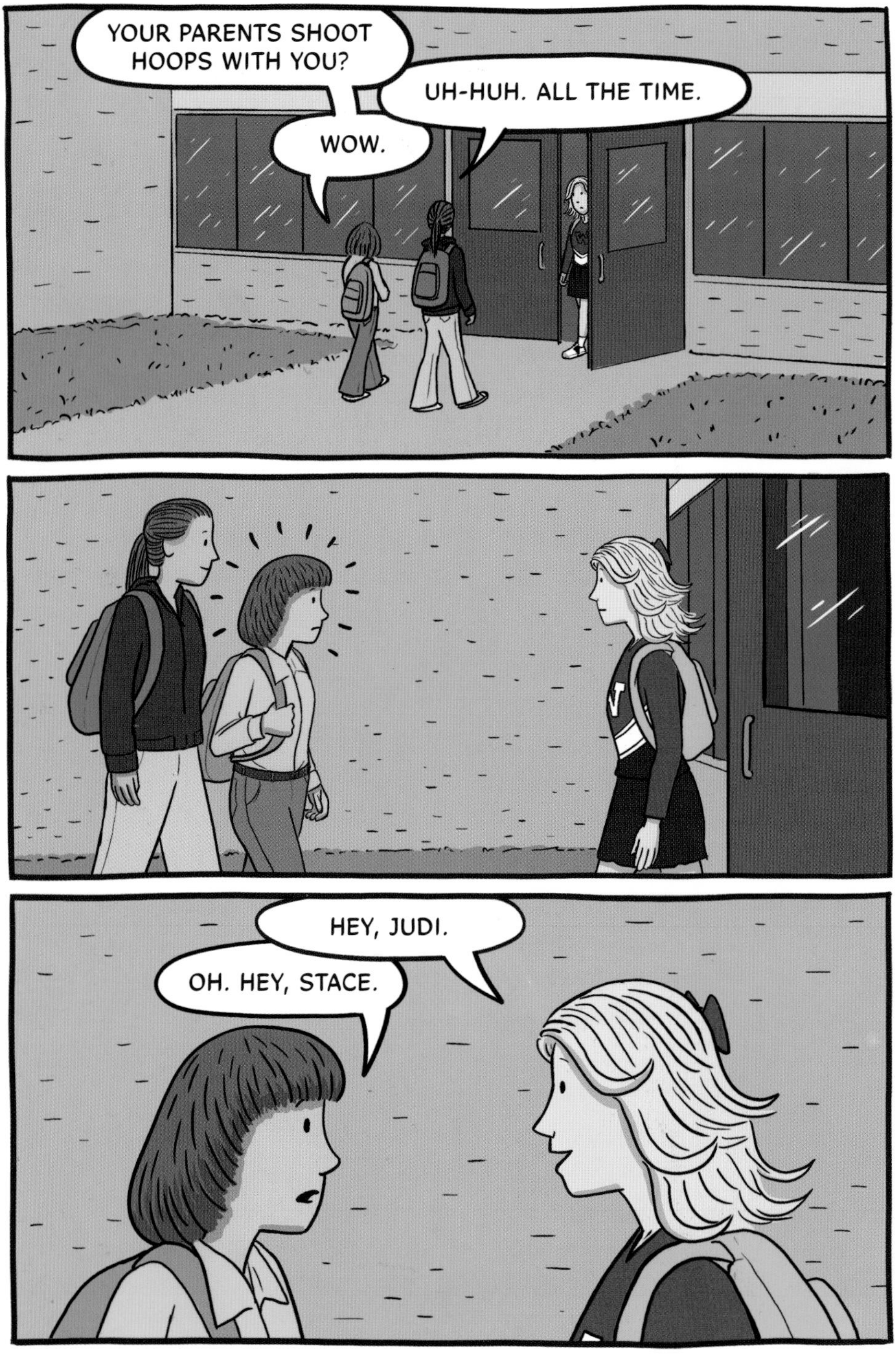
YOUR PARENTS SHOOT HOOPS WITH YOU?
UH-HUH. ALL THE TIME.
WOW.
HEY, JUDI.
OH. HEY, STACE.

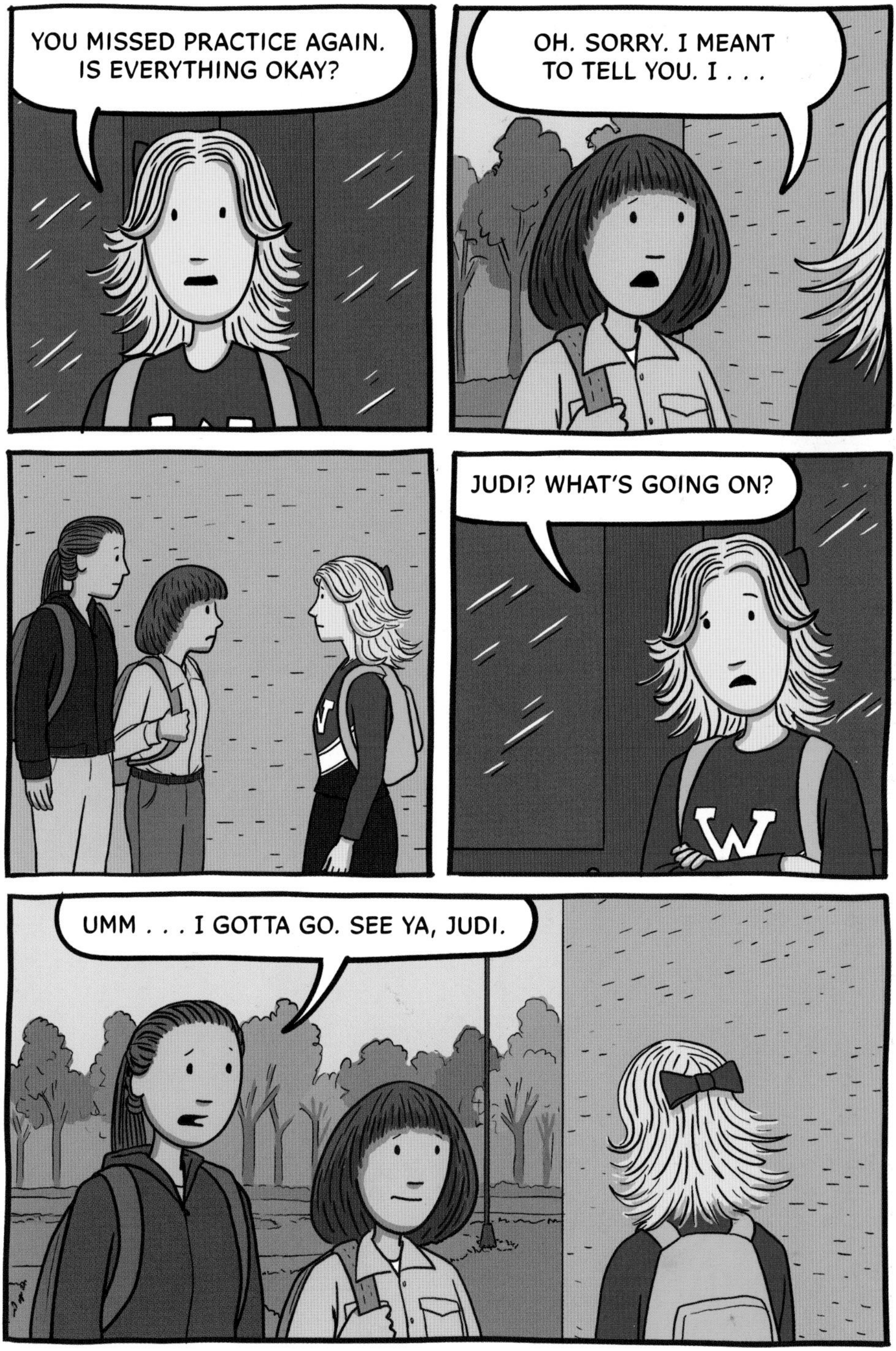
YOU MISSED PRACTICE AGAIN. IS EVERYTHING OKAY?
OH. SORRY. I MEANT TO TELL YOU. I . . .
JUDI? WHAT'S GOING ON?
UMM . . . I GOTTA GO. SEE YA, JUDI.

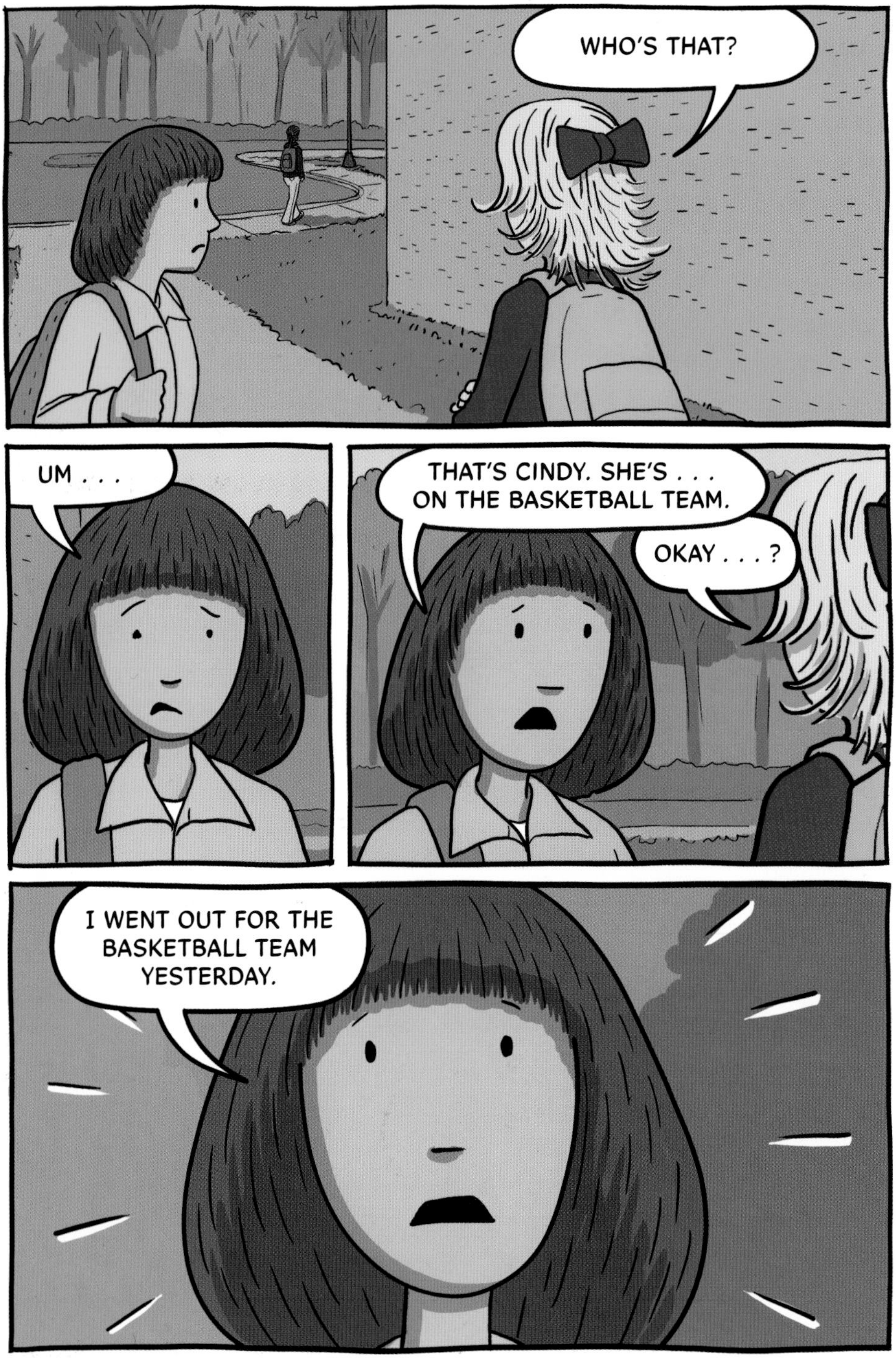
WHO'S THAT?
UM . . .
THAT'S CINDY. SHE'S . . . ON THE BASKETBALL TEAM.
OKAY . . . ?
I WENT OUT FOR THE BASKETBALL TEAM YESTERDAY.

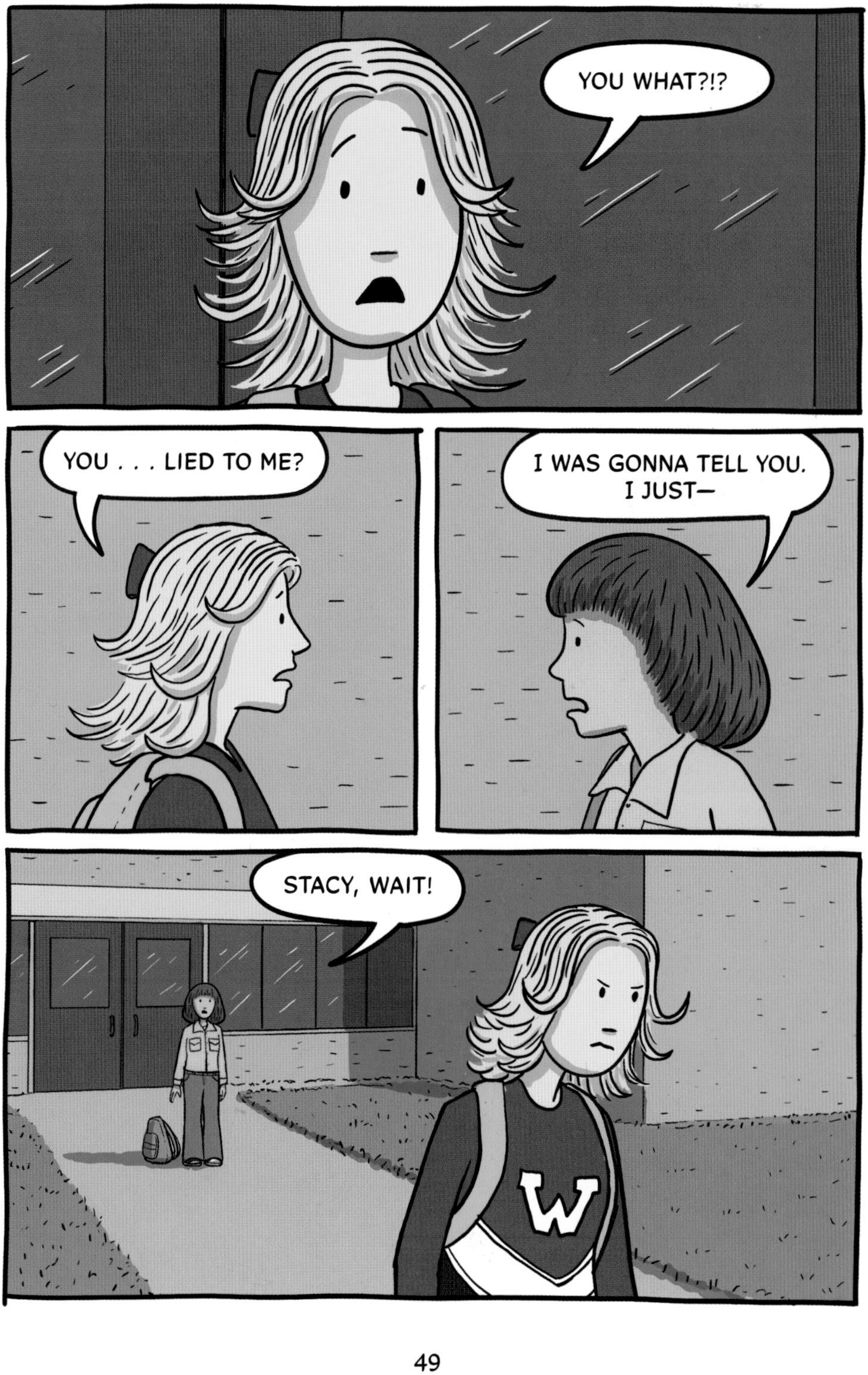
YOU WHAT?!?
YOU . . . LIED TO ME?
I WAS GONNA TELL YOU. I JUST—
STACY, WAIT!
W

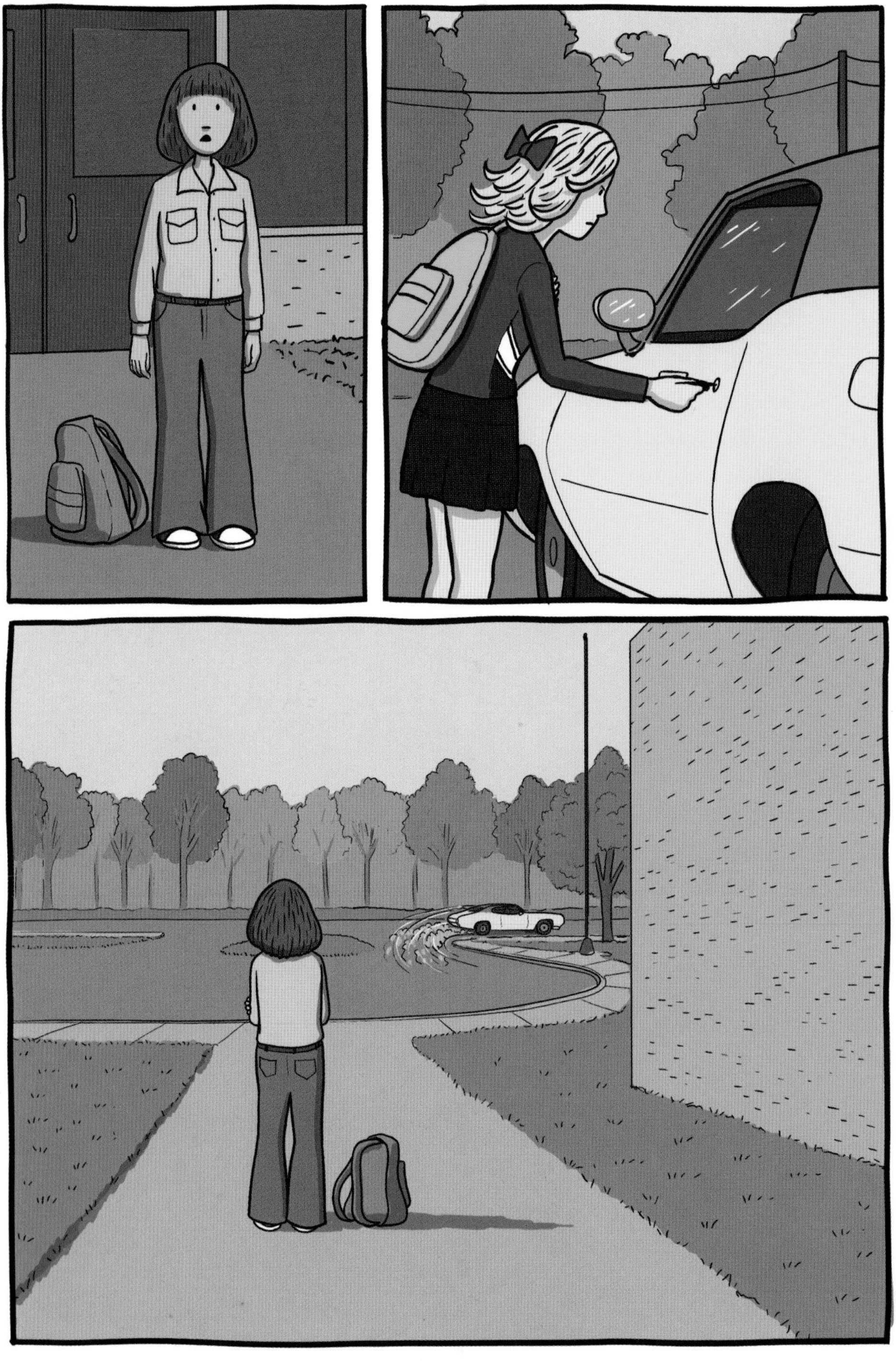

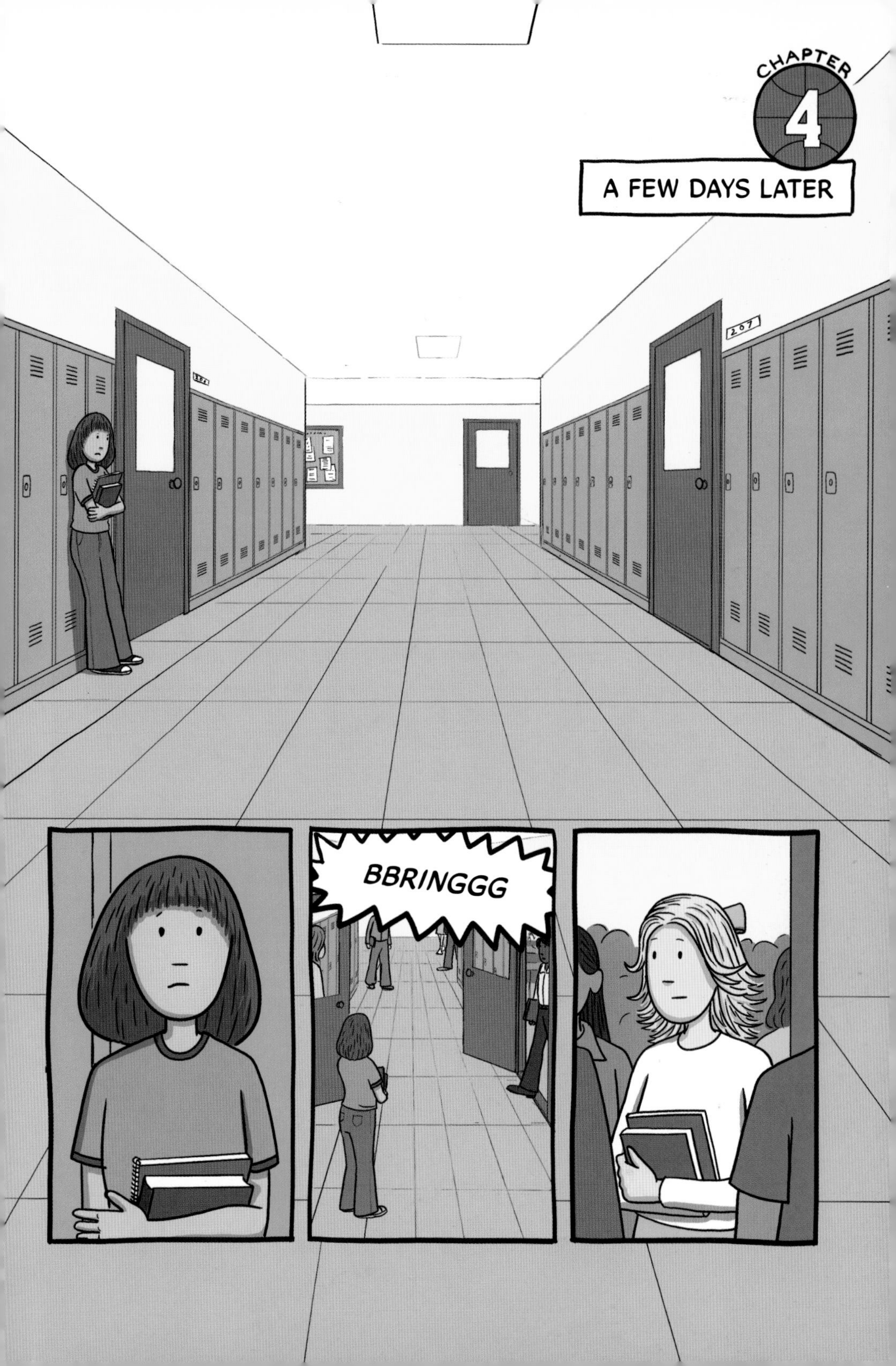
CHAPTER
4
A FEW DAYS LATER
207
BBRINGGG

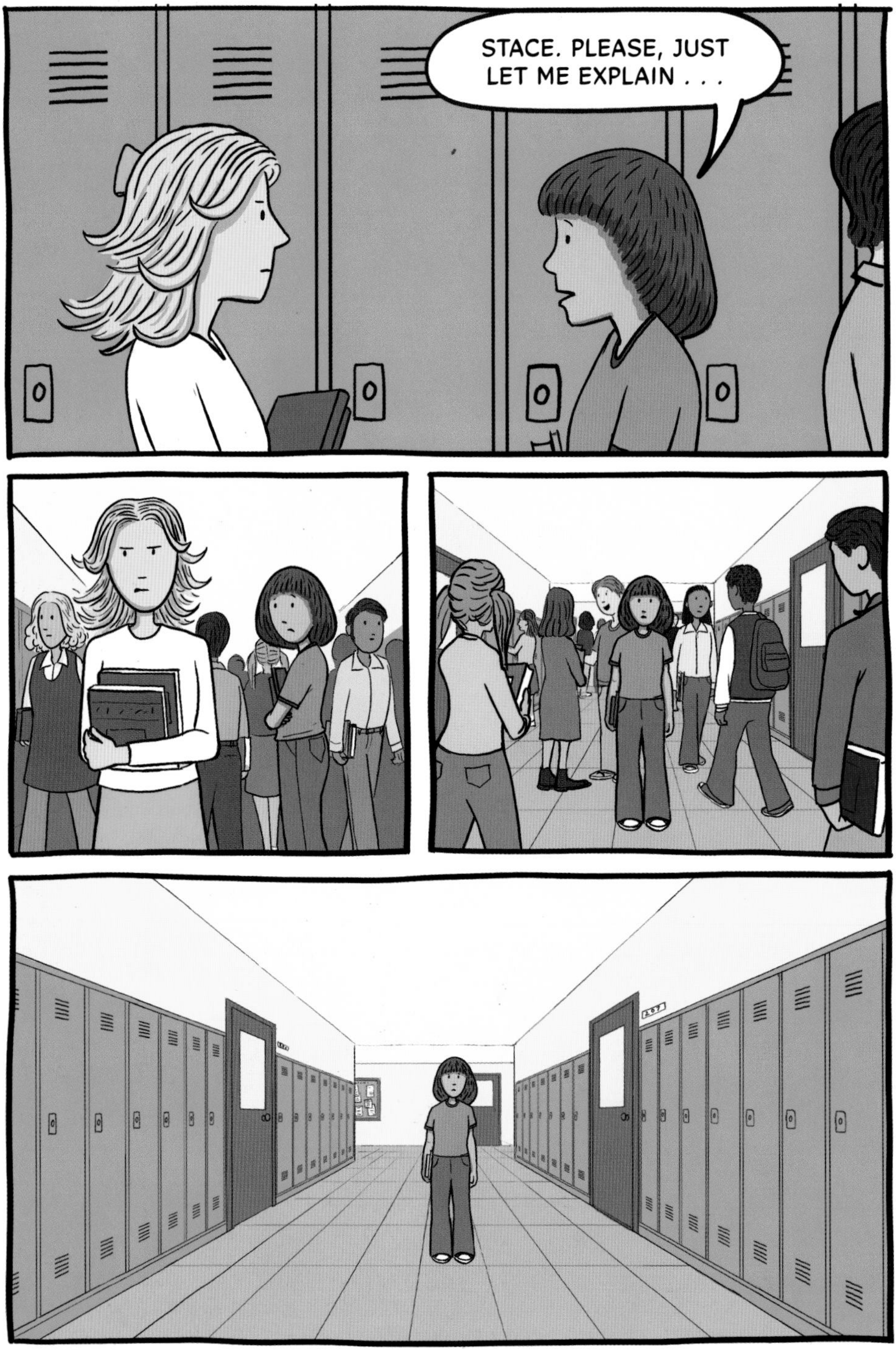
STACE. PLEASE, JUST LET ME EXPLAIN . . .

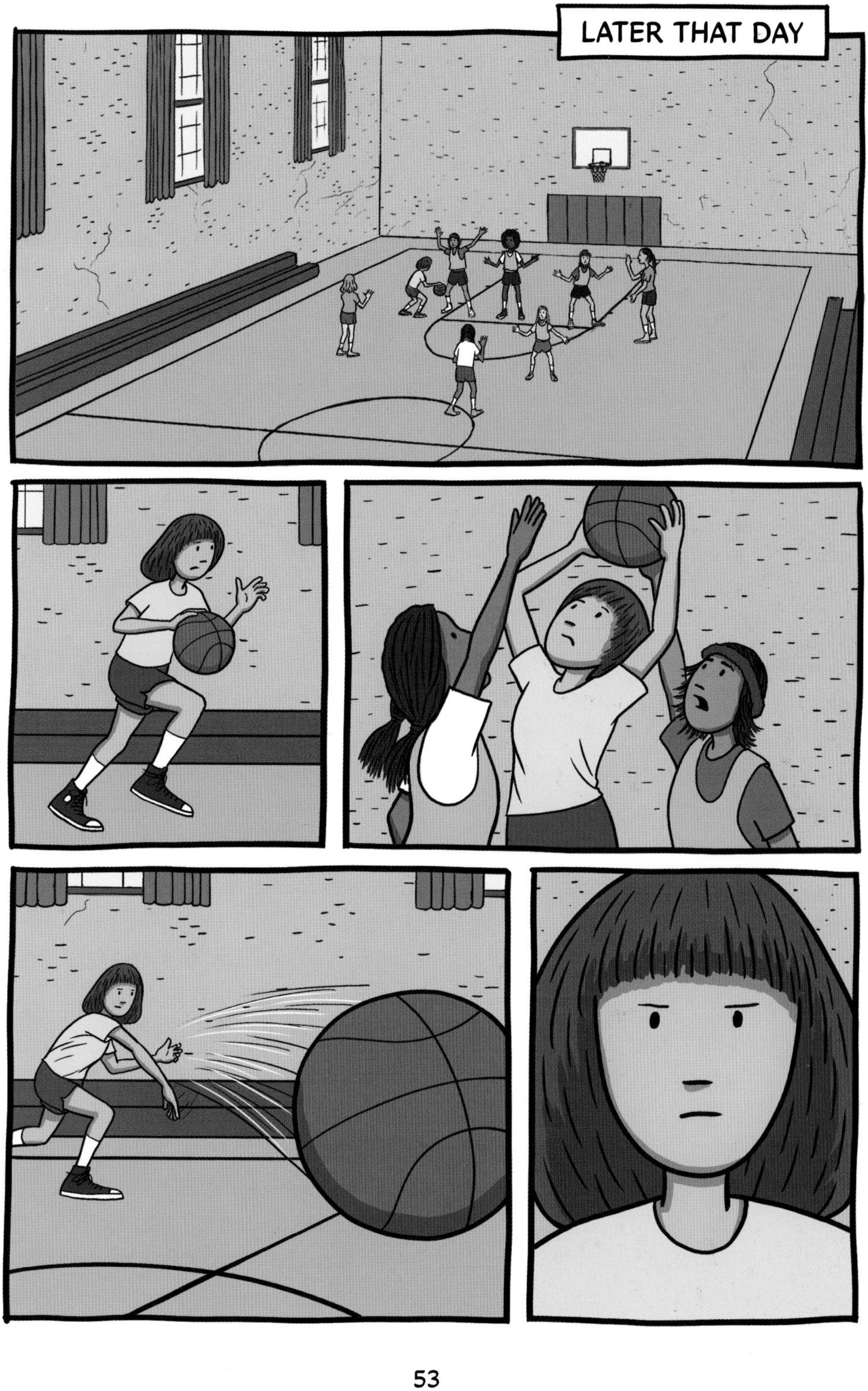
LATER THAT DAY

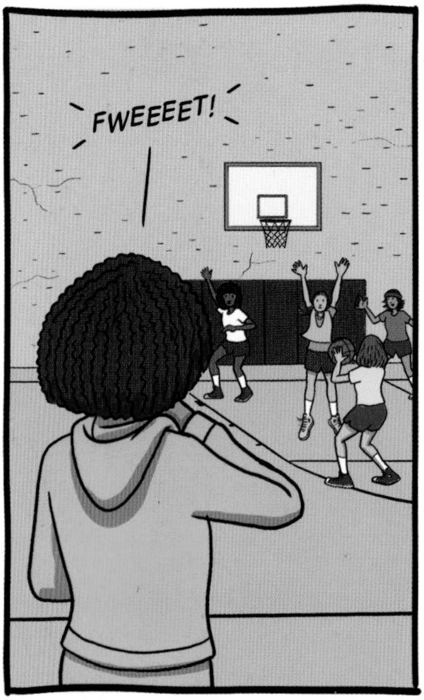
FWEEEET!

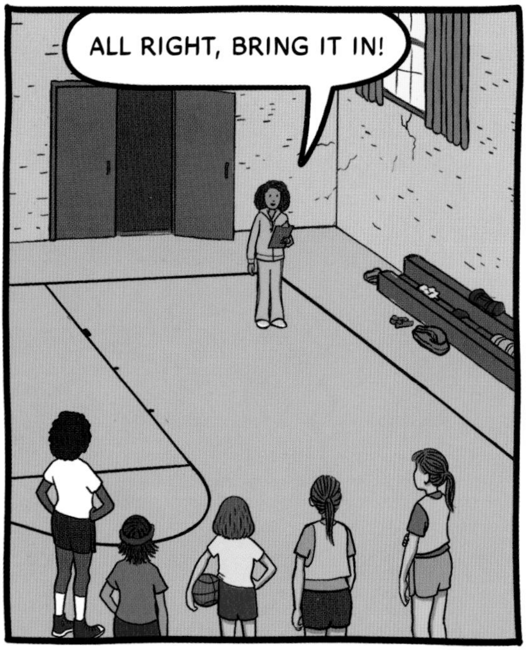
ALL RIGHT, BRING IT IN!

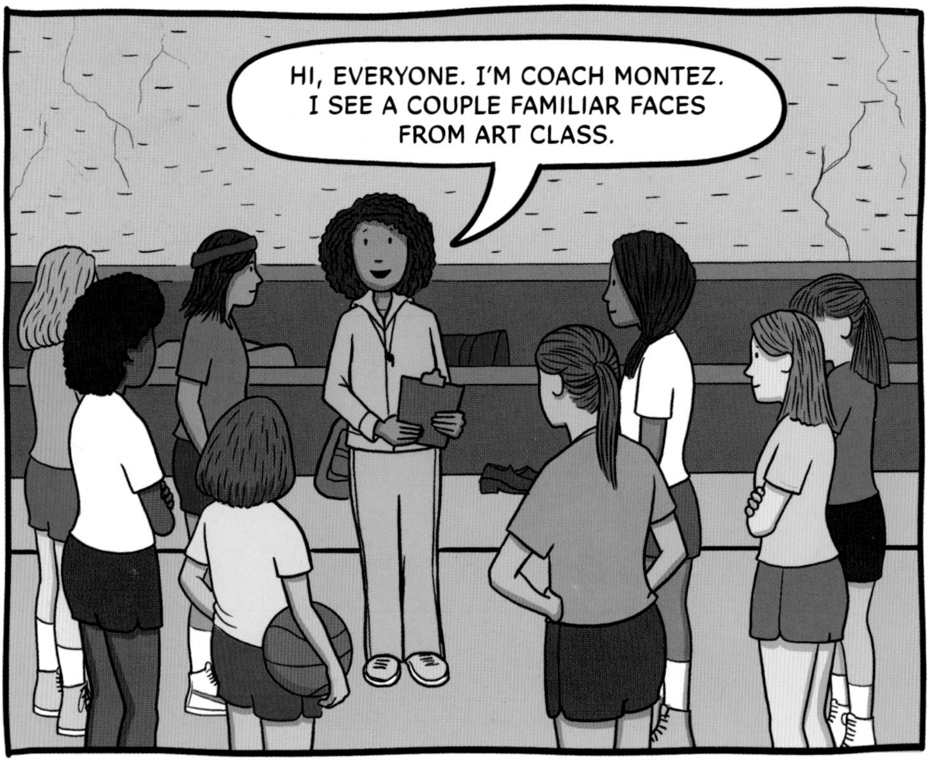
HI, EVERYONE. I'M COACH MONTEZ. I SEE A COUPLE FAMILIAR FACES FROM ART CLASS.

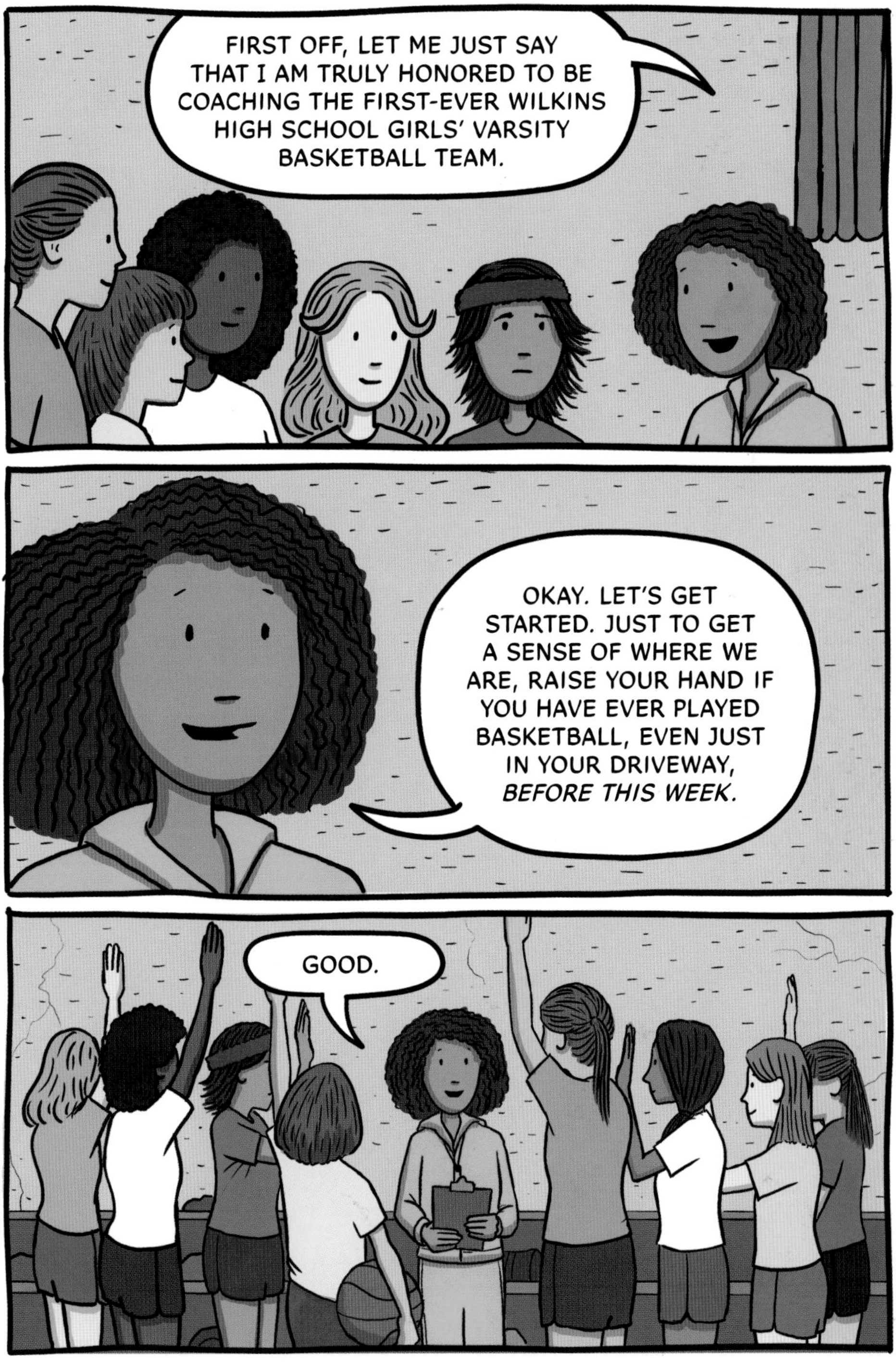
FIRST OFF, LET ME JUST SAY THAT I AM TRULY HONORED TO BE COACHING THE FIRST-EVER WILKINS HIGH SCHOOL GIRLS' VARSITY BASKETBALL TEAM.
OKAY. LET'S GET STARTED. JUST TO GET A SENSE OF WHERE WE ARE, RAISE YOUR HAND IF YOU HAVE EVER PLAYED BASKETBALL, EVEN JUST IN YOUR DRIVEWAY, *BEFORE THIS WEEK.*
GOOD.

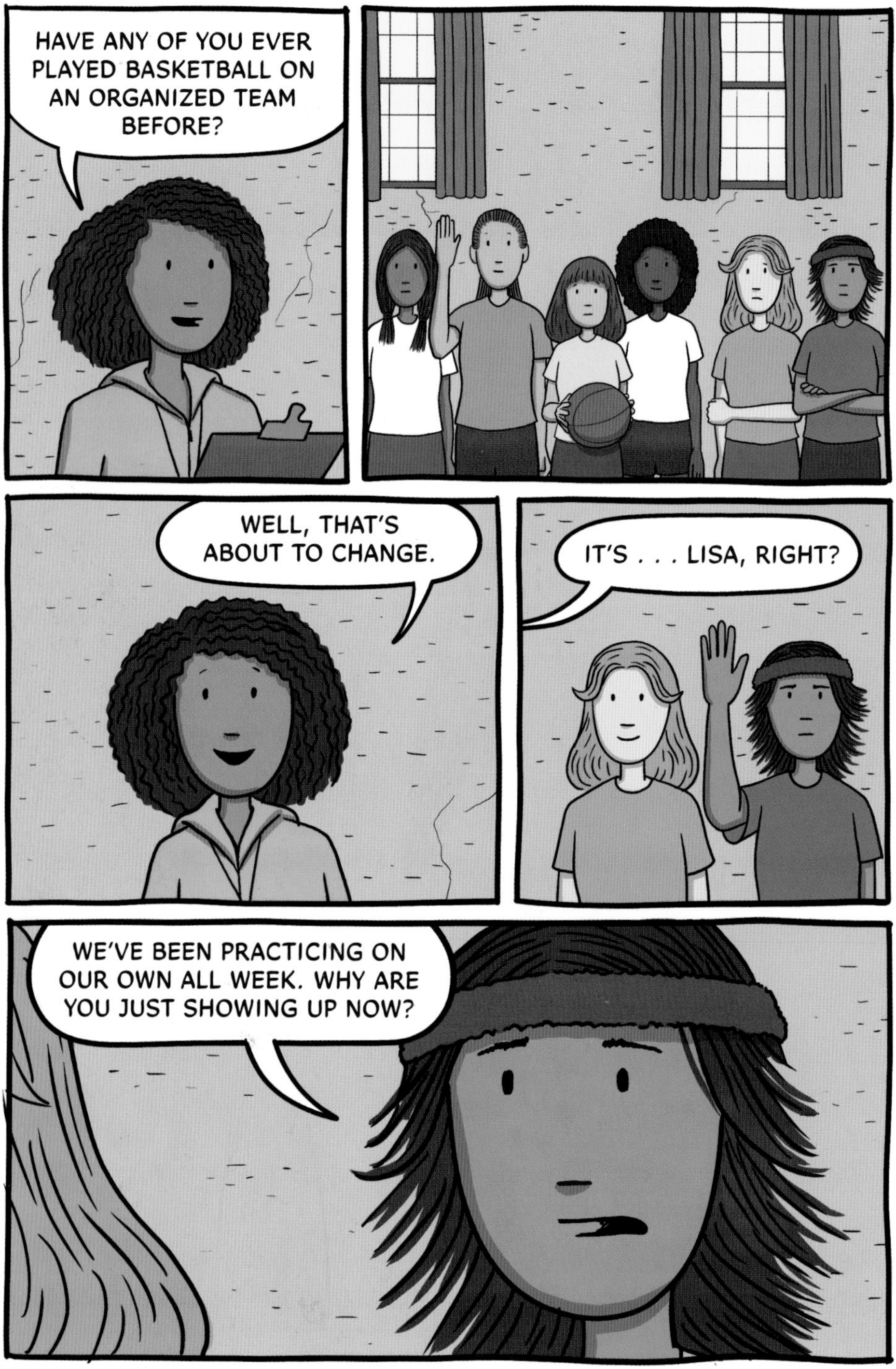
HAVE ANY OF YOU EVER PLAYED BASKETBALL ON AN ORGANIZED TEAM BEFORE?
WELL, THAT'S ABOUT TO CHANGE.
IT'S . . . LISA, RIGHT?
WE'VE BEEN PRACTICING ON OUR OWN ALL WEEK. WHY ARE YOU JUST SHOWING UP NOW?

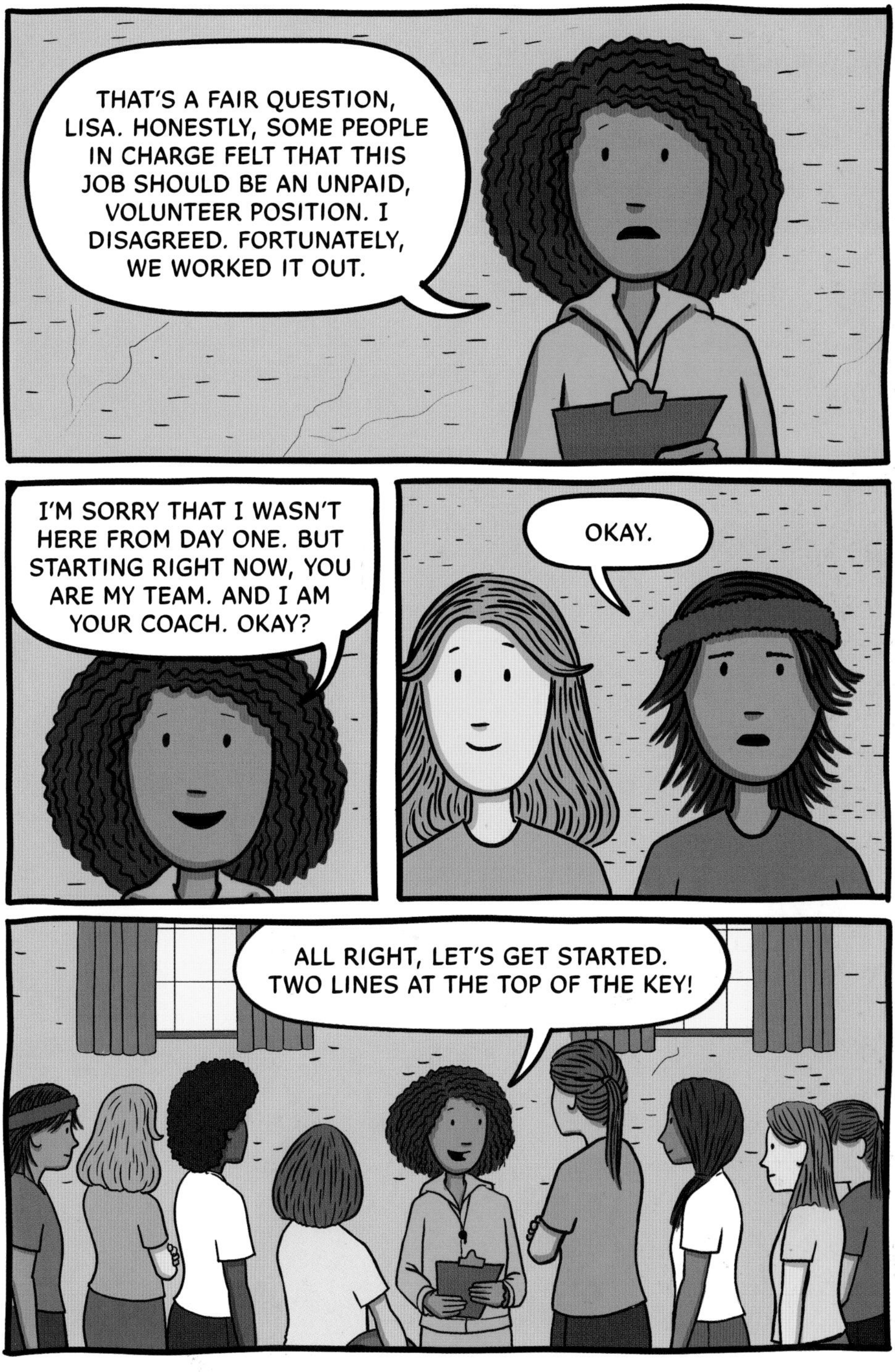
THAT'S A FAIR QUESTION, LISA. HONESTLY, SOME PEOPLE IN CHARGE FELT THAT THIS JOB SHOULD BE AN UNPAID, VOLUNTEER POSITION. I DISAGREED. FORTUNATELY, WE WORKED IT OUT.
I'M SORRY THAT I WASN'T HERE FROM DAY ONE. BUT STARTING RIGHT NOW, YOU ARE MY TEAM. AND I AM YOUR COACH. OKAY?
OKAY.
ALL RIGHT, LET'S GET STARTED. TWO LINES AT THE TOP OF THE KEY!

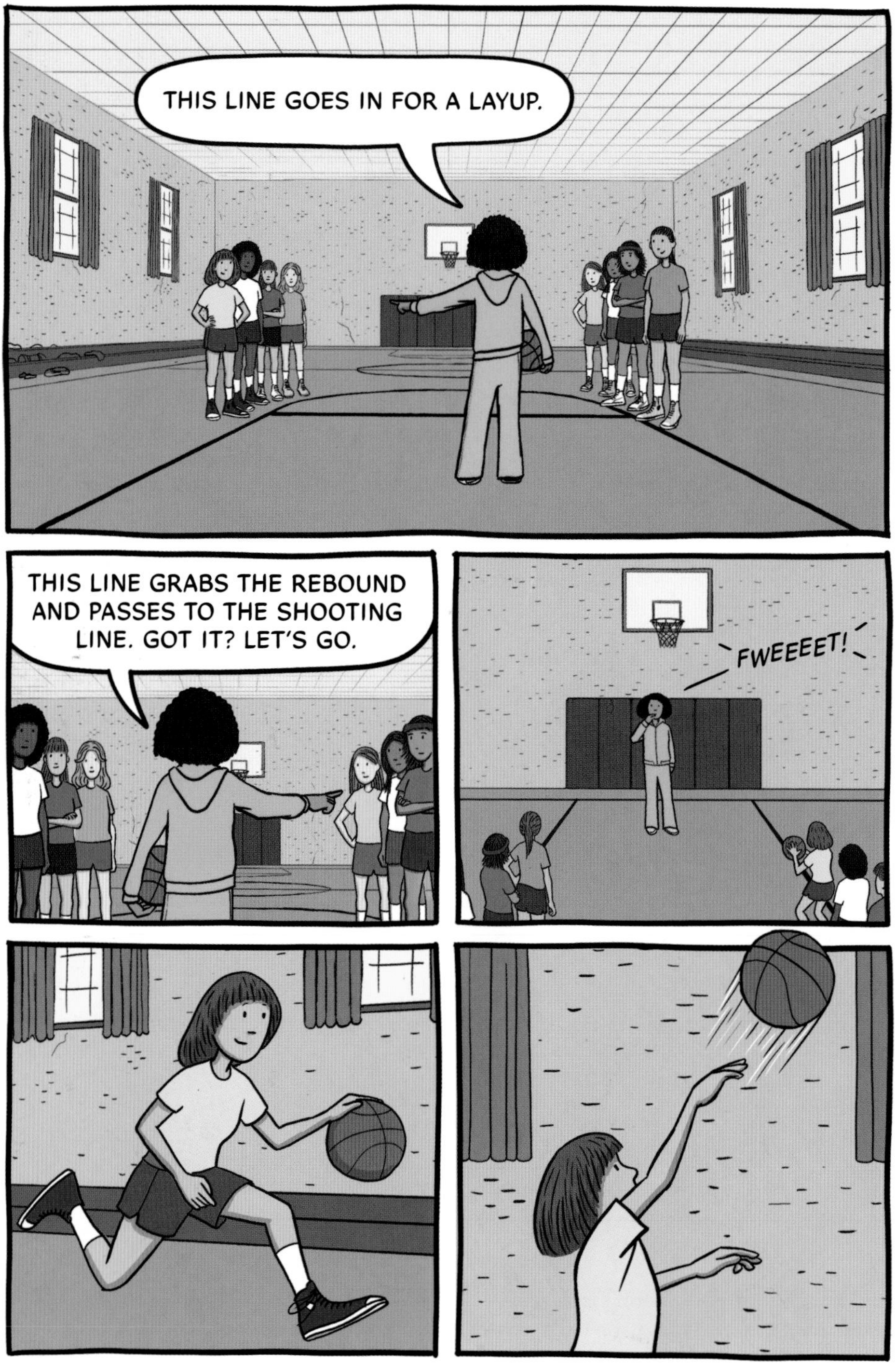
THIS LINE GOES IN FOR A LAYUP.
THIS LINE GRABS THE REBOUND AND PASSES TO THE SHOOTING LINE. GOT IT? LET'S GO.
FWEEEET!

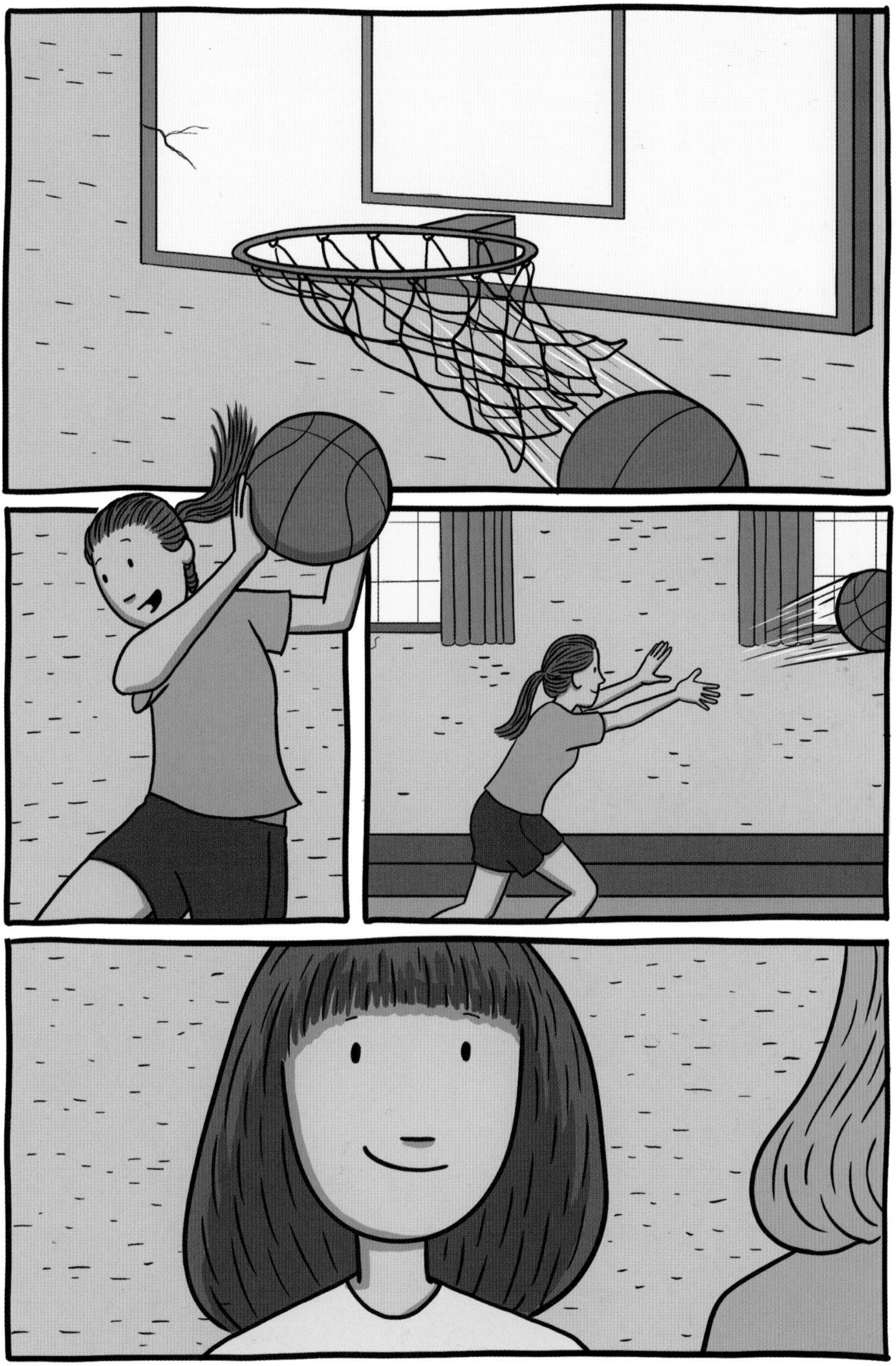

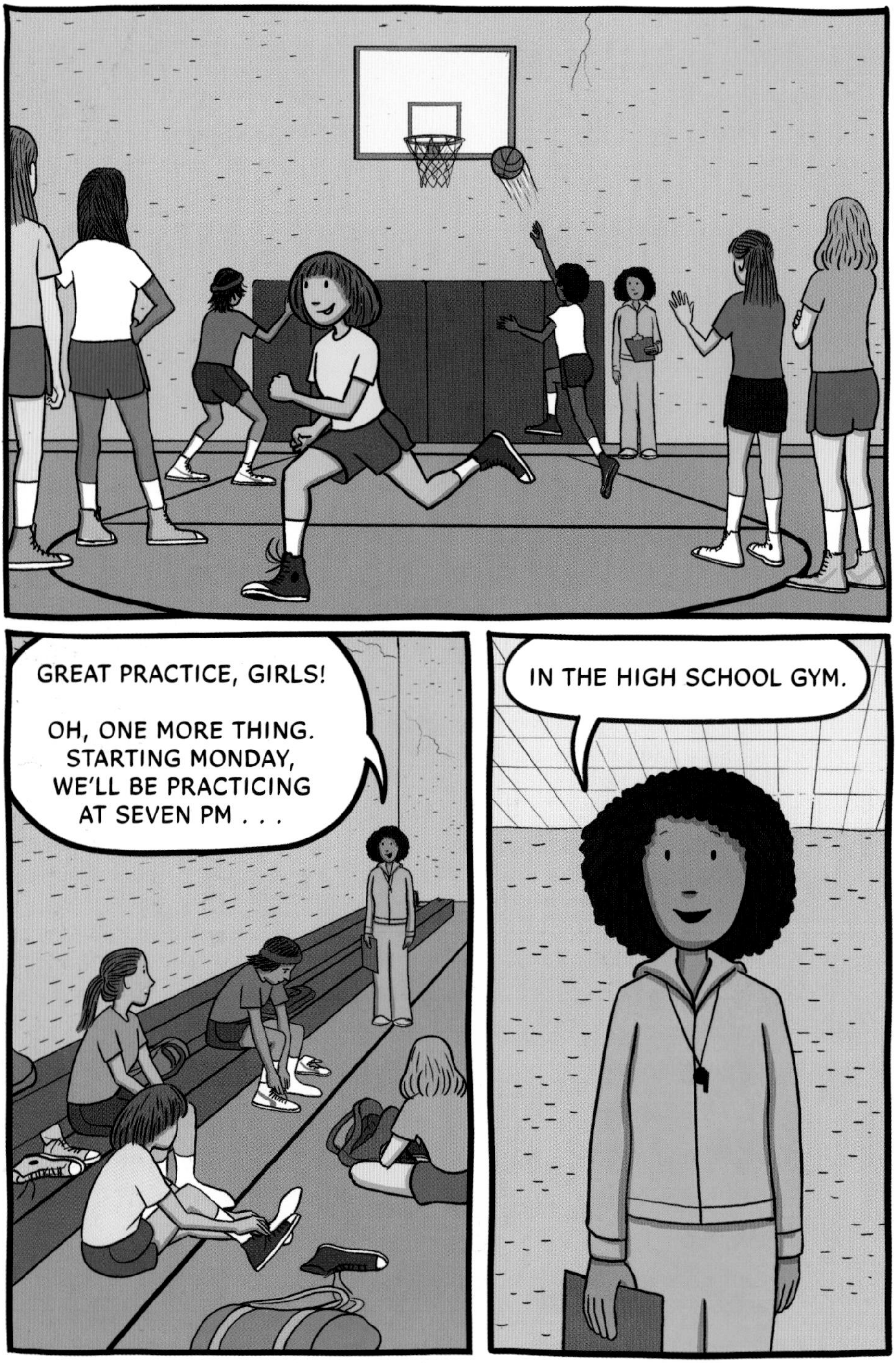
GREAT PRACTICE, GIRLS!
OH, ONE MORE THING. STARTING MONDAY, WE'LL BE PRACTICING AT SEVEN PM . . .
IN THE HIGH SCHOOL GYM.

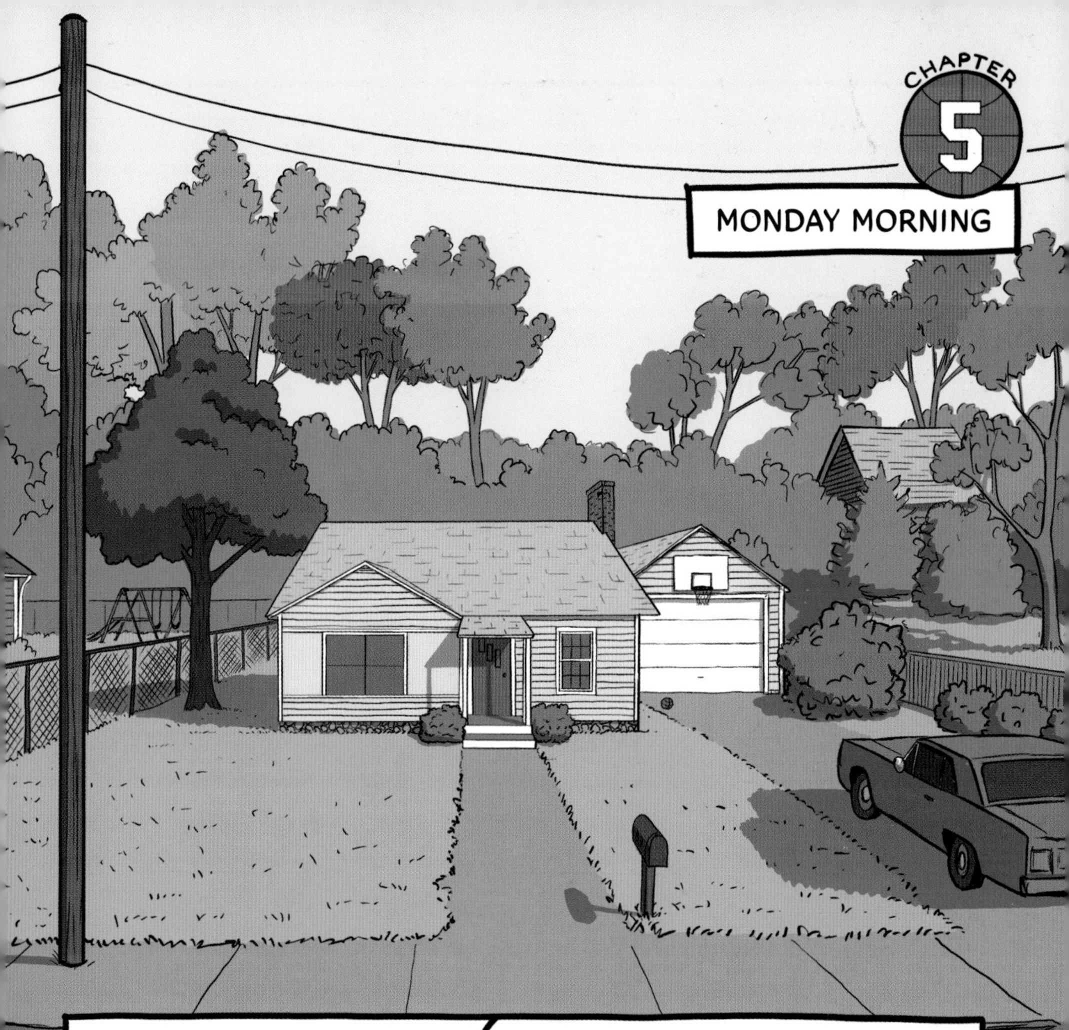
CHAPTER
5
MONDAY MORNING

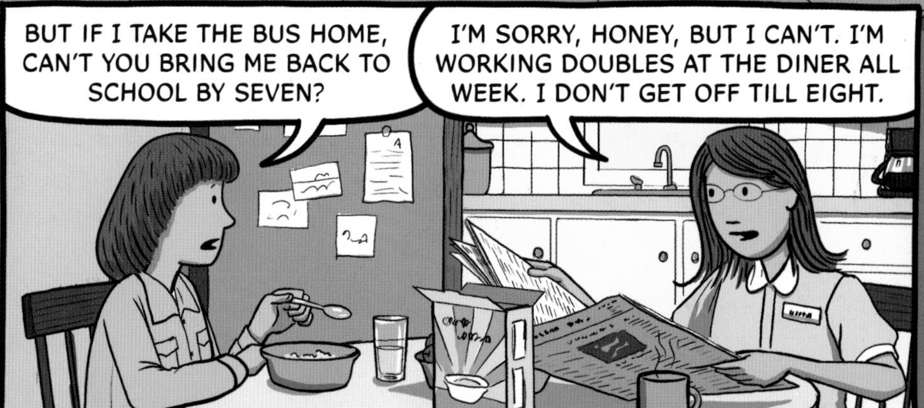
BUT IF I TAKE THE BUS HOME, CAN'T YOU BRING ME BACK TO SCHOOL BY SEVEN?
I'M SORRY, HONEY, BUT I CAN'T. I'M WORKING DOUBLES AT THE DINER ALL WEEK. I DON'T GET OFF TILL EIGHT.

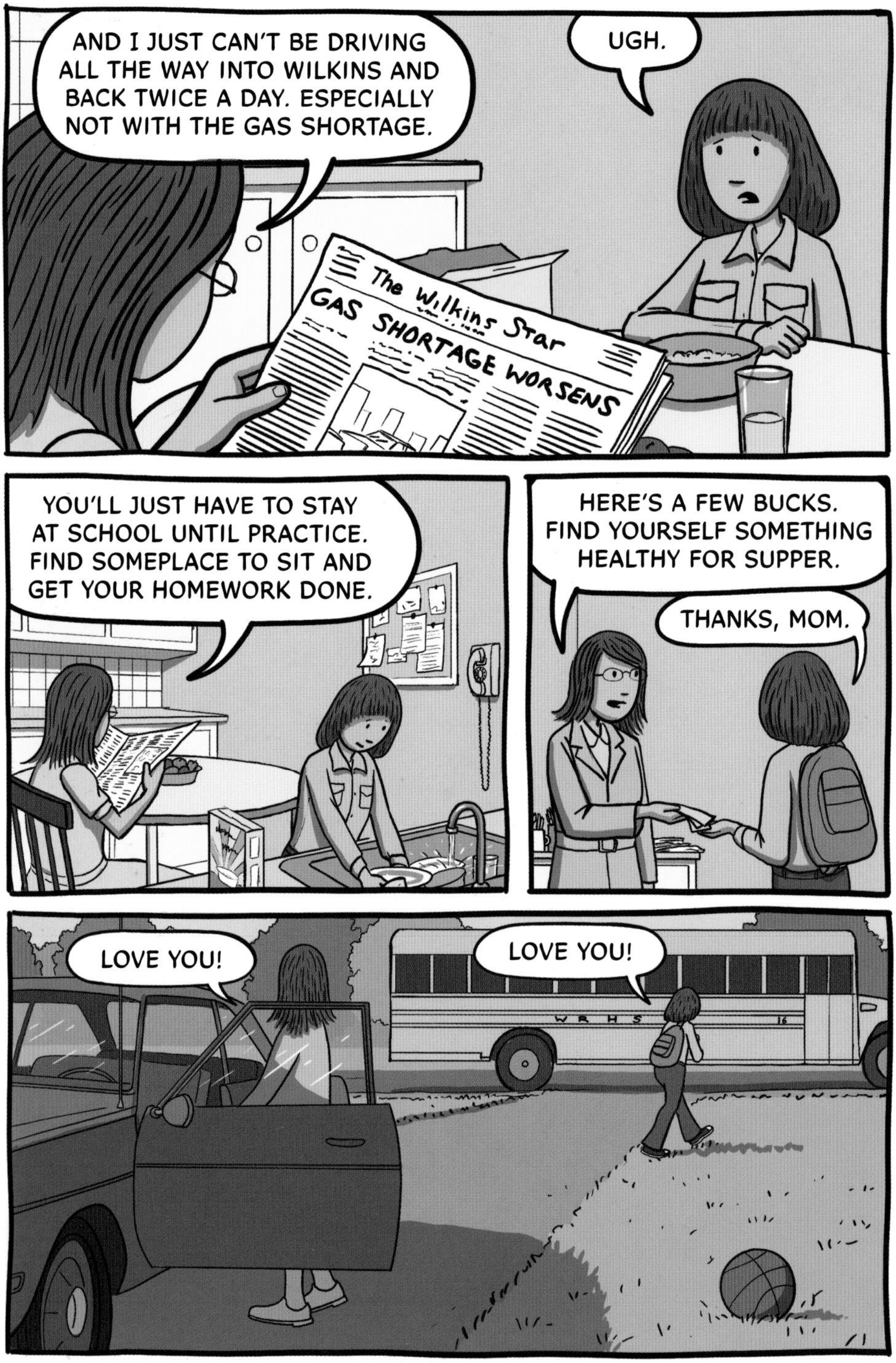
AND I JUST CAN'T BE DRIVING ALL THE WAY INTO WILKINS AND BACK TWICE A DAY. ESPECIALLY NOT WITH THE GAS SHORTAGE.
UGH.
The Wilkins Star
GAS SHORTAGE WORSENS
YOU'LL JUST HAVE TO STAY AT SCHOOL UNTIL PRACTICE. FIND SOMEPLACE TO SIT AND GET YOUR HOMEWORK DONE.
HERE'S A FEW BUCKS. FIND YOURSELF SOMETHING HEALTHY FOR SUPPER.
THANKS, MOM.
LOVE YOU!
LOVE YOU!
WRHS
16

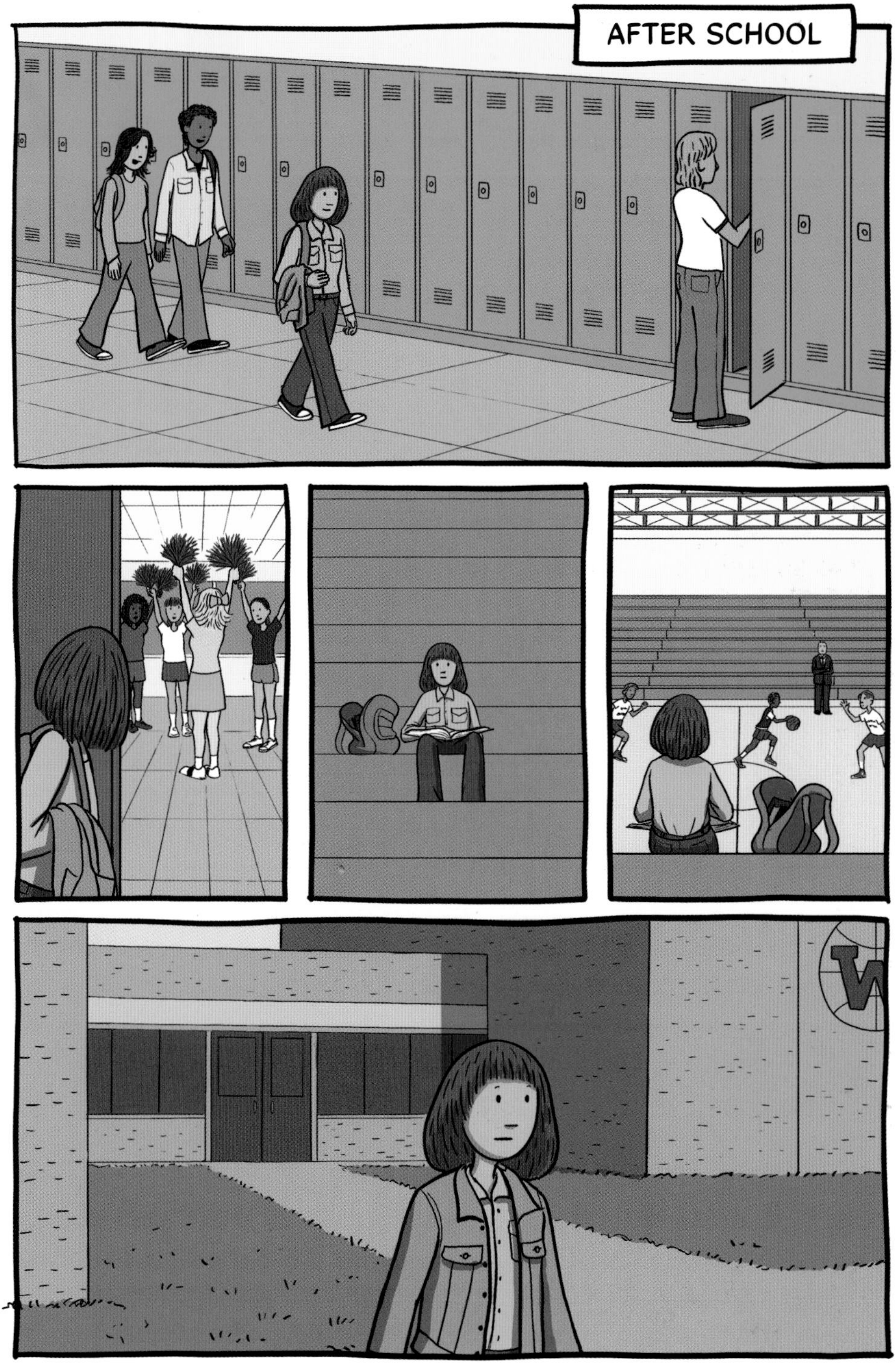
AFTER SCHOOL

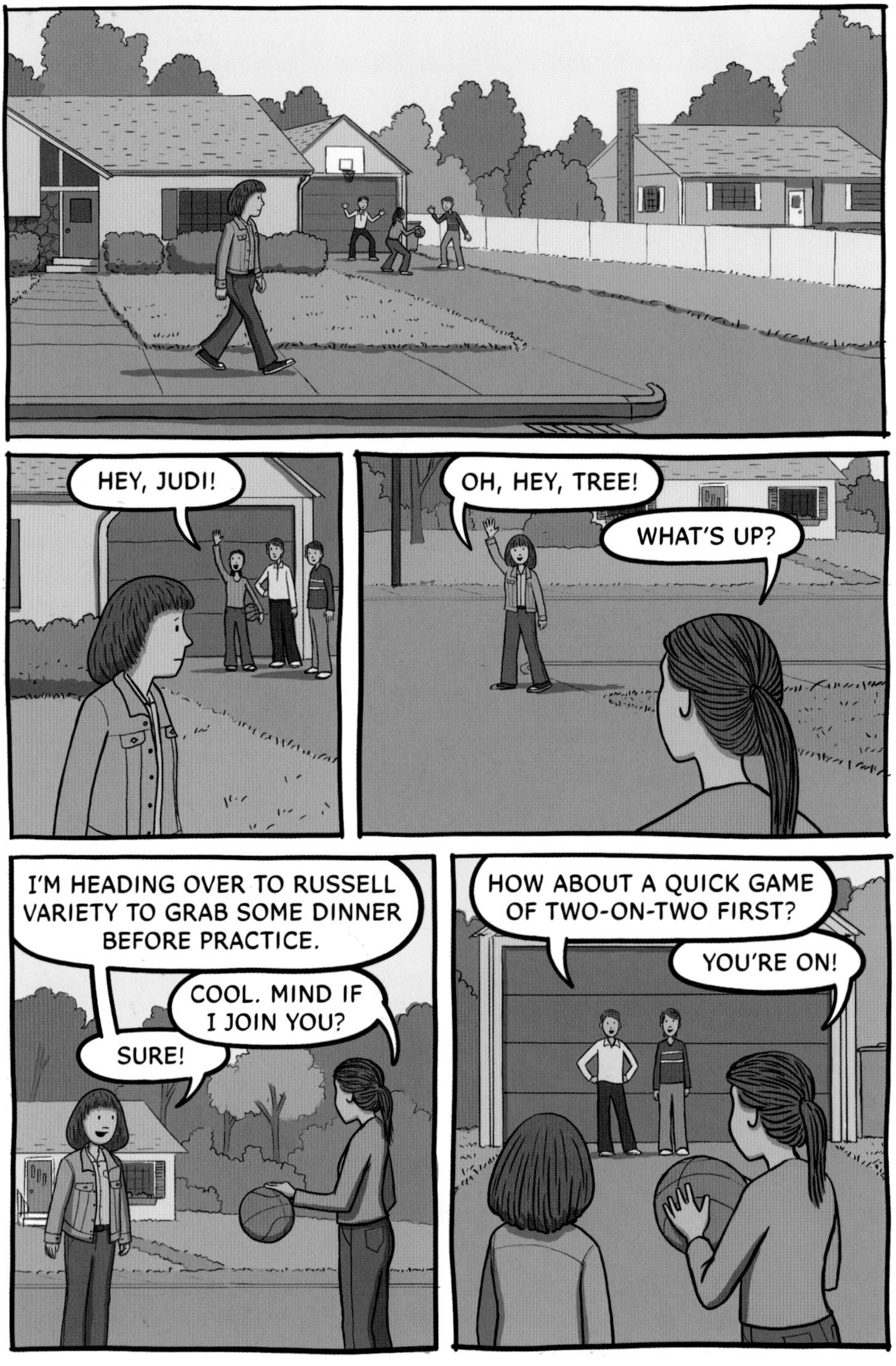
HEY, JUDI!
OH, HEY, TREE!
WHAT'S UP?
I'M HEADING OVER TO RUSSELL VARIETY TO GRAB SOME DINNER BEFORE PRACTICE.
COOL. MIND IF I JOIN YOU?
SURE!
HOW ABOUT A QUICK GAME OF TWO-ON-TWO FIRST?
YOU'RE ON!

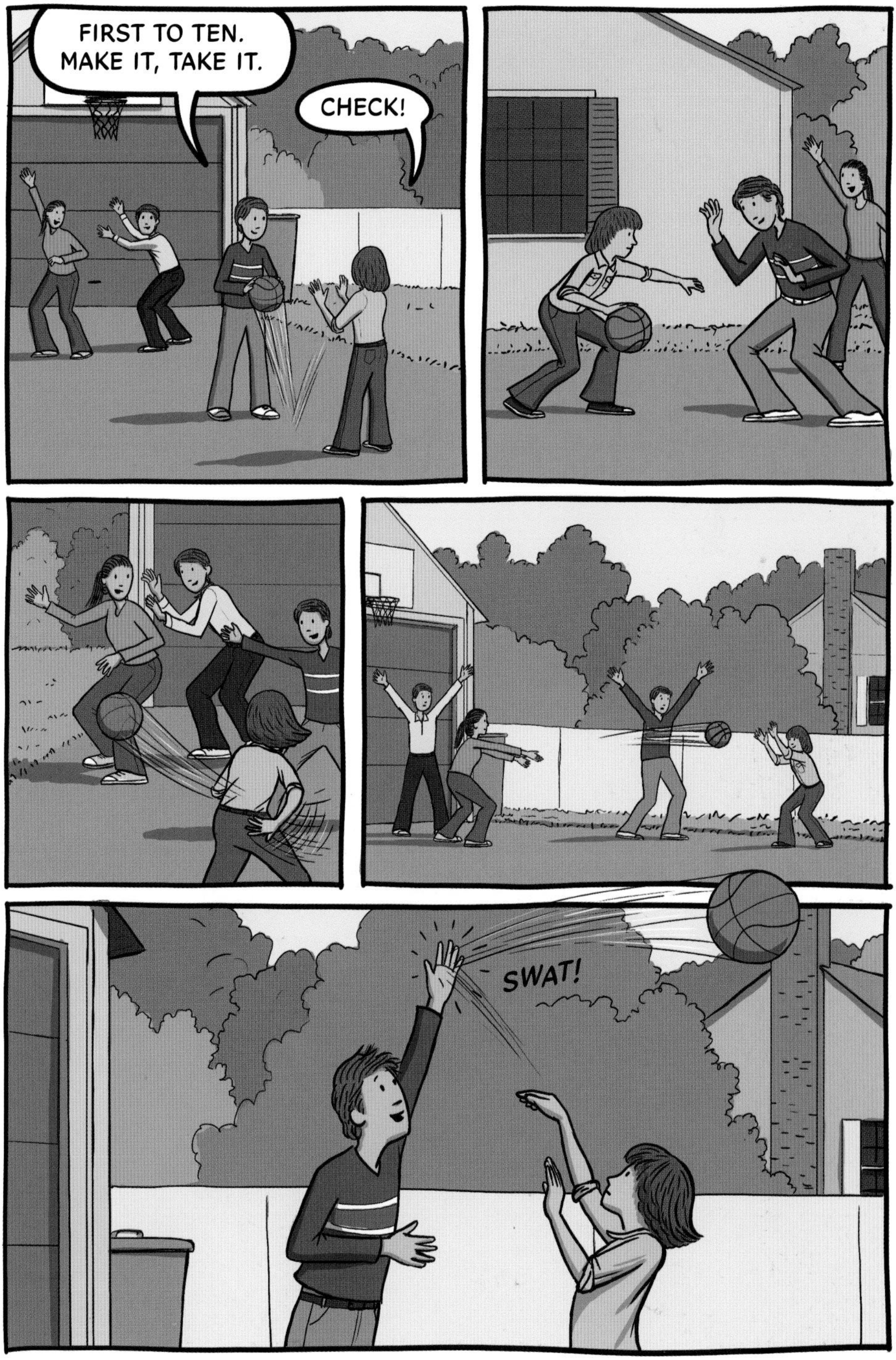
FIRST TO TEN.
MAKE IT, TAKE IT.
CHECK!
SWAT!

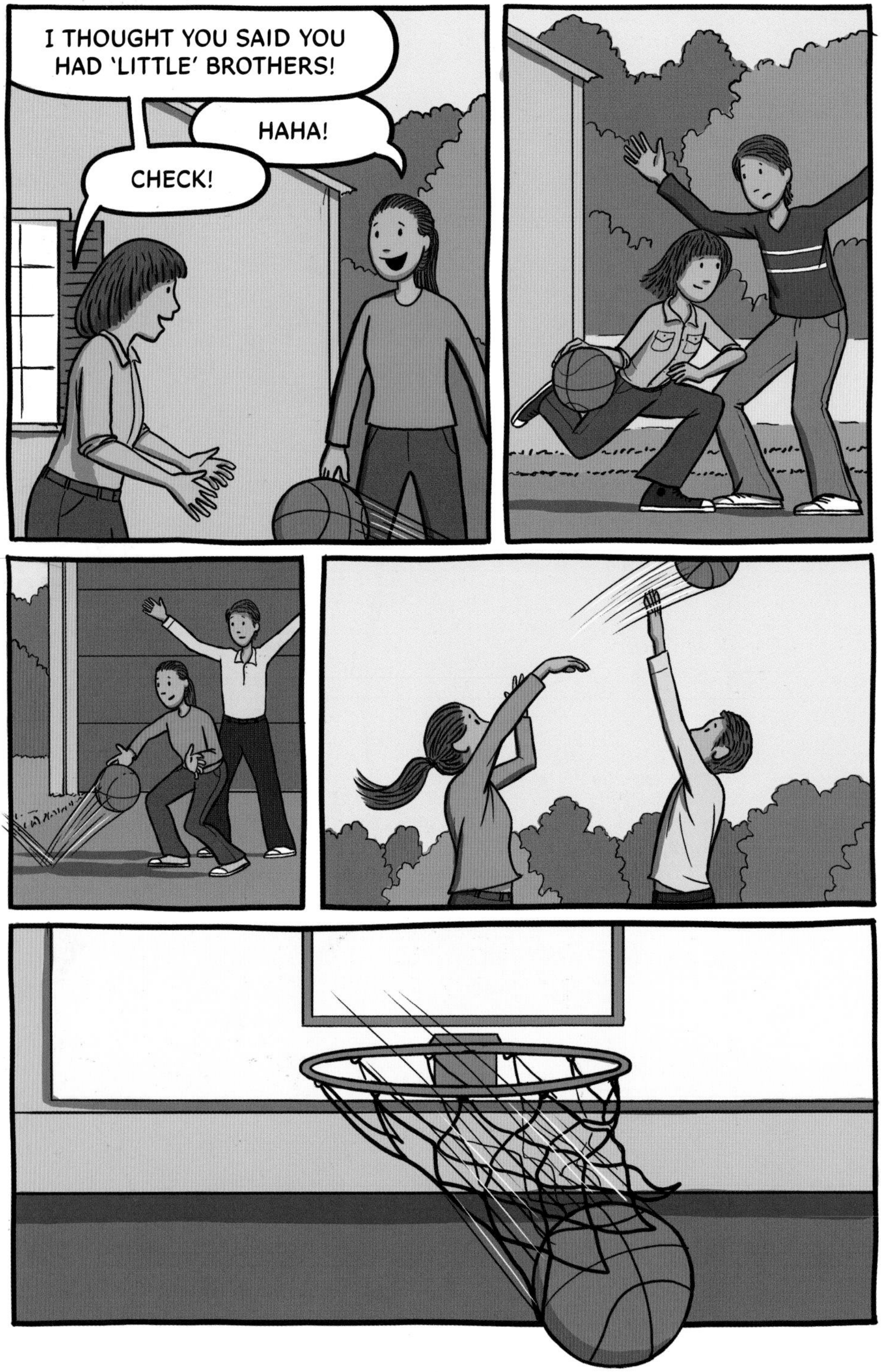
I THOUGHT YOU SAID YOU HAD 'LITTLE' BROTHERS!
HAHA!
CHECK!

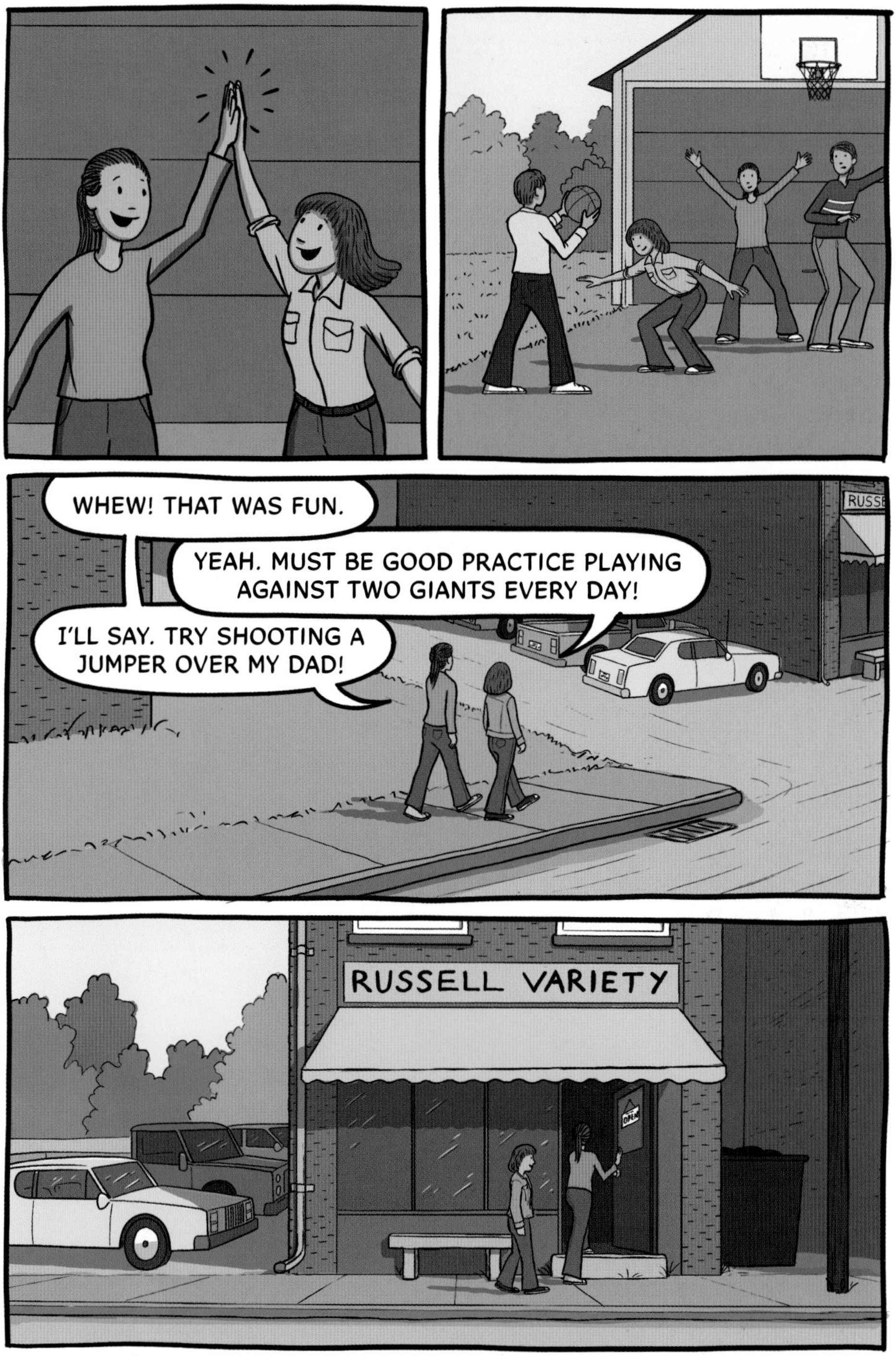

WHEW! THAT WAS FUN.
YEAH. MUST BE GOOD PRACTICE PLAYING AGAINST TWO GIANTS EVERY DAY!
I'LL SAY. TRY SHOOTING A JUMPER OVER MY DAD!
RUSSELL VARIETY
OPEN

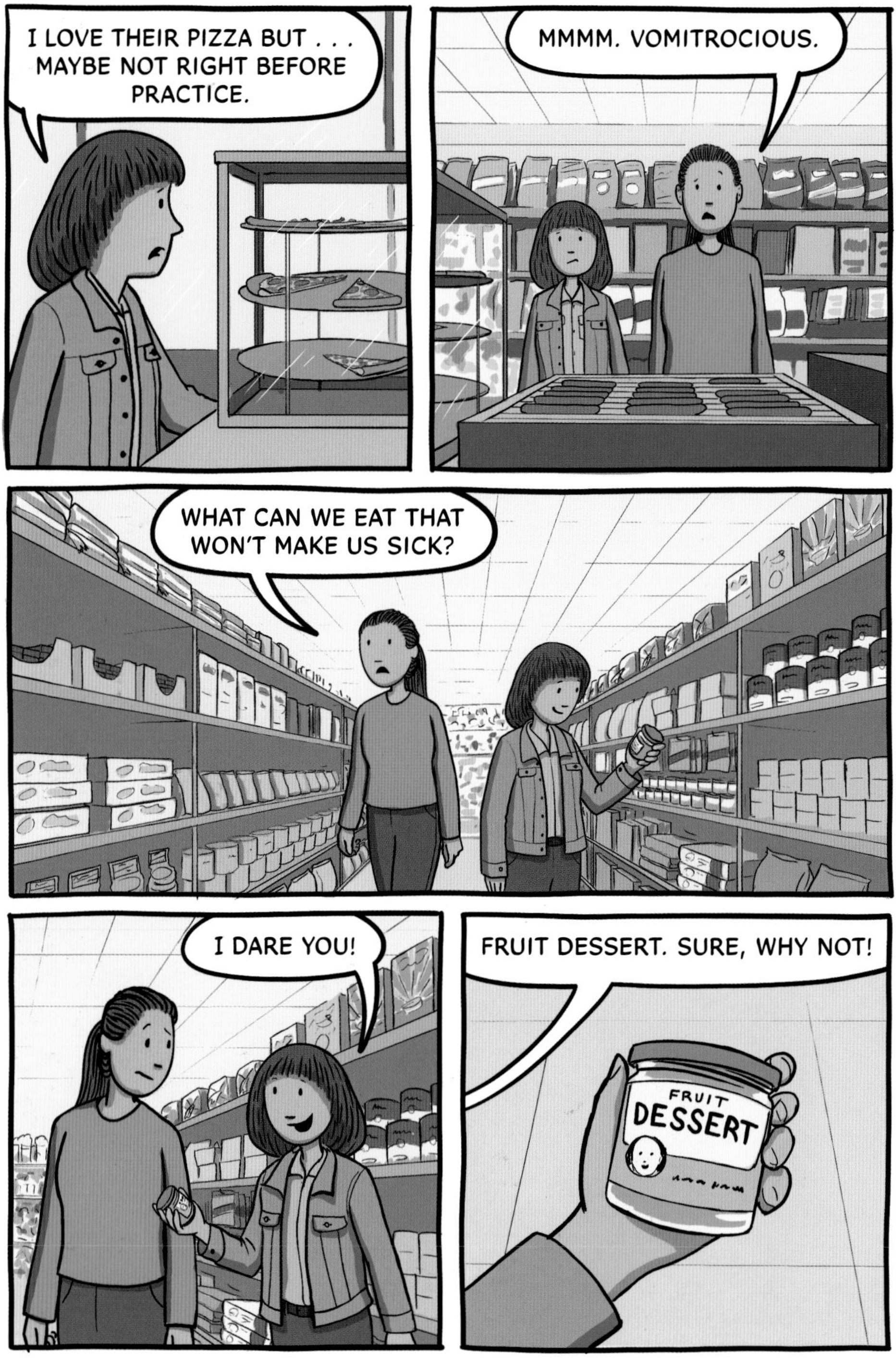
I LOVE THEIR PIZZA BUT . . . MAYBE NOT RIGHT BEFORE PRACTICE.
MMMM. VOMITROCIOUS.
WHAT CAN WE EAT THAT WON'T MAKE US SICK?
I DARE YOU!
FRUIT DESSERT. SURE, WHY NOT!
FRUIT DESSERT

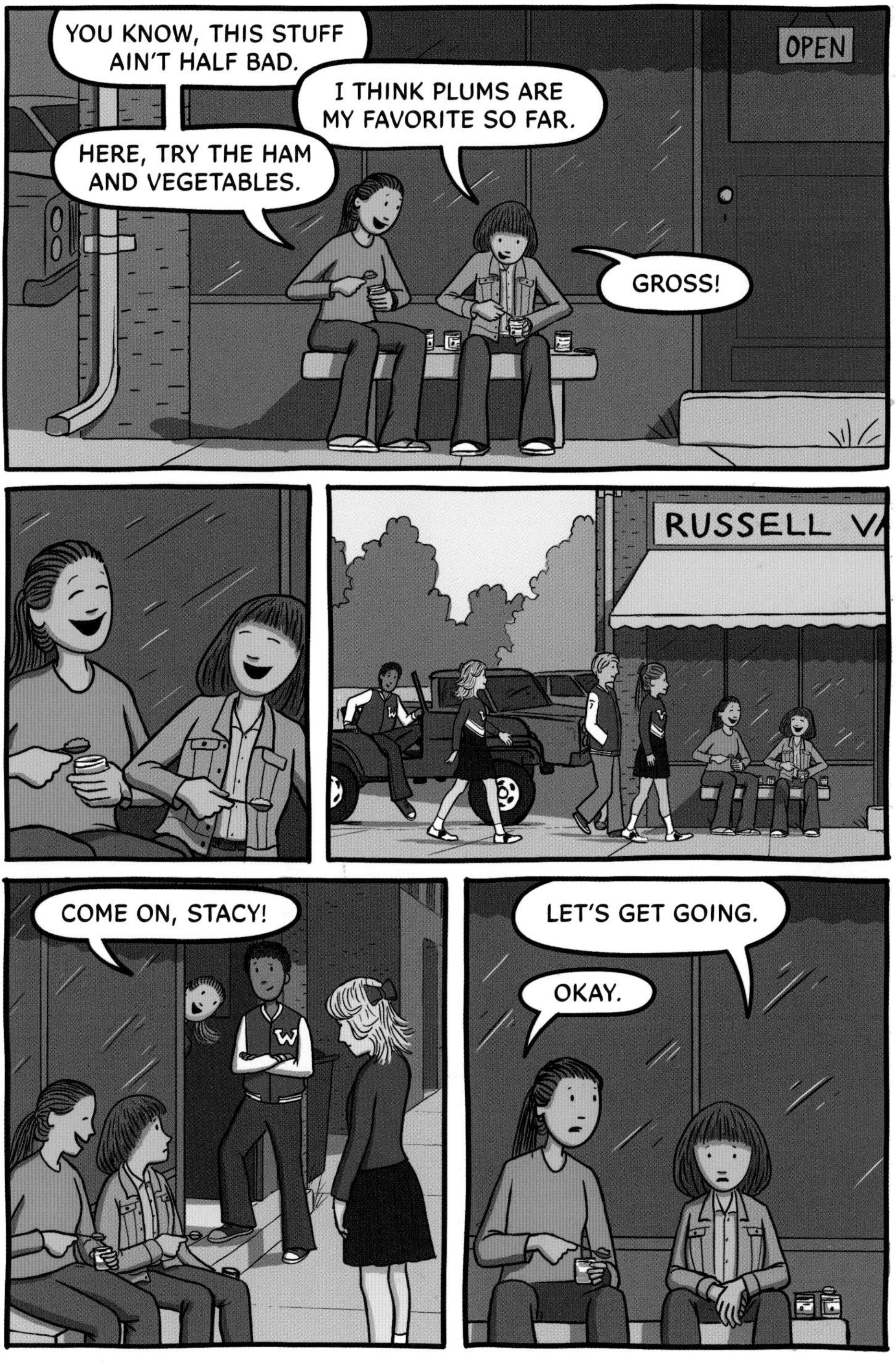
OPEN
YOU KNOW, THIS STUFF AIN'T HALF BAD.
HERE, TRY THE HAM AND VEGETABLES.
I THINK PLUMS ARE MY FAVORITE SO FAR.
GROSS!
RUSSELL V
COME ON, STACY!
LET'S GET GOING.
OKAY.

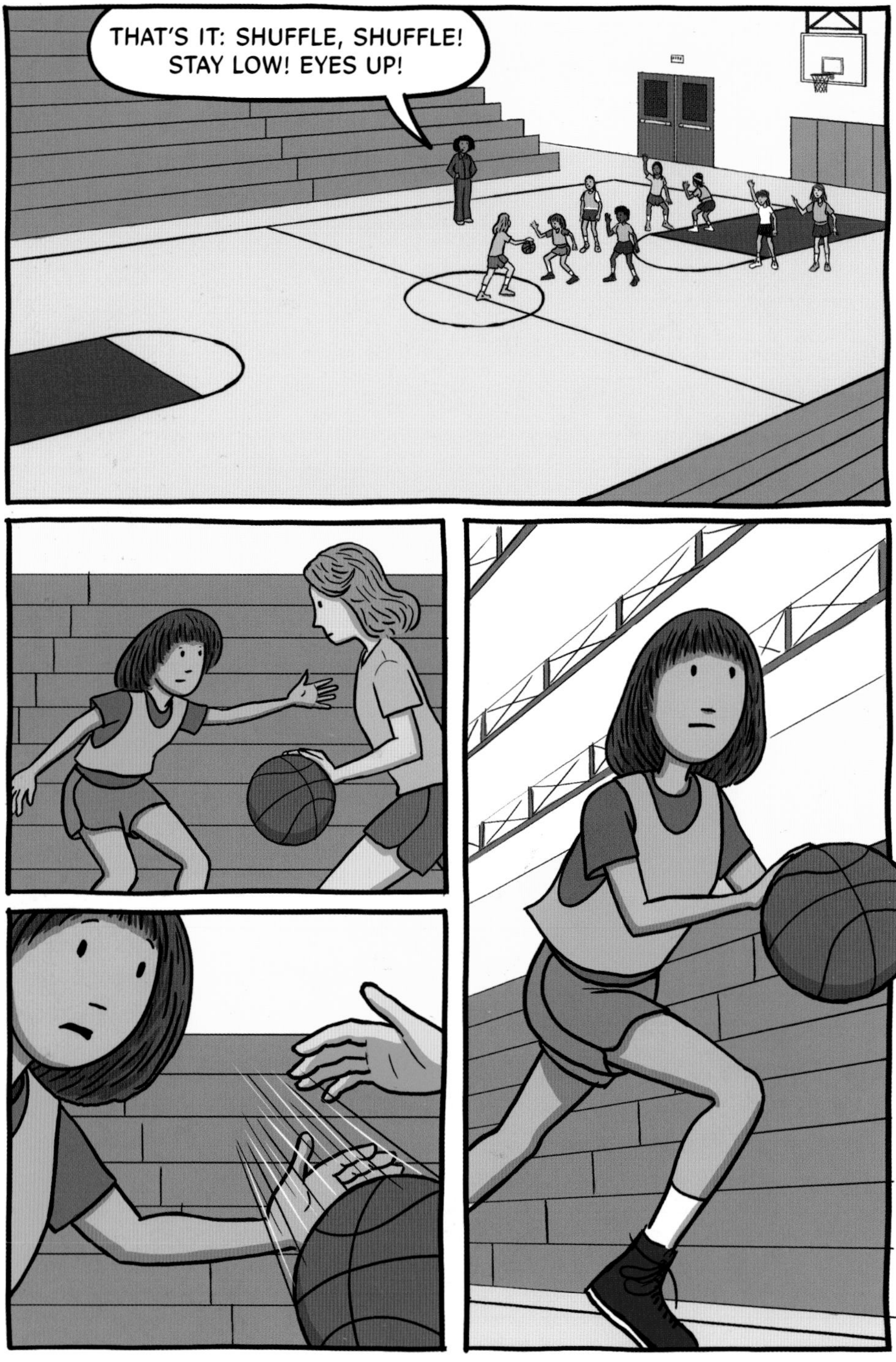
THAT'S IT: SHUFFLE, SHUFFLE! STAY LOW! EYES UP!

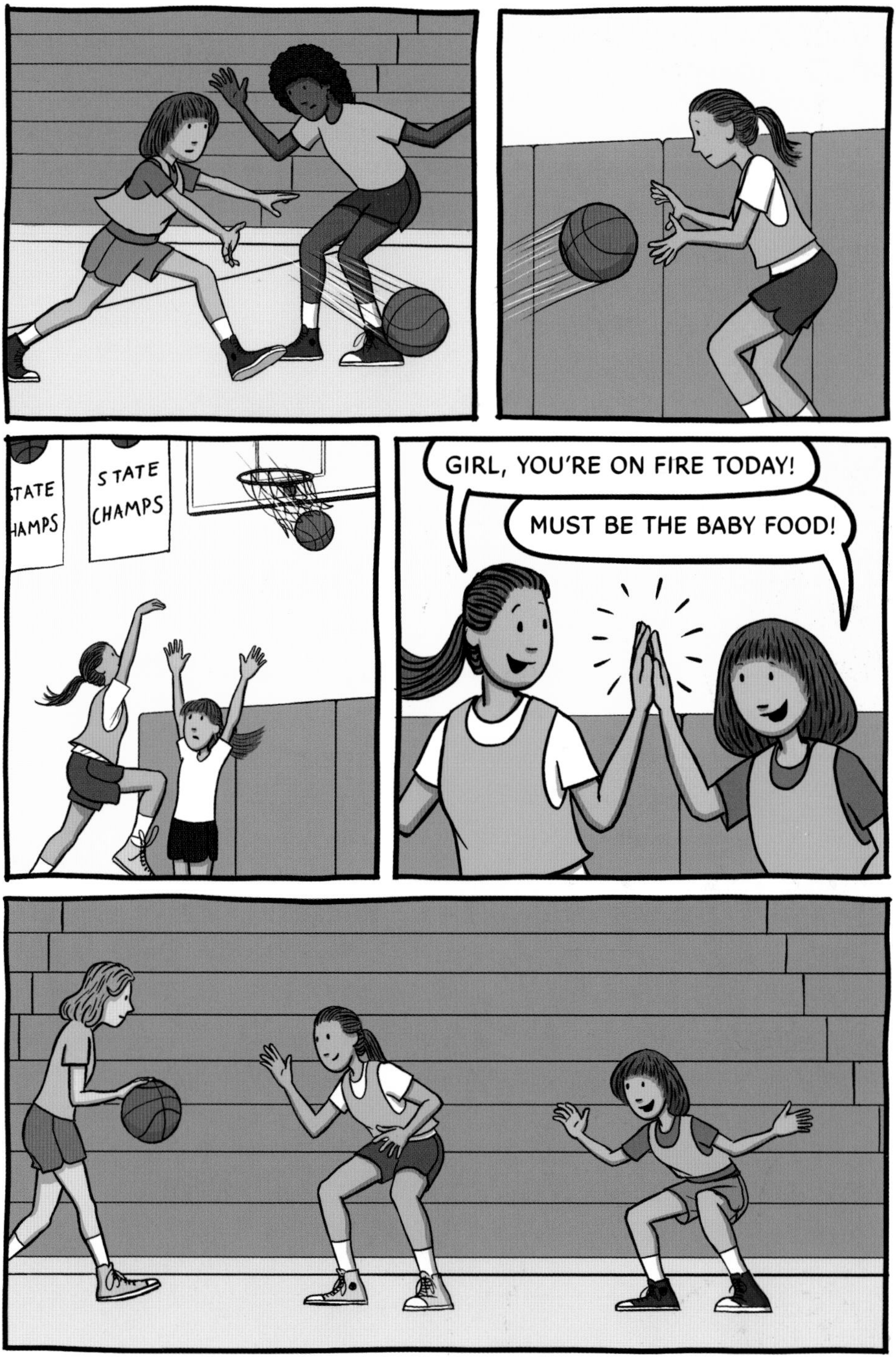
STATE CHAMPS
STATE CHAMPS
GIRL, YOU'RE ON FIRE TODAY!
MUST BE THE BABY FOOD!

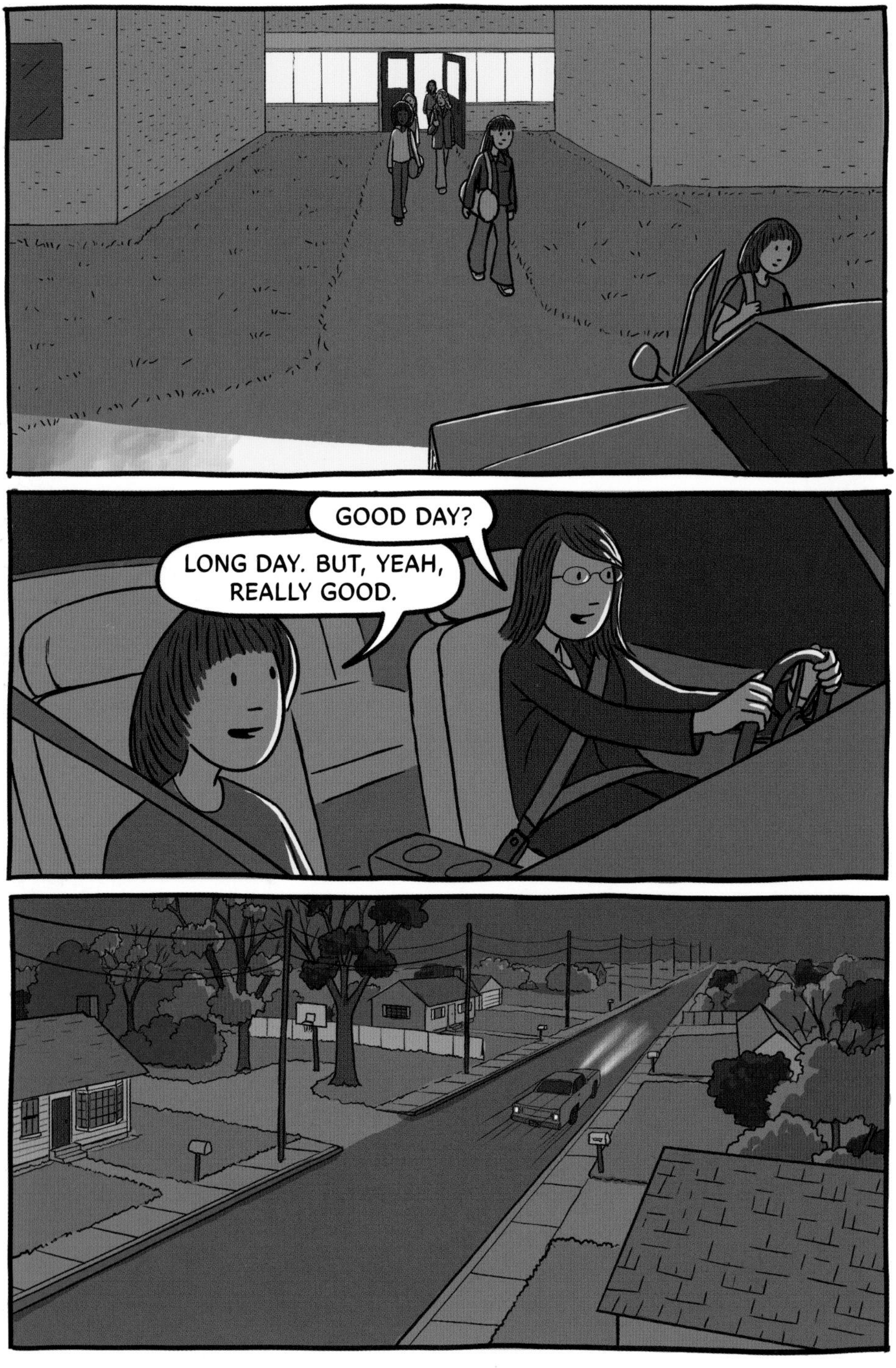
GOOD DAY?
LONG DAY. BUT, YEAH, REALLY GOOD.

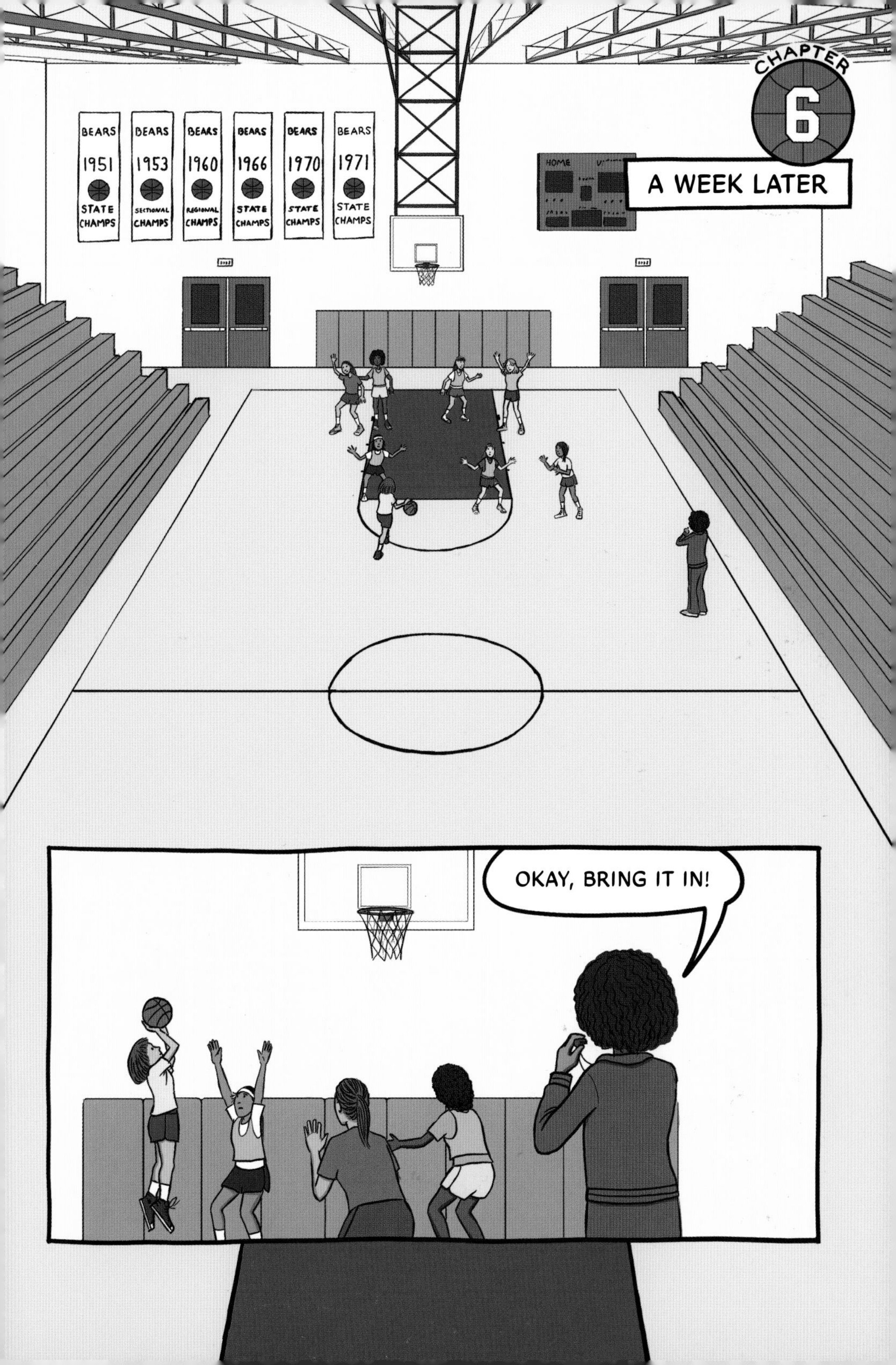

CHAPTER 6
A WEEK LATER
BEARS 1951 STATE CHAMPS
BEARS 1953 SECTIONAL CHAMPS
BEARS 1960 REGIONAL CHAMPS
BEARS 1966 STATE CHAMPS
BEARS 1970 STATE CHAMPS
BEARS 1971 STATE CHAMPS
HOME
OKAY, BRING IT IN!

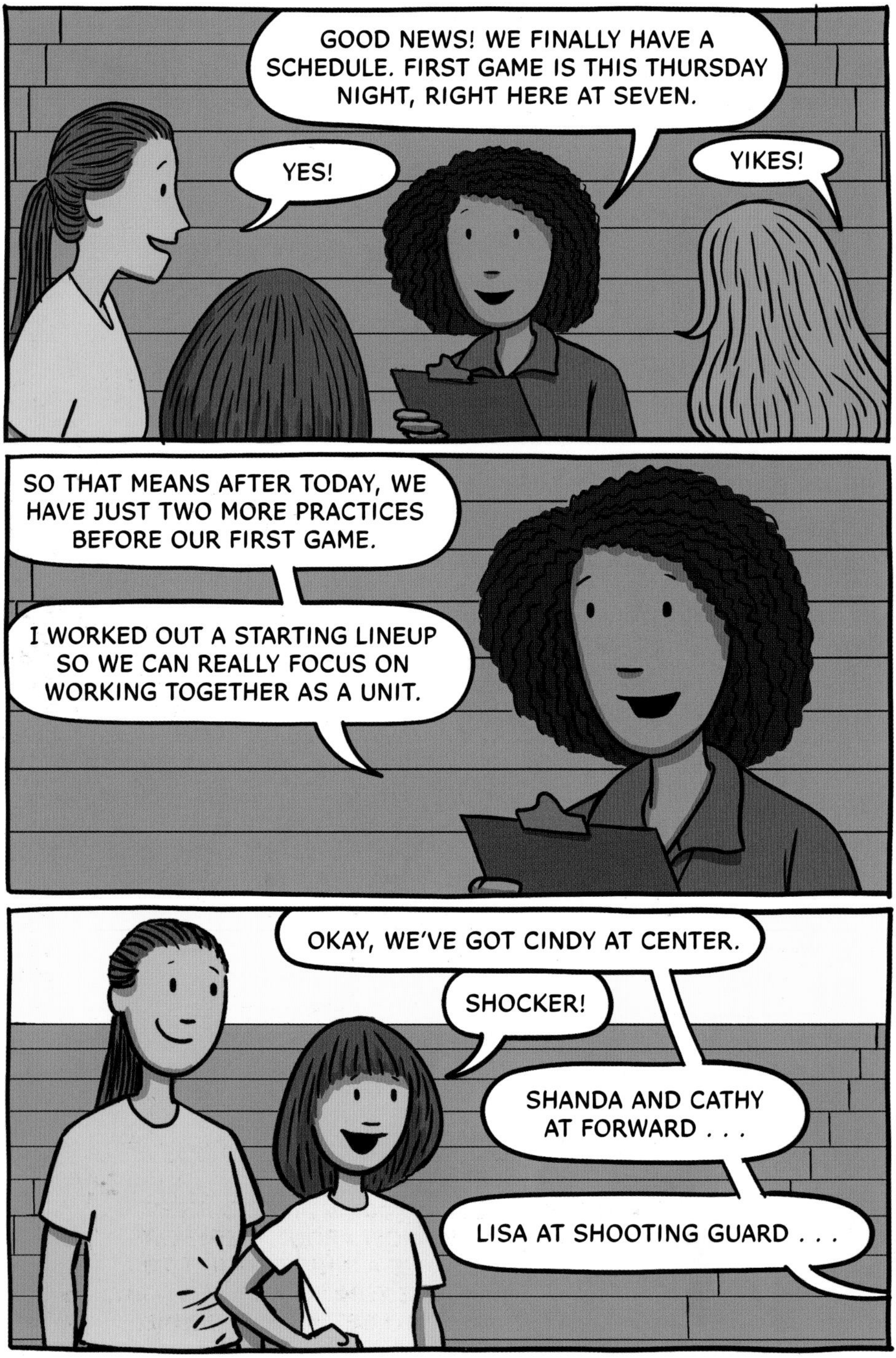
GOOD NEWS! WE FINALLY HAVE A SCHEDULE. FIRST GAME IS THIS THURSDAY NIGHT, RIGHT HERE AT SEVEN.
YES!
YIKES!
SO THAT MEANS AFTER TODAY, WE HAVE JUST TWO MORE PRACTICES BEFORE OUR FIRST GAME.
I WORKED OUT A STARTING LINEUP SO WE CAN REALLY FOCUS ON WORKING TOGETHER AS A UNIT.
OKAY, WE'VE GOT CINDY AT CENTER.
SHOCKER!
SHANDA AND CATHY AT FORWARD . . .
LISA AT SHOOTING GUARD . . .

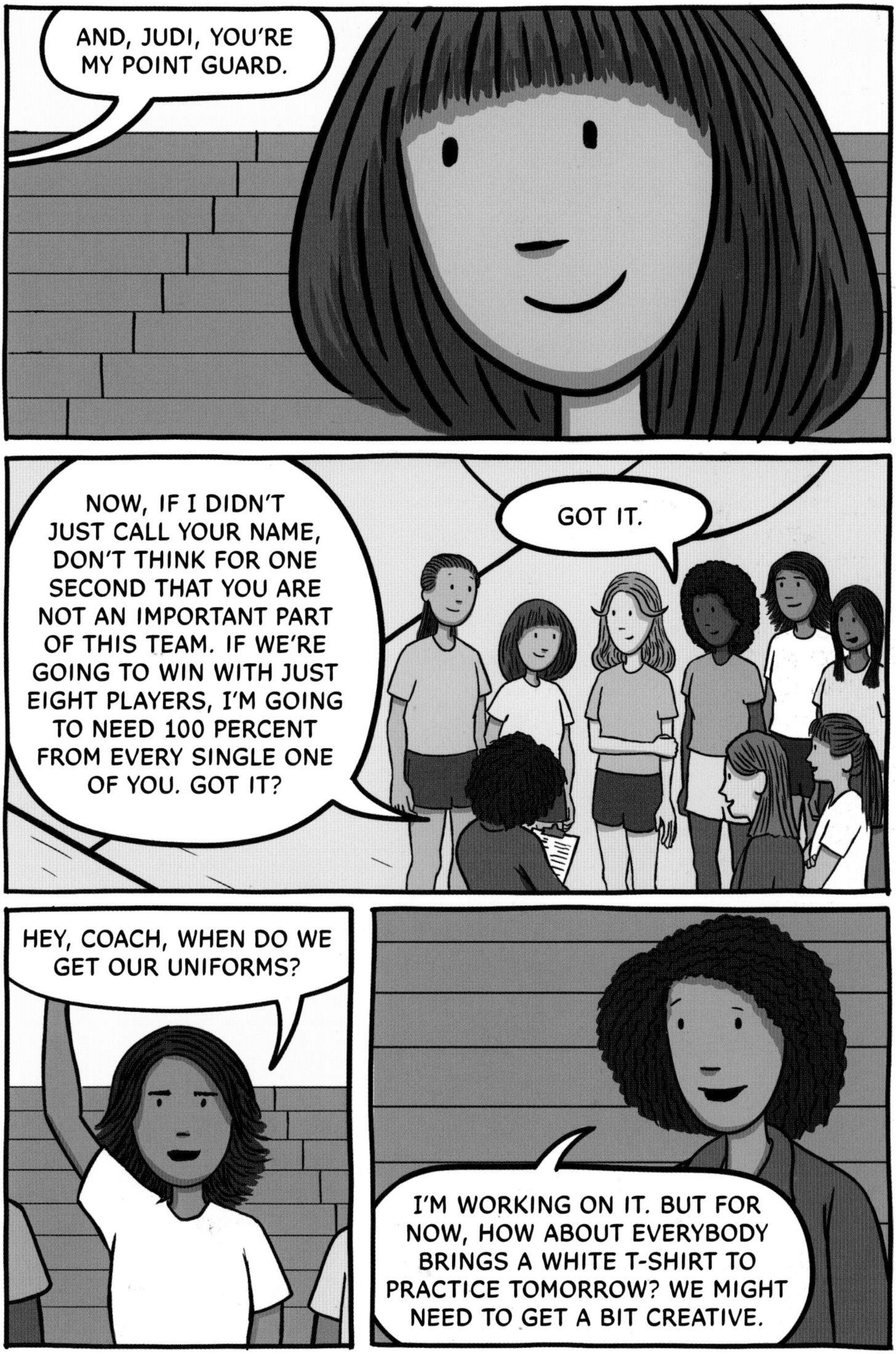
AND, JUDI, YOU'RE MY POINT GUARD.
NOW, IF I DIDN'T JUST CALL YOUR NAME, DON'T THINK FOR ONE SECOND THAT YOU ARE NOT AN IMPORTANT PART OF THIS TEAM. IF WE'RE GOING TO WIN WITH JUST EIGHT PLAYERS, I'M GOING TO NEED 100 PERCENT FROM EVERY SINGLE ONE OF YOU. GOT IT?
GOT IT.
HEY, COACH, WHEN DO WE GET OUR UNIFORMS?
I'M WORKING ON IT. BUT FOR NOW, HOW ABOUT EVERYBODY BRINGS A WHITE T-SHIRT TO PRACTICE TOMORROW? WE MIGHT NEED TO GET A BIT CREATIVE.

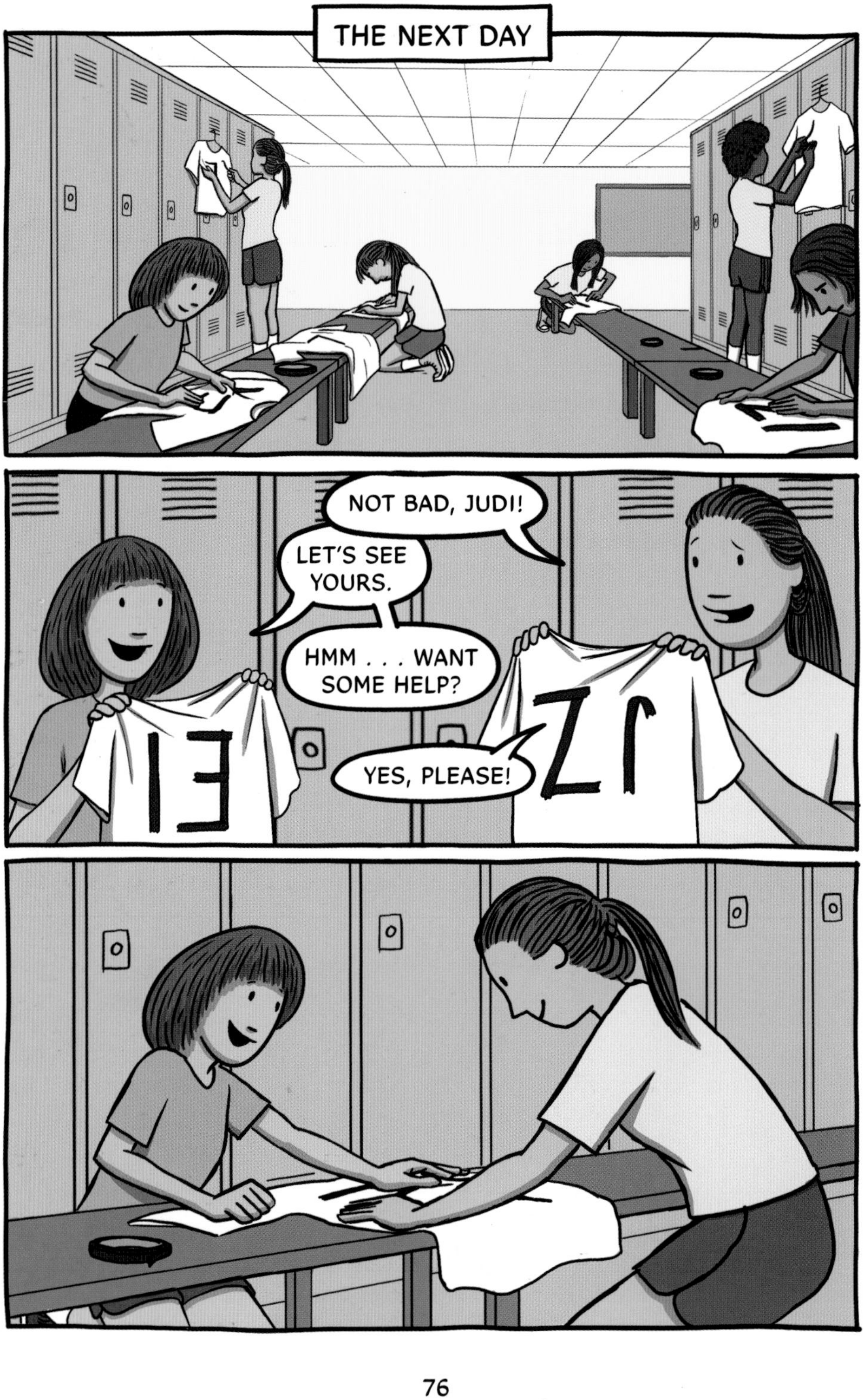
THE NEXT DAY
NOT BAD, JUDI!
LET'S SEE YOURS.
HMM . . . WANT SOME HELP?
YES, PLEASE!

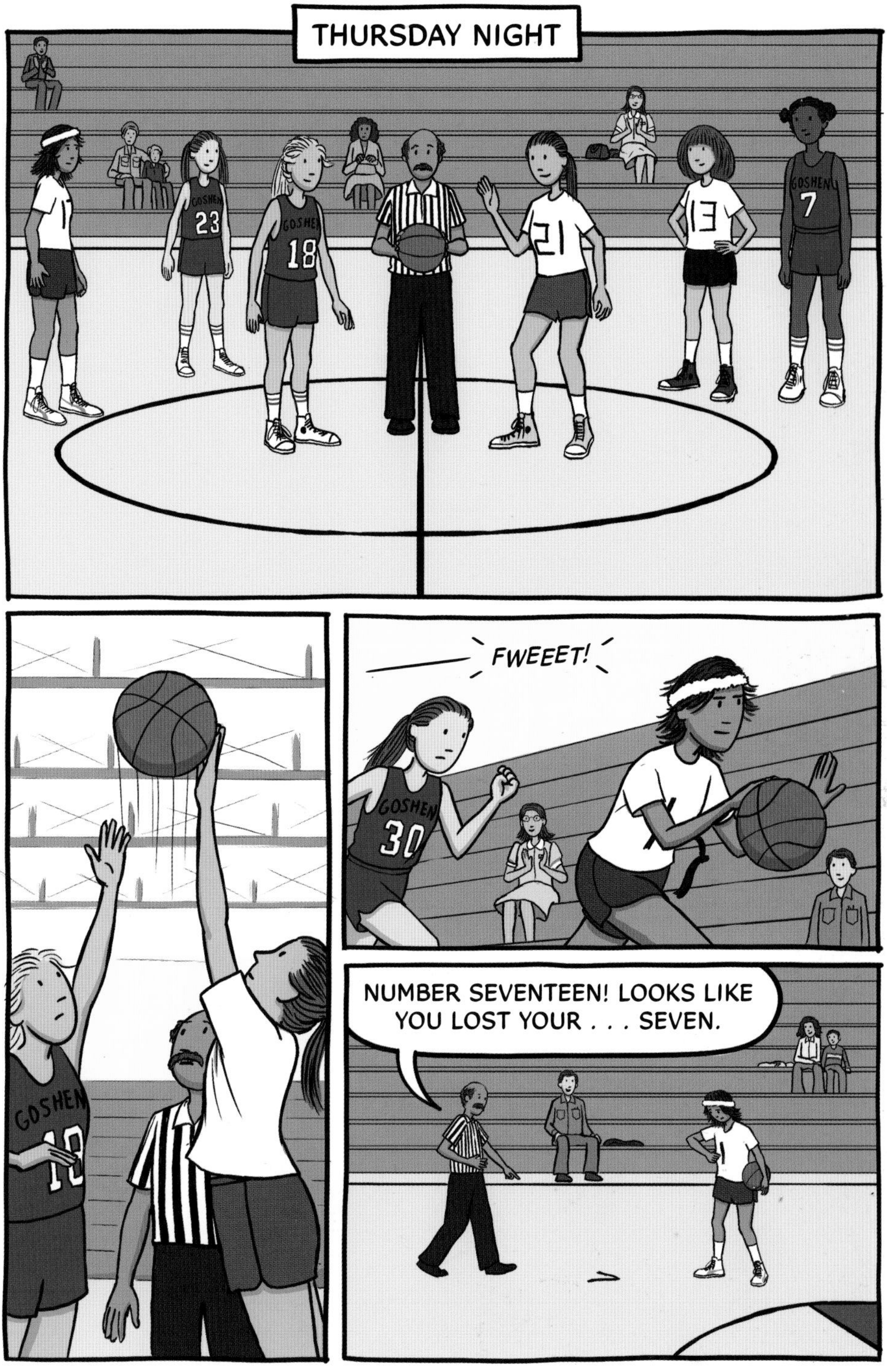
THURSDAY NIGHT
FWEEET!
NUMBER SEVENTEEN! LOOKS LIKE YOU LOST YOUR . . . SEVEN.

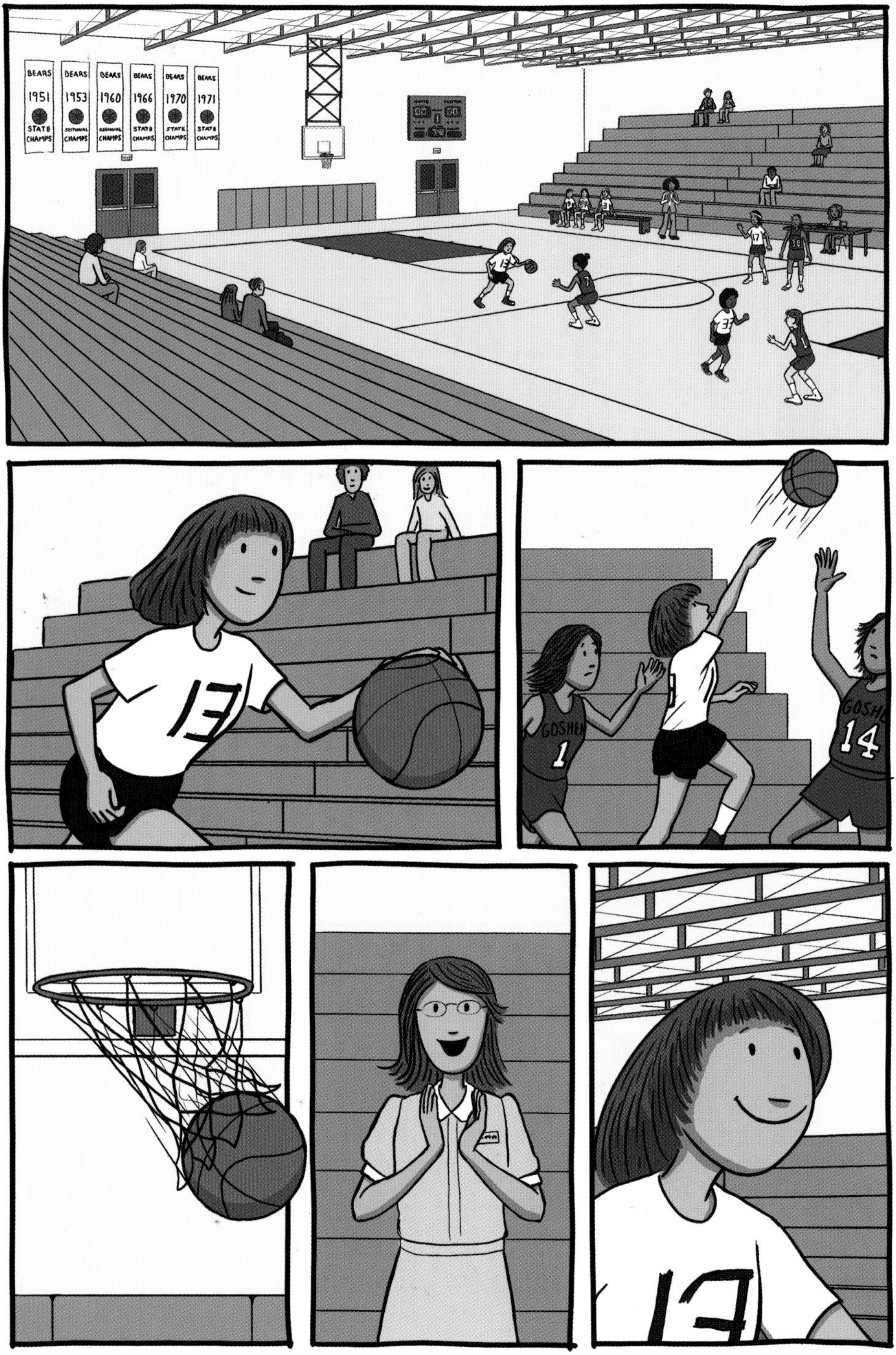
BEARS 1951 STATE CHAMPS
BEARS 1953 SECTIONAL CHAMPS
BEARS 1960 REGIONAL CHAMPS
BEARS 1966 STATE CHAMPS
BEARS 1970 STATE CHAMPS
BEARS 1971 STATE CHAMPS
13
GOSHEN 1
GOSHEN 14
13

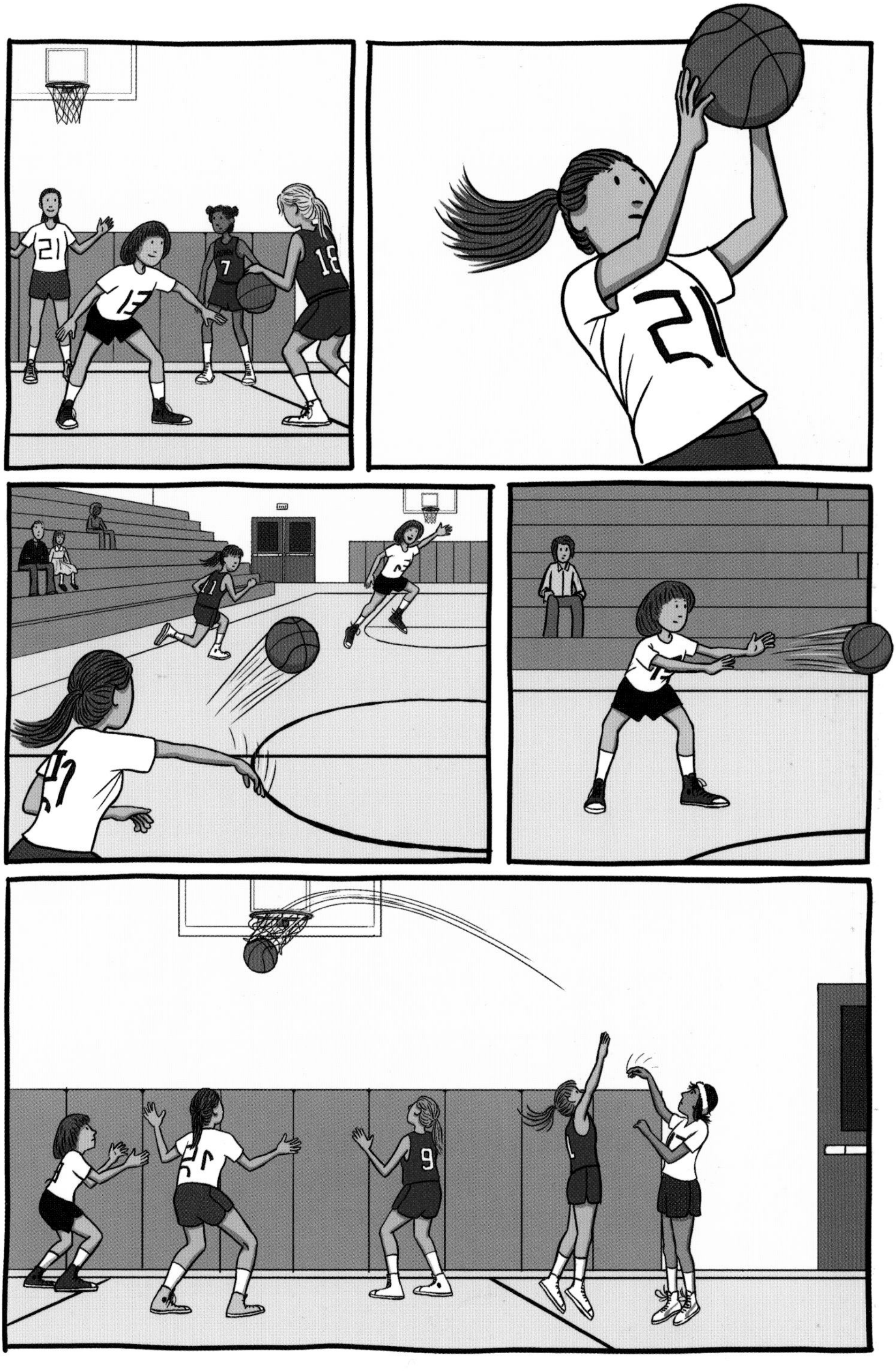

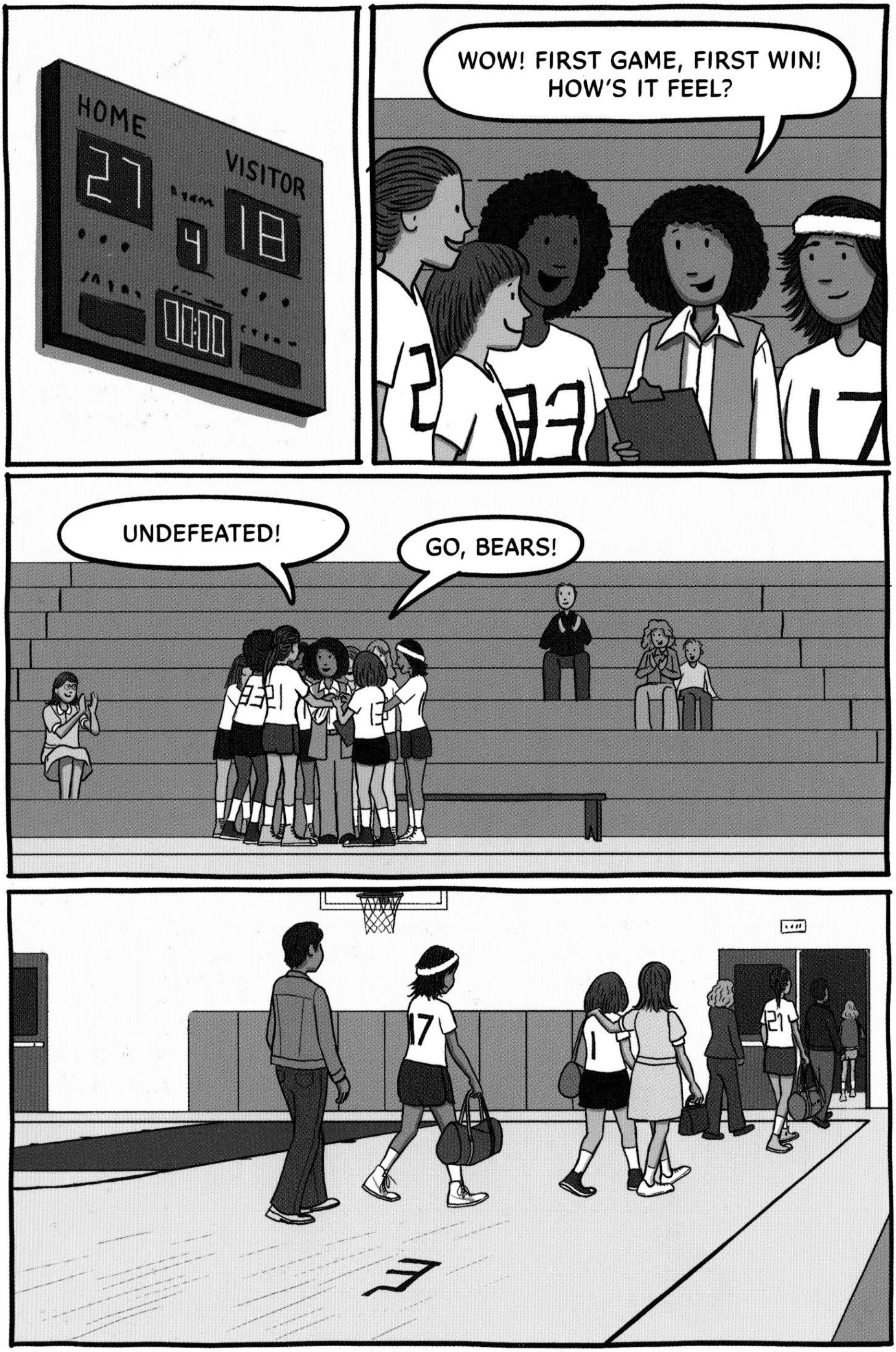
HOME
27
VISITOR
18
4
00:00
WOW! FIRST GAME, FIRST WIN! HOW'S IT FEEL?
UNDEFEATED!
GO, BEARS!

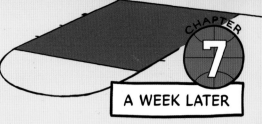

CHAPTER 7

A WEEK LATER

OKAY, OUR FIRST ROAD GAME IS TOMORROW. I'M STILL WAITING TO HEAR BACK ABOUT A BUS, BUT JUST IN CASE, CAN ANYONE HERE DRIVE?

I CAN FIT FOUR OF YOU IN MY CAR. SO ONE OTHER CAR SHOULD DO IT.

AND THE GAME IS IN SOUTH BEND, ABOUT FORTY MINUTES AWAY. SO YOU MIGHT WANT TO PACK SANDWICHES, SNACKS, POP, WHATEVER YOU NEED TO GET YOU THROUGH.

AND IF ANYONE WANTS TO REDO THEIR NUMBERS, I BROUGHT SOME ELECTRICAL TAPE. IT'LL STAY ON WAY BETTER THAN THAT OTHER STUFF.

TRUST ME—I'VE BEEN WORKING AT MY DAD'S HARDWARE STORE SINCE I WAS LIKE FIVE.

THANK YOU, LISA. I THINK WE'LL BE NEEDING IT, FOR THE NEXT FEW GAMES AT LEAST.

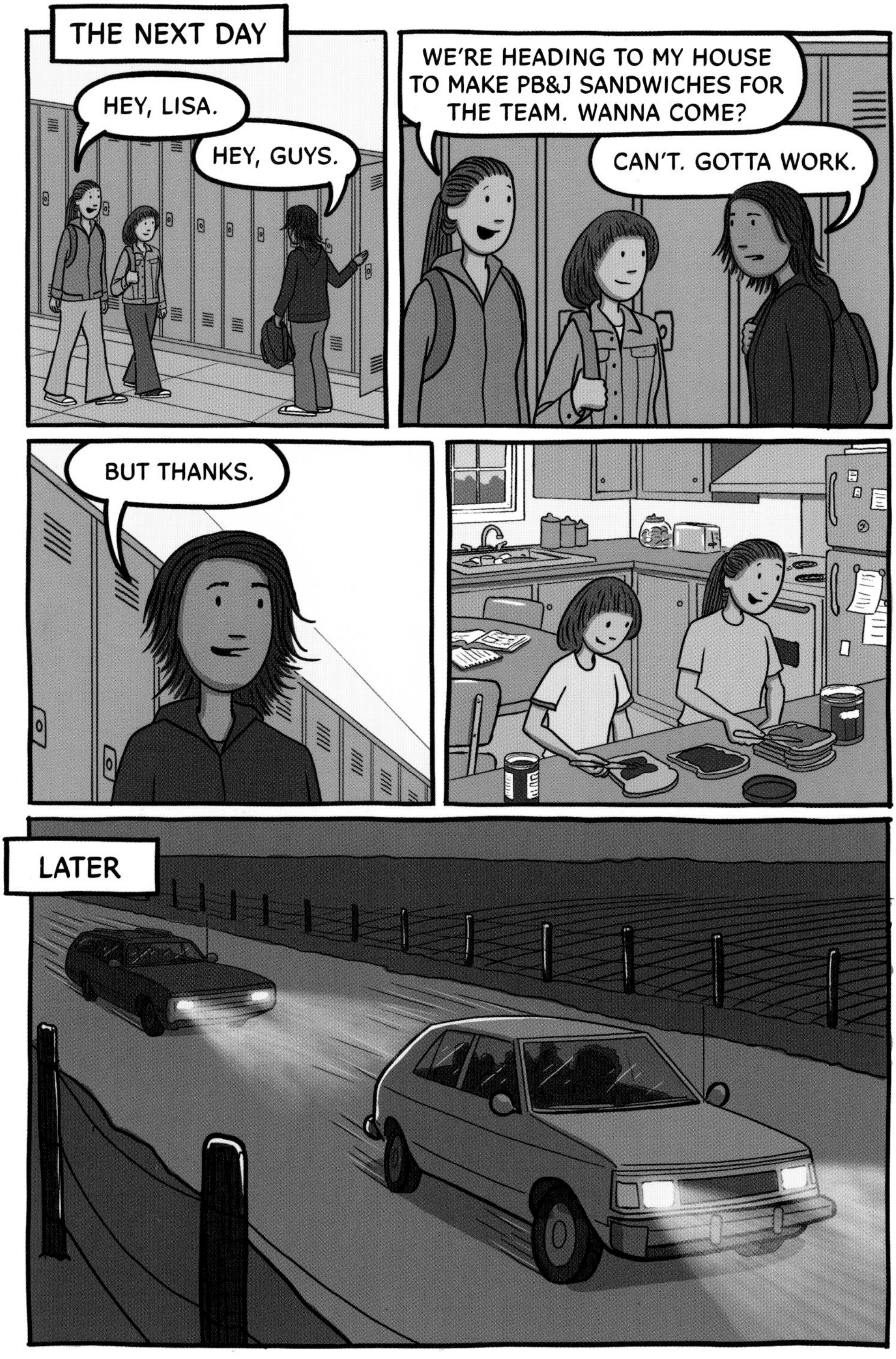
THE NEXT DAY
HEY, LISA.
HEY, GUYS.
WE'RE HEADING TO MY HOUSE TO MAKE PB&J SANDWICHES FOR THE TEAM. WANNA COME?
CAN'T. GOTTA WORK.
BUT THANKS.
LATER

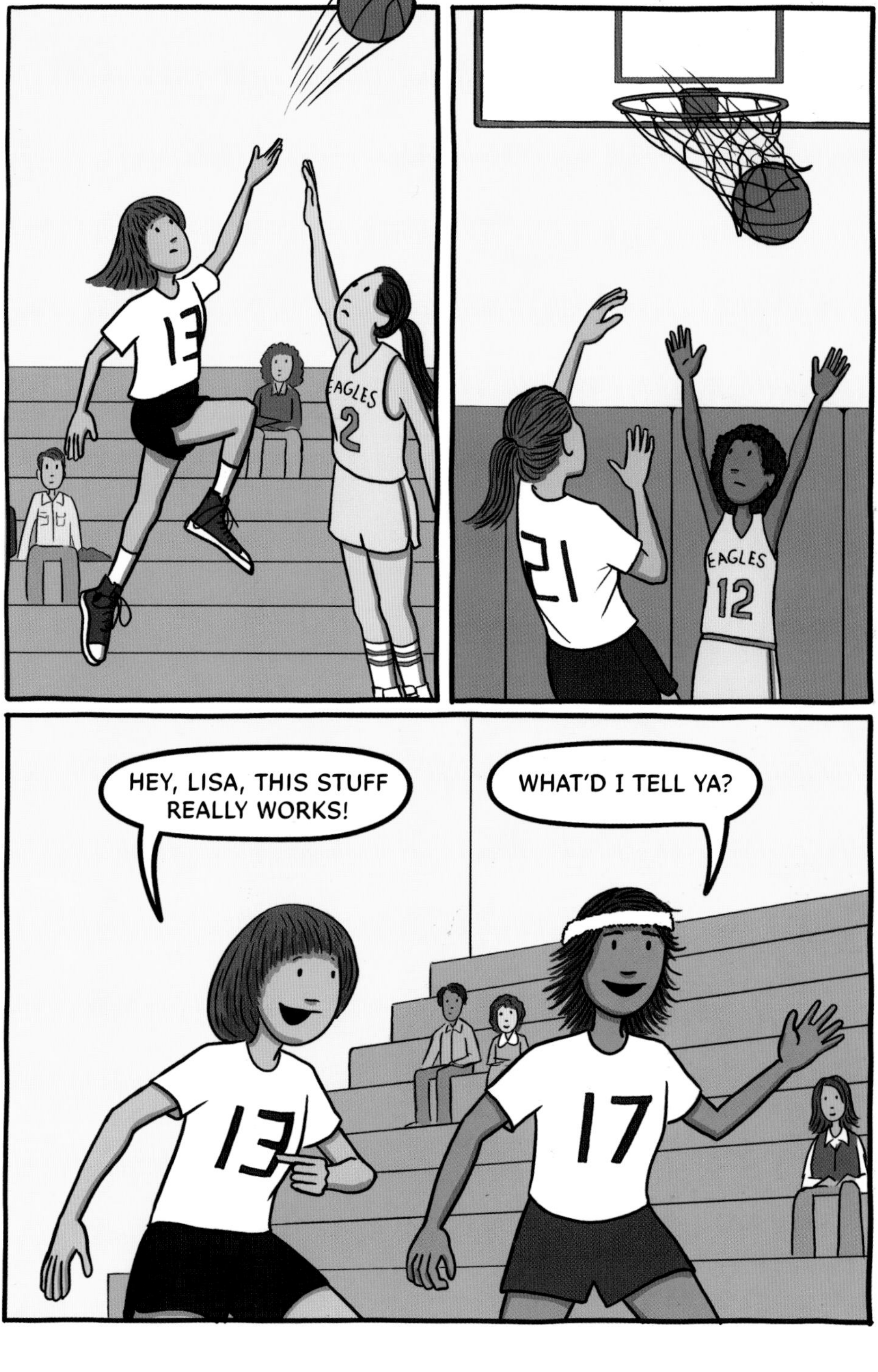
EAGLES
2
13
21
EAGLES
12
HEY, LISA, THIS STUFF REALLY WORKS!
WHAT'D I TELL YA?
13
17

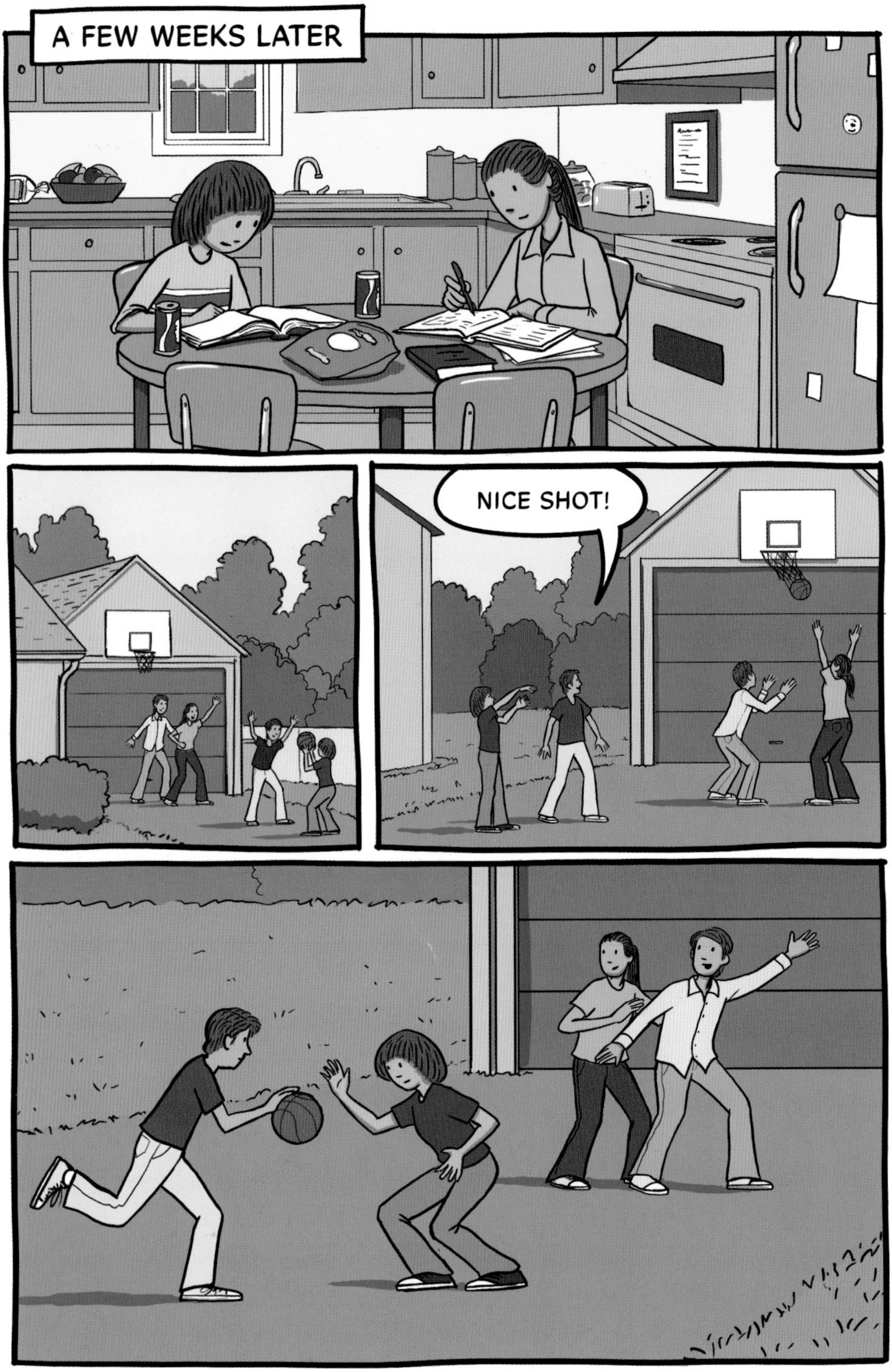
A FEW WEEKS LATER
NICE SHOT!

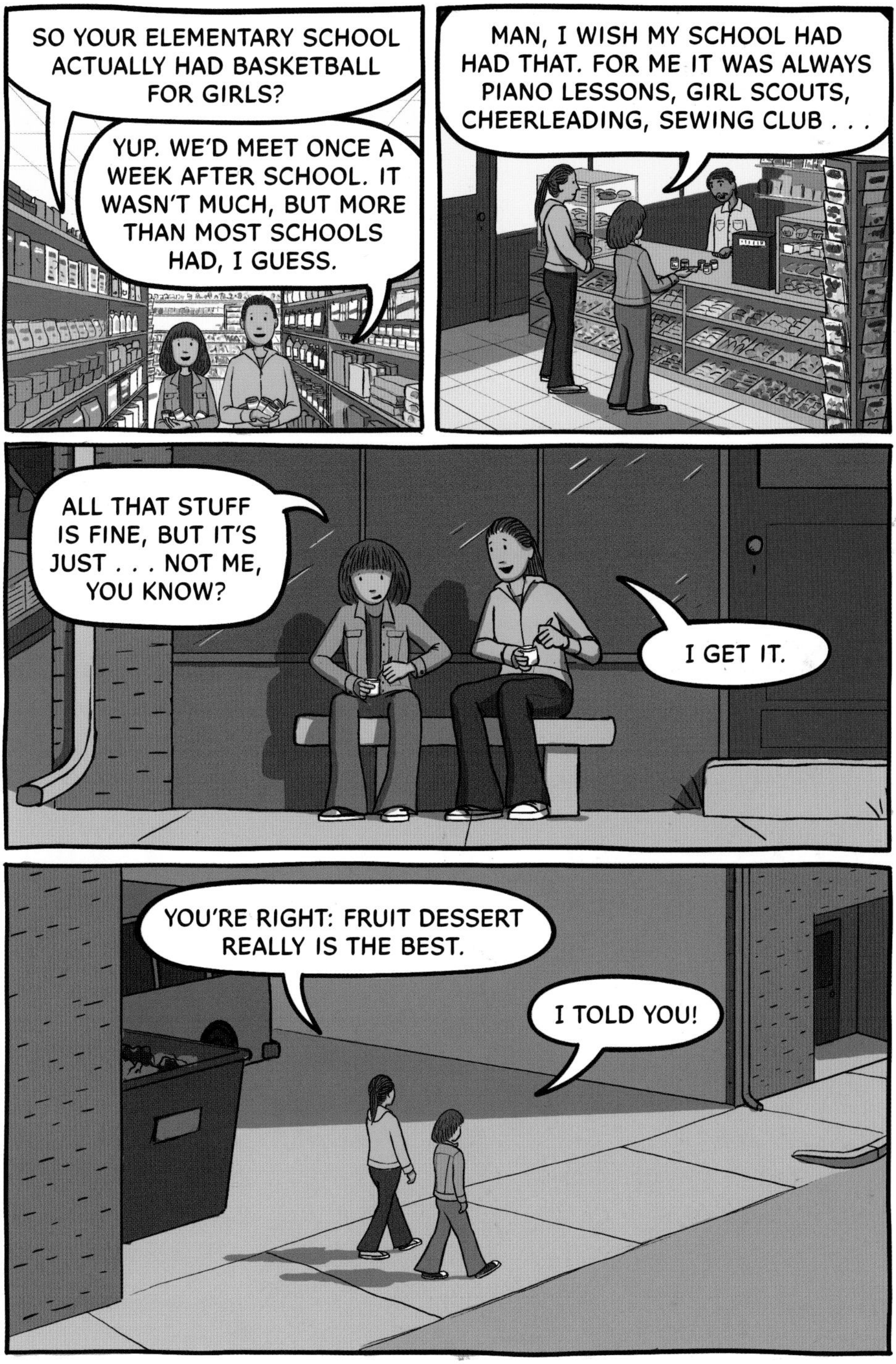
SO YOUR ELEMENTARY SCHOOL ACTUALLY HAD BASKETBALL FOR GIRLS?
YUP. WE'D MEET ONCE A WEEK AFTER SCHOOL. IT WASN'T MUCH, BUT MORE THAN MOST SCHOOLS HAD, I GUESS.
MAN, I WISH MY SCHOOL HAD HAD THAT. FOR ME IT WAS ALWAYS PIANO LESSONS, GIRL SCOUTS, CHEERLEADING, SEWING CLUB . . .
ALL THAT STUFF IS FINE, BUT IT'S JUST . . . NOT ME, YOU KNOW?
I GET IT.
YOU'RE RIGHT: FRUIT DESSERT REALLY IS THE BEST.
I TOLD YOU!

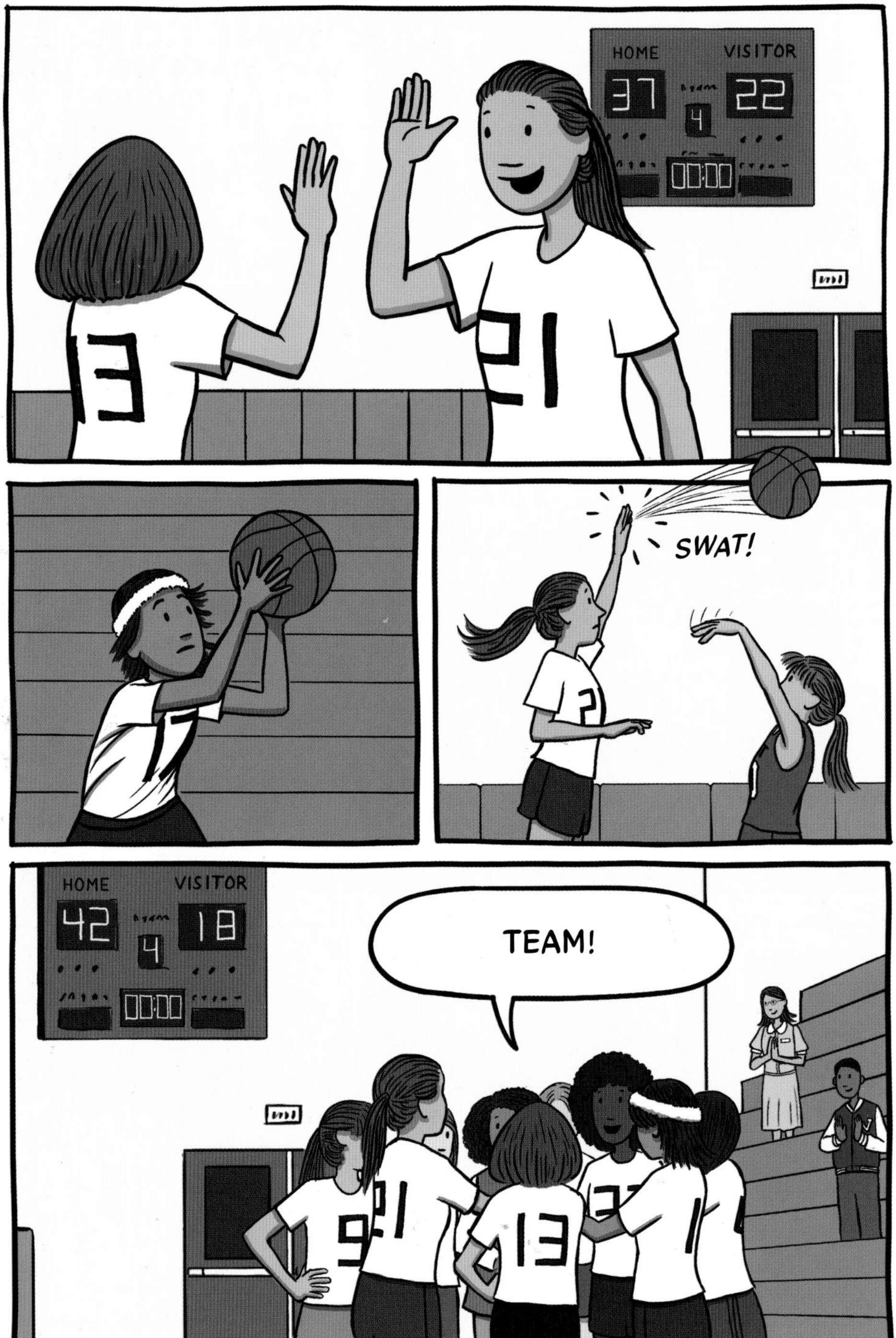
HOME
VISITOR
37
22
4
00:00
SWAT!
HOME
VISITOR
42
18
4
00:00
TEAM!

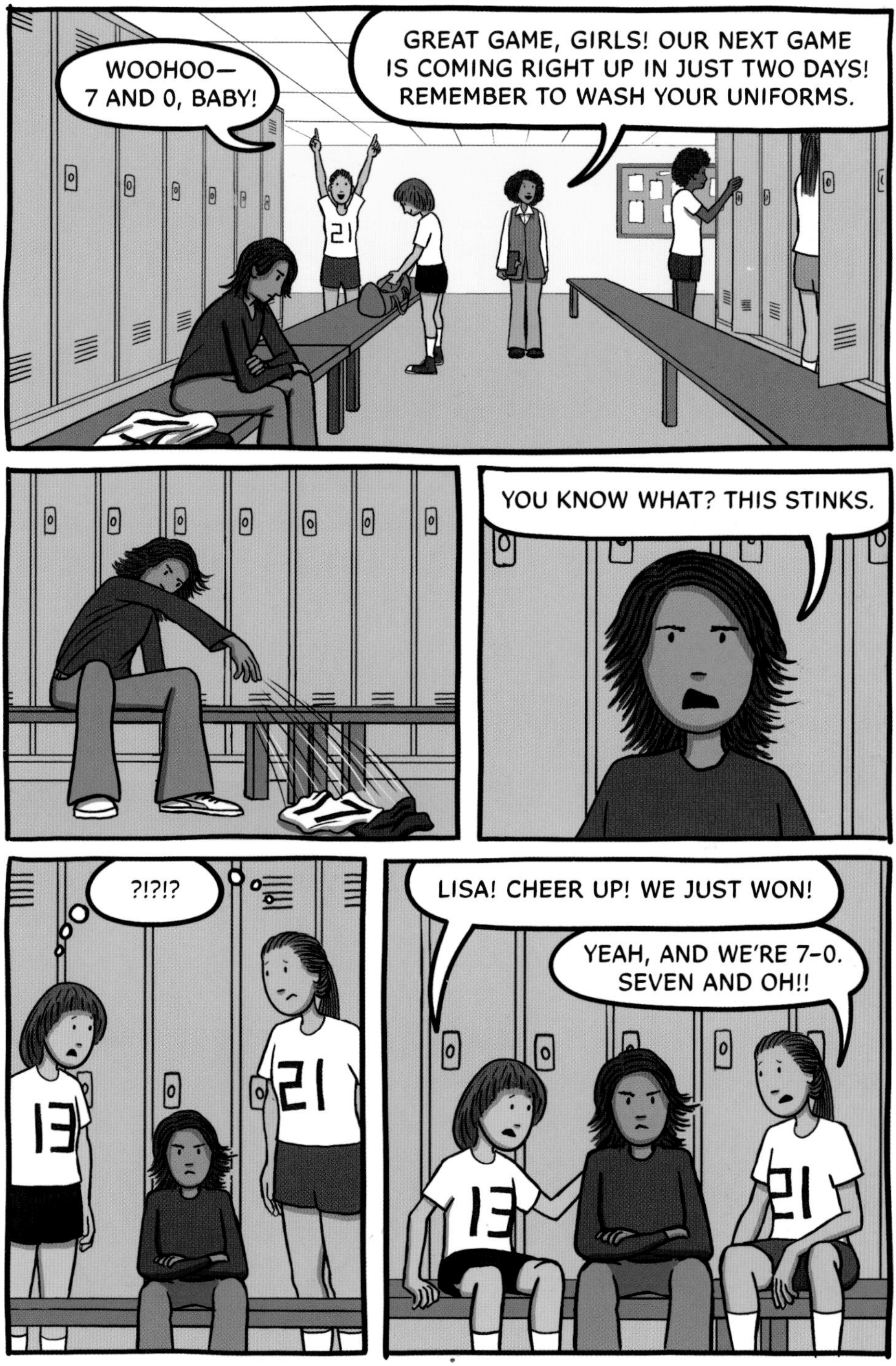
WOOHOO—
7 AND 0, BABY!
GREAT GAME, GIRLS! OUR NEXT GAME IS COMING RIGHT UP IN JUST TWO DAYS! REMEMBER TO WASH YOUR UNIFORMS.
YOU KNOW WHAT? THIS STINKS.
?!?!?
LISA! CHEER UP! WE JUST WON!
YEAH, AND WE'RE 7–0. SEVEN AND OH!!

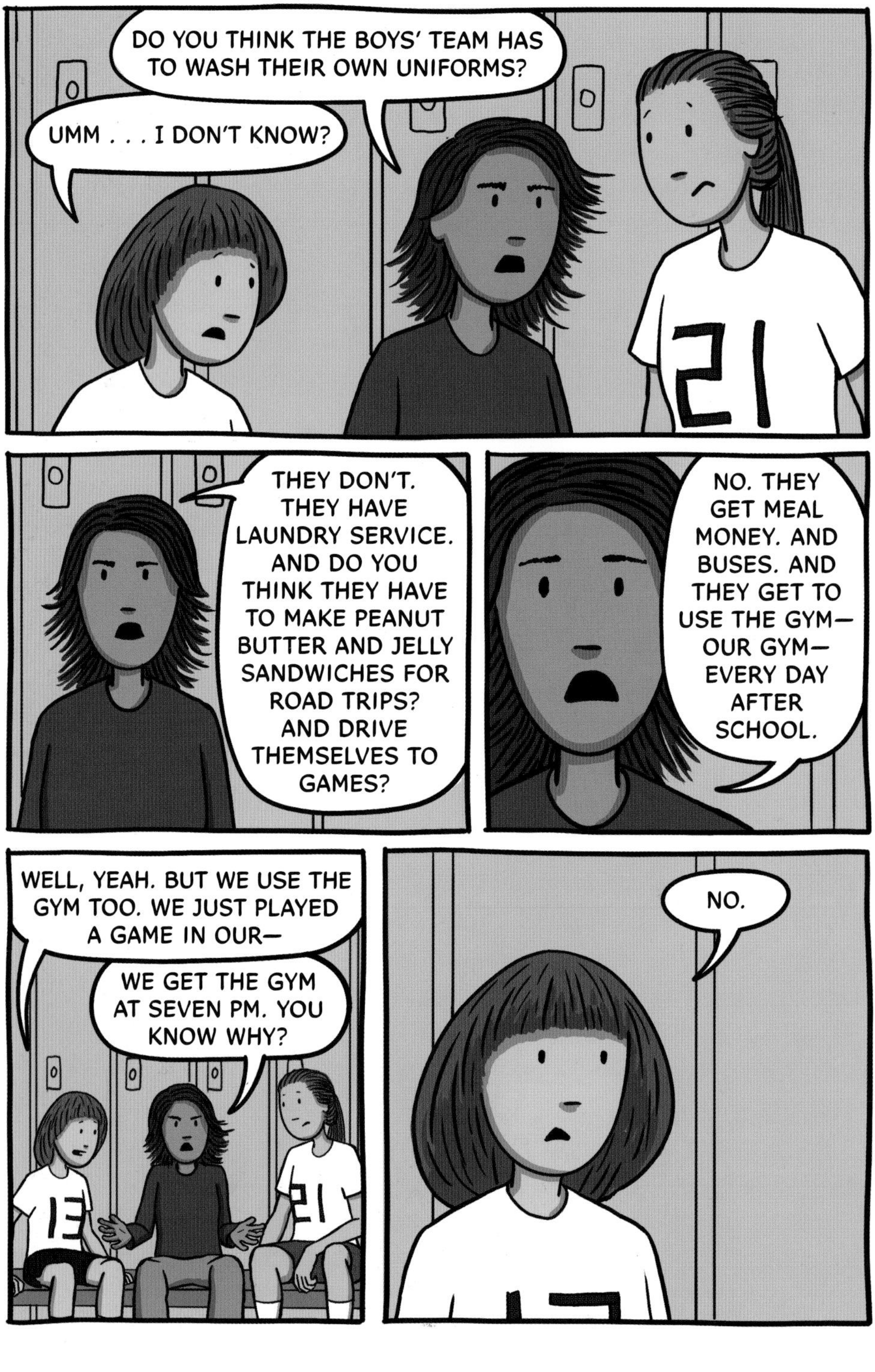
DO YOU THINK THE BOYS' TEAM HAS TO WASH THEIR OWN UNIFORMS?
UMM . . . I DON'T KNOW?
THEY DON'T. THEY HAVE LAUNDRY SERVICE. AND DO YOU THINK THEY HAVE TO MAKE PEANUT BUTTER AND JELLY SANDWICHES FOR ROAD TRIPS? AND DRIVE THEMSELVES TO GAMES?
NO. THEY GET MEAL MONEY. AND BUSES. AND THEY GET TO USE THE GYM— OUR GYM— EVERY DAY AFTER SCHOOL.
WELL, YEAH. BUT WE USE THE GYM TOO. WE JUST PLAYED A GAME IN OUR—
WE GET THE GYM AT SEVEN PM. YOU KNOW WHY?
NO.

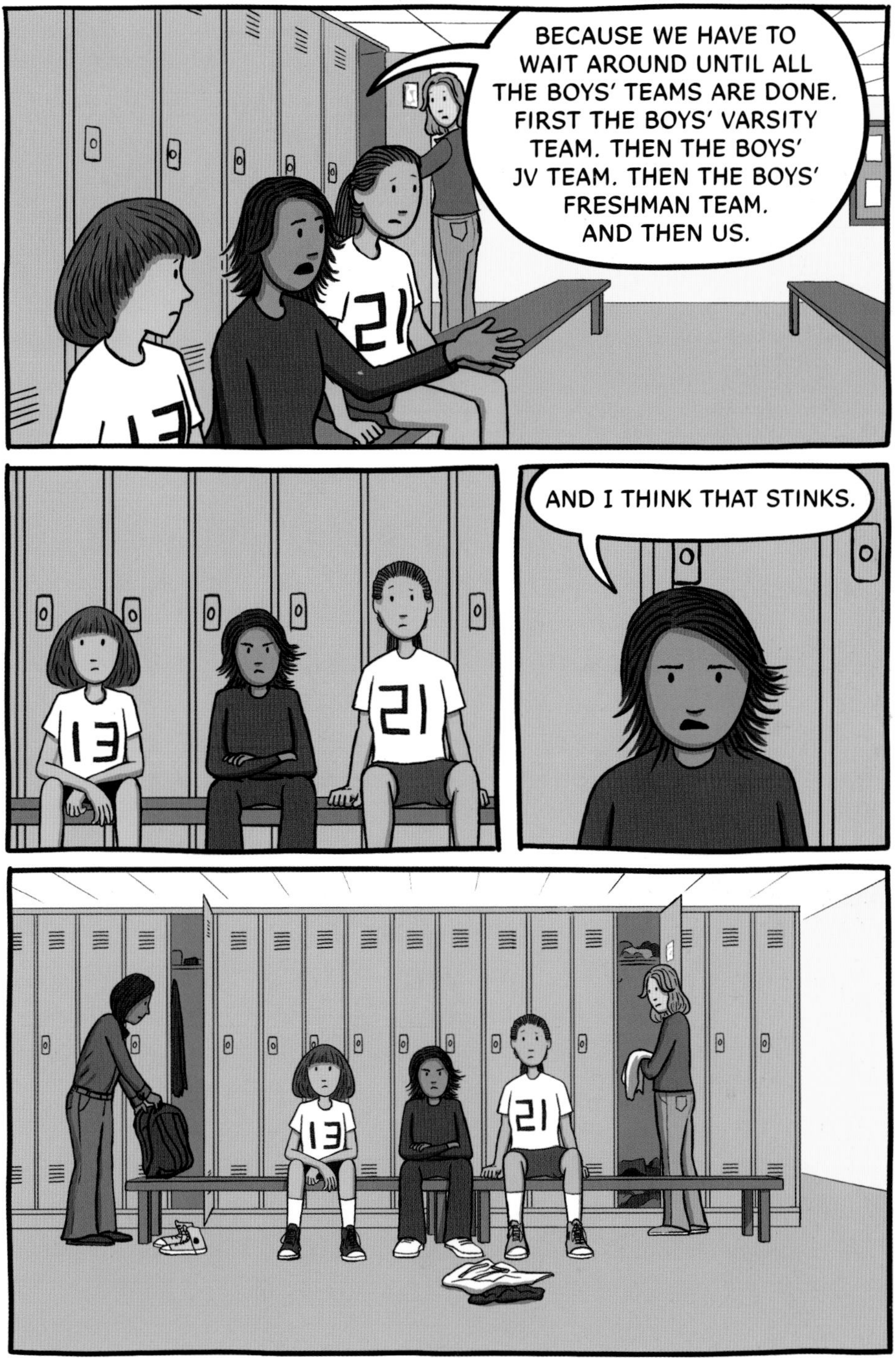
BECAUSE WE HAVE TO WAIT AROUND UNTIL ALL THE BOYS' TEAMS ARE DONE. FIRST THE BOYS' VARSITY TEAM. THEN THE BOYS' JV TEAM. THEN THE BOYS' FRESHMAN TEAM. AND THEN US.
13
21
13
21
AND I THINK THAT STINKS.
13
21

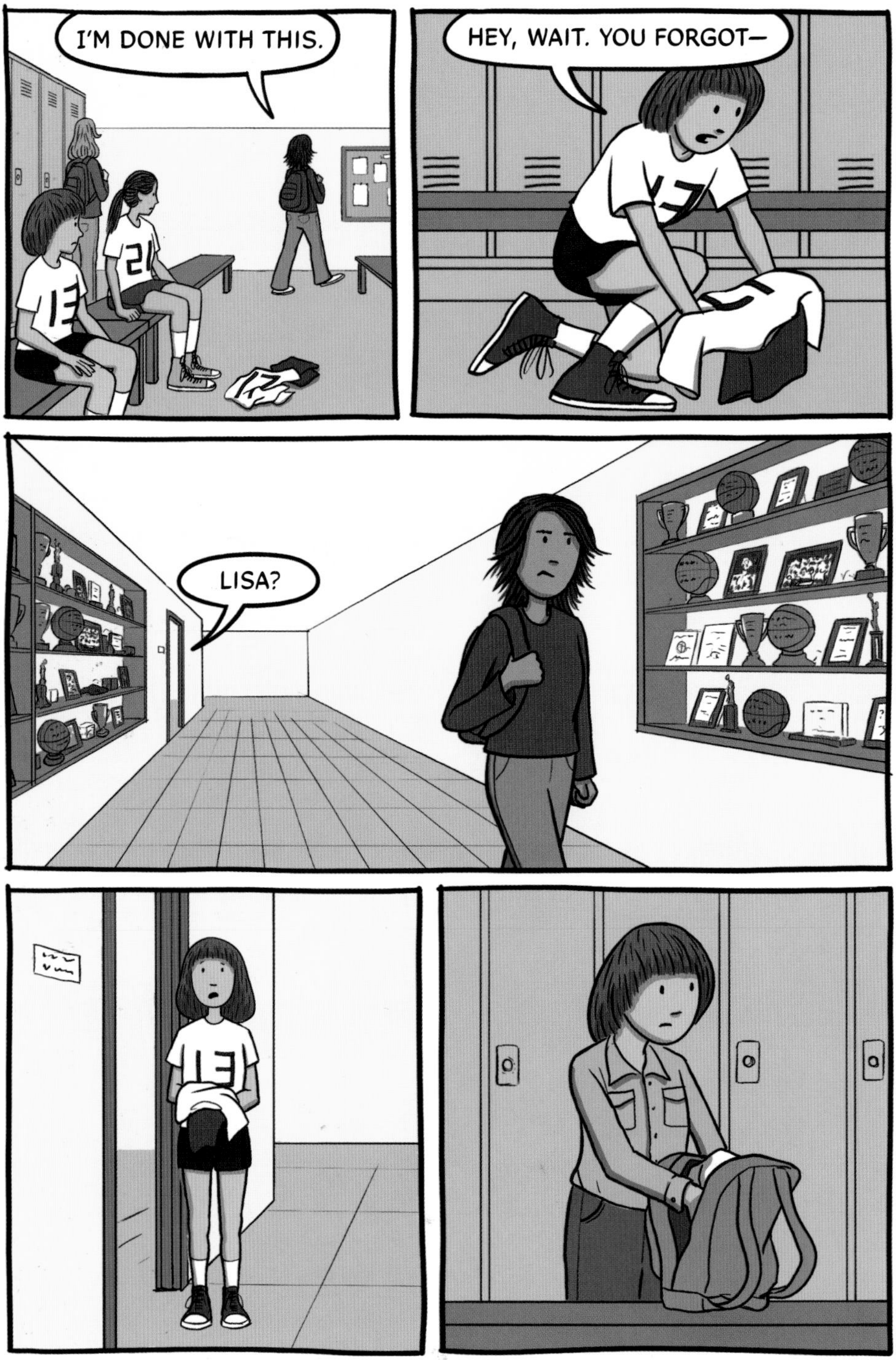
I'M DONE WITH THIS.
HEY, WAIT. YOU FORGOT—
LISA?

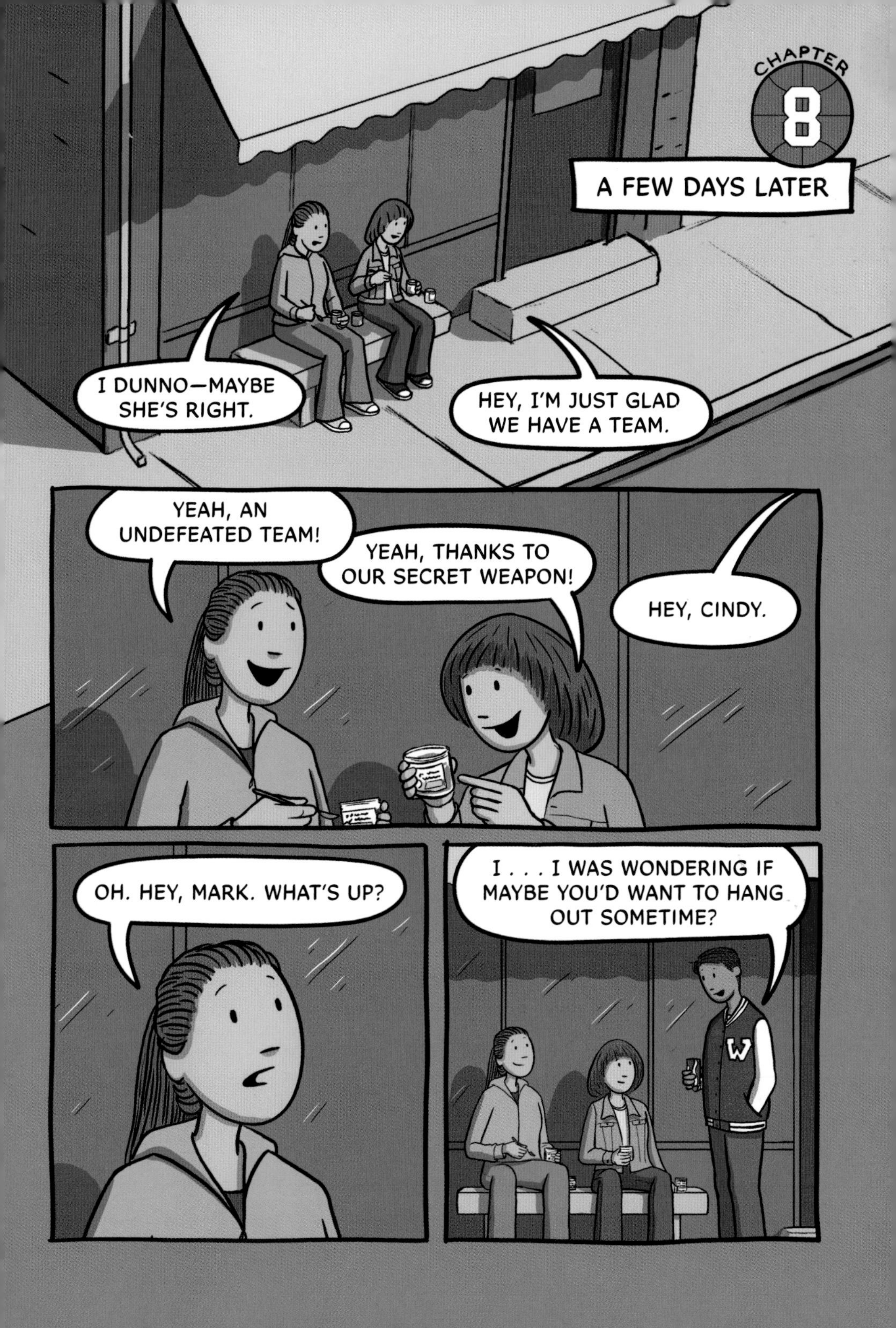
CHAPTER 8
A FEW DAYS LATER
I DUNNO—MAYBE SHE'S RIGHT.
HEY, I'M JUST GLAD WE HAVE A TEAM.
YEAH, AN UNDEFEATED TEAM!
YEAH, THANKS TO OUR SECRET WEAPON!
HEY, CINDY.
OH. HEY, MARK. WHAT'S UP?
I . . . I WAS WONDERING IF MAYBE YOU'D WANT TO HANG OUT SOMETIME?

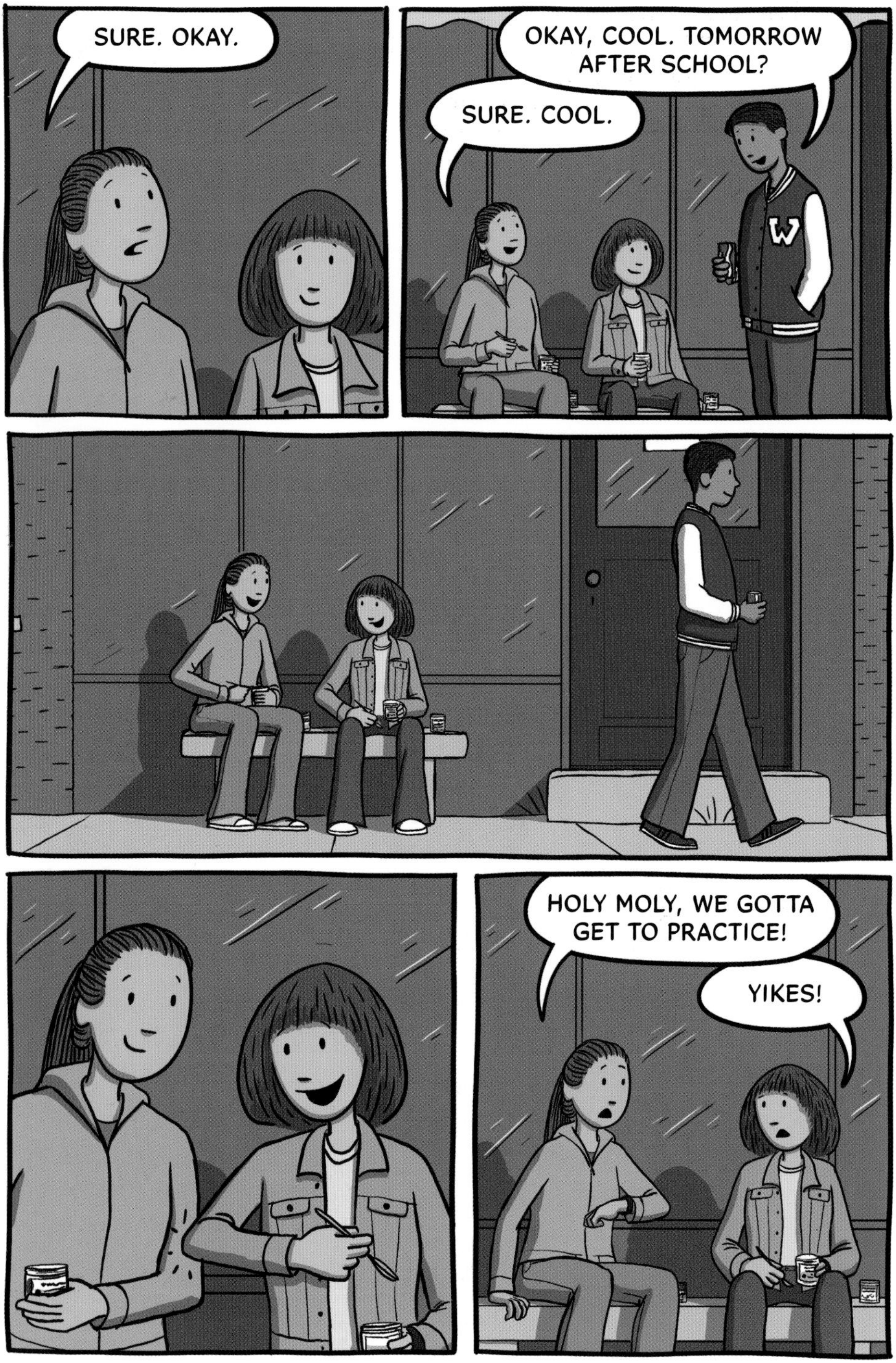
SURE. OKAY.
OKAY, COOL. TOMORROW AFTER SCHOOL?
SURE. COOL.
HOLY MOLY, WE GOTTA GET TO PRACTICE!
YIKES!

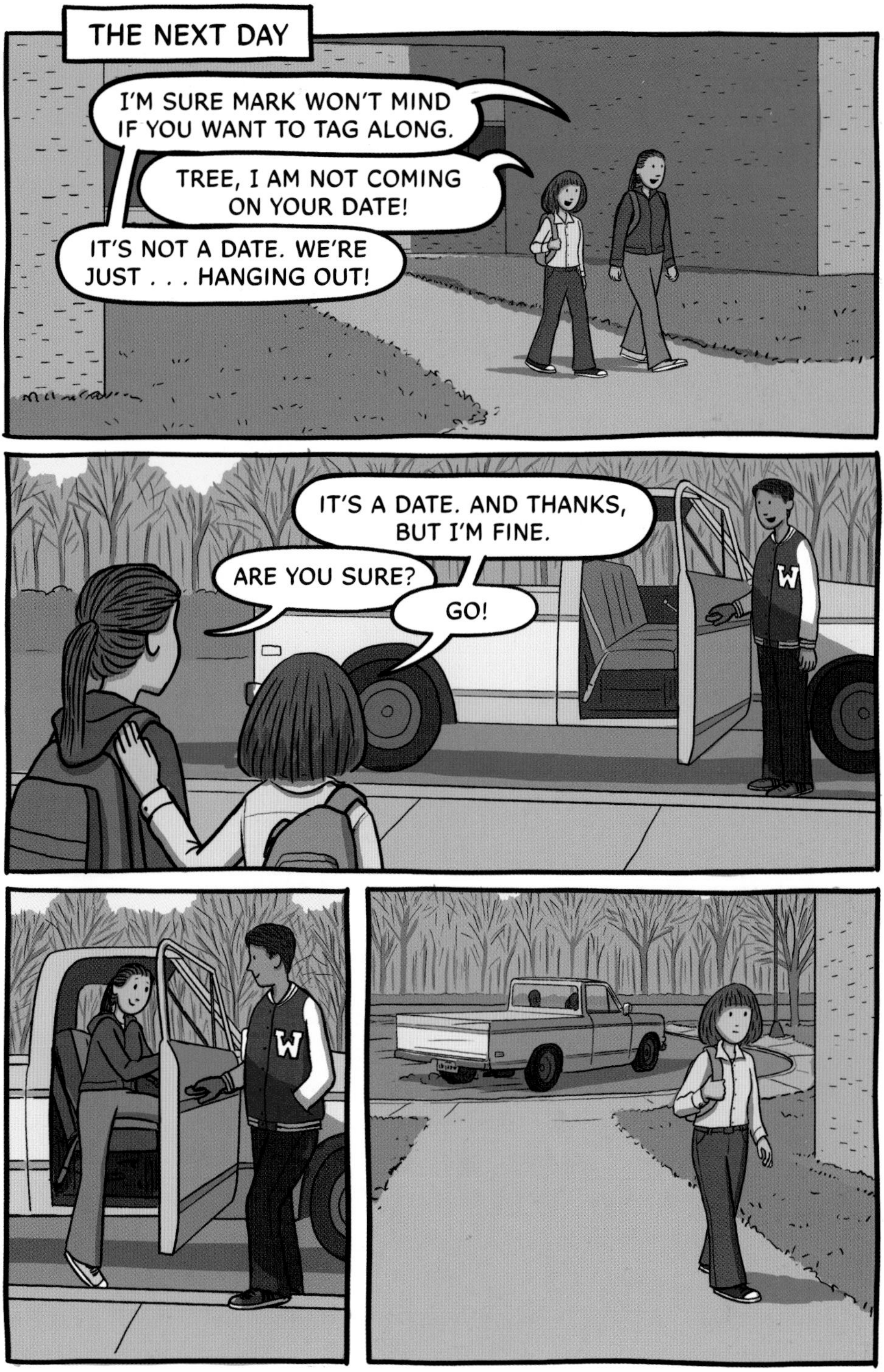
THE NEXT DAY
I'M SURE MARK WON'T MIND IF YOU WANT TO TAG ALONG.
TREE, I AM NOT COMING ON YOUR DATE!
IT'S NOT A DATE. WE'RE JUST . . . HANGING OUT!
IT'S A DATE. AND THANKS, BUT I'M FINE.
ARE YOU SURE?
GO!
W
W

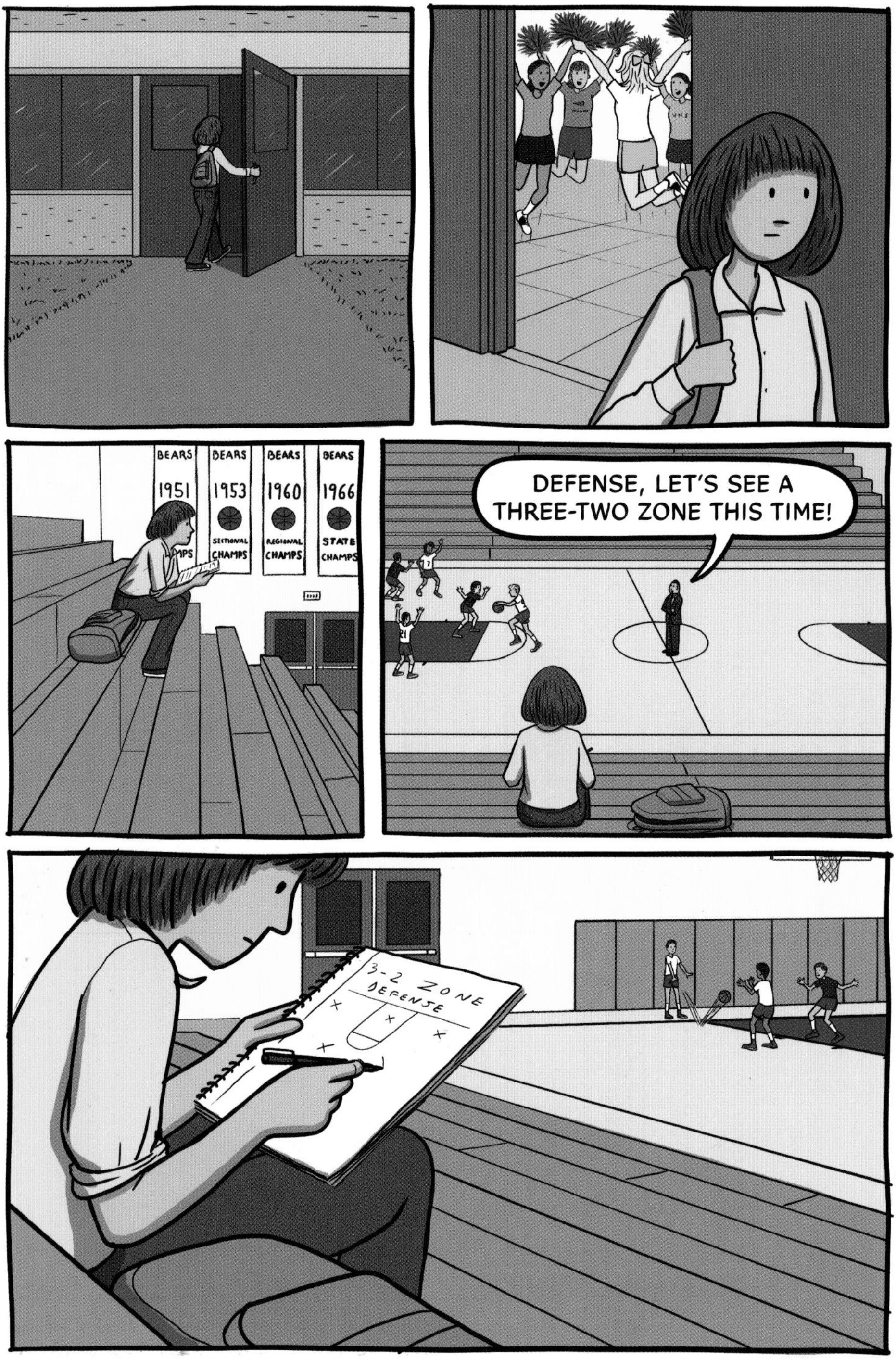
BEARS
1951
BEARS
1953
SECTIONAL
CHAMPS
BEARS
1960
REGIONAL
CHAMPS
BEARS
1966
STATE
CHAMPS
DEFENSE, LET'S SEE A THREE-TWO ZONE THIS TIME!
3-2 ZONE
DEFENSE

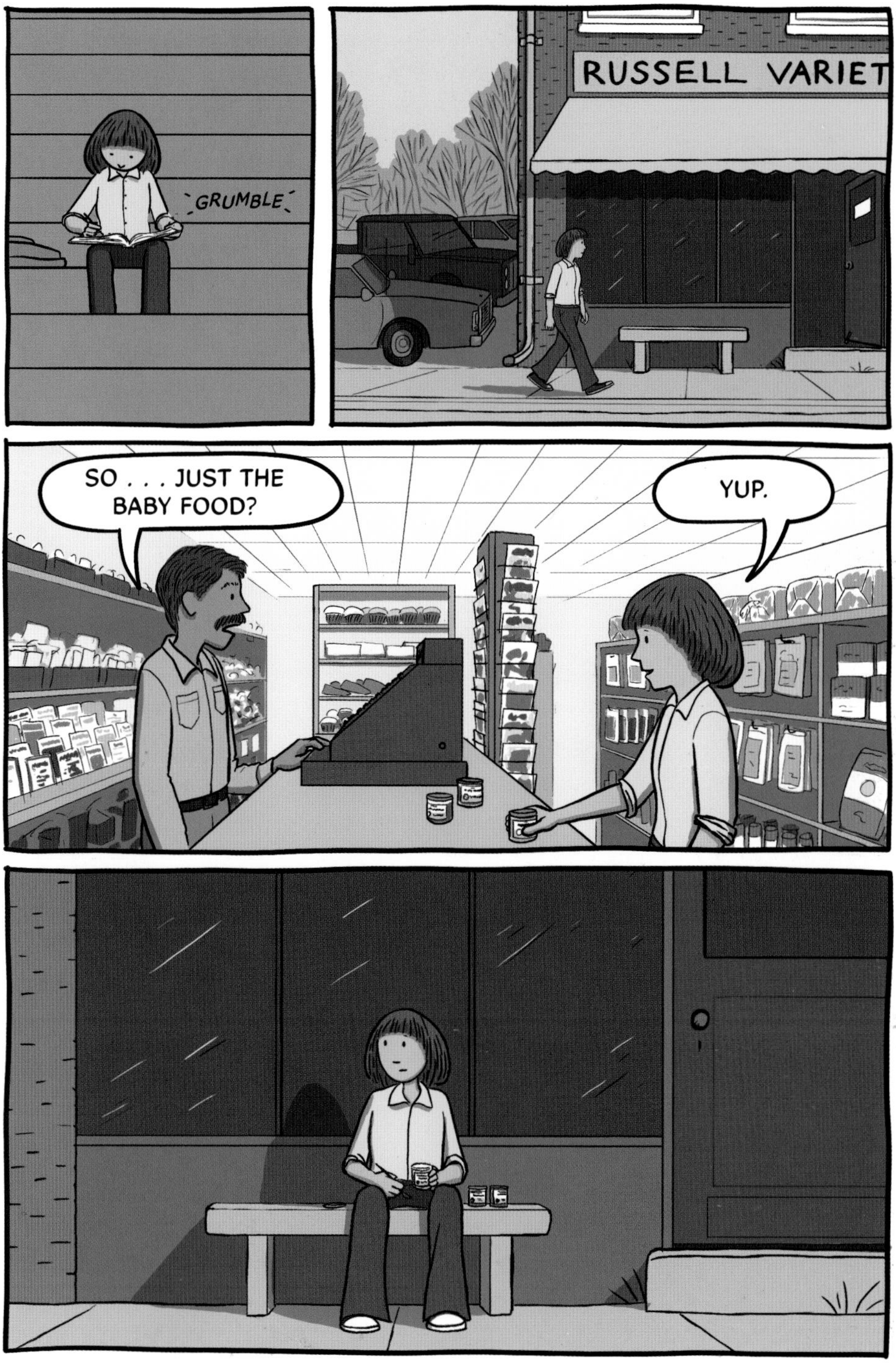
GRUMBLE
RUSSELL VARIET
SO . . . JUST THE BABY FOOD?
YUP.

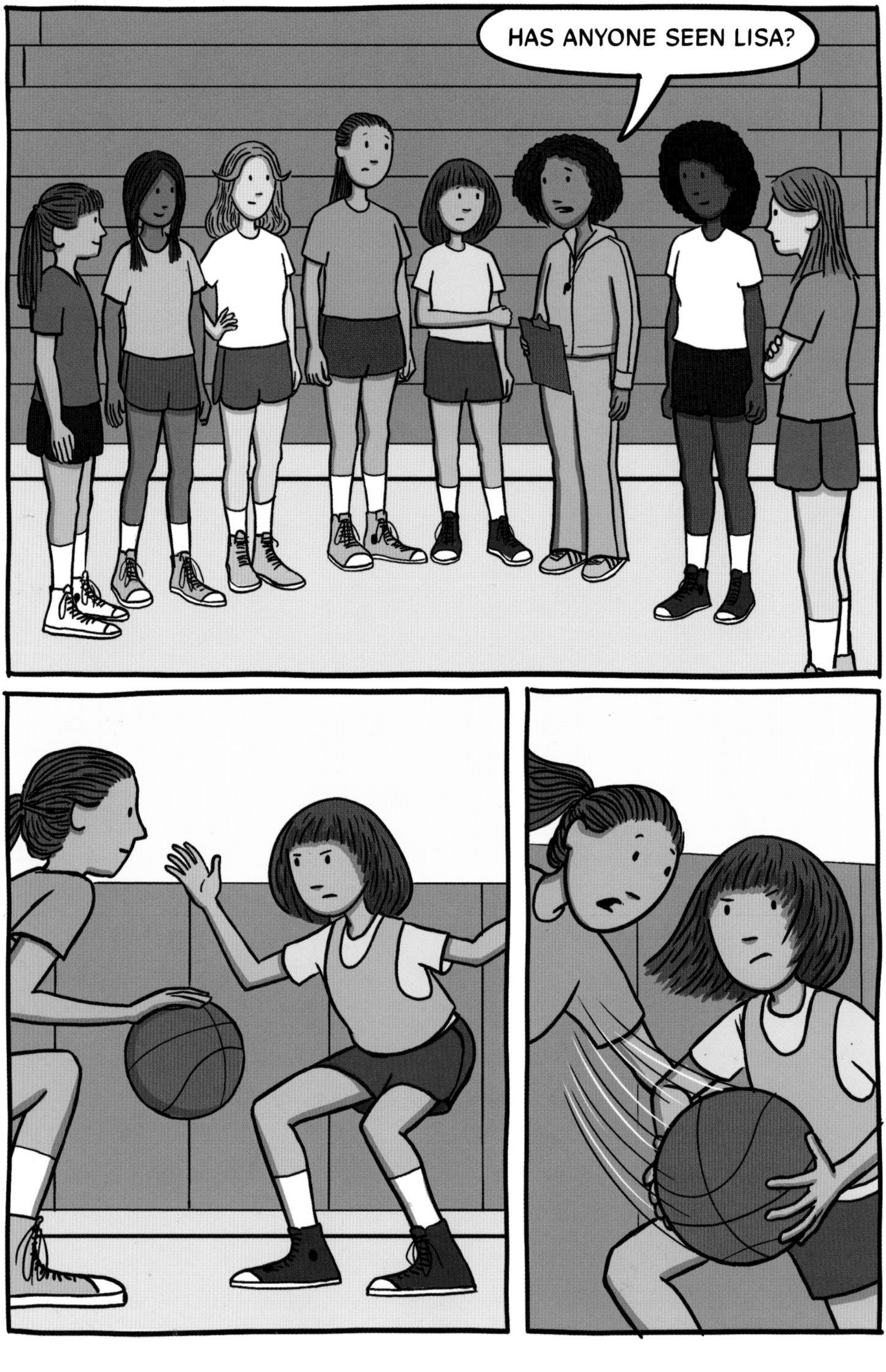
HAS ANYONE SEEN LISA?

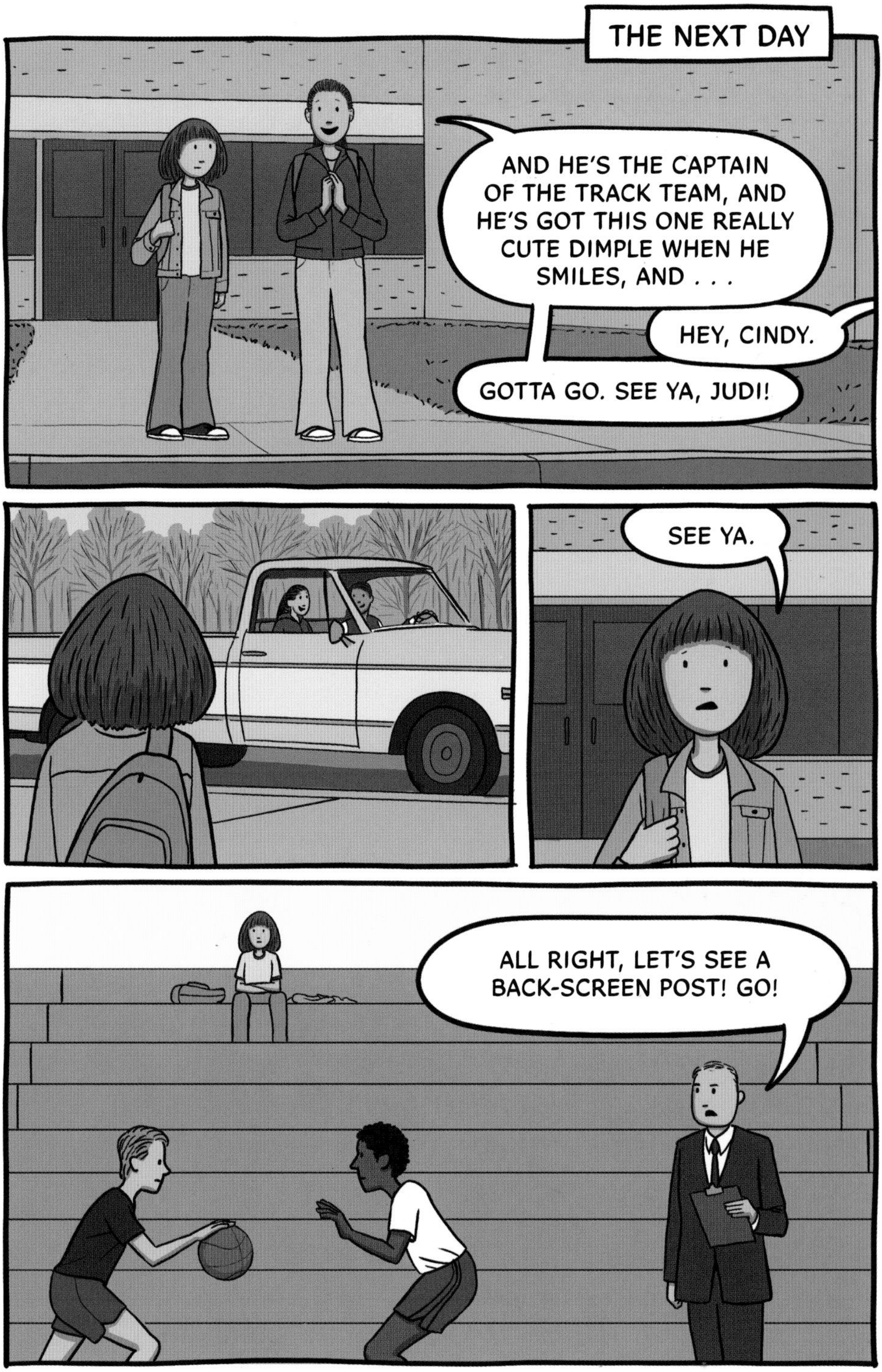
THE NEXT DAY
AND HE'S THE CAPTAIN OF THE TRACK TEAM, AND HE'S GOT THIS ONE REALLY CUTE DIMPLE WHEN HE SMILES, AND . . .
HEY, CINDY.
GOTTA GO. SEE YA, JUDI!
SEE YA.
ALL RIGHT, LET'S SEE A BACK-SCREEN POST! GO!

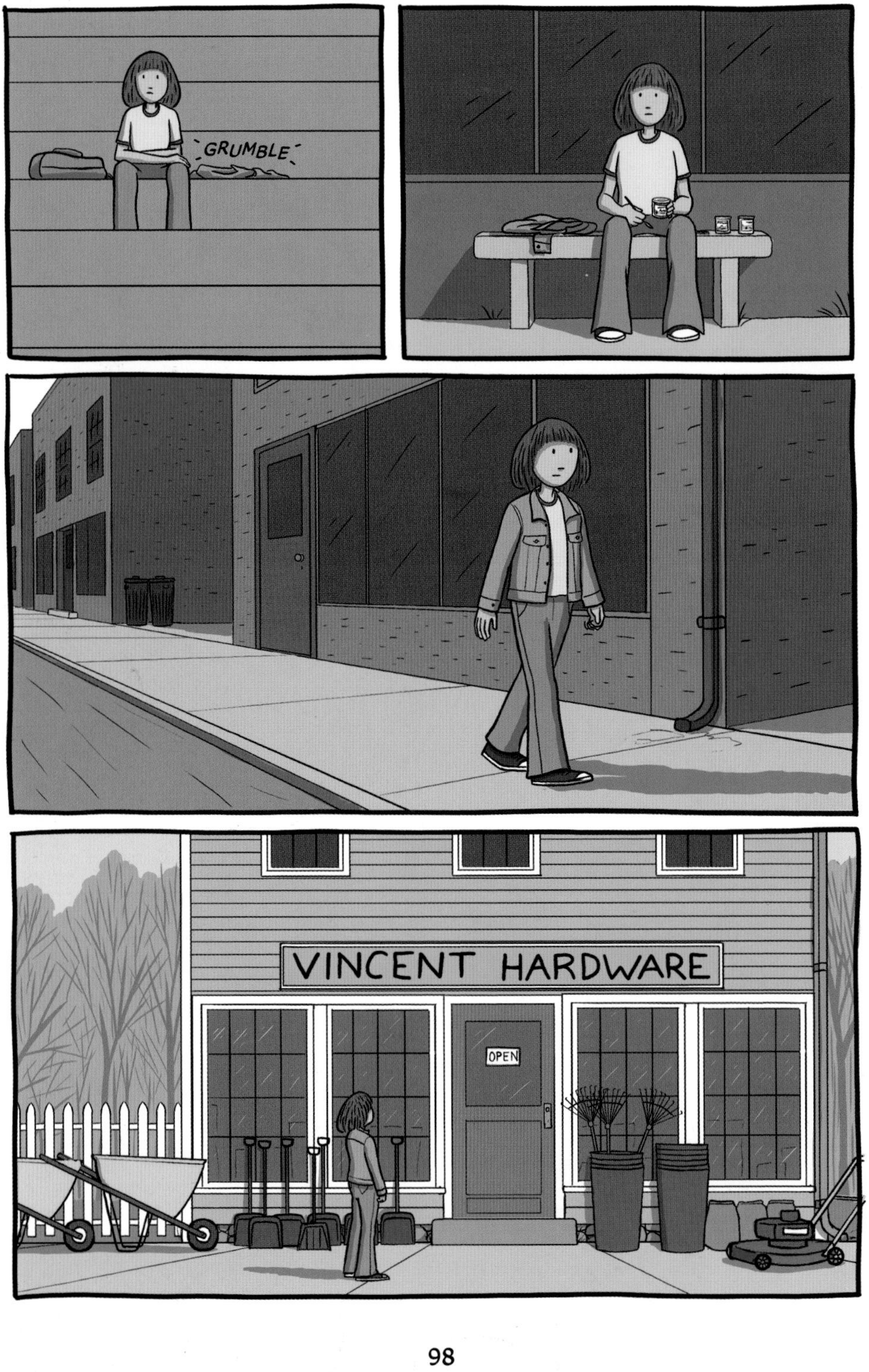
GRUMBLE
VINCENT HARDWARE
OPEN

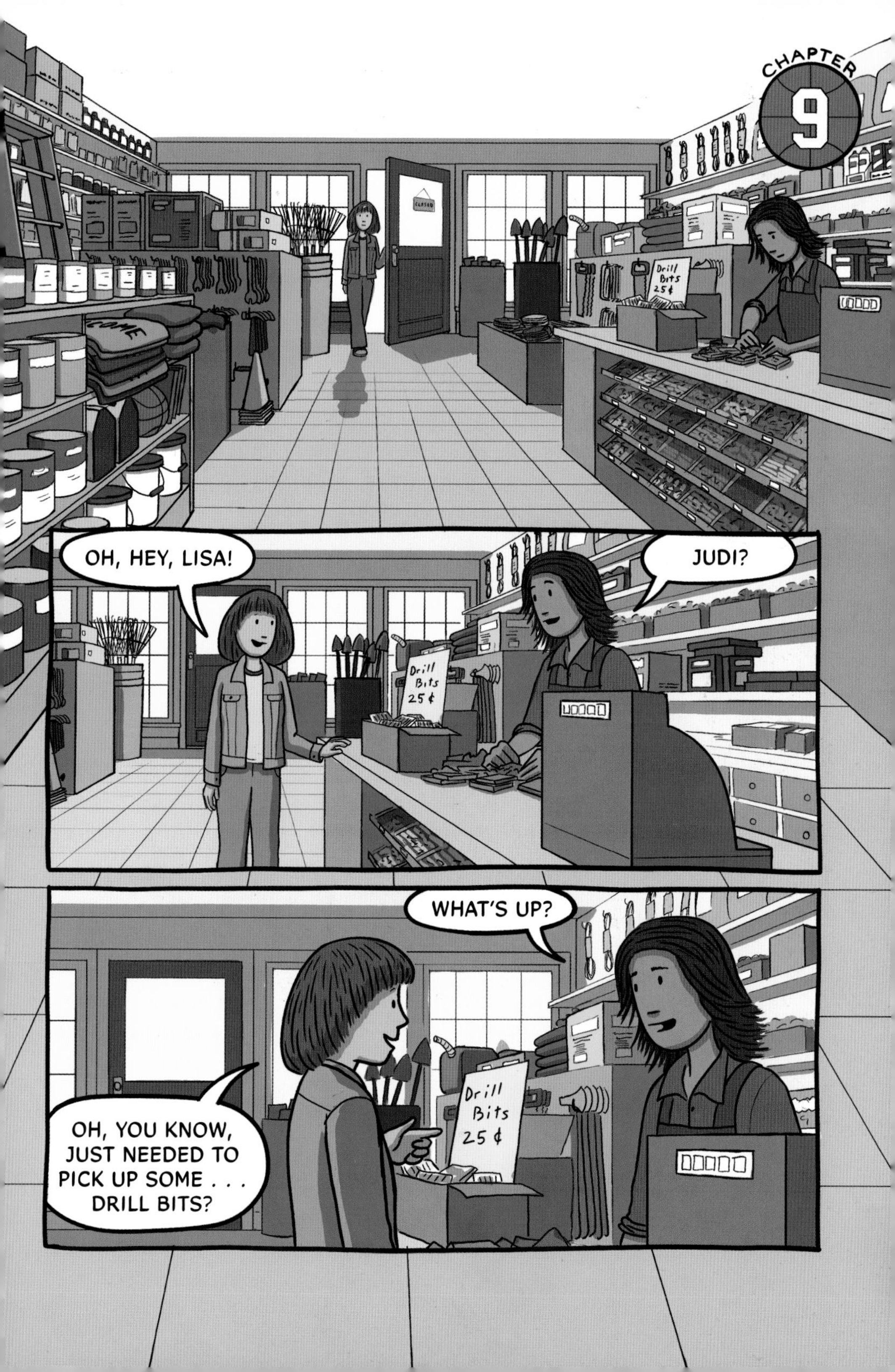
CHAPTER
9
CLOSED
Drill Bits 25¢
OH, HEY, LISA!
JUDI?
WHAT'S UP?
OH, YOU KNOW, JUST NEEDED TO PICK UP SOME . . . DRILL BITS?

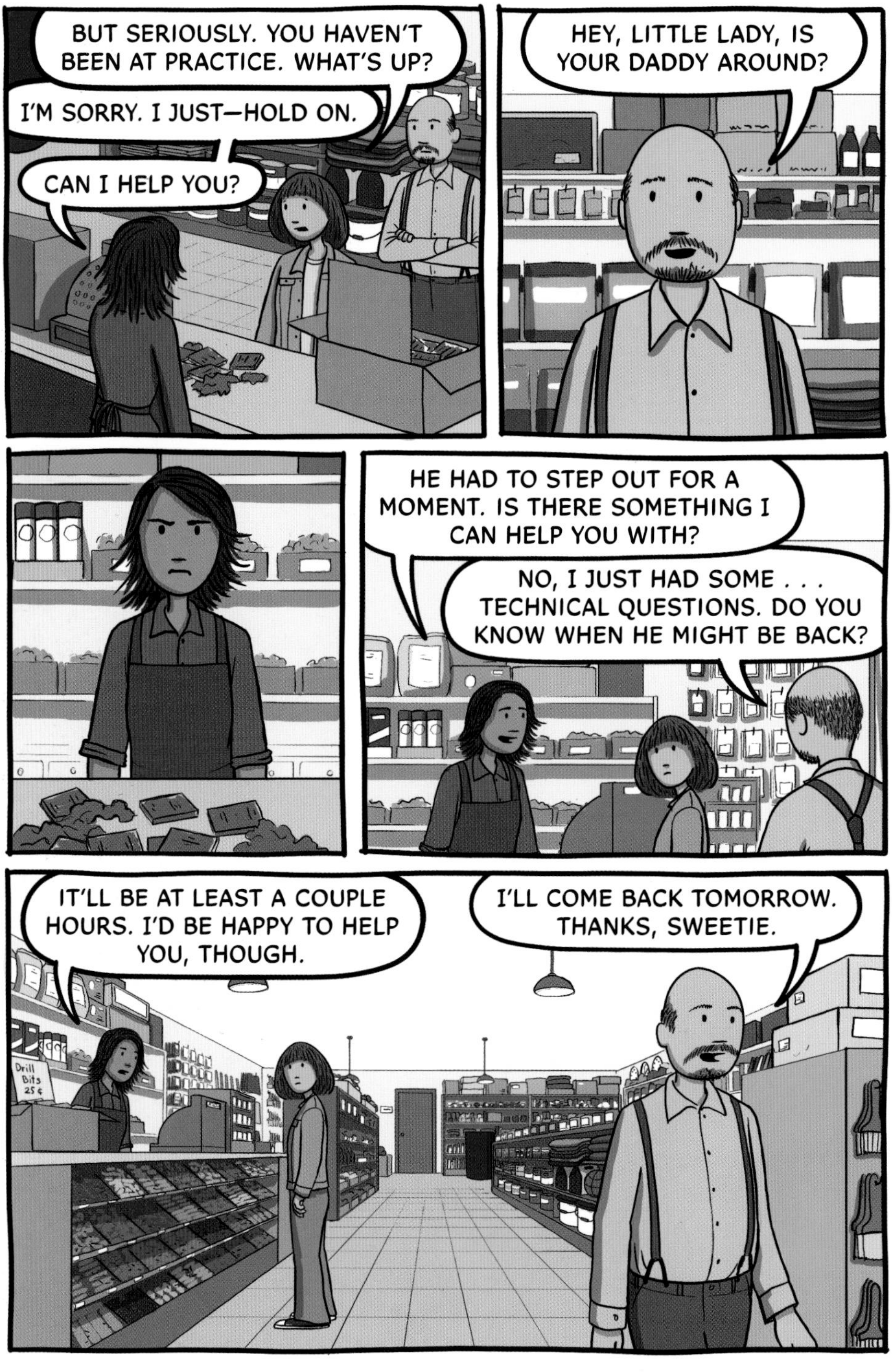
BUT SERIOUSLY. YOU HAVEN'T BEEN AT PRACTICE. WHAT'S UP?
I'M SORRY. I JUST—HOLD ON.
CAN I HELP YOU?
HEY, LITTLE LADY, IS YOUR DADDY AROUND?
HE HAD TO STEP OUT FOR A MOMENT. IS THERE SOMETHING I CAN HELP YOU WITH?
NO, I JUST HAD SOME . . . TECHNICAL QUESTIONS. DO YOU KNOW WHEN HE MIGHT BE BACK?
IT'LL BE AT LEAST A COUPLE HOURS. I'D BE HAPPY TO HELP YOU, THOUGH.
Drill Bits 25¢
I'LL COME BACK TOMORROW. THANKS, SWEETIE.

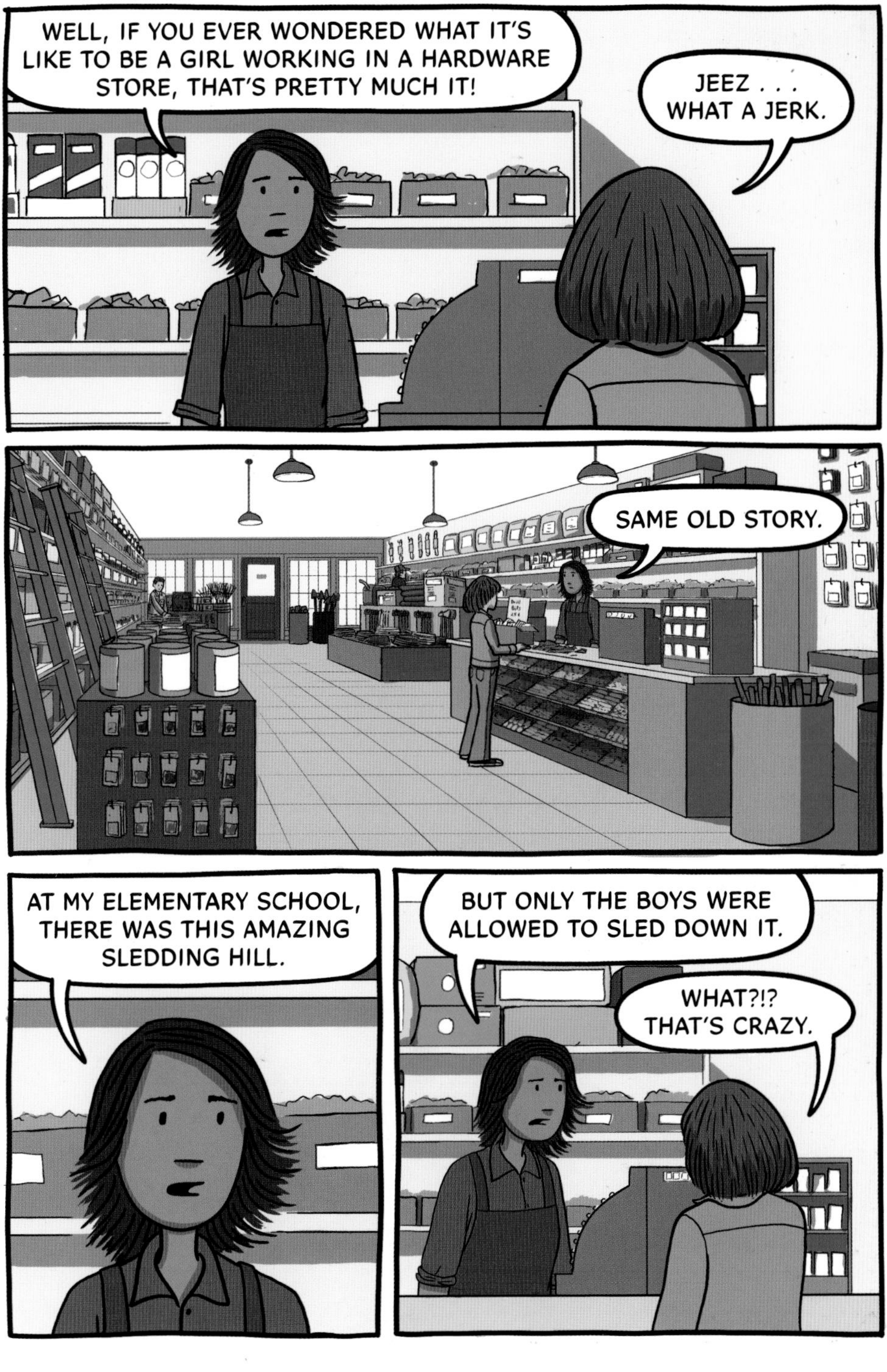
WELL, IF YOU EVER WONDERED WHAT IT'S LIKE TO BE A GIRL WORKING IN A HARDWARE STORE, THAT'S PRETTY MUCH IT!
JEEZ . . . WHAT A JERK.
SAME OLD STORY.
AT MY ELEMENTARY SCHOOL, THERE WAS THIS AMAZING SLEDDING HILL.
BUT ONLY THE BOYS WERE ALLOWED TO SLED DOWN IT.
WHAT?!? THAT'S CRAZY.

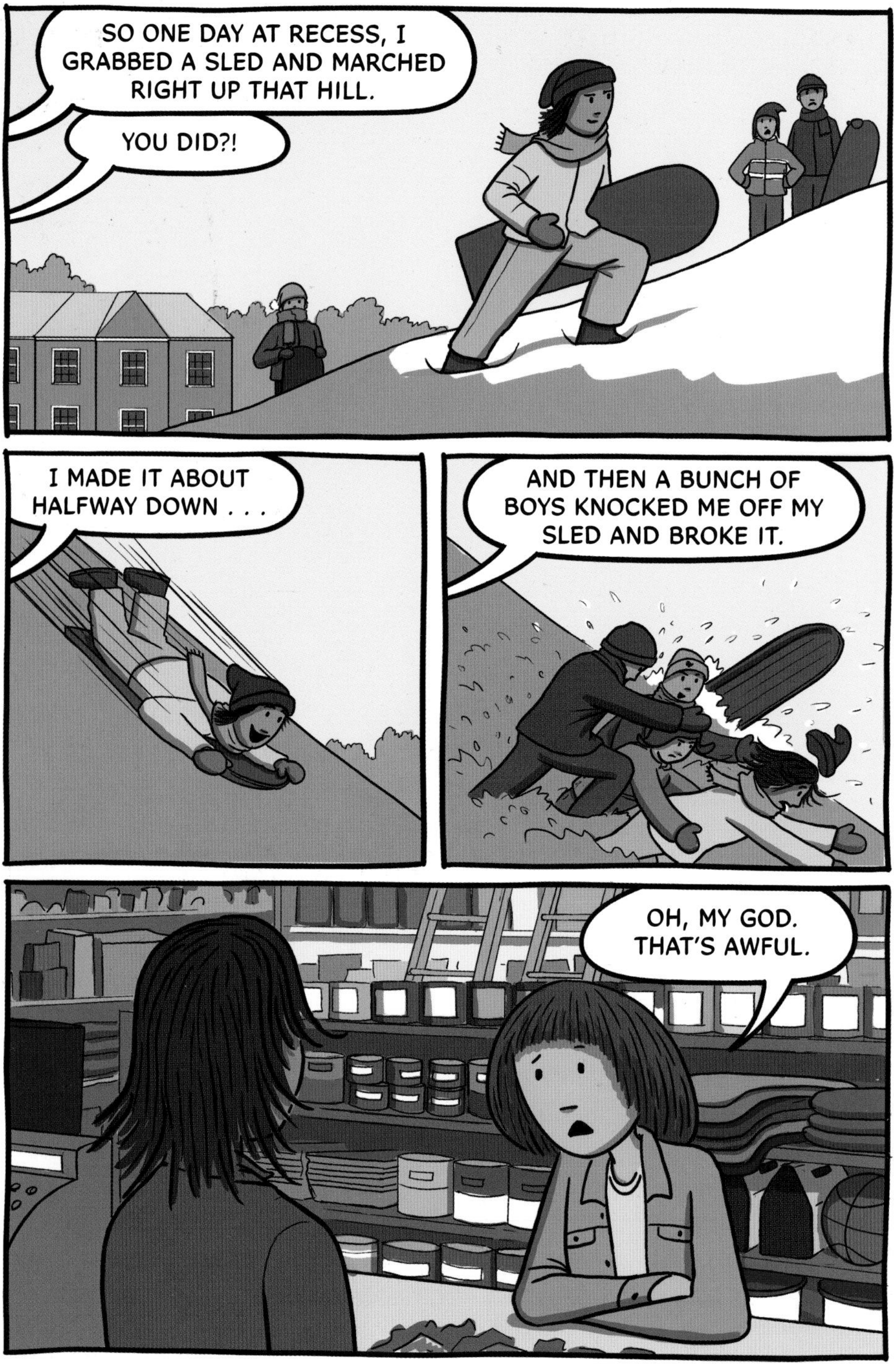
SO ONE DAY AT RECESS, I GRABBED A SLED AND MARCHED RIGHT UP THAT HILL.
YOU DID?!
I MADE IT ABOUT HALFWAY DOWN . . .
AND THEN A BUNCH OF BOYS KNOCKED ME OFF MY SLED AND BROKE IT.
OH, MY GOD. THAT'S AWFUL.

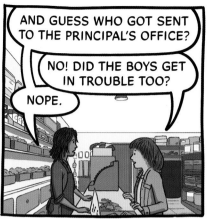

AND GUESS WHO GOT SENT TO THE PRINCIPAL'S OFFICE?

NO! DID THE BOYS GET IN TROUBLE TOO?

NOPE.

OH, MY GOD. I'M SO SORRY THAT HAPPENED TO YOU.

LISTEN, I'M SORRY I HAVEN'T BEEN AT PRACTICE. I JUST . . . I'M SO SICK OF BEING TREATED LIKE I DON'T MATTER JUST BECAUSE I'M A GIRL.

I JUST FEEL LIKE . . . IF I KEEP LETTING IT HAPPEN, IT'S LIKE I'M SAYING IT'S OKAY.

AND IT'S NOT OKAY. IT'S JUST NOT.

CAN I HELP YOU?

IS YOUR DAD AROUND?

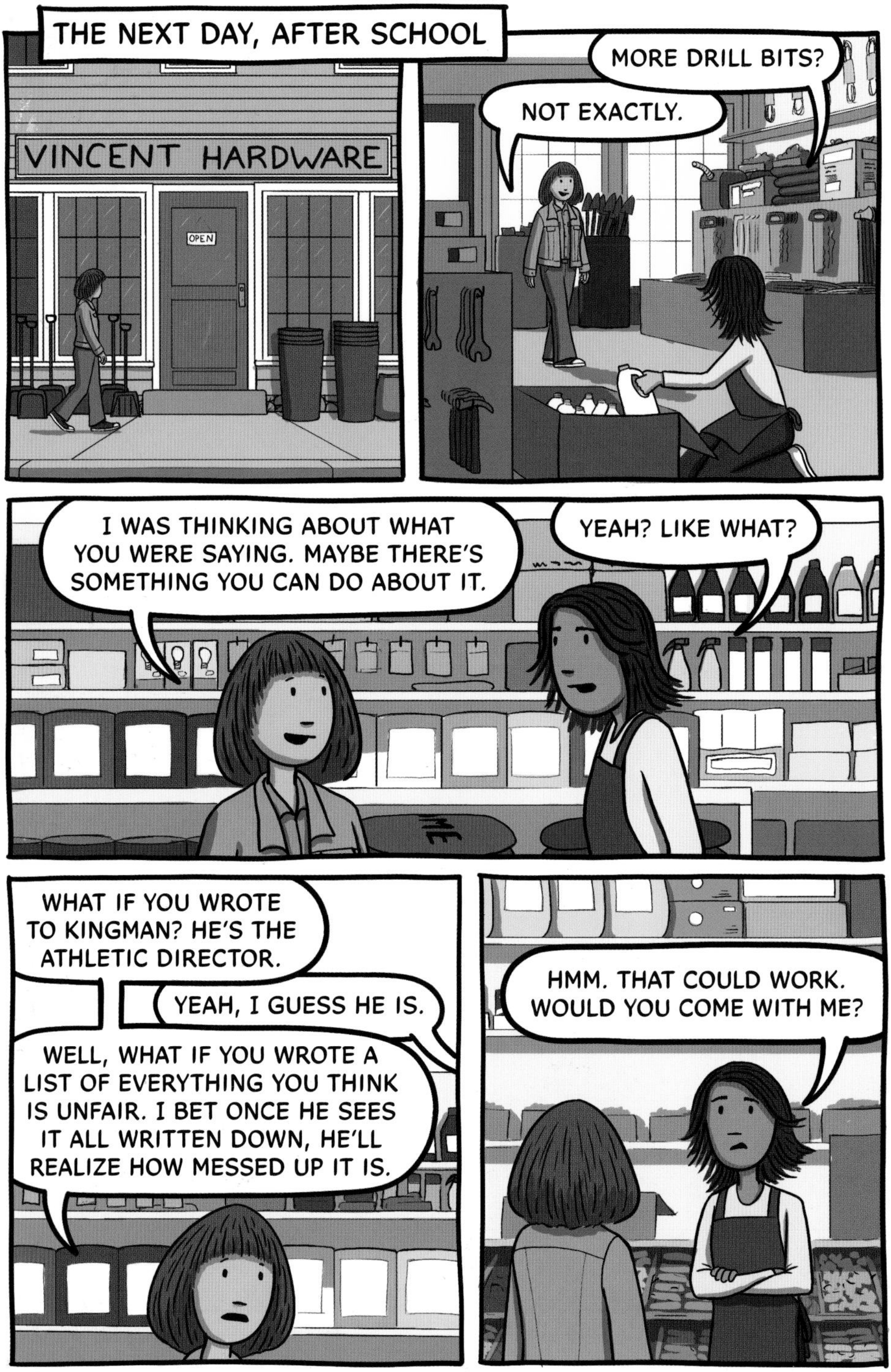
THE NEXT DAY, AFTER SCHOOL
VINCENT HARDWARE
OPEN
MORE DRILL BITS?
NOT EXACTLY.
I WAS THINKING ABOUT WHAT YOU WERE SAYING. MAYBE THERE'S SOMETHING YOU CAN DO ABOUT IT.
YEAH? LIKE WHAT?
WHAT IF YOU WROTE TO KINGMAN? HE'S THE ATHLETIC DIRECTOR.
YEAH, I GUESS HE IS.
WELL, WHAT IF YOU WROTE A LIST OF EVERYTHING YOU THINK IS UNFAIR. I BET ONCE HE SEES IT ALL WRITTEN DOWN, HE'LL REALIZE HOW MESSED UP IT IS.
HMM. THAT COULD WORK. WOULD YOU COME WITH ME?

COME WITH YOU WHERE?

TO HIS OFFICE.

OH, I WAS THINKING YOU COULD . . . MAIL IT OR SOMETHING.

NO. I WANT TO LOOK HIM IN THE EYE. LET'S GO TO HIS OFFICE. TOMORROW AFTER SCHOOL.

WHOA, OKAY. UM . . .

OKAY. HOW ABOUT THIS: IF I GO WITH YOU, WILL YOU COME BACK TO PRACTICE?

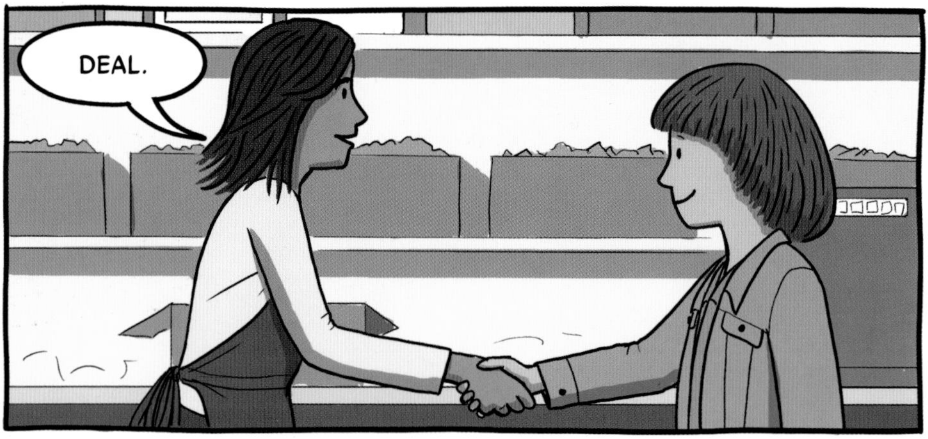
DEAL.

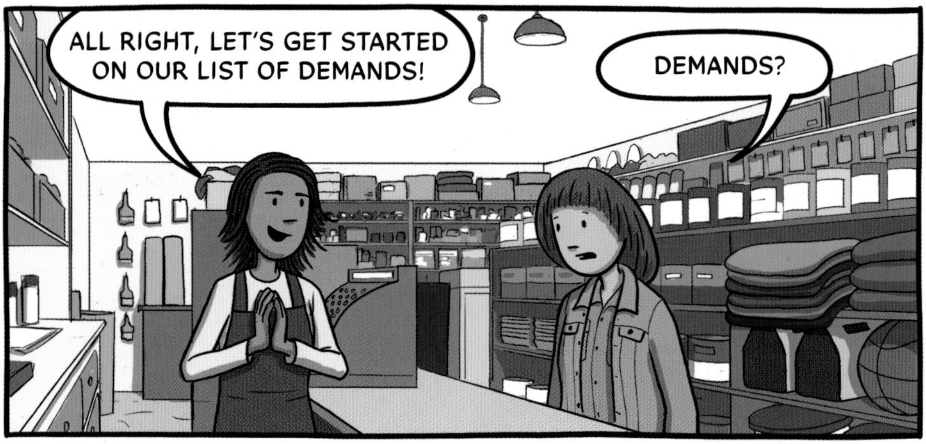
ALL RIGHT, LET'S GET STARTED ON OUR LIST OF DEMANDS!
DEMANDS?

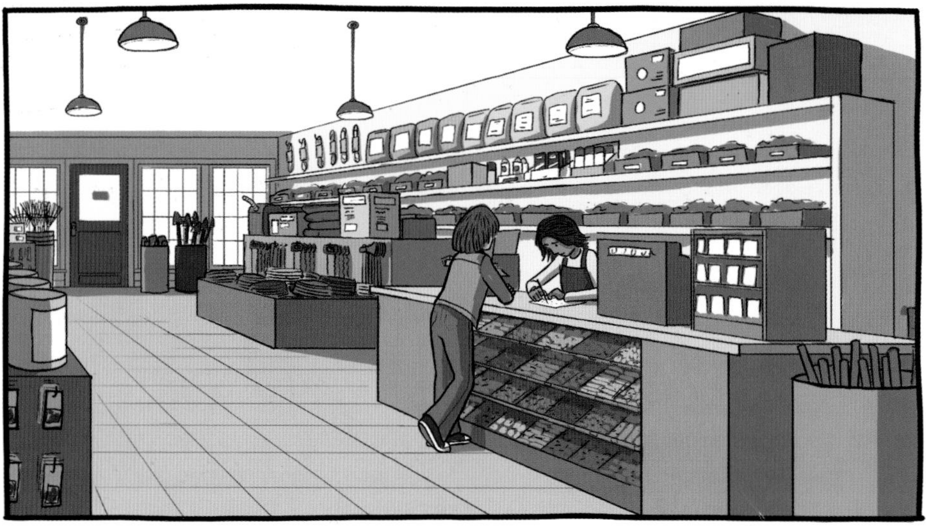

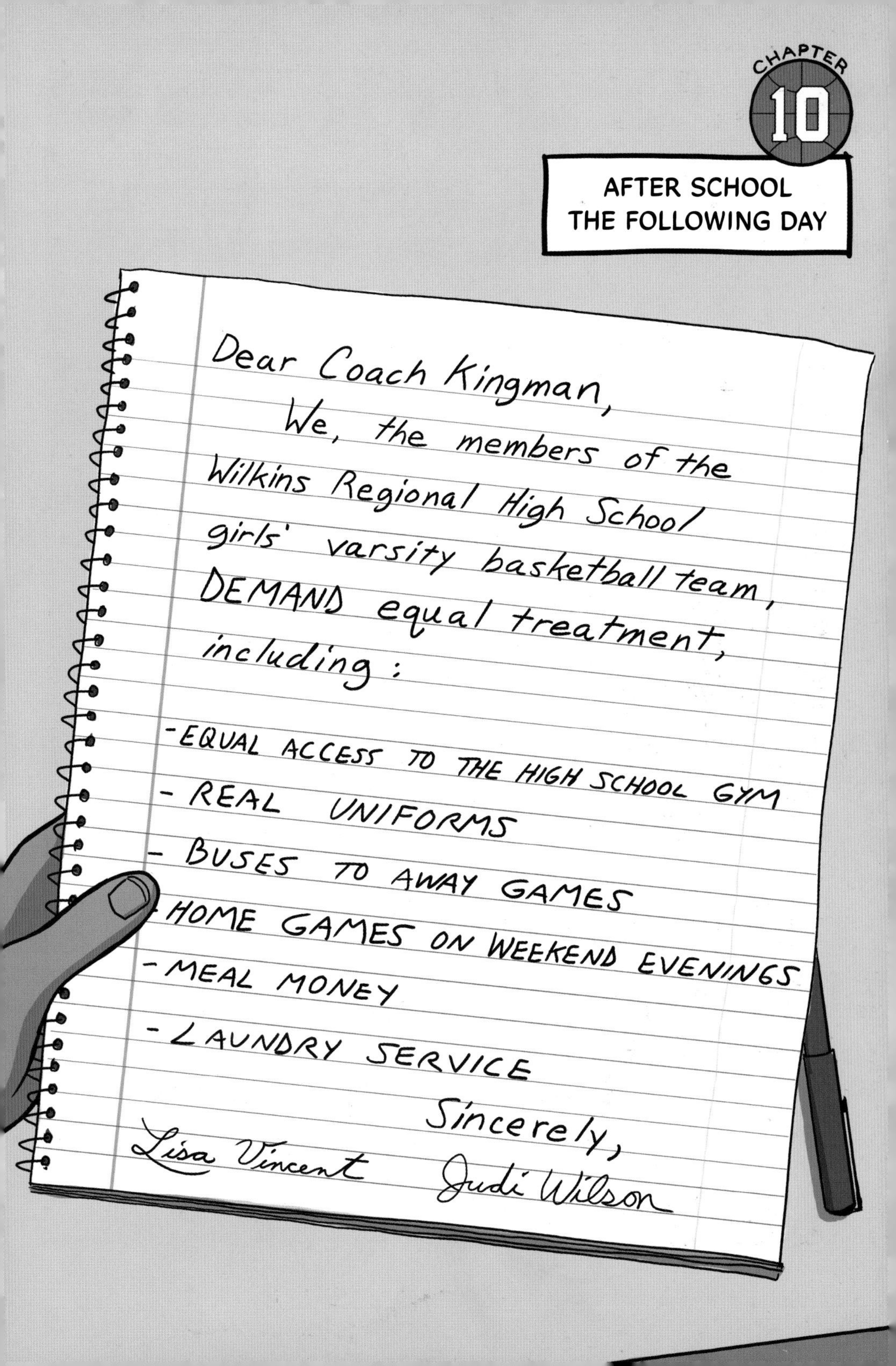
CHAPTER
10
AFTER SCHOOL
THE FOLLOWING DAY
Dear Coach Kingman,
We, the members of the Wilkins Regional High School girls' varsity basketball team, DEMAND equal treatment, including:
-EQUAL ACCESS TO THE HIGH SCHOOL GYM
-REAL UNIFORMS
-BUSES TO AWAY GAMES
-HOME GAMES ON WEEKEND EVENINGS
-MEAL MONEY
-LAUNDRY SERVICE
Sincerely,
Lisa Vincent
Judi Wilson

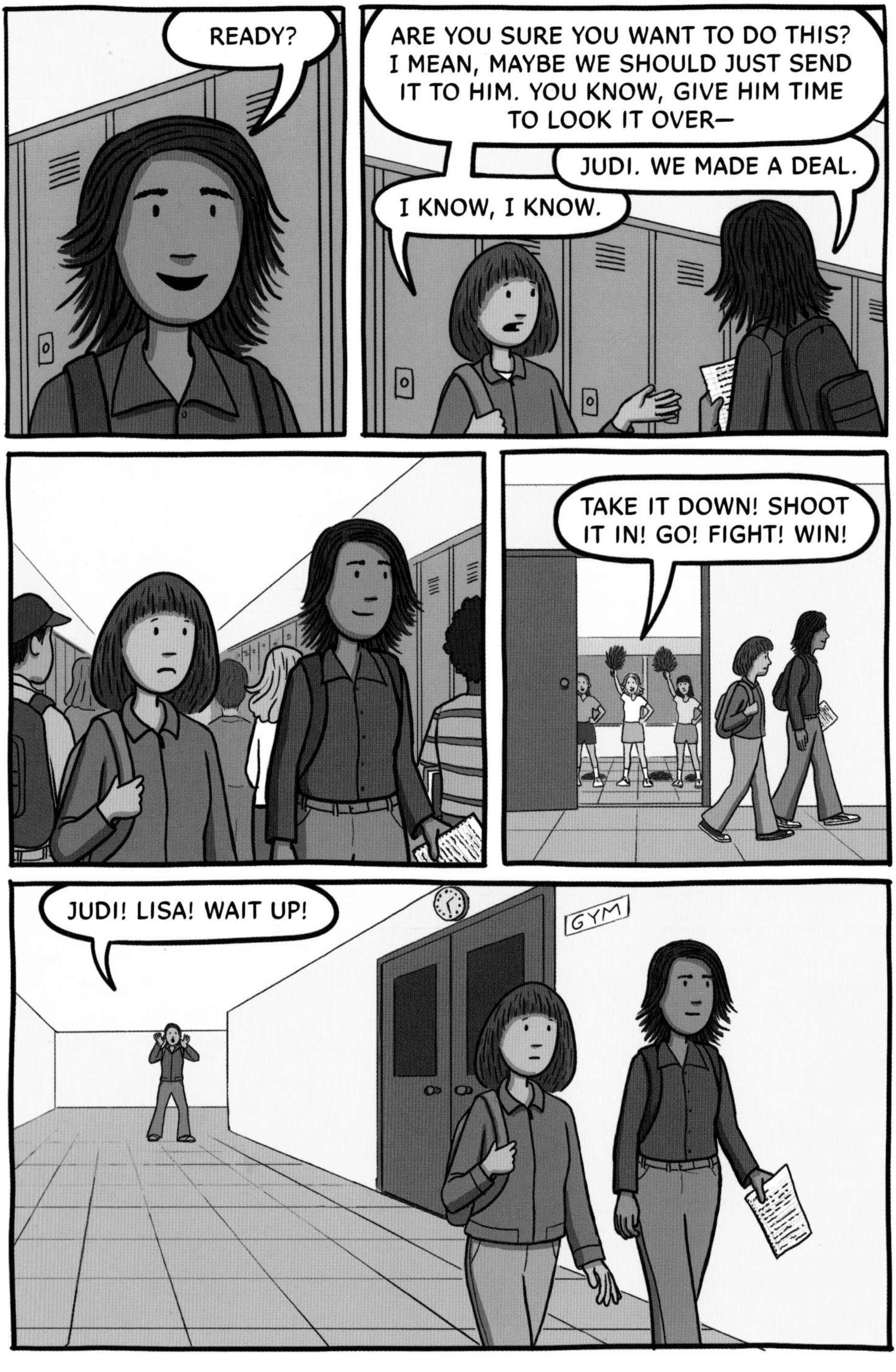
READY?
ARE YOU SURE YOU WANT TO DO THIS? I MEAN, MAYBE WE SHOULD JUST SEND IT TO HIM. YOU KNOW, GIVE HIM TIME TO LOOK IT OVER—
JUDI. WE MADE A DEAL.
I KNOW, I KNOW.
TAKE IT DOWN! SHOOT IT IN! GO! FIGHT! WIN!
JUDI! LISA! WAIT UP!
GYM

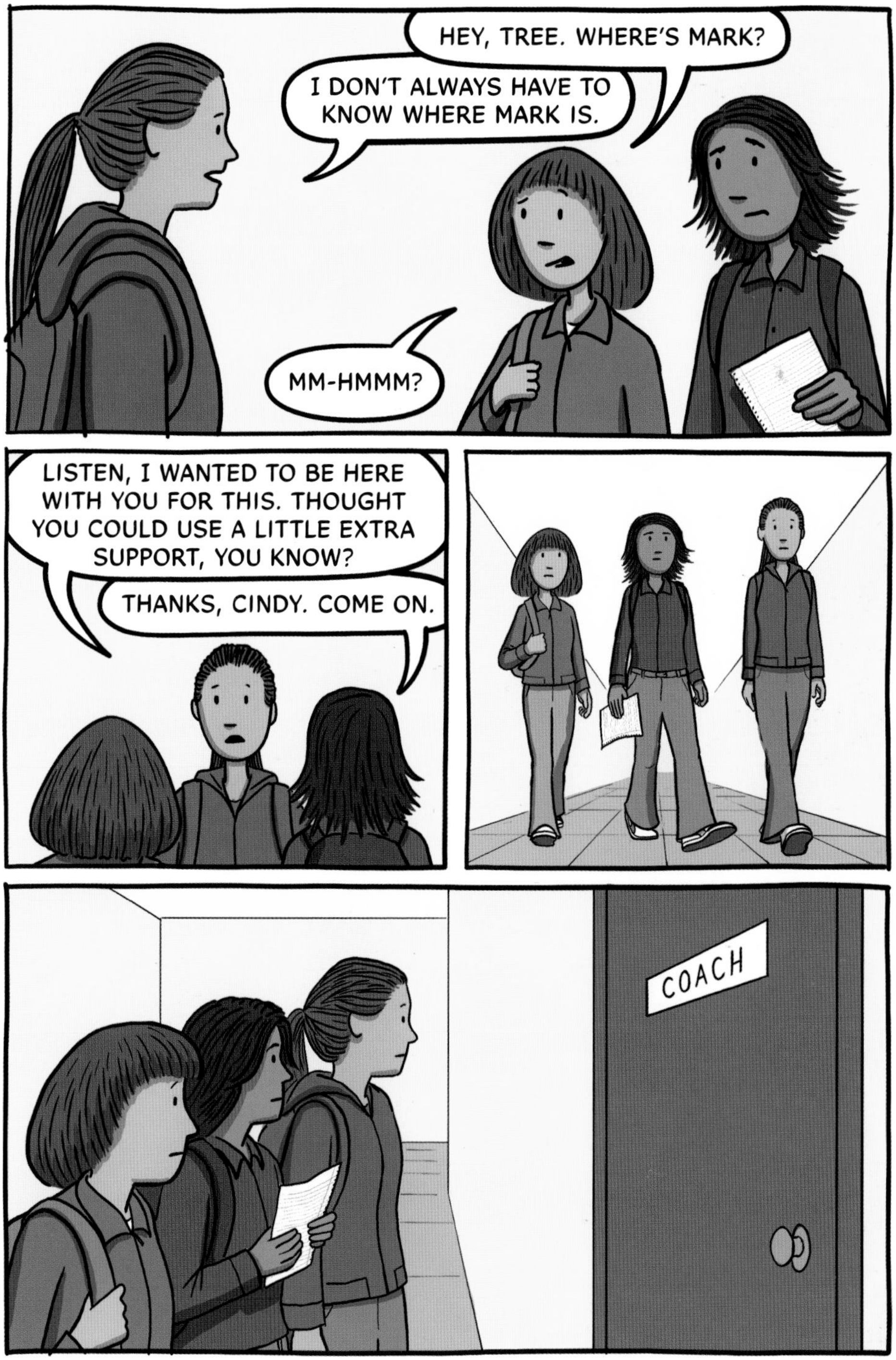
HEY, TREE. WHERE'S MARK?
I DON'T ALWAYS HAVE TO KNOW WHERE MARK IS.
MM-HMMM?
LISTEN, I WANTED TO BE HERE WITH YOU FOR THIS. THOUGHT YOU COULD USE A LITTLE EXTRA SUPPORT, YOU KNOW?
THANKS, CINDY. COME ON.
COACH

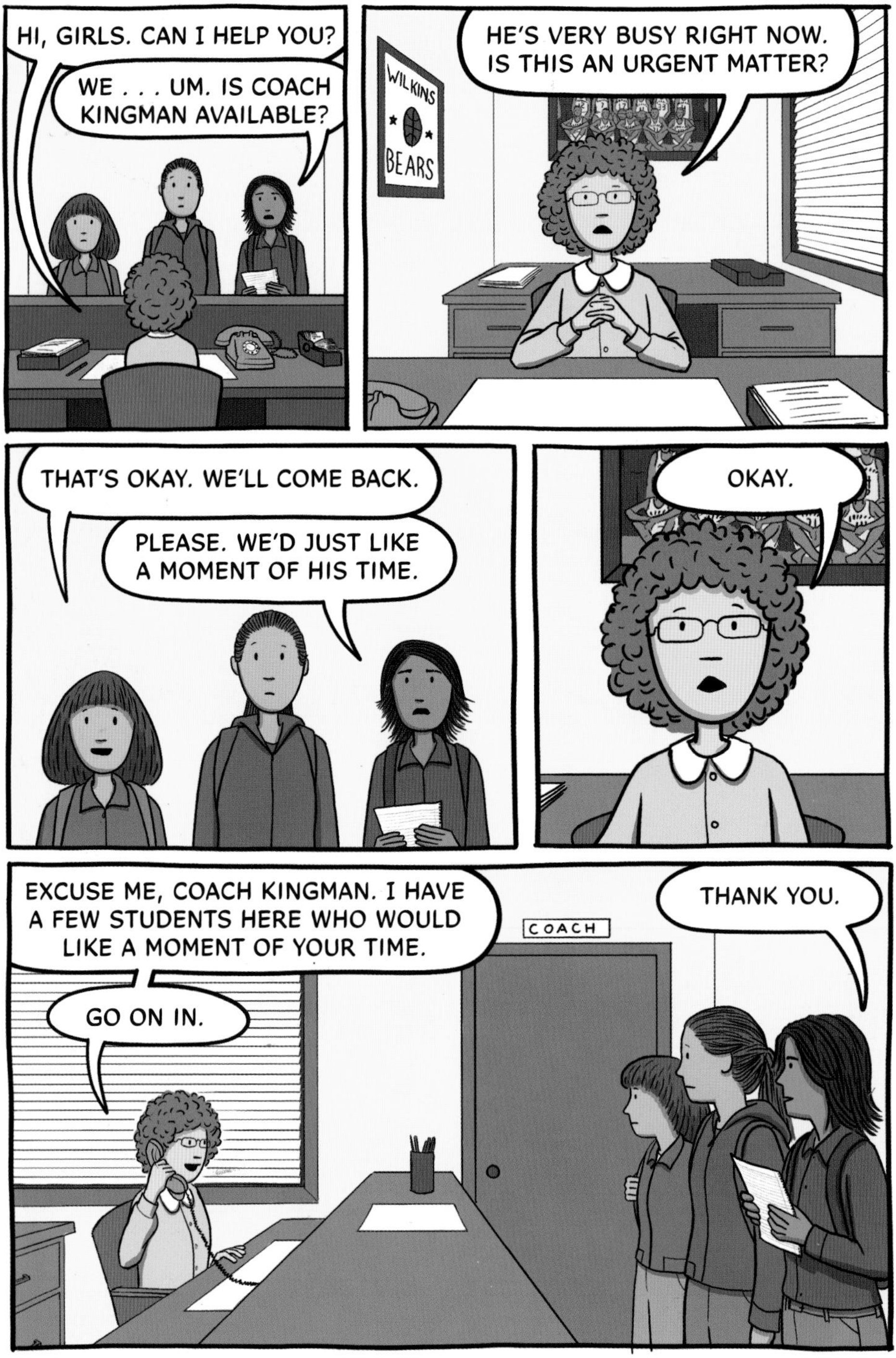
HI, GIRLS. CAN I HELP YOU?
WE . . . UM. IS COACH KINGMAN AVAILABLE?
WILKINS BEARS
HE'S VERY BUSY RIGHT NOW. IS THIS AN URGENT MATTER?
THAT'S OKAY. WE'LL COME BACK.
PLEASE. WE'D JUST LIKE A MOMENT OF HIS TIME.
OKAY.
EXCUSE ME, COACH KINGMAN. I HAVE A FEW STUDENTS HERE WHO WOULD LIKE A MOMENT OF YOUR TIME.
GO ON IN.
COACH
THANK YOU.

COACH OF THE YEAR 1960
COACH OF THE YEAR 1966
WELL?
I . . . WE . . .

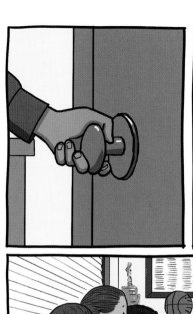

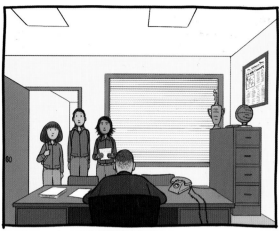

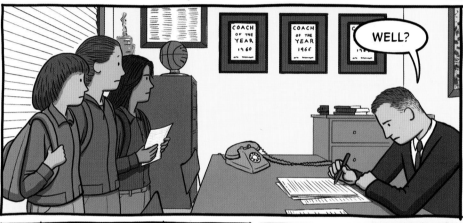

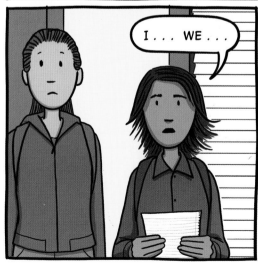

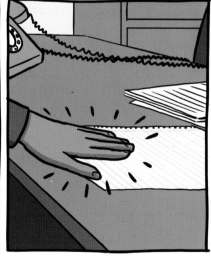

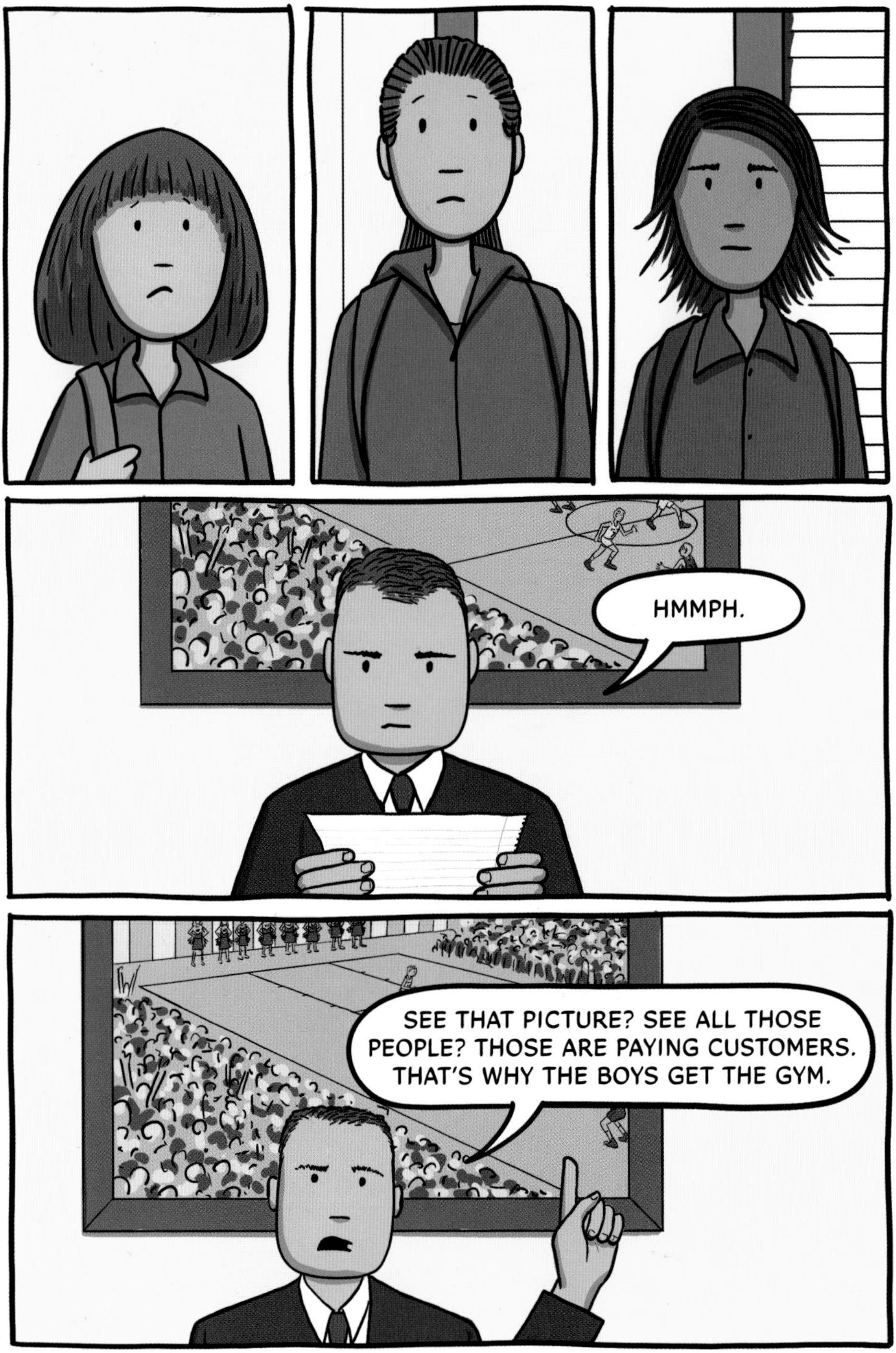
HMMPH.
SEE THAT PICTURE? SEE ALL THOSE PEOPLE? THOSE ARE PAYING CUSTOMERS. THAT'S WHY THE BOYS GET THE GYM.

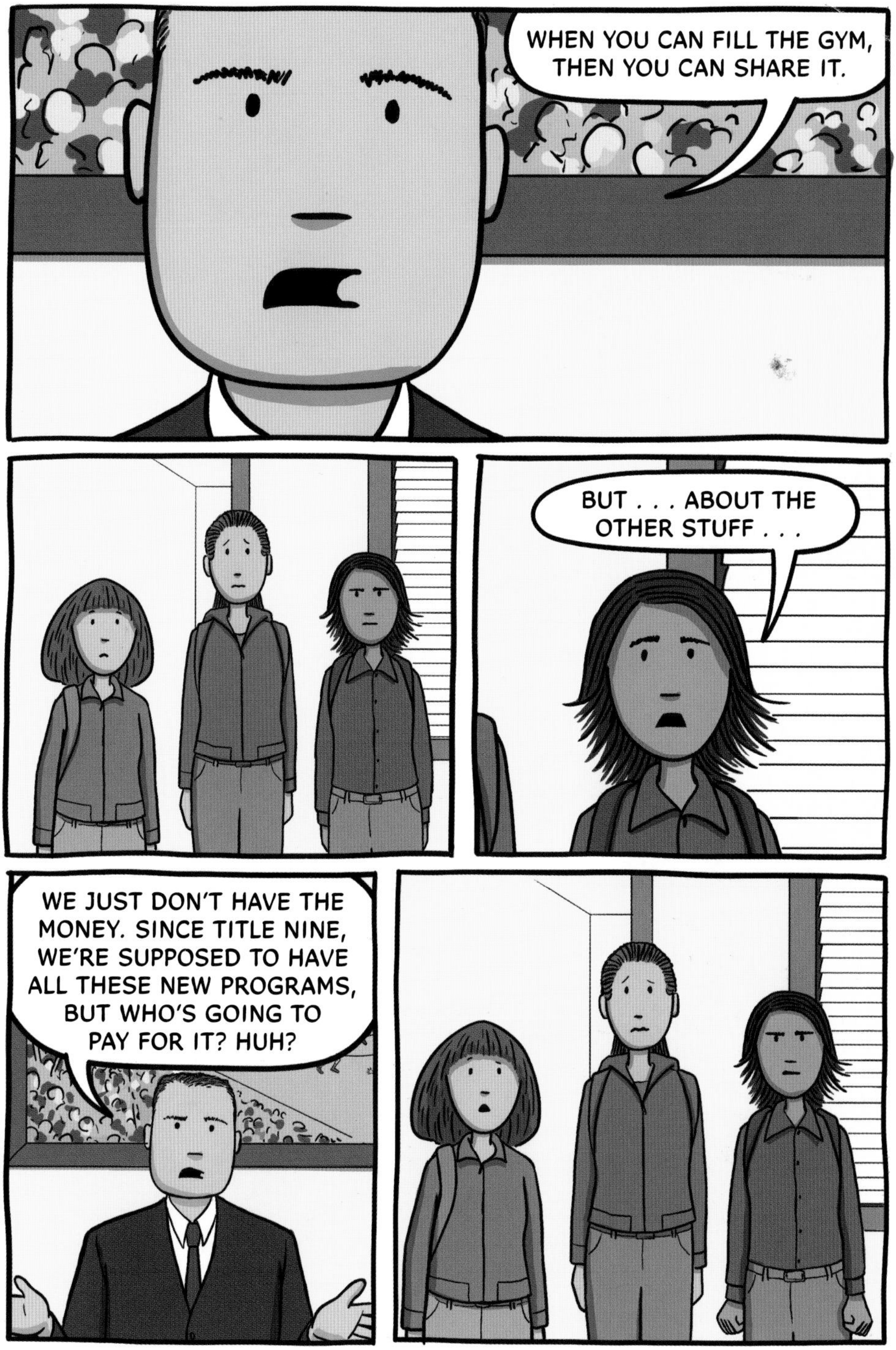
WHEN YOU CAN FILL THE GYM, THEN YOU CAN SHARE IT.
BUT . . . ABOUT THE OTHER STUFF . . .
WE JUST DON'T HAVE THE MONEY. SINCE TITLE NINE, WE'RE SUPPOSED TO HAVE ALL THESE NEW PROGRAMS, BUT WHO'S GOING TO PAY FOR IT? HUH?

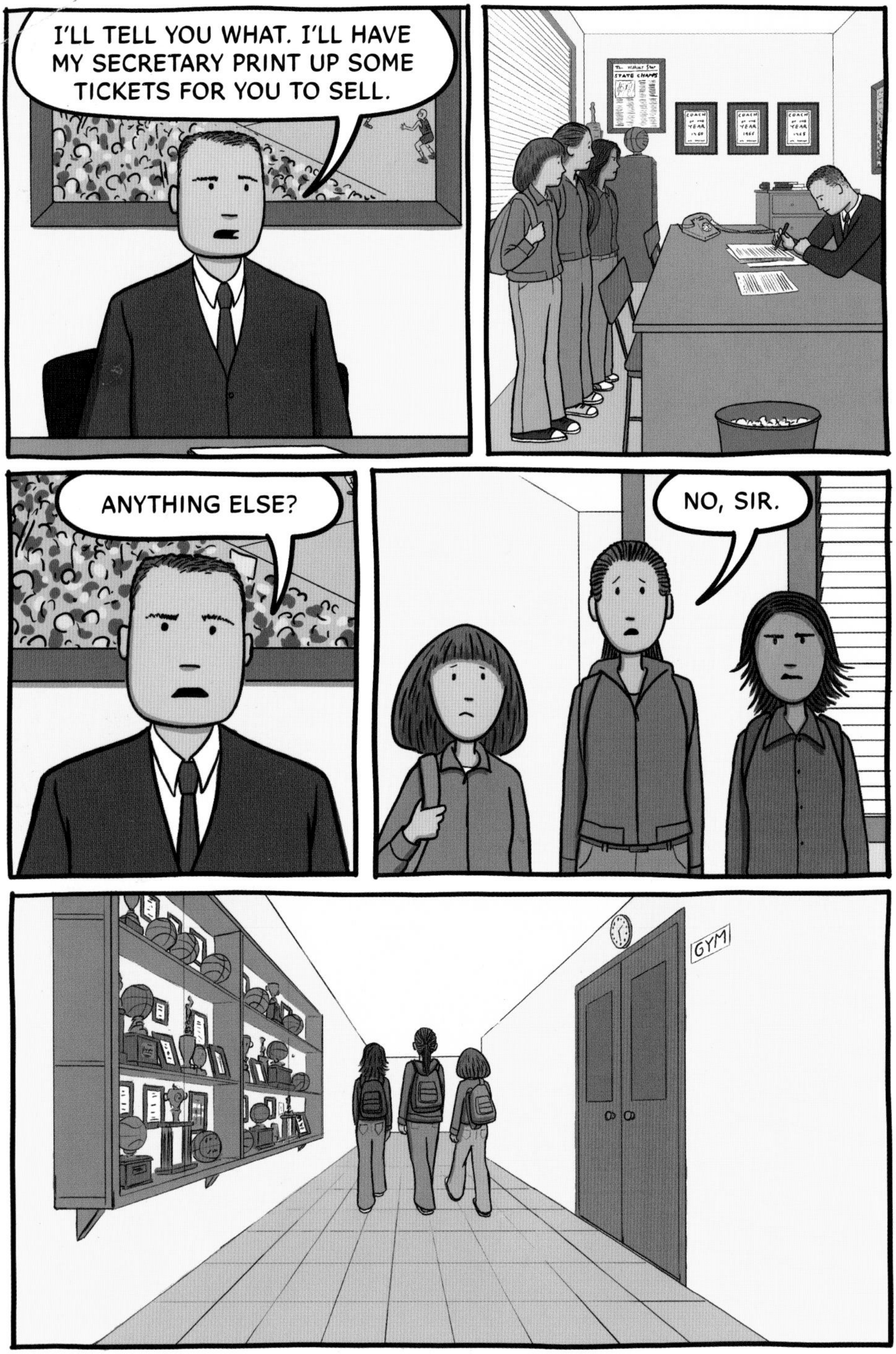
I'LL TELL YOU WHAT. I'LL HAVE MY SECRETARY PRINT UP SOME TICKETS FOR YOU TO SELL.
ANYTHING ELSE?
NO, SIR.
GYM

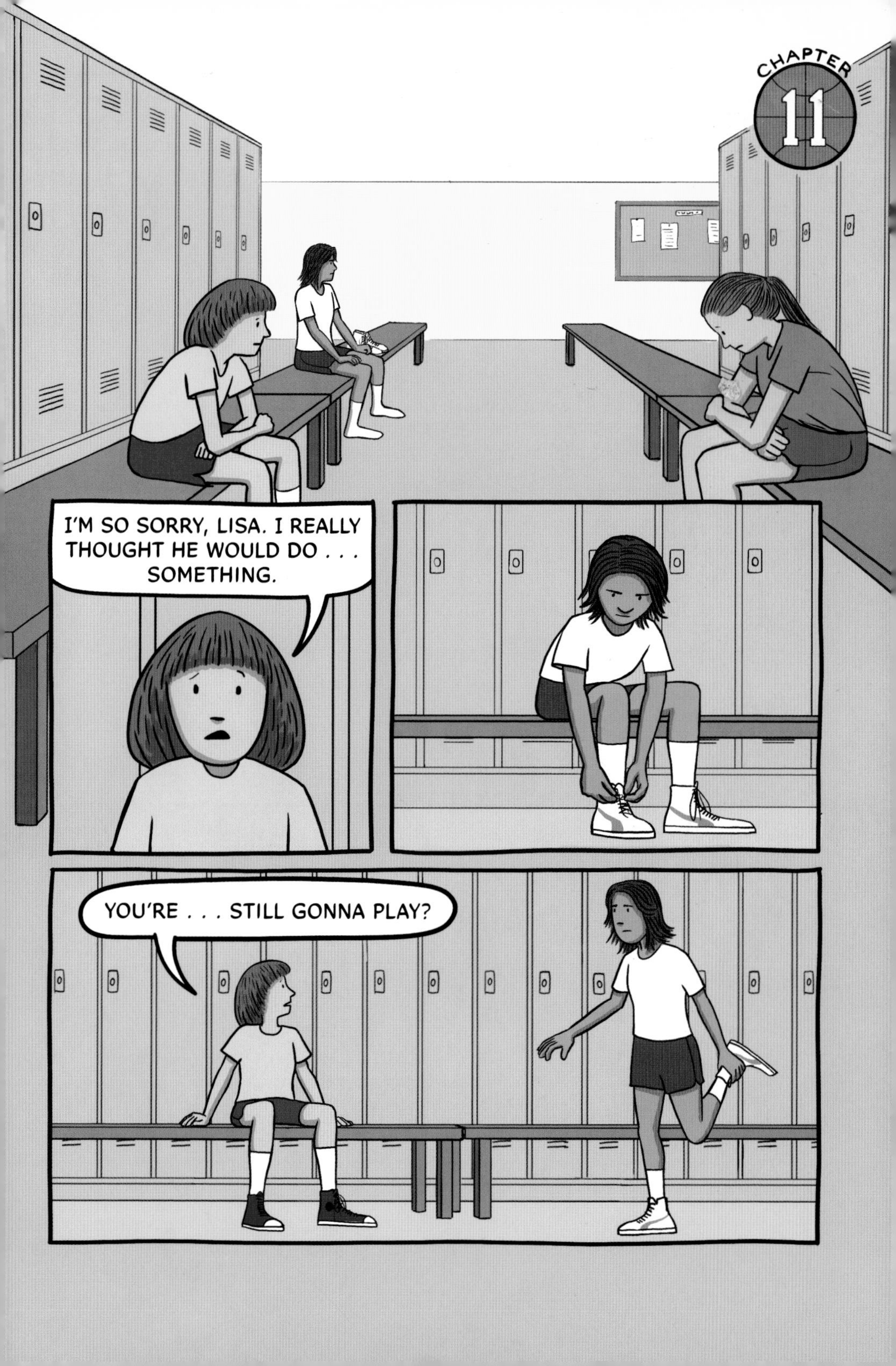
CHAPTER
11
I'M SO SORRY, LISA. I REALLY THOUGHT HE WOULD DO . . . SOMETHING.
YOU'RE . . . STILL GONNA PLAY?

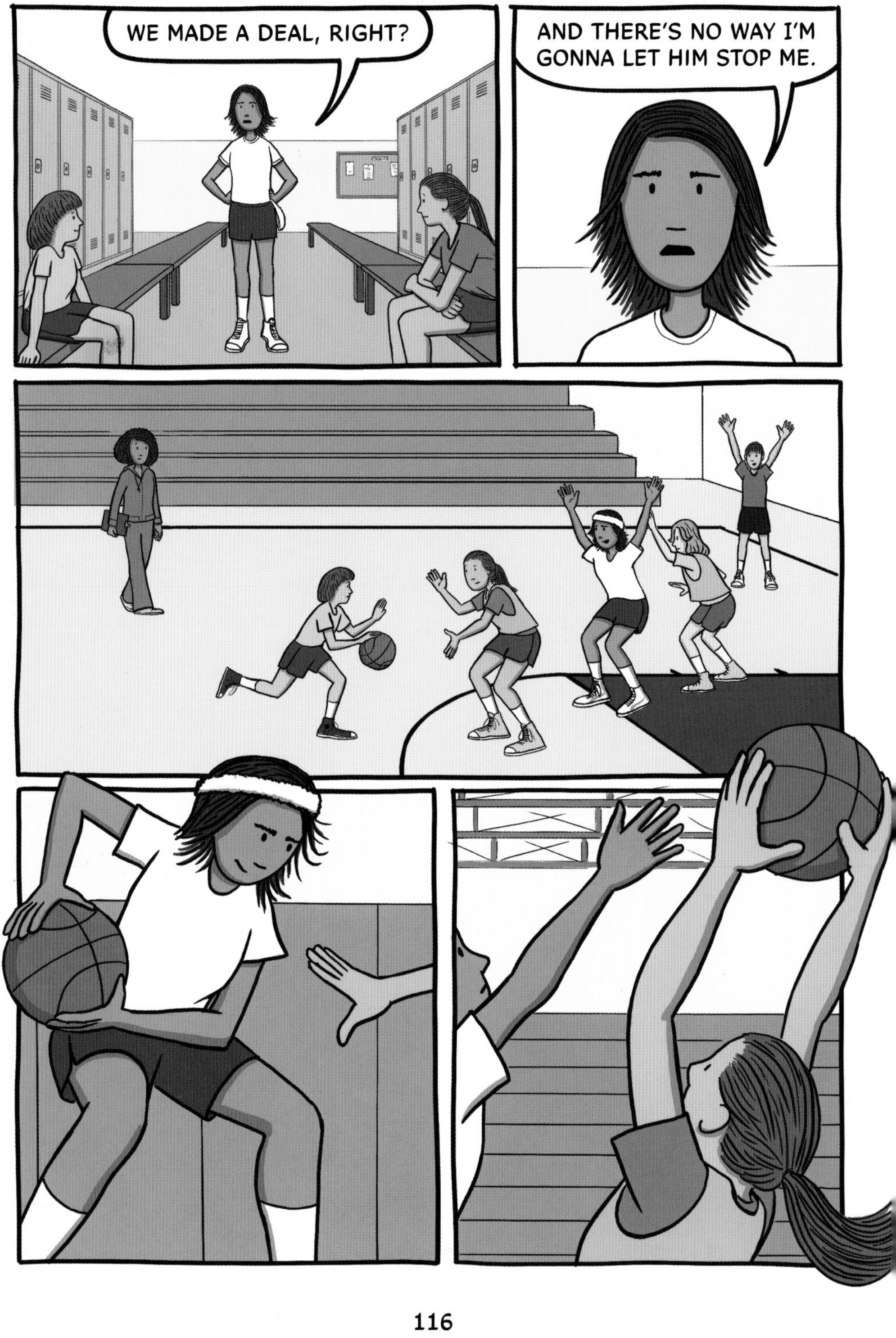
WE MADE A DEAL, RIGHT?
AND THERE'S NO WAY I'M GONNA LET HIM STOP ME.

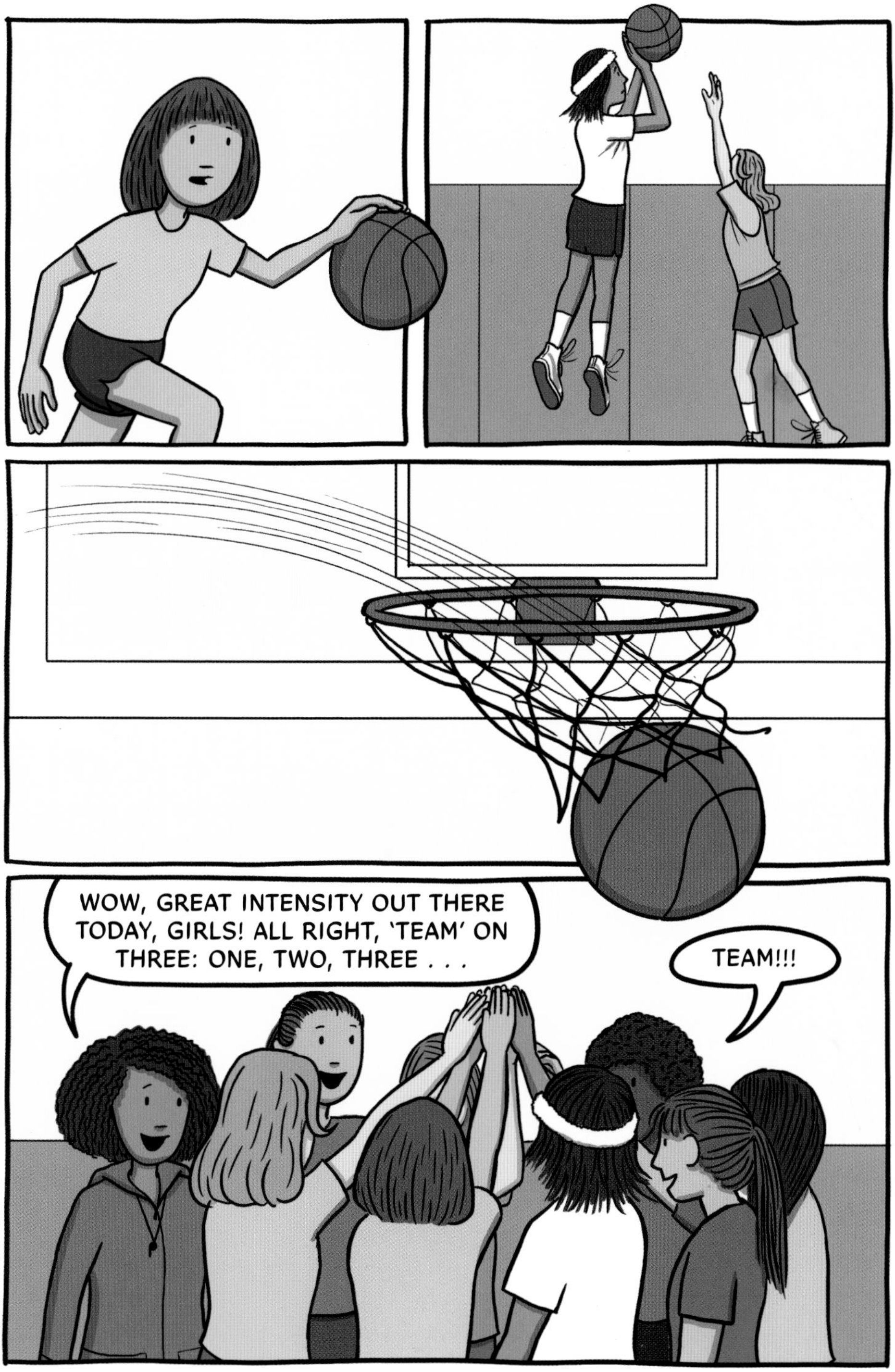
WOW, GREAT INTENSITY OUT THERE TODAY, GIRLS! ALL RIGHT, 'TEAM' ON THREE: ONE, TWO, THREE . . .
TEAM!!!

HE SAID WE COULD SHARE THE GYM IF WE CAN FILL IT, RIGHT?

UH-HUH.

SO . . . ?

LET'S FILL THE GYM!

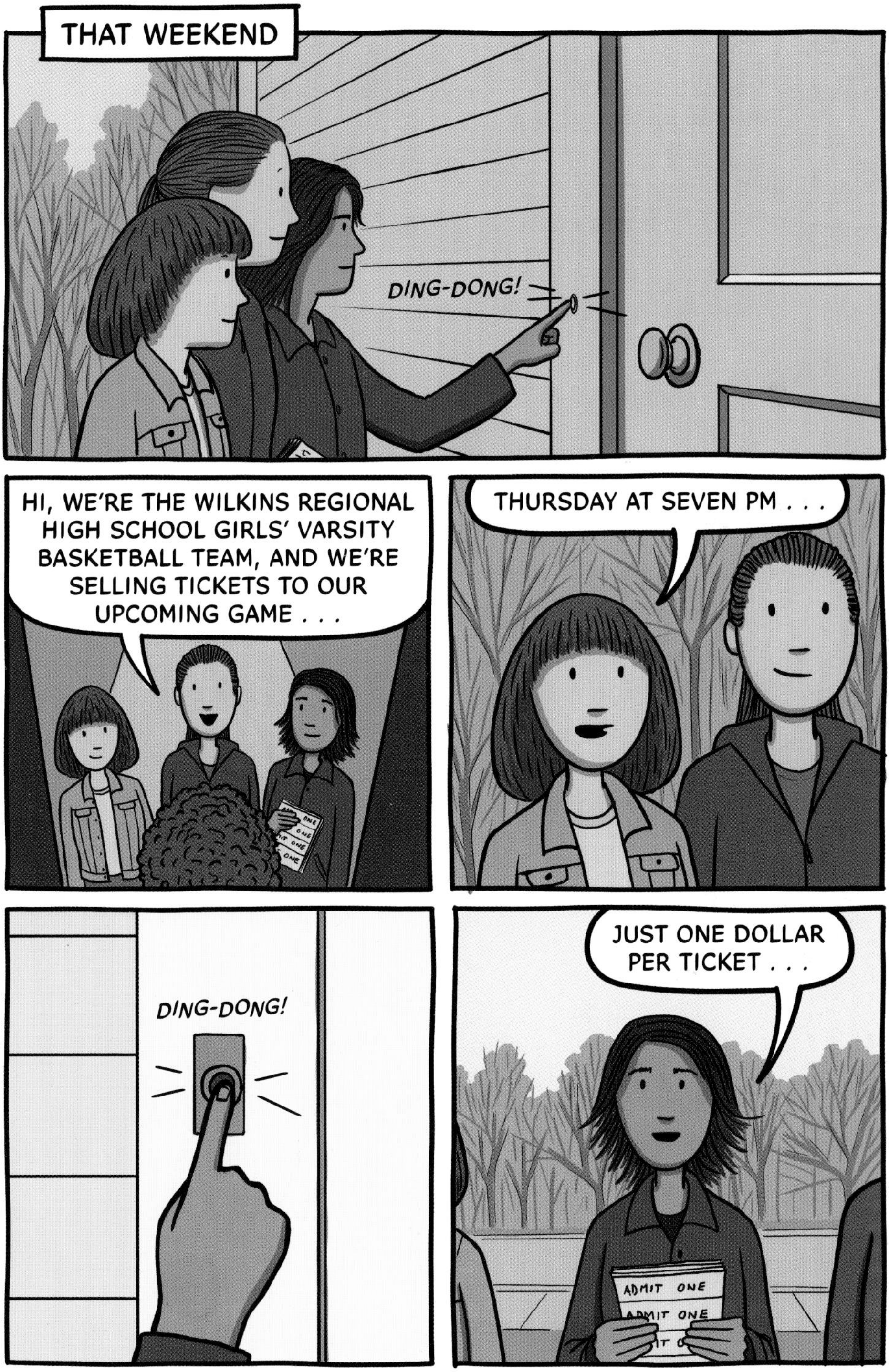
THAT WEEKEND
DING-DONG!
HI, WE'RE THE WILKINS REGIONAL HIGH SCHOOL GIRLS' VARSITY BASKETBALL TEAM, AND WE'RE SELLING TICKETS TO OUR UPCOMING GAME . . .
THURSDAY AT SEVEN PM . . .
DING-DONG!
JUST ONE DOLLAR PER TICKET . . .
ADMIT ONE
ADMIT ONE

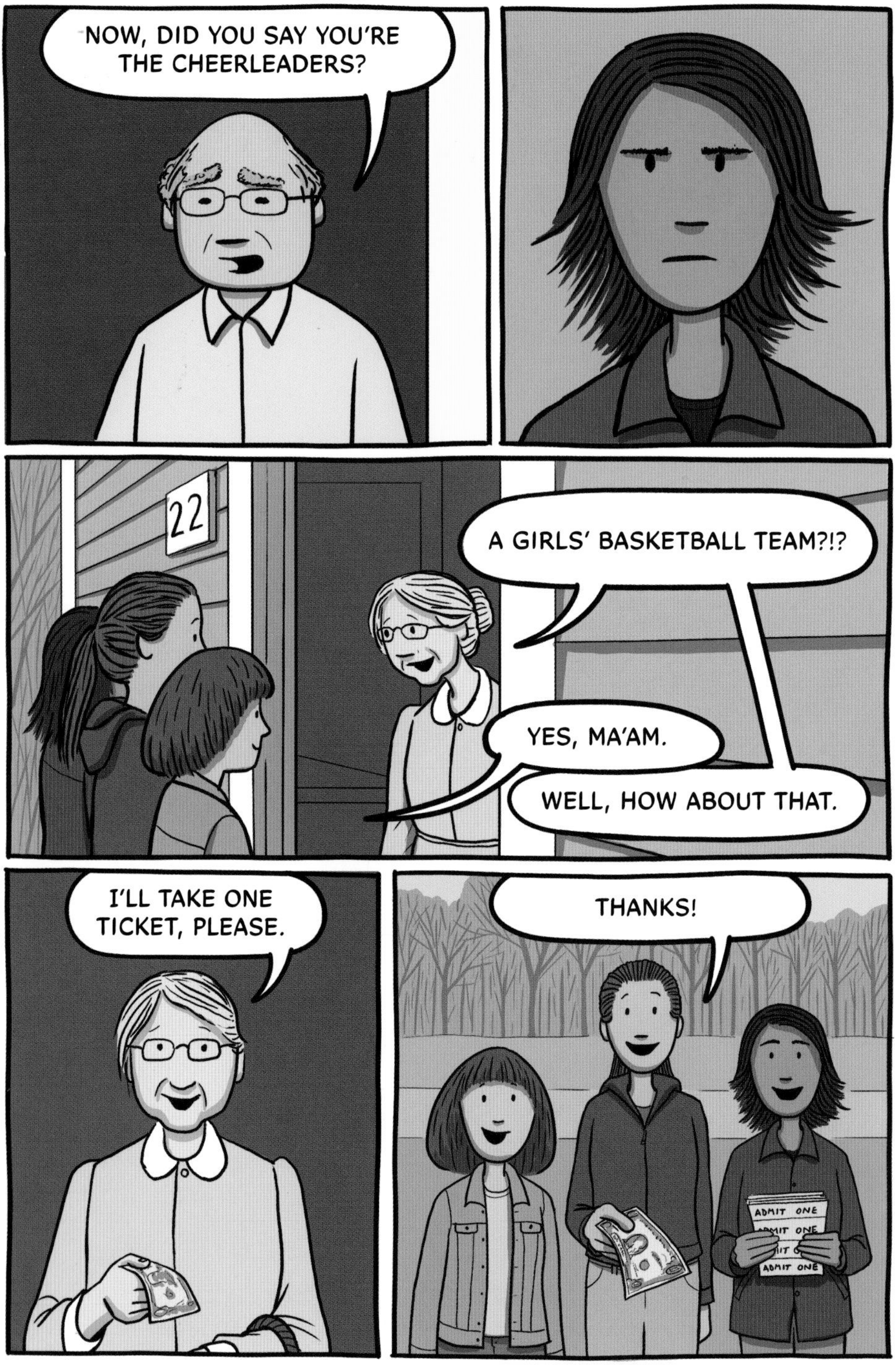
NOW, DID YOU SAY YOU'RE THE CHEERLEADERS?
22
A GIRLS' BASKETBALL TEAM?!?
YES, MA'AM.
WELL, HOW ABOUT THAT.
I'LL TAKE ONE TICKET, PLEASE.
THANKS!
ADMIT ONE

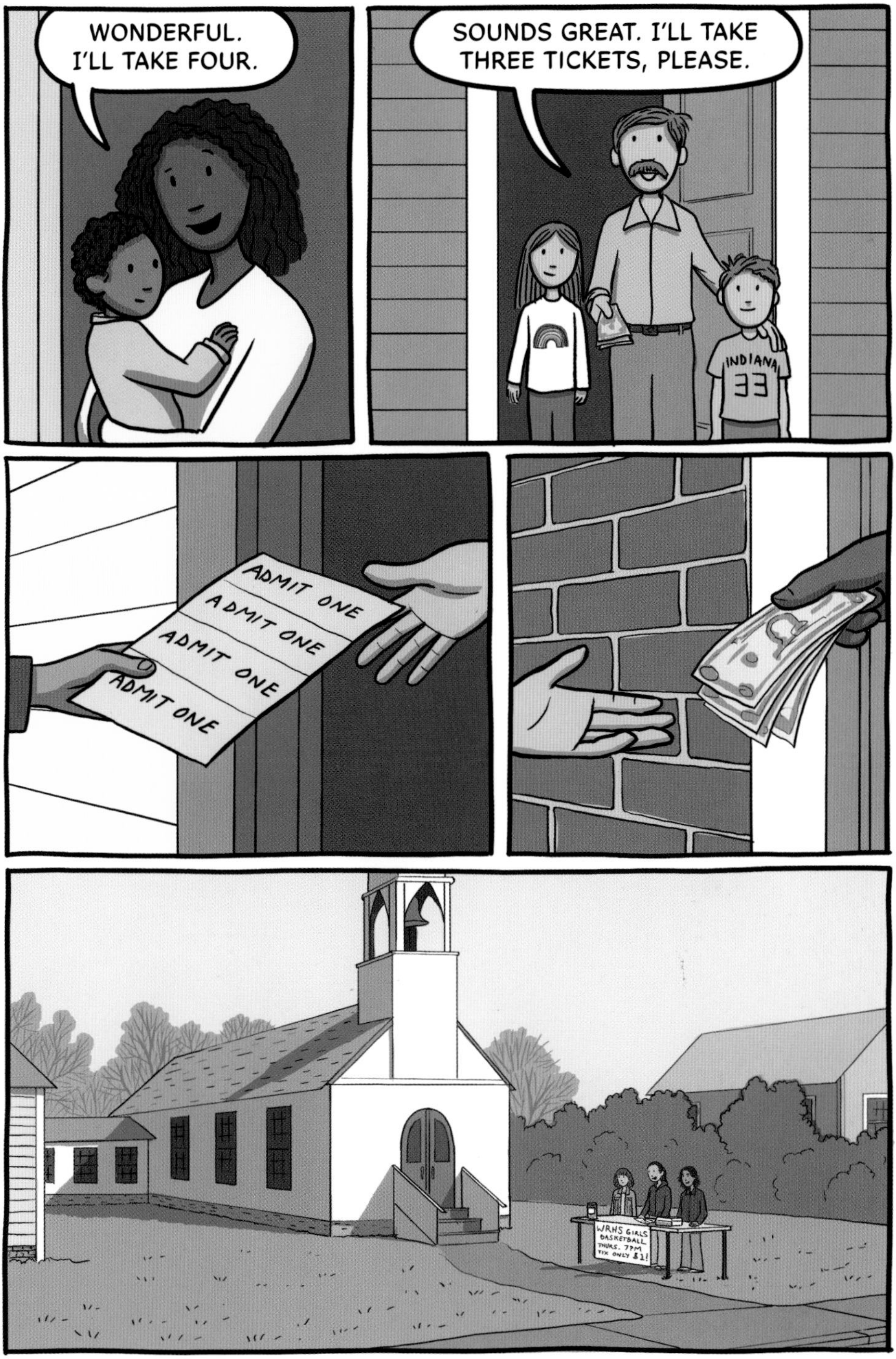
WONDERFUL. I'LL TAKE FOUR.
SOUNDS GREAT. I'LL TAKE THREE TICKETS, PLEASE.
INDIANA
33
ADMIT ONE
ADMIT ONE
ADMIT ONE
ADMIT ONE
WRHS GIRLS BASKETBALL THURS. 7PM TIX ONLY $1!

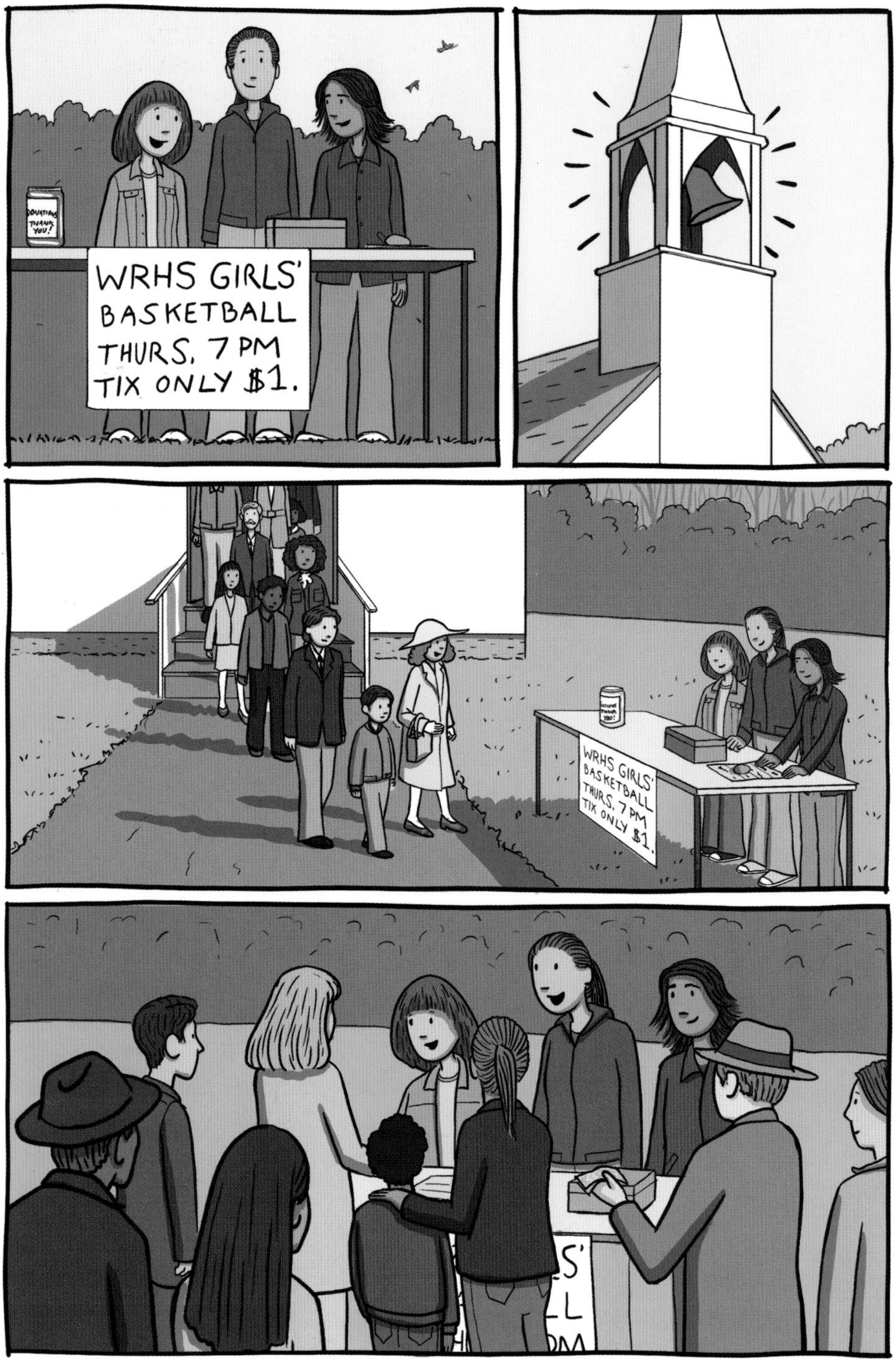
DONATIONS
THANK YOU!
WRHS GIRLS'
BASKETBALL
THURS. 7 PM
TIX ONLY $1.
WRHS GIRLS'
BASKETBALL
THURS. 7 PM
TIX ONLY $1.

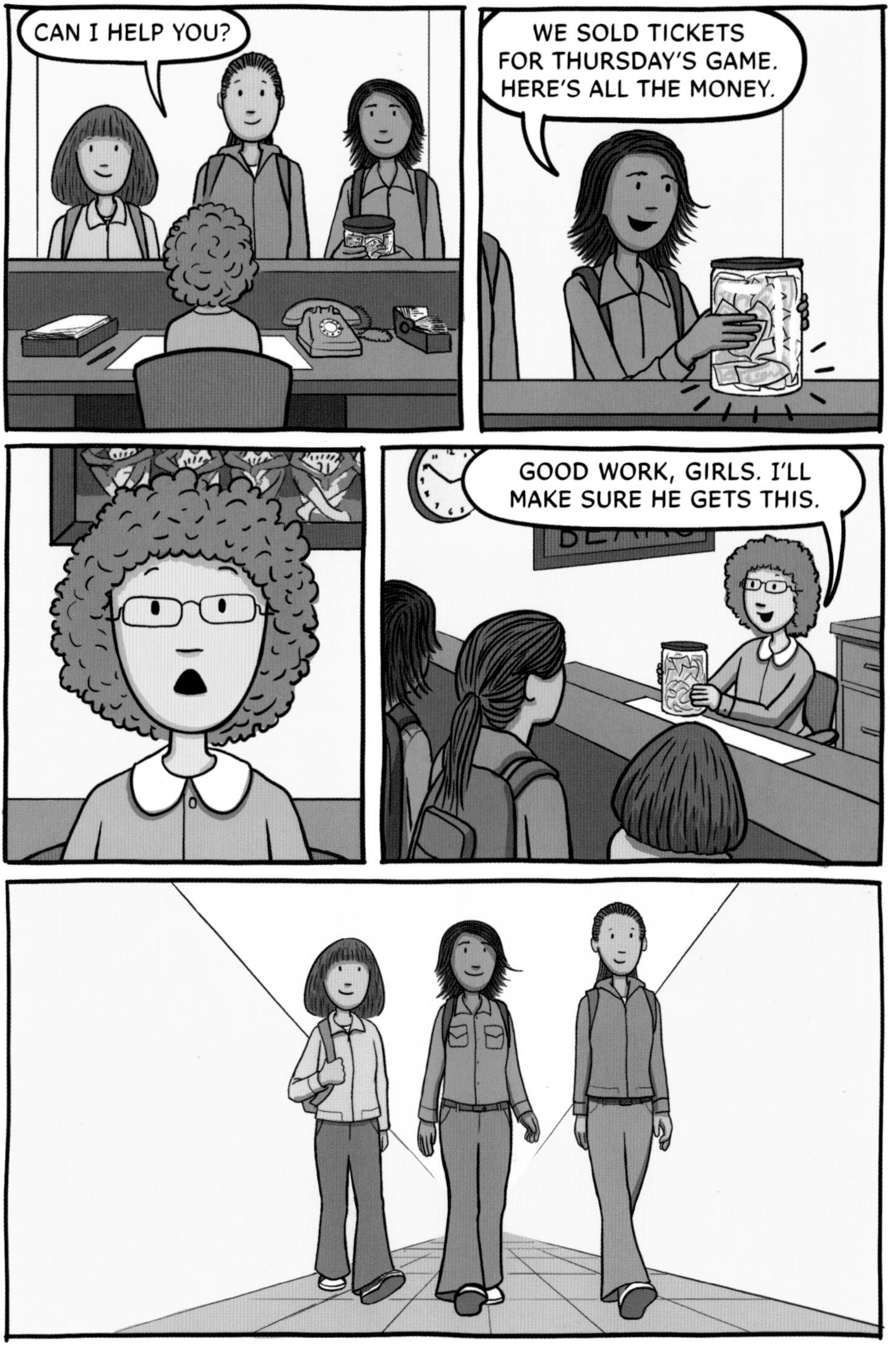
CAN I HELP YOU?
WE SOLD TICKETS FOR THURSDAY'S GAME. HERE'S ALL THE MONEY.
GOOD WORK, GIRLS. I'LL MAKE SURE HE GETS THIS.

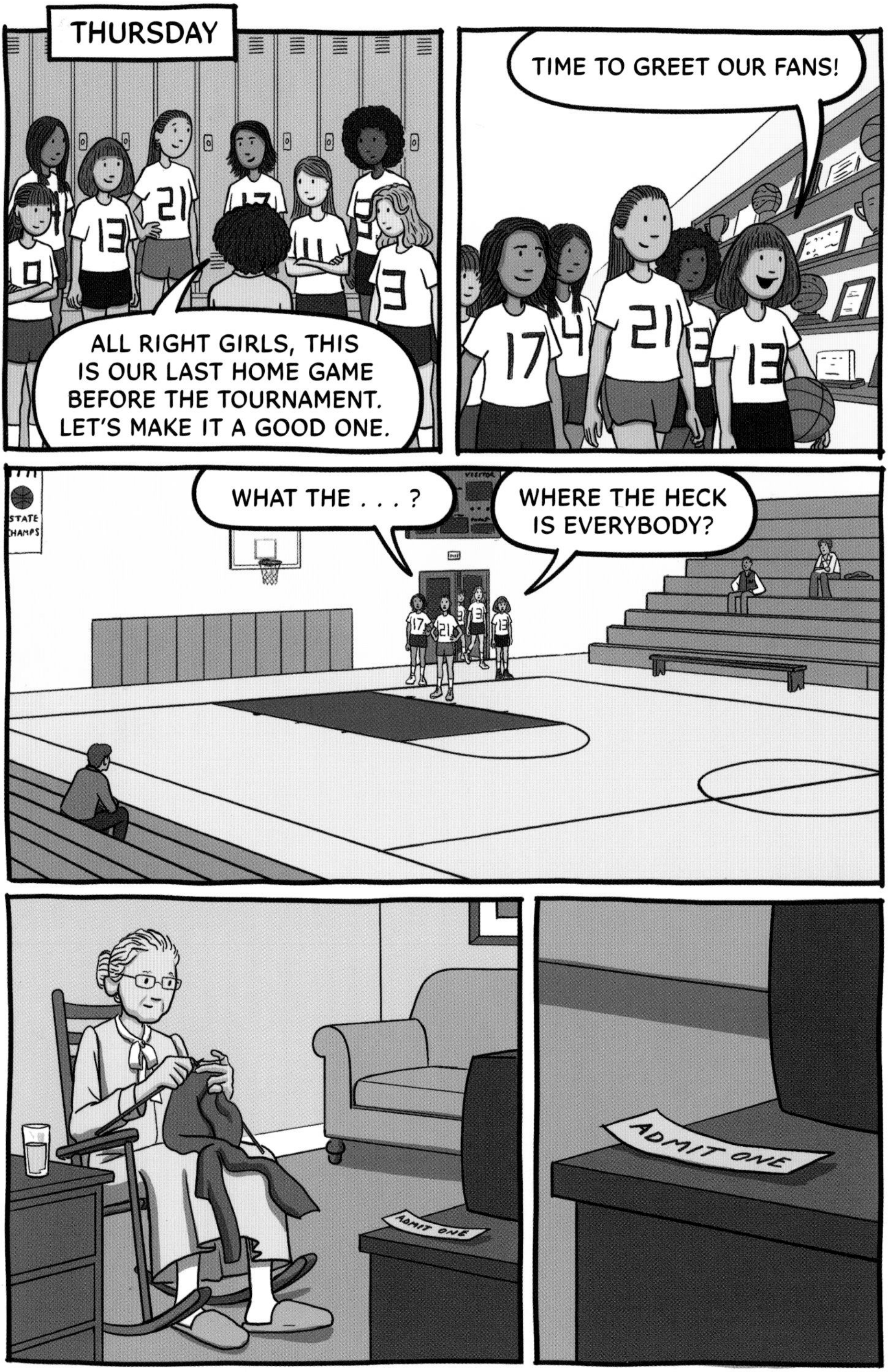
THURSDAY
ALL RIGHT GIRLS, THIS IS OUR LAST HOME GAME BEFORE THE TOURNAMENT. LET'S MAKE IT A GOOD ONE.
TIME TO GREET OUR FANS!
STATE CHAMPS
WHAT THE . . . ?
WHERE THE HECK IS EVERYBODY?
ADMIT ONE
ADMIT ONE

CHAPTER 12
FRIDAY NIGHT

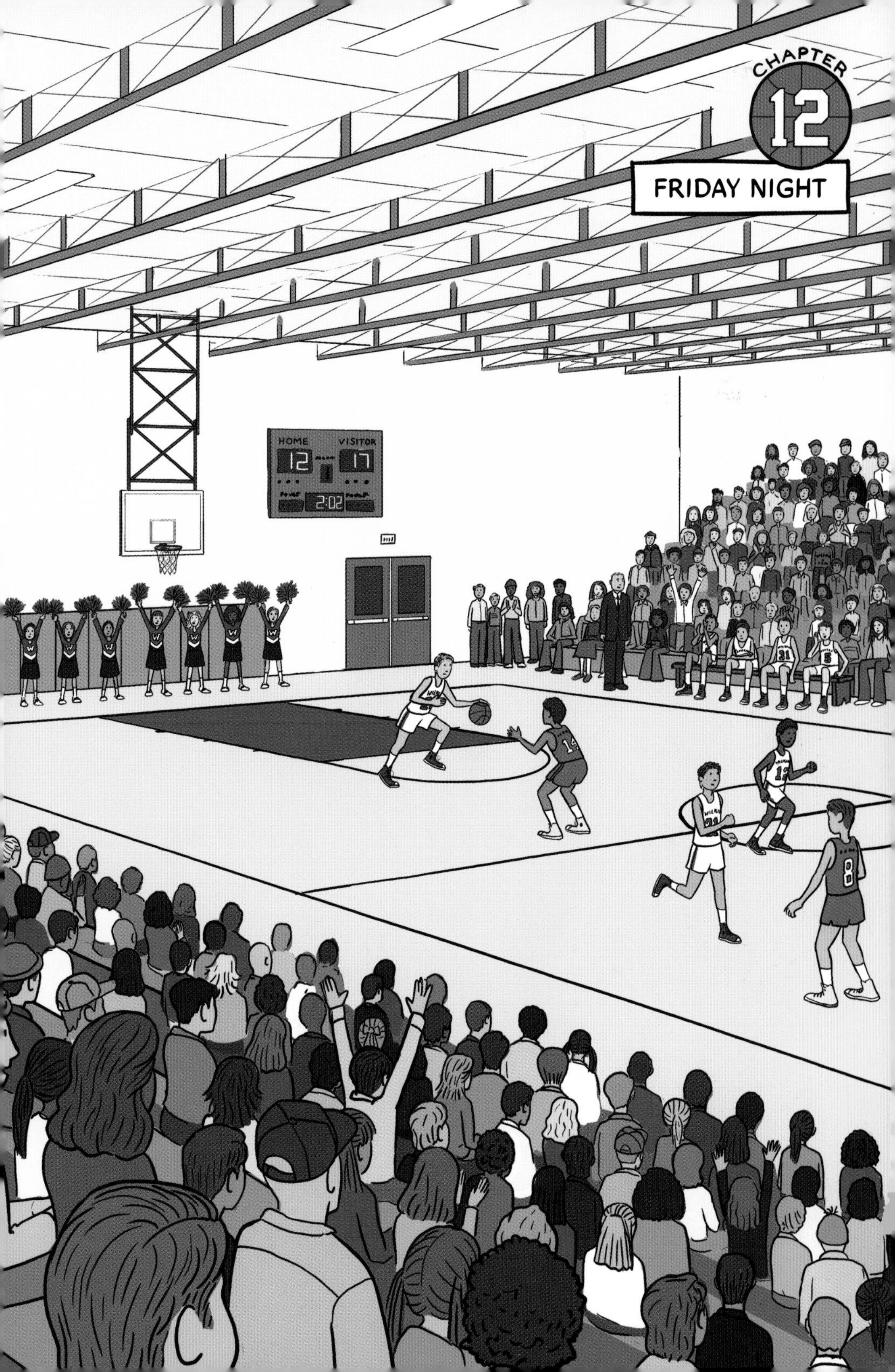
HOME
VISITOR
12
17
2:02

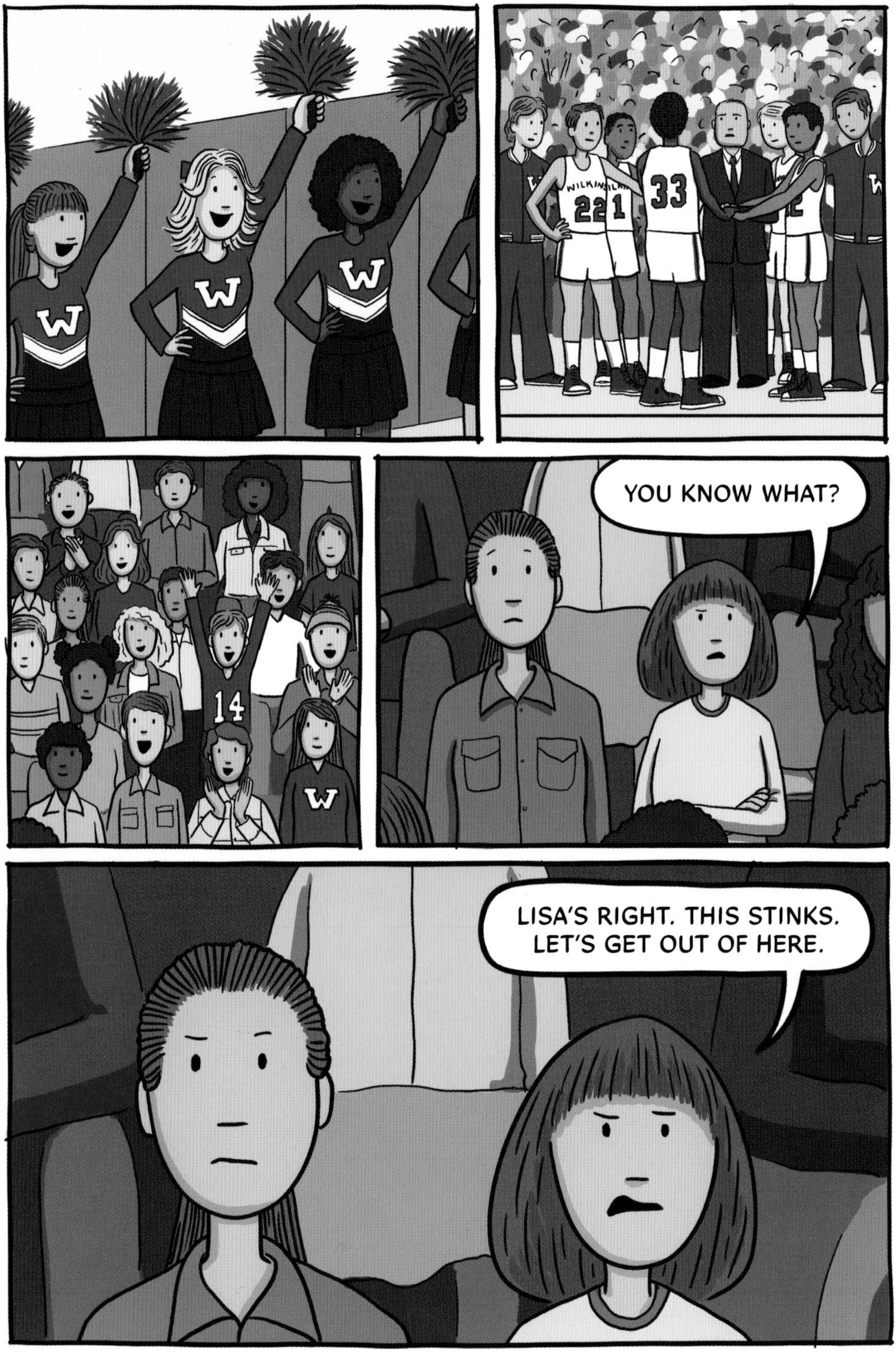
WILKINS
22
1
33
14
W
YOU KNOW WHAT?
LISA'S RIGHT. THIS STINKS. LET'S GET OUT OF HERE.

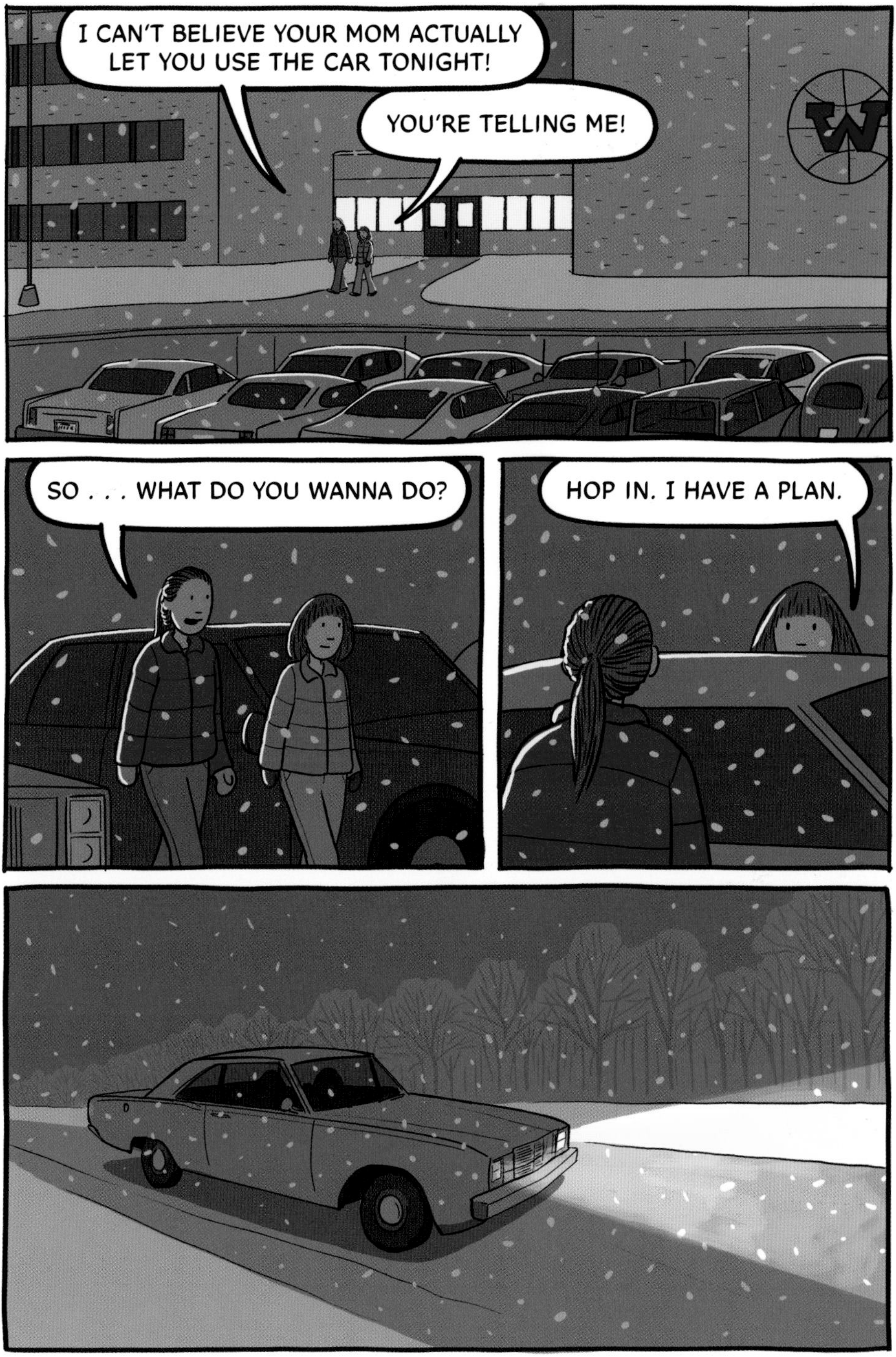
I CAN'T BELIEVE YOUR MOM ACTUALLY LET YOU USE THE CAR TONIGHT!
YOU'RE TELLING ME!
SO . . . WHAT DO YOU WANNA DO?
HOP IN. I HAVE A PLAN.

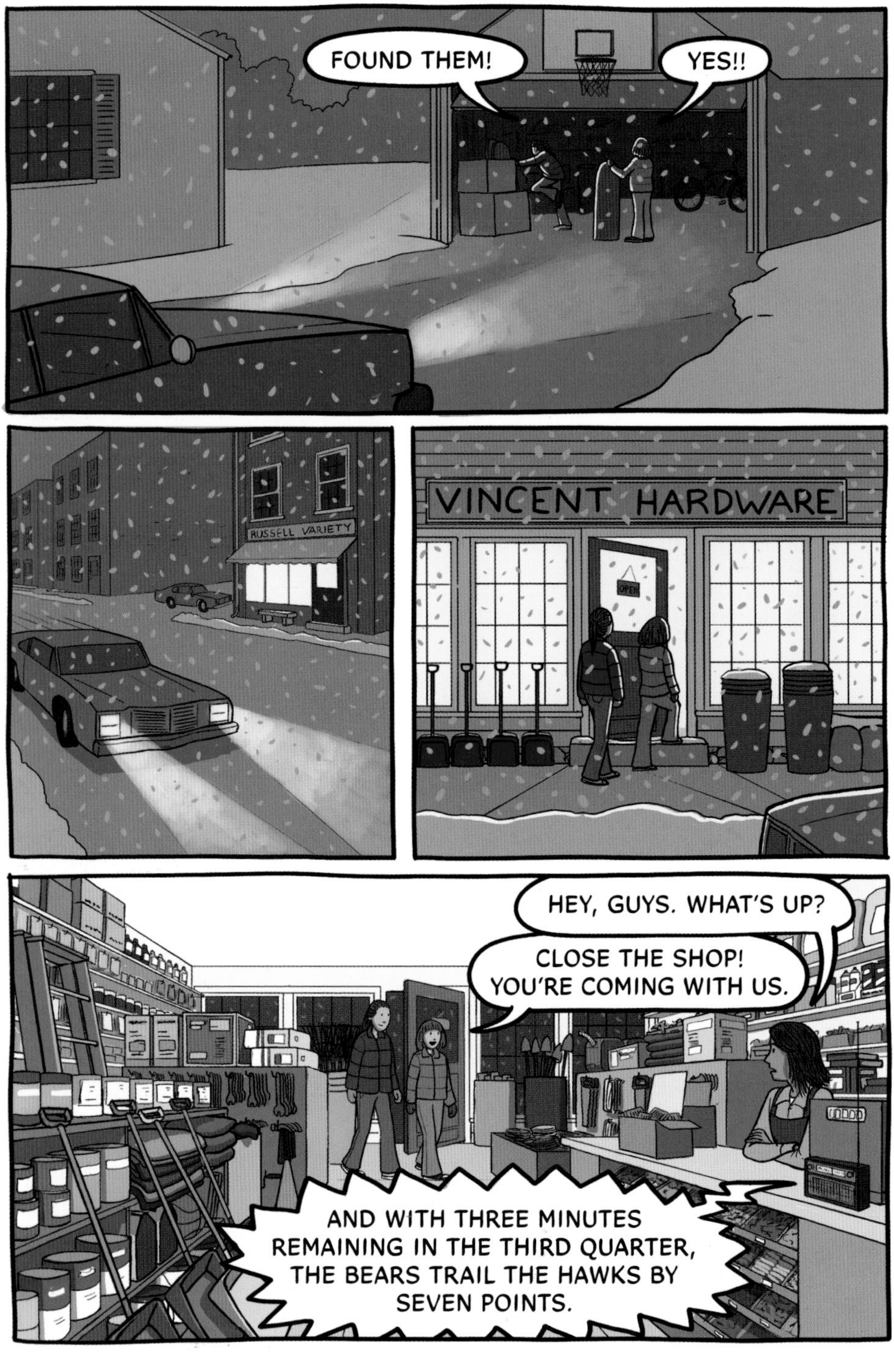
FOUND THEM!
YES!!
RUSSELL VARIETY
VINCENT HARDWARE
HEY, GUYS. WHAT'S UP?
CLOSE THE SHOP! YOU'RE COMING WITH US.
AND WITH THREE MINUTES REMAINING IN THE THIRD QUARTER, THE BEARS TRAIL THE HAWKS BY SEVEN POINTS.

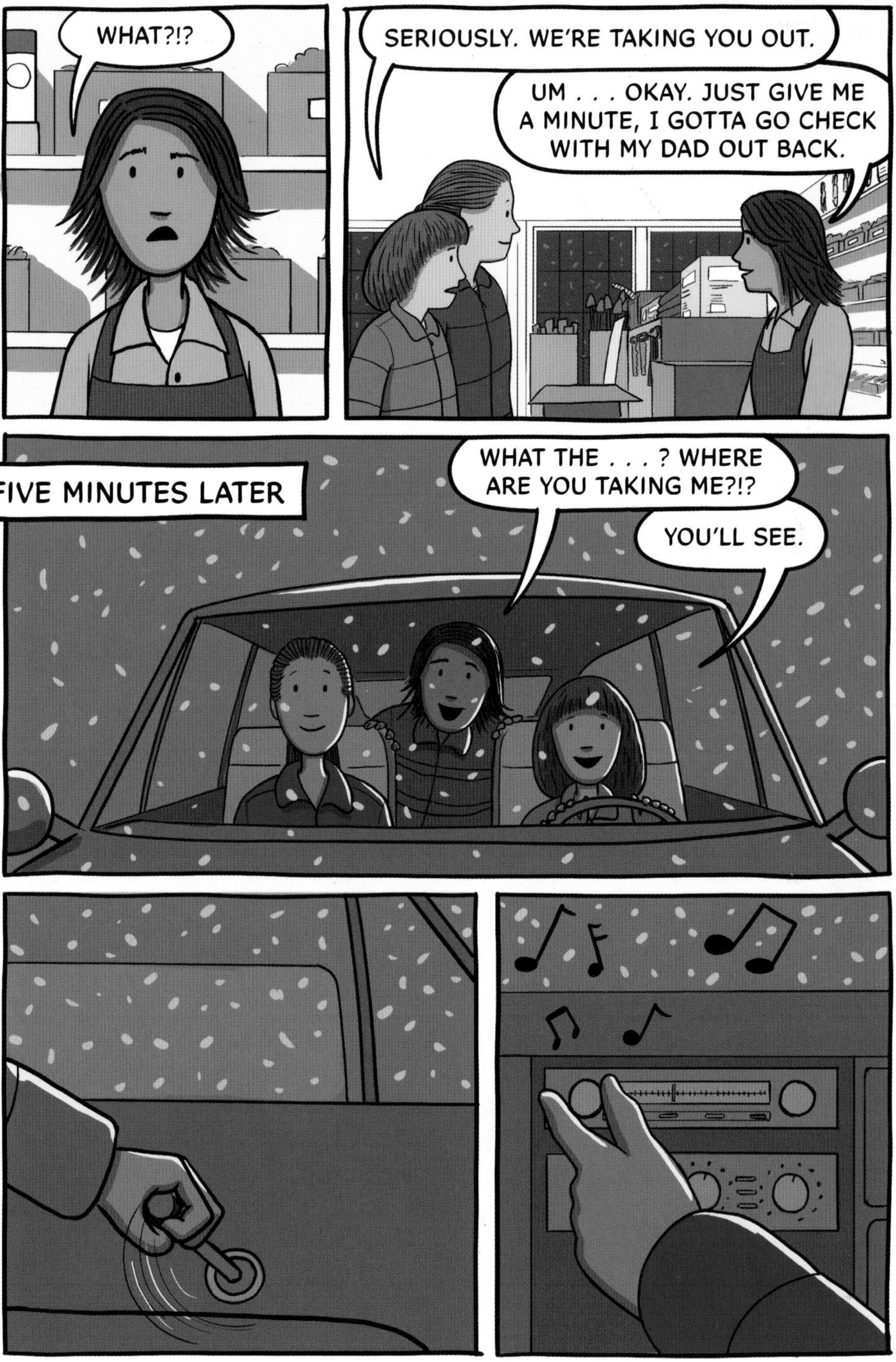
WHAT?!?
SERIOUSLY. WE'RE TAKING YOU OUT.
UM . . . OKAY. JUST GIVE ME A MINUTE, I GOTTA GO CHECK WITH MY DAD OUT BACK.
FIVE MINUTES LATER
WHAT THE . . . ? WHERE ARE YOU TAKING ME?!?
YOU'LL SEE.

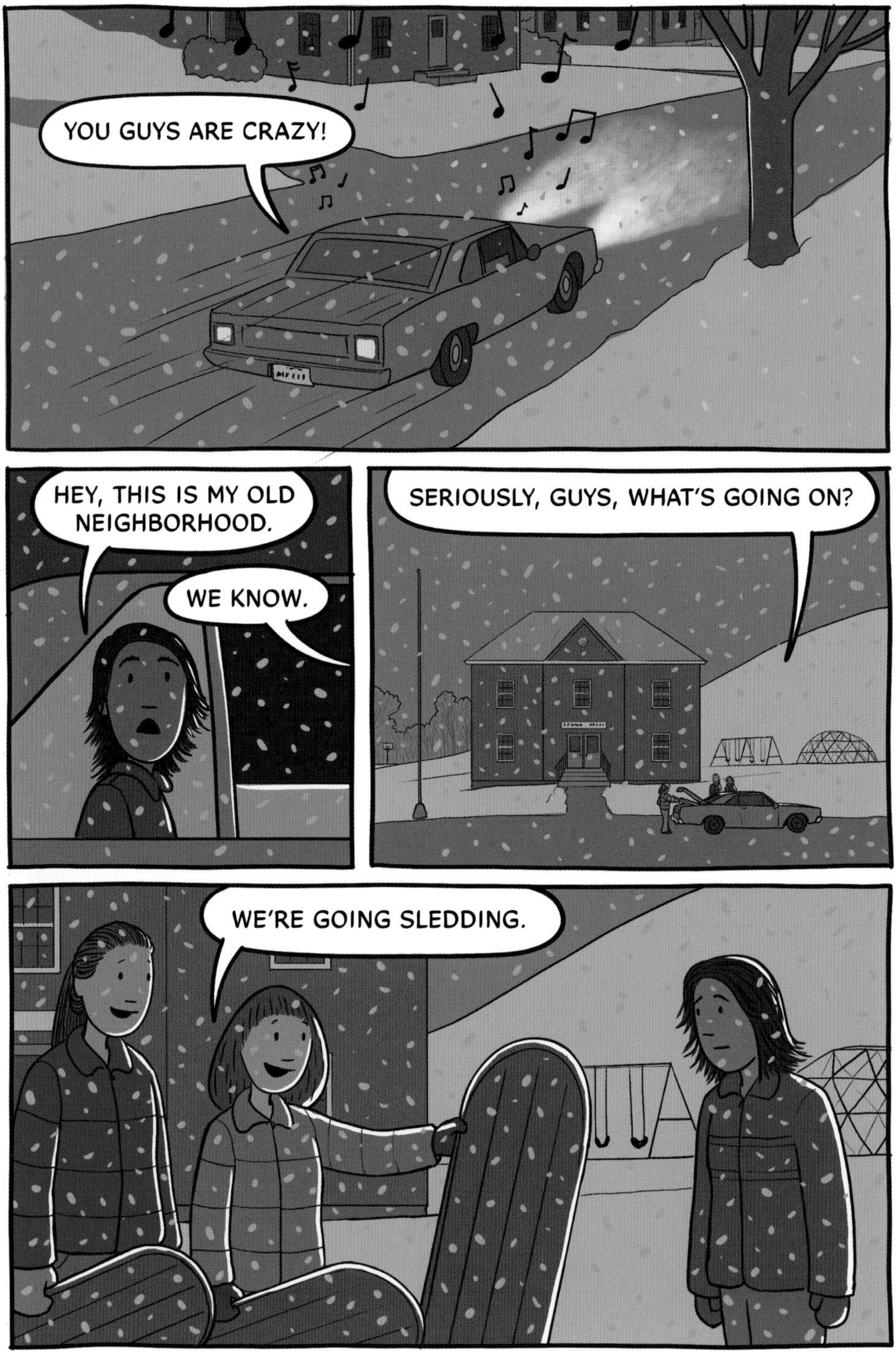
YOU GUYS ARE CRAZY!
HEY, THIS IS MY OLD NEIGHBORHOOD.
WE KNOW.
SERIOUSLY, GUYS, WHAT'S GOING ON?
WE'RE GOING SLEDDING.

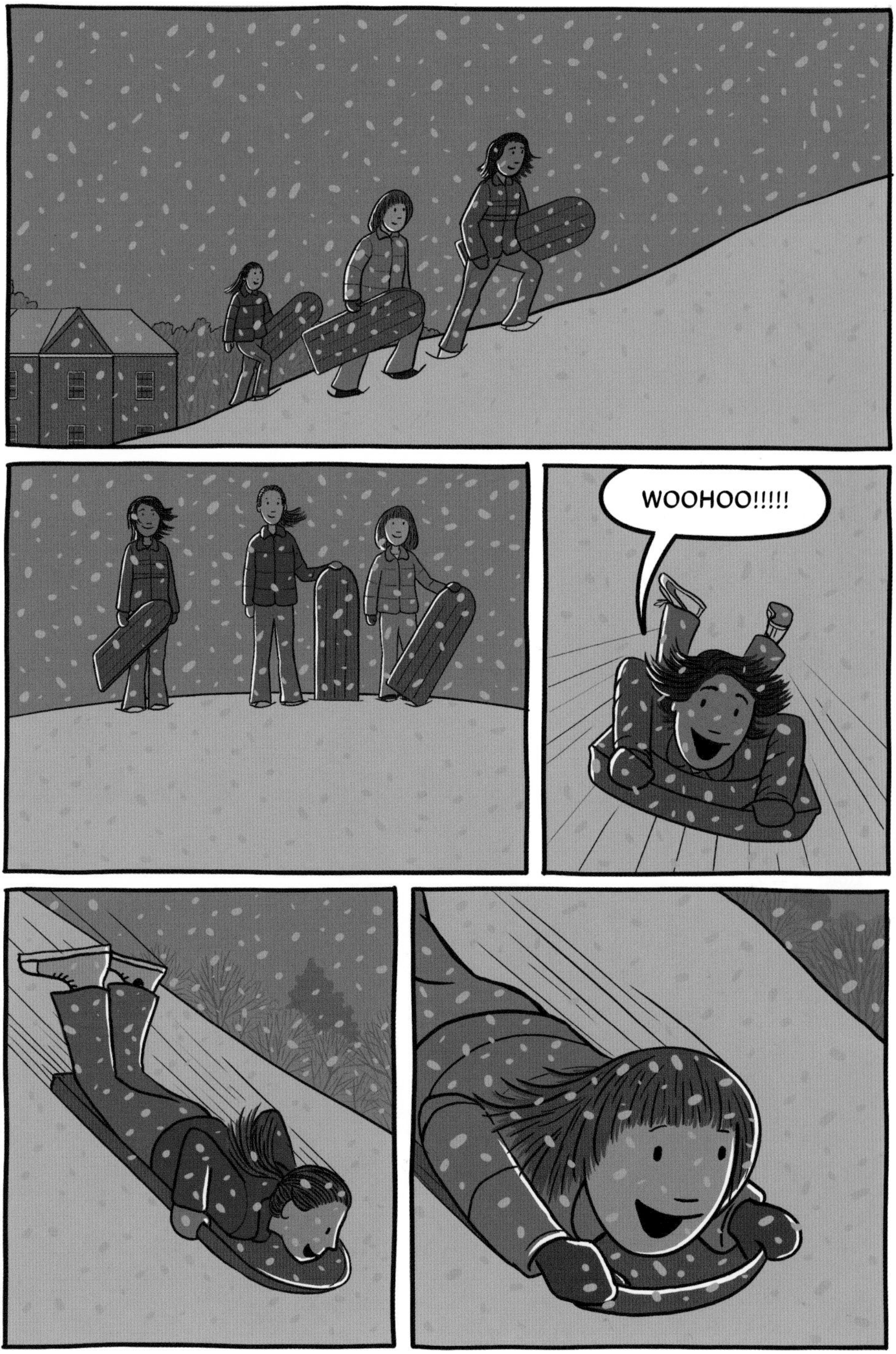
WOOHOO!!!!!

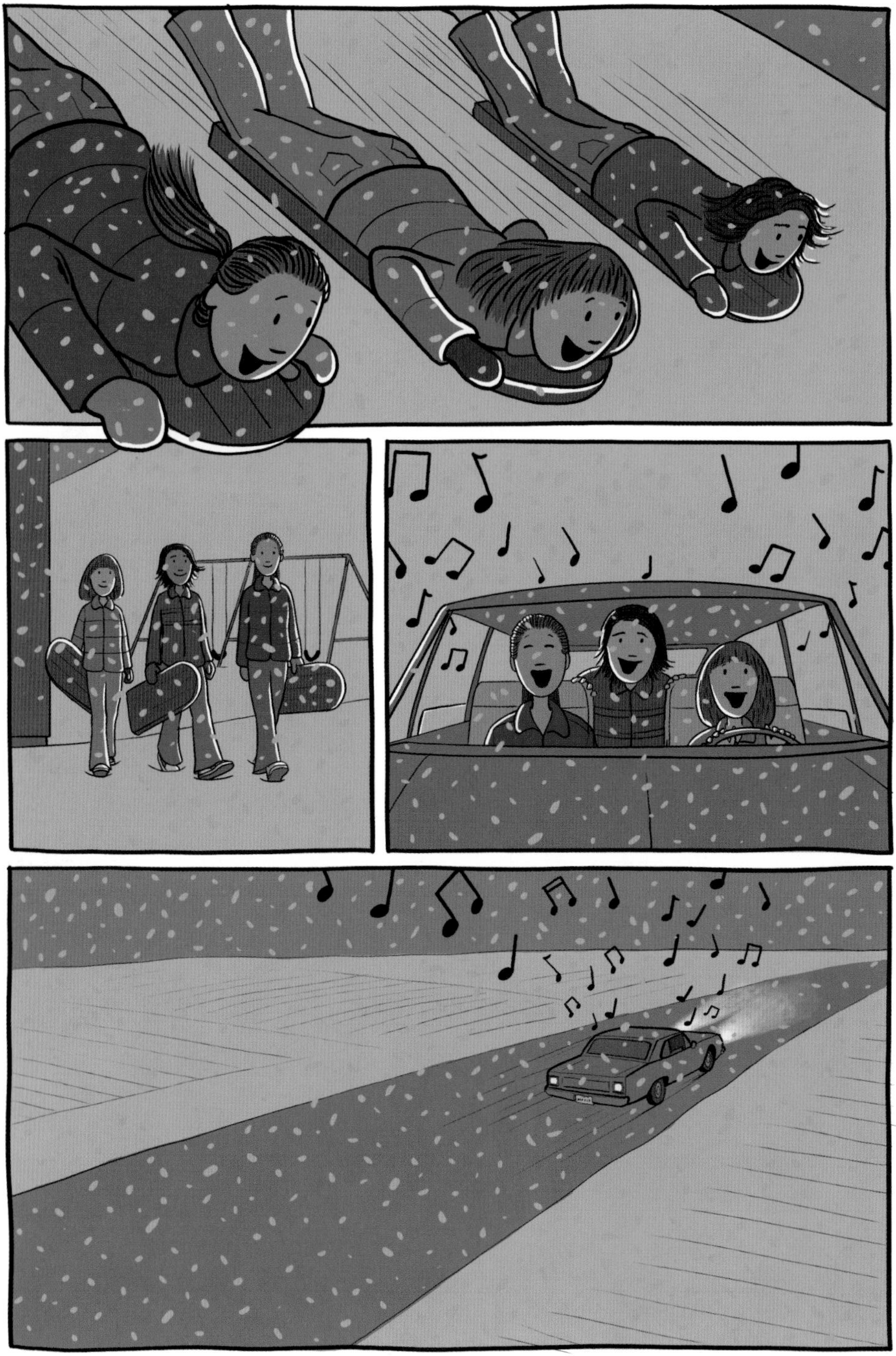

CHAPTER 13

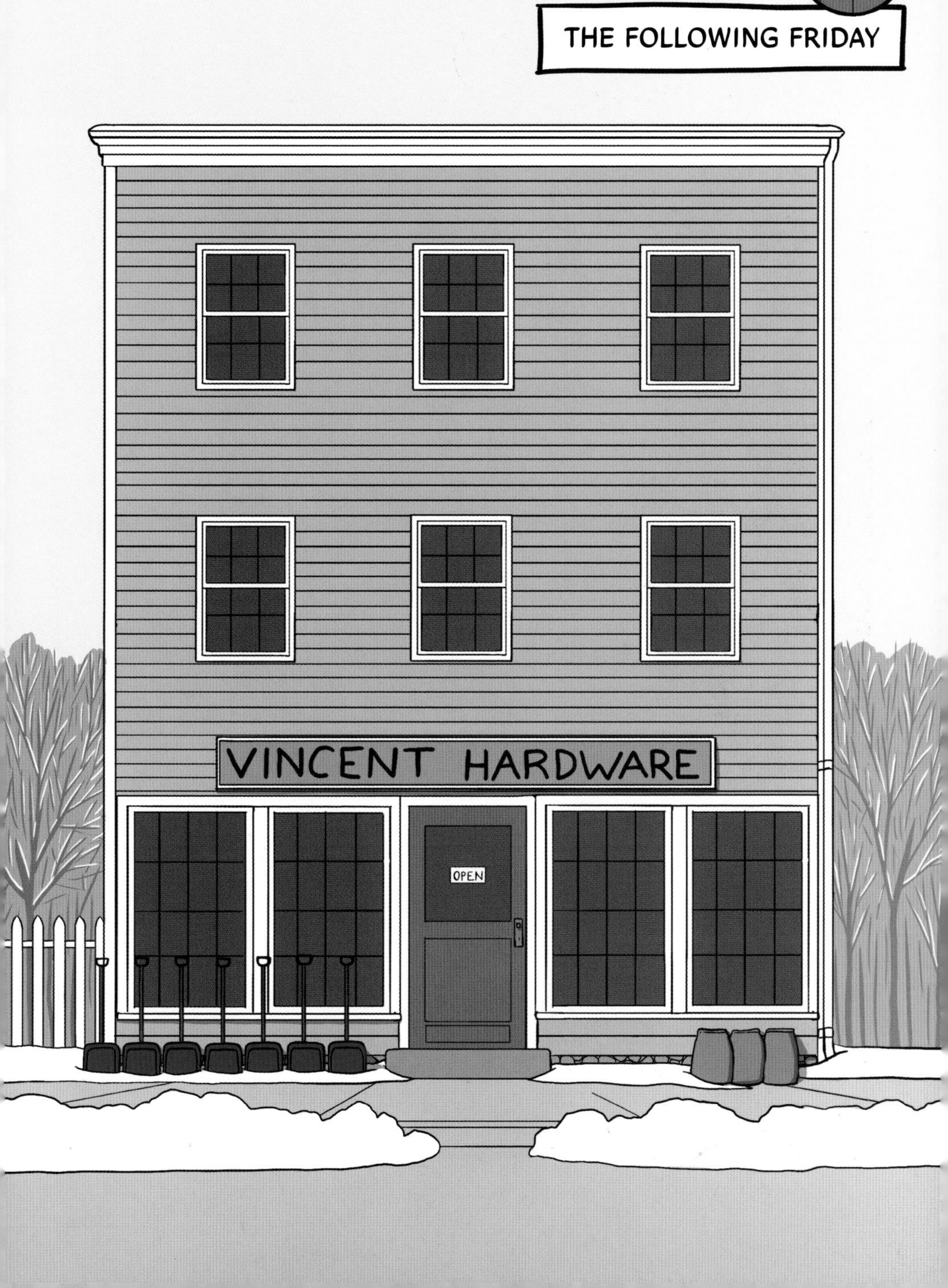
THE FOLLOWING FRIDAY
VINCENT HARDWARE
OPEN

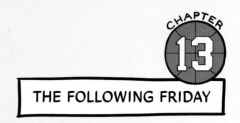

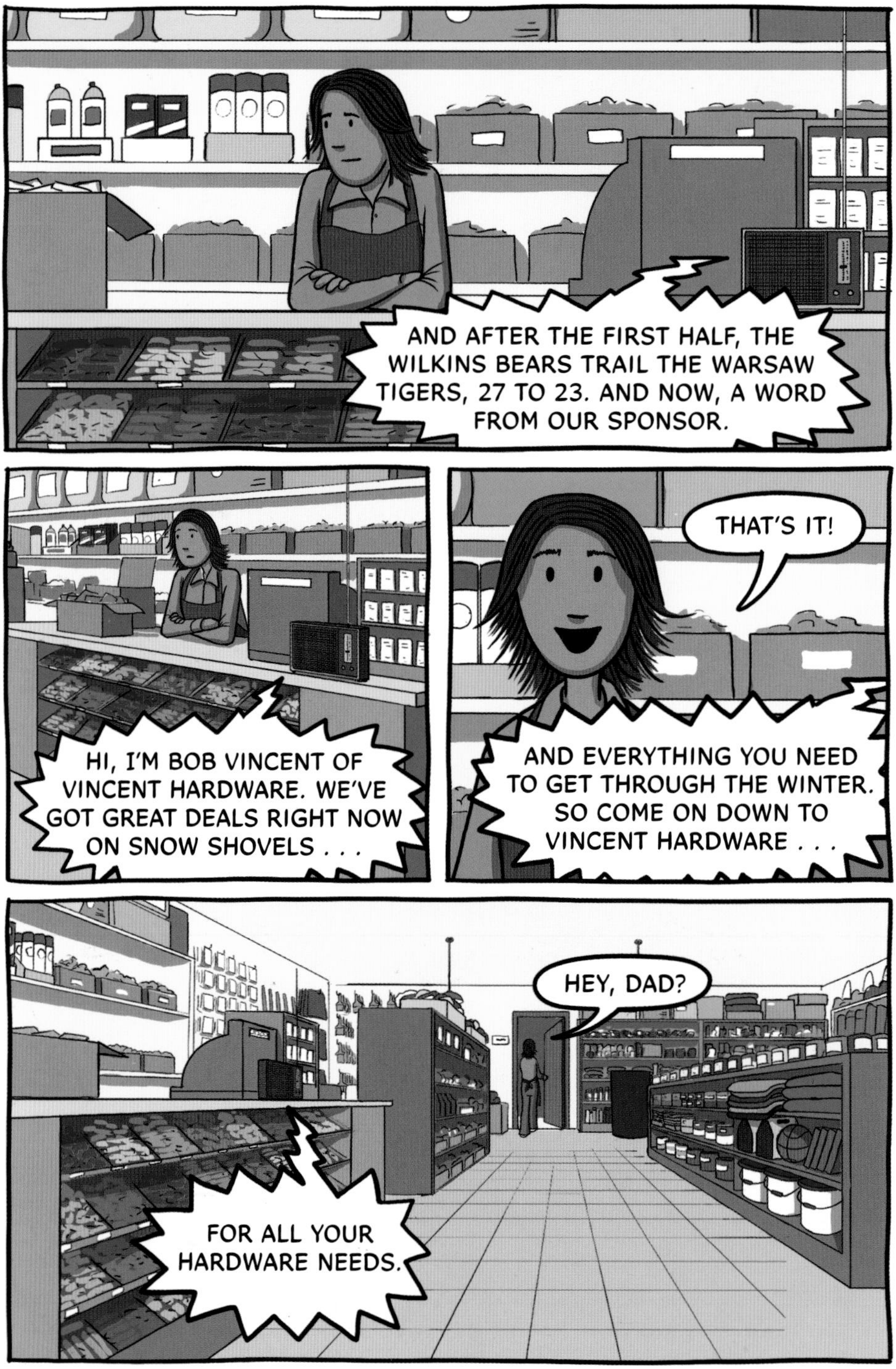
AND AFTER THE FIRST HALF, THE WILKINS BEARS TRAIL THE WARSAW TIGERS, 27 TO 23. AND NOW, A WORD FROM OUR SPONSOR.
HI, I'M BOB VINCENT OF VINCENT HARDWARE. WE'VE GOT GREAT DEALS RIGHT NOW ON SNOW SHOVELS . . .
THAT'S IT!
AND EVERYTHING YOU NEED TO GET THROUGH THE WINTER. SO COME ON DOWN TO VINCENT HARDWARE . . .
HEY, DAD?
FOR ALL YOUR HARDWARE NEEDS.

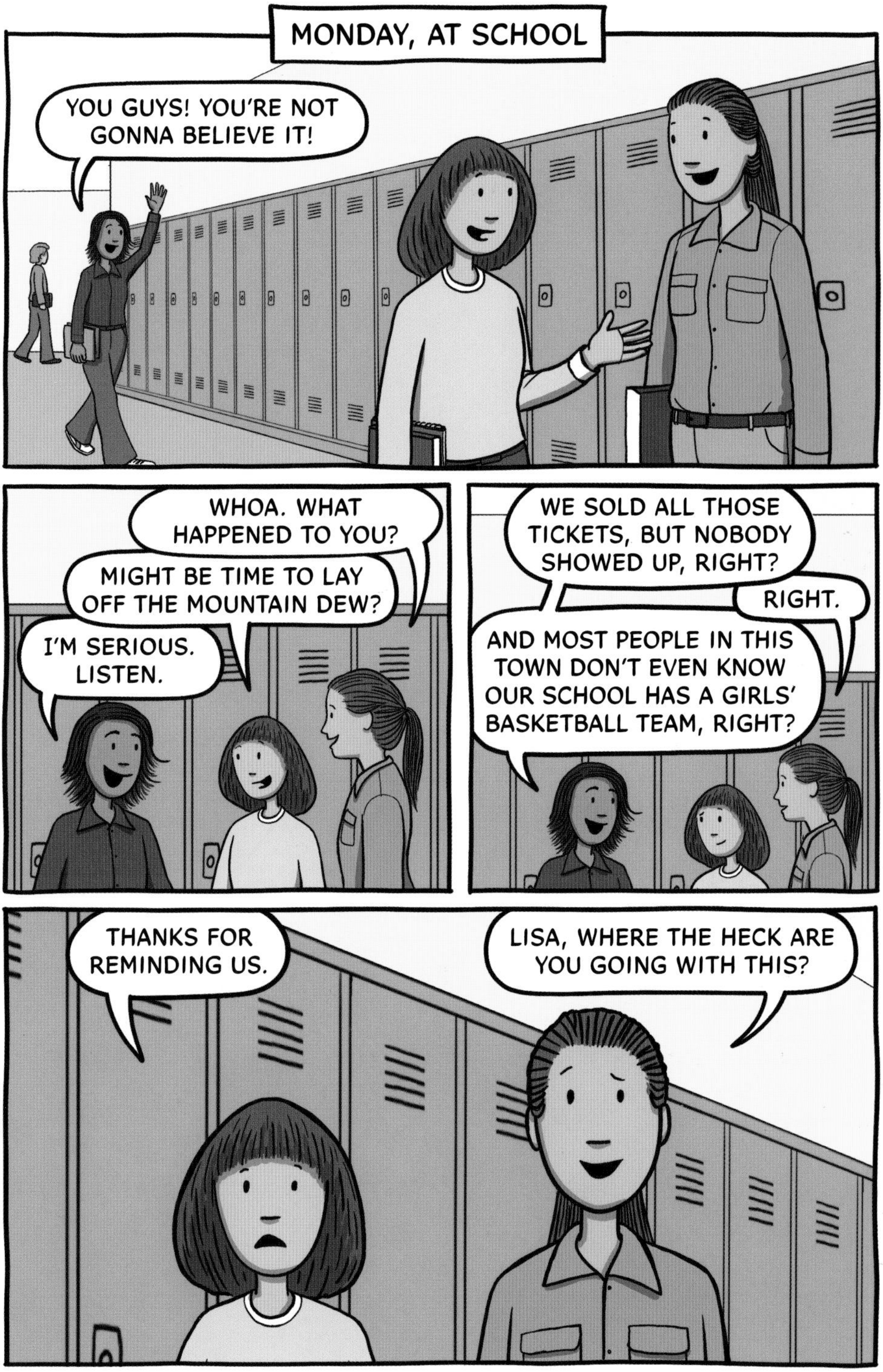
MONDAY, AT SCHOOL
YOU GUYS! YOU'RE NOT GONNA BELIEVE IT!
WHOA. WHAT HAPPENED TO YOU?
MIGHT BE TIME TO LAY OFF THE MOUNTAIN DEW?
I'M SERIOUS. LISTEN.
WE SOLD ALL THOSE TICKETS, BUT NOBODY SHOWED UP, RIGHT?
RIGHT.
AND MOST PEOPLE IN THIS TOWN DON'T EVEN KNOW OUR SCHOOL HAS A GIRLS' BASKETBALL TEAM, RIGHT?
THANKS FOR REMINDING US.
LISA, WHERE THE HECK ARE YOU GOING WITH THIS?

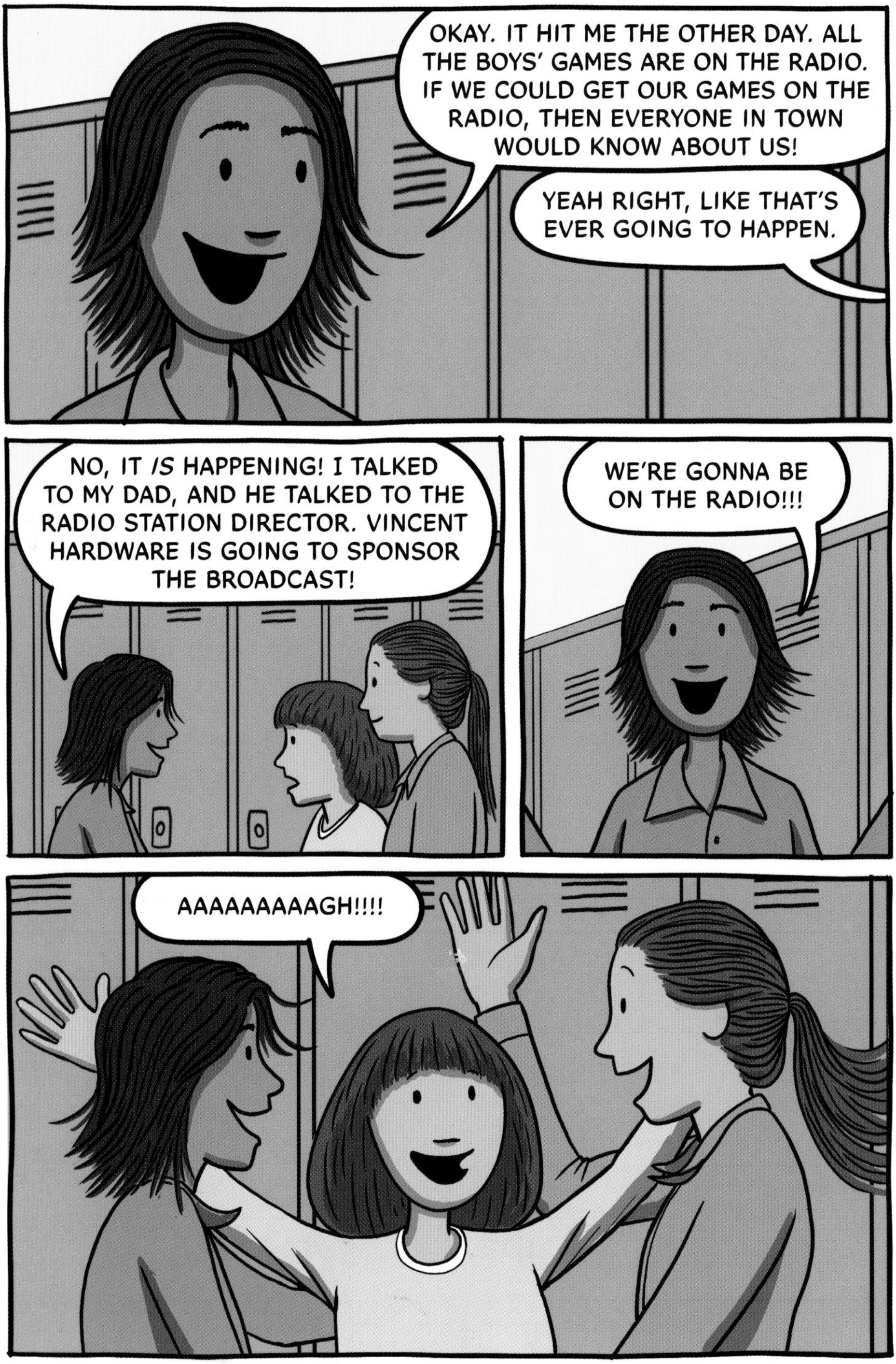
OKAY. IT HIT ME THE OTHER DAY. ALL THE BOYS' GAMES ARE ON THE RADIO. IF WE COULD GET OUR GAMES ON THE RADIO, THEN EVERYONE IN TOWN WOULD KNOW ABOUT US!
YEAH RIGHT, LIKE THAT'S EVER GOING TO HAPPEN.
NO, IT *IS* HAPPENING! I TALKED TO MY DAD, AND HE TALKED TO THE RADIO STATION DIRECTOR. VINCENT HARDWARE IS GOING TO SPONSOR THE BROADCAST!
WE'RE GONNA BE ON THE RADIO!!!
AAAAAAAAAGH!!!!

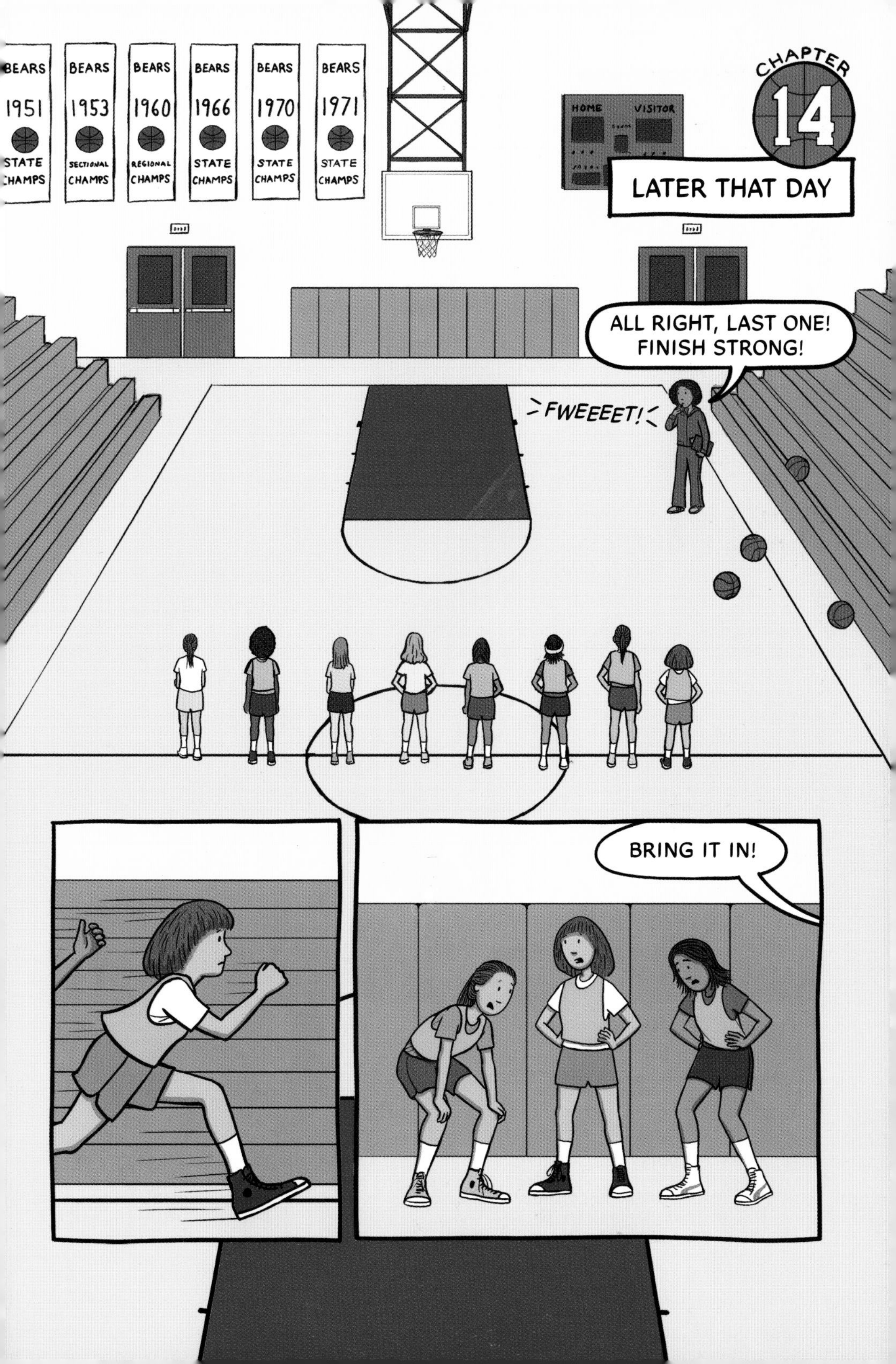
CHAPTER 14
LATER THAT DAY
BEARS 1951 STATE CHAMPS
BEARS 1953 SECTIONAL CHAMPS
BEARS 1960 REGIONAL CHAMPS
BEARS 1966 STATE CHAMPS
BEARS 1970 STATE CHAMPS
BEARS 1971 STATE CHAMPS
HOME
VISITOR
ALL RIGHT, LAST ONE! FINISH STRONG!
FWEEEET!
BRING IT IN!

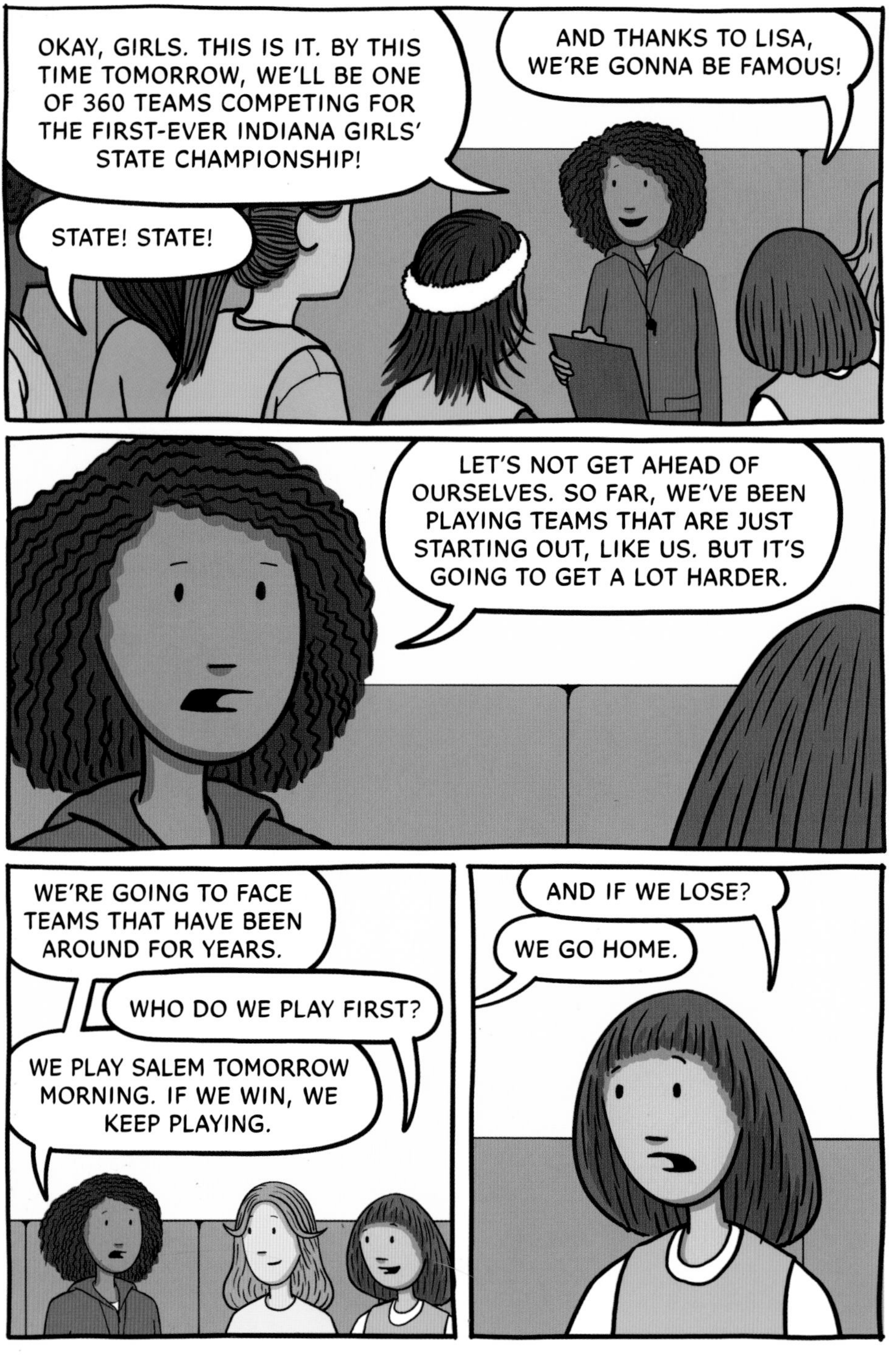
OKAY, GIRLS. THIS IS IT. BY THIS TIME TOMORROW, WE'LL BE ONE OF 360 TEAMS COMPETING FOR THE FIRST-EVER INDIANA GIRLS' STATE CHAMPIONSHIP!
AND THANKS TO LISA, WE'RE GONNA BE FAMOUS!
STATE! STATE!
LET'S NOT GET AHEAD OF OURSELVES. SO FAR, WE'VE BEEN PLAYING TEAMS THAT ARE JUST STARTING OUT, LIKE US. BUT IT'S GOING TO GET A LOT HARDER.
WE'RE GOING TO FACE TEAMS THAT HAVE BEEN AROUND FOR YEARS.
WHO DO WE PLAY FIRST?
WE PLAY SALEM TOMORROW MORNING. IF WE WIN, WE KEEP PLAYING.
AND IF WE LOSE?
WE GO HOME.

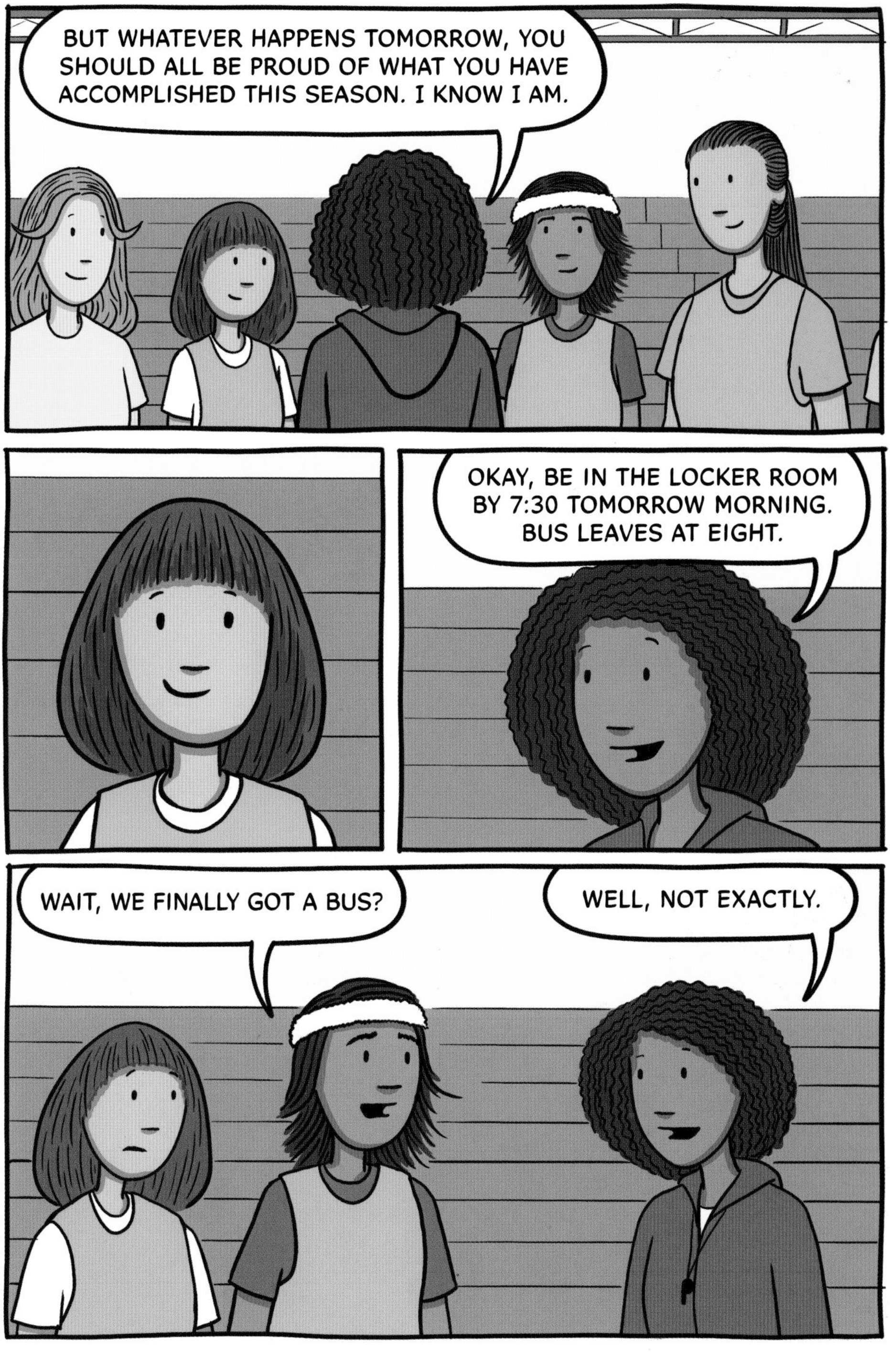
BUT WHATEVER HAPPENS TOMORROW, YOU SHOULD ALL BE PROUD OF WHAT YOU HAVE ACCOMPLISHED THIS SEASON. I KNOW I AM.
OKAY, BE IN THE LOCKER ROOM BY 7:30 TOMORROW MORNING. BUS LEAVES AT EIGHT.
WAIT, WE FINALLY GOT A BUS?
WELL, NOT EXACTLY.

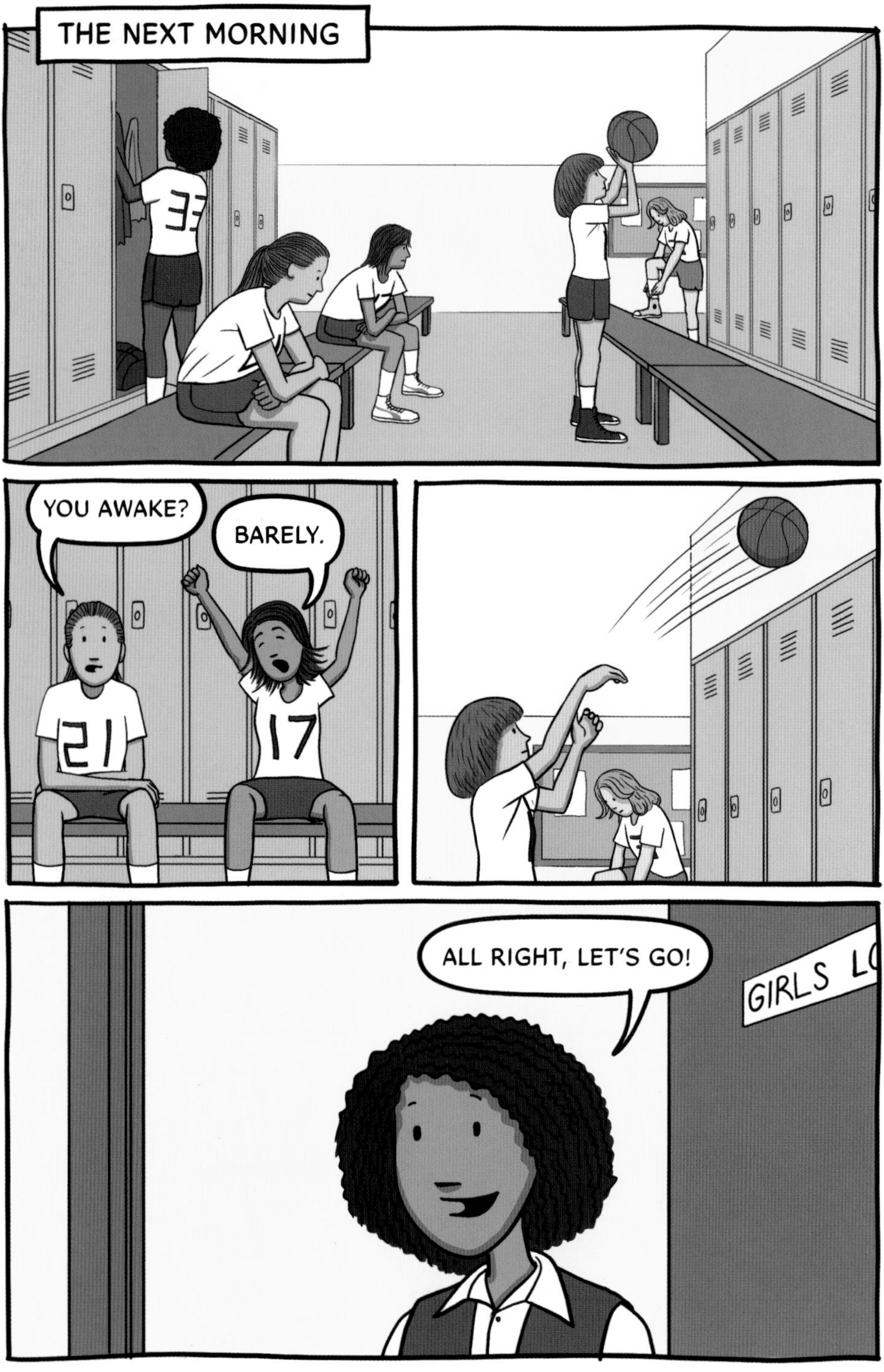
THE NEXT MORNING
33
YOU AWAKE?
BARELY.
21
17
ALL RIGHT, LET'S GO!
GIRLS LO

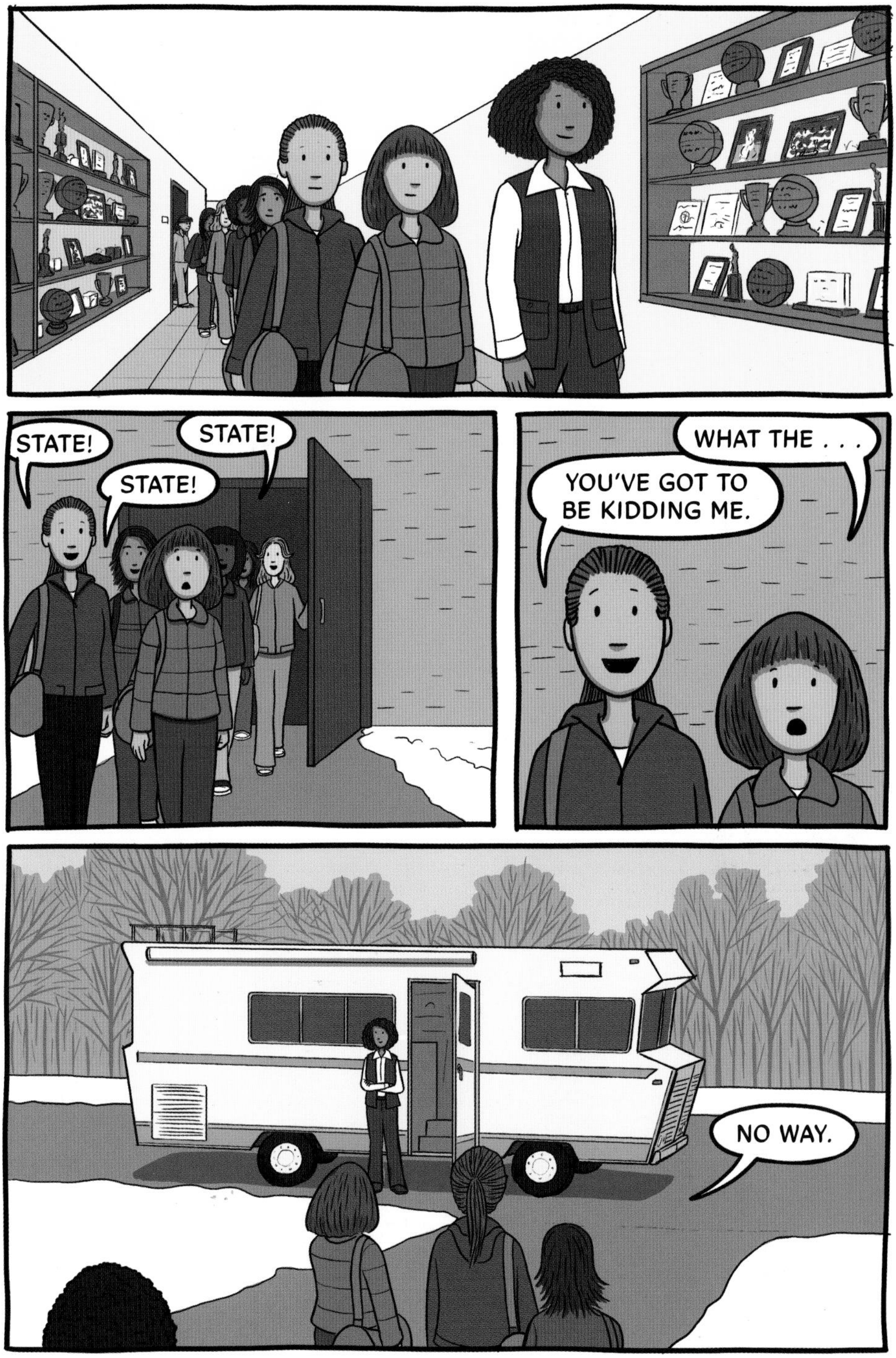
STATE!
STATE!
STATE!
WHAT THE . . .
YOU'VE GOT TO BE KIDDING ME.
NO WAY.

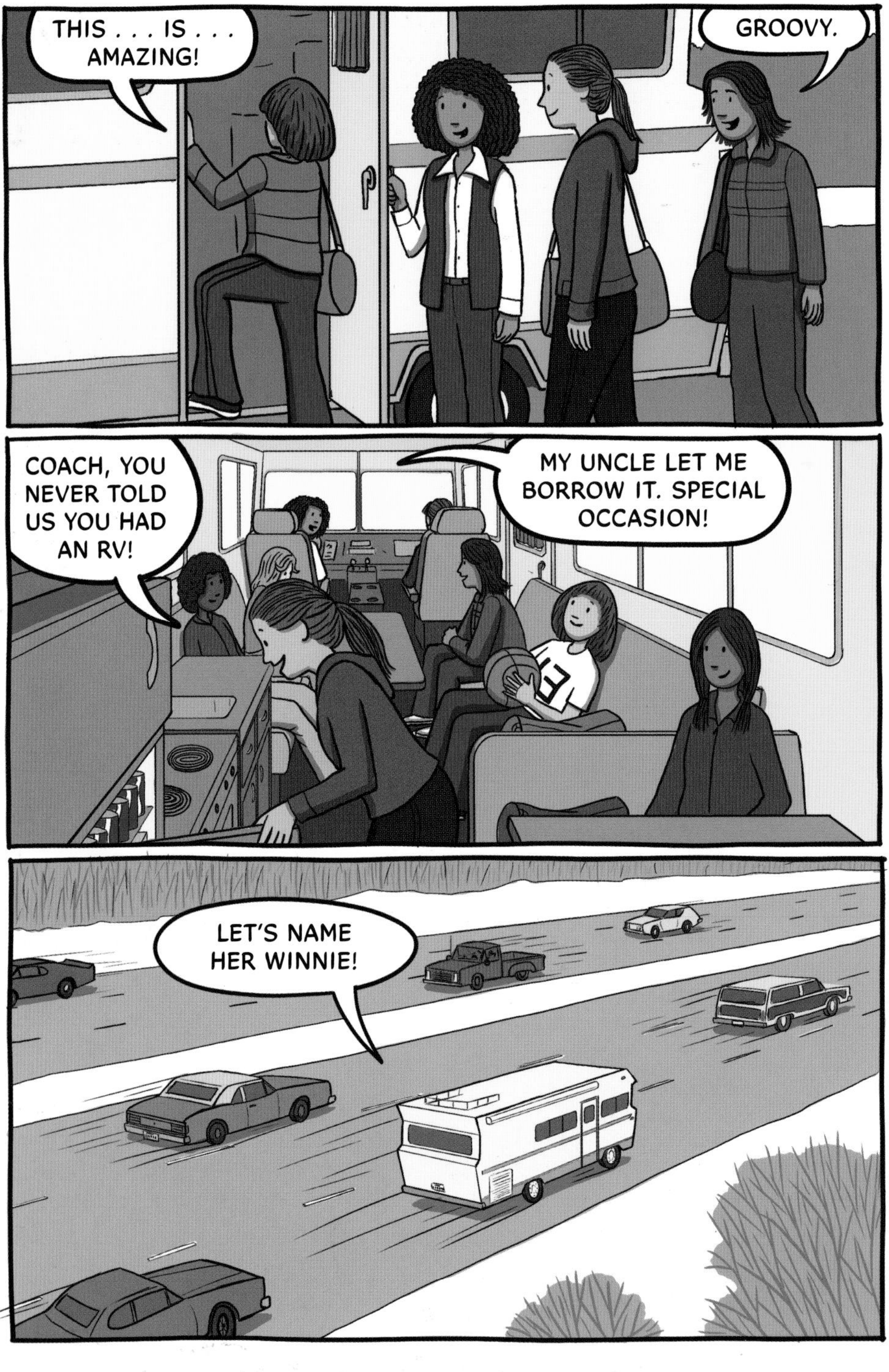
THIS . . . IS . . . AMAZING!
GROOVY.
COACH, YOU NEVER TOLD US YOU HAD AN RV!
MY UNCLE LET ME BORROW IT. SPECIAL OCCASION!
LET'S NAME HER WINNIE!

THIS IS RITA MILLER, COMING TO YOU LIVE FROM THE SECTIONALS ROUND OF THE FIRST-EVER INDIANA GIRLS' HIGH SCHOOL BASKETBALL TOURNAMENT.

SIXTEEN TEAMS ARE HERE AT SPRINGFIELD HIGH SCHOOL TODAY . . .

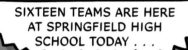

REMEMBER: TOUGH ON DEFENSE. FAST BREAKS. THAT'S OUR GAME. 'TEAM' ON THREE: ONE, TWO, THREE . . .

TEAM!!

BUT ONLY ONE WILL ADVANCE TO REGIONALS NEXT WEEK IN SOUTH BEND.

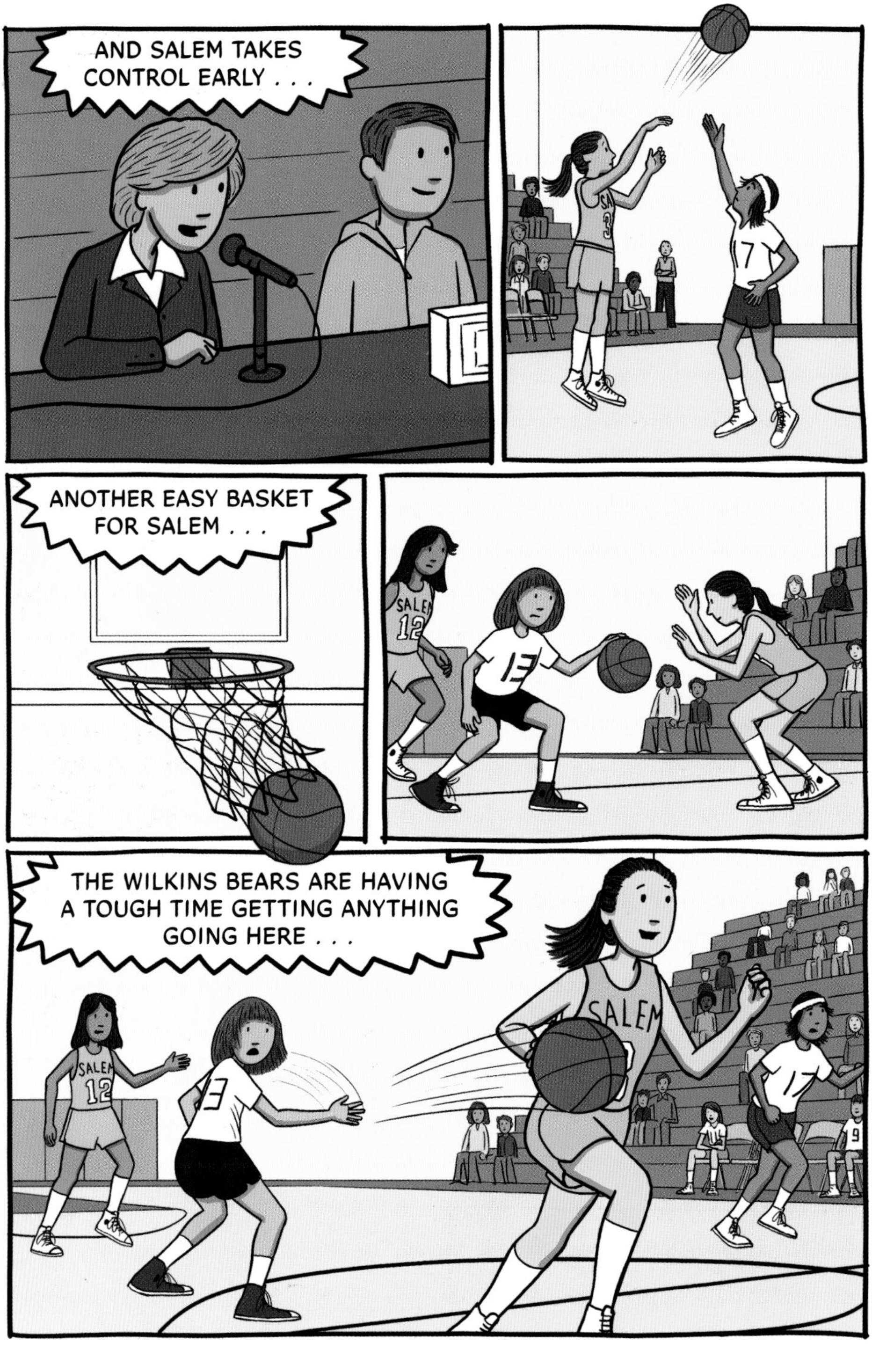
AND SALEM TAKES CONTROL EARLY . . .
SAL
3
17
ANOTHER EASY BASKET FOR SALEM . . .
SALEM
12
13
THE WILKINS BEARS ARE HAVING A TOUGH TIME GETTING ANYTHING GOING HERE . . .
SALEM
12
13
SALEM
17
9

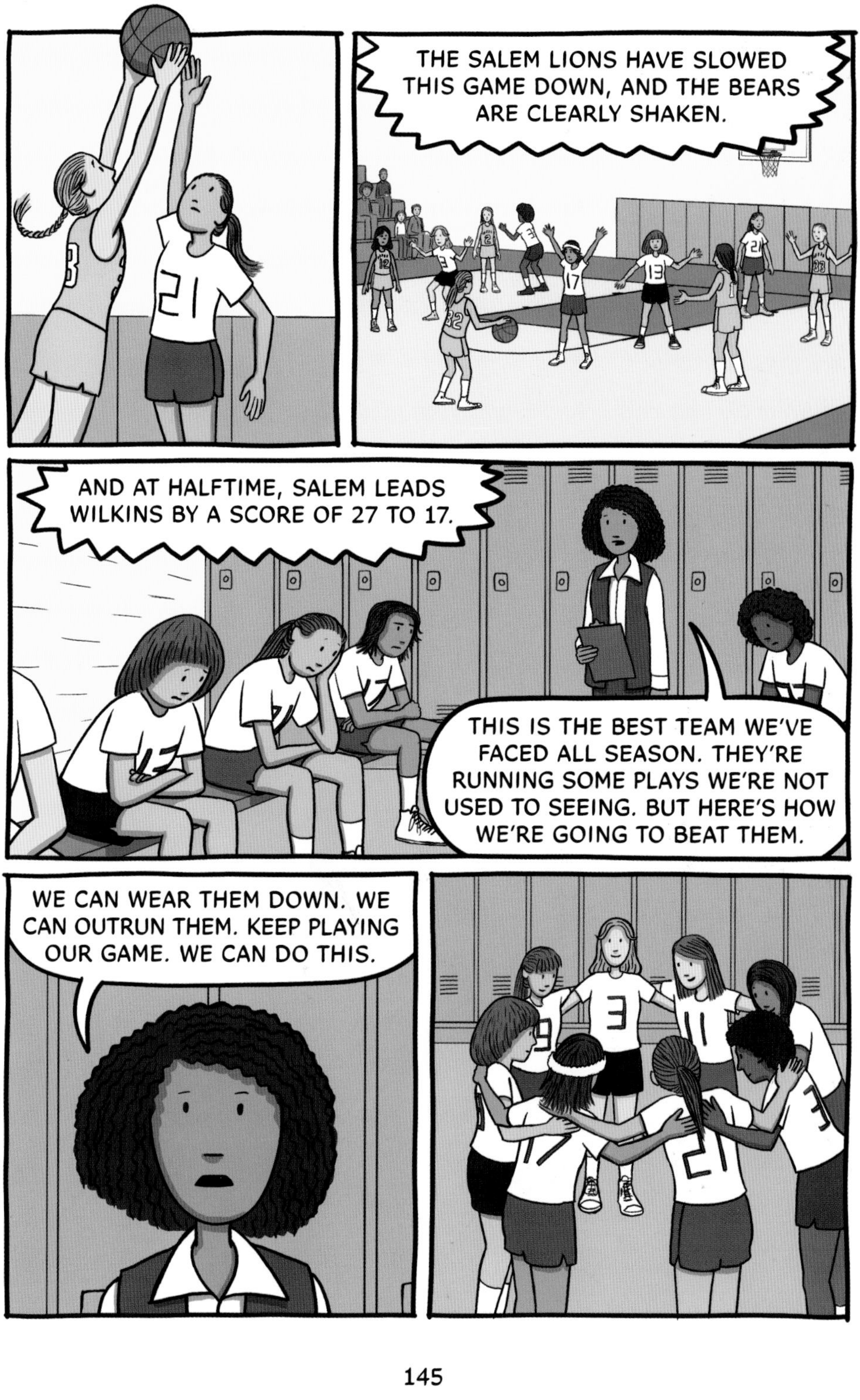
THE SALEM LIONS HAVE SLOWED THIS GAME DOWN, AND THE BEARS ARE CLEARLY SHAKEN.
AND AT HALFTIME, SALEM LEADS WILKINS BY A SCORE OF 27 TO 17.
THIS IS THE BEST TEAM WE'VE FACED ALL SEASON. THEY'RE RUNNING SOME PLAYS WE'RE NOT USED TO SEEING. BUT HERE'S HOW WE'RE GOING TO BEAT THEM.
WE CAN WEAR THEM DOWN. WE CAN OUTRUN THEM. KEEP PLAYING OUR GAME. WE CAN DO THIS.

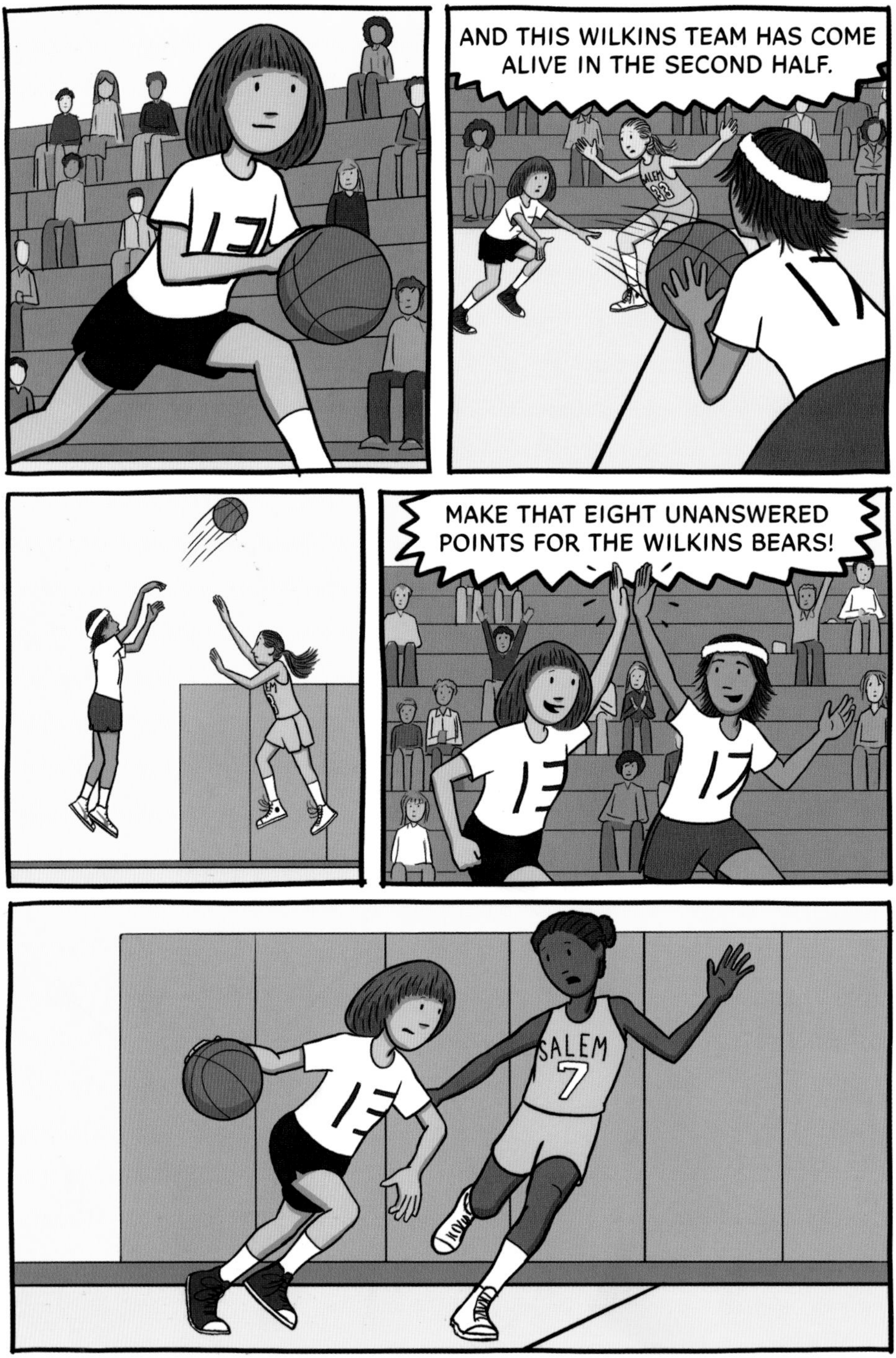
AND THIS WILKINS TEAM HAS COME ALIVE IN THE SECOND HALF.
SALEM
33
SALEM
MAKE THAT EIGHT UNANSWERED POINTS FOR THE WILKINS BEARS!
SALEM
7

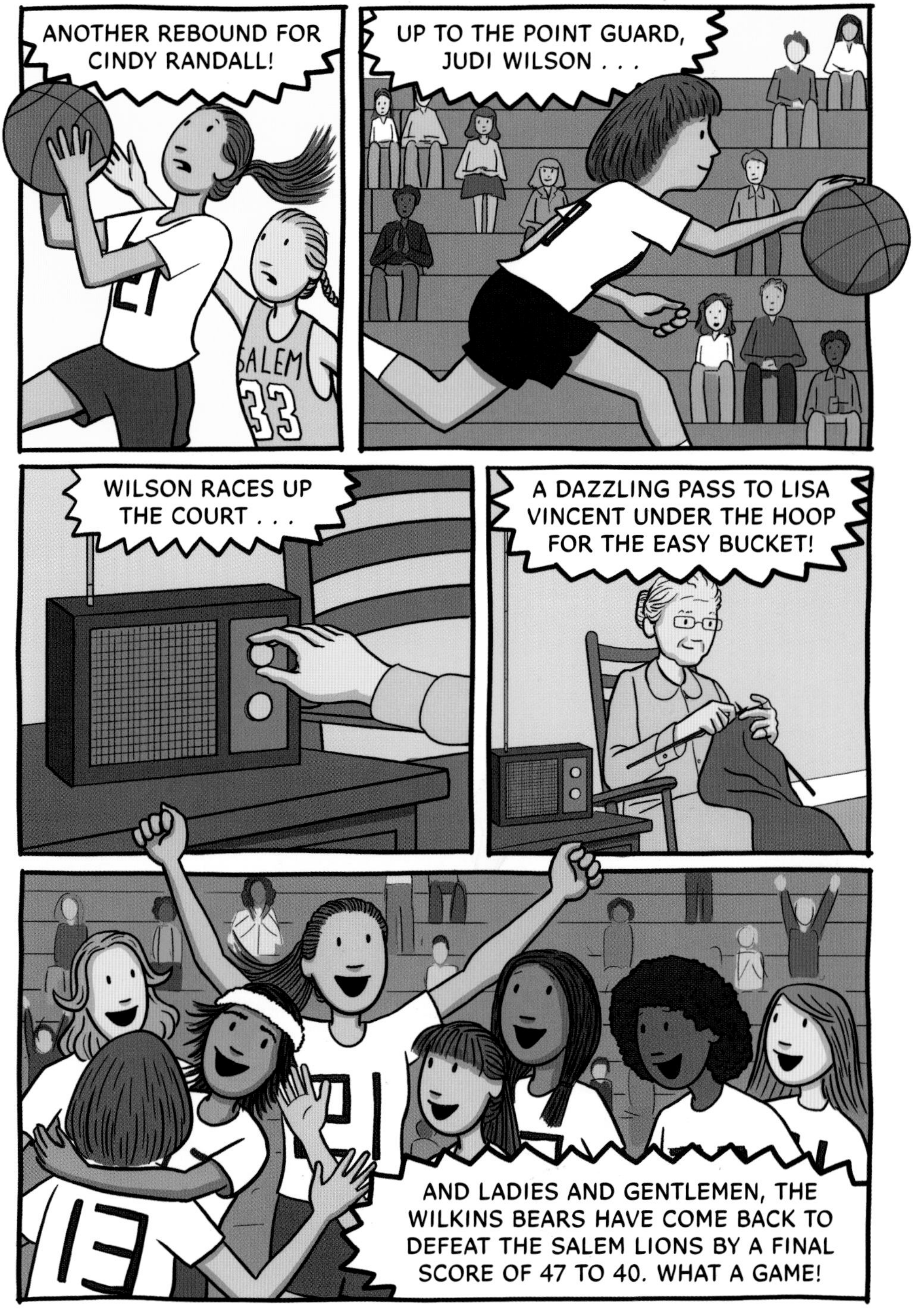
ANOTHER REBOUND FOR CINDY RANDALL!
27
SALEM 33
UP TO THE POINT GUARD, JUDI WILSON . . .
WILSON RACES UP THE COURT . . .
A DAZZLING PASS TO LISA VINCENT UNDER THE HOOP FOR THE EASY BUCKET!
13
AND LADIES AND GENTLEMEN, THE WILKINS BEARS HAVE COME BACK TO DEFEAT THE SALEM LIONS BY A FINAL SCORE OF 47 TO 40. WHAT A GAME!

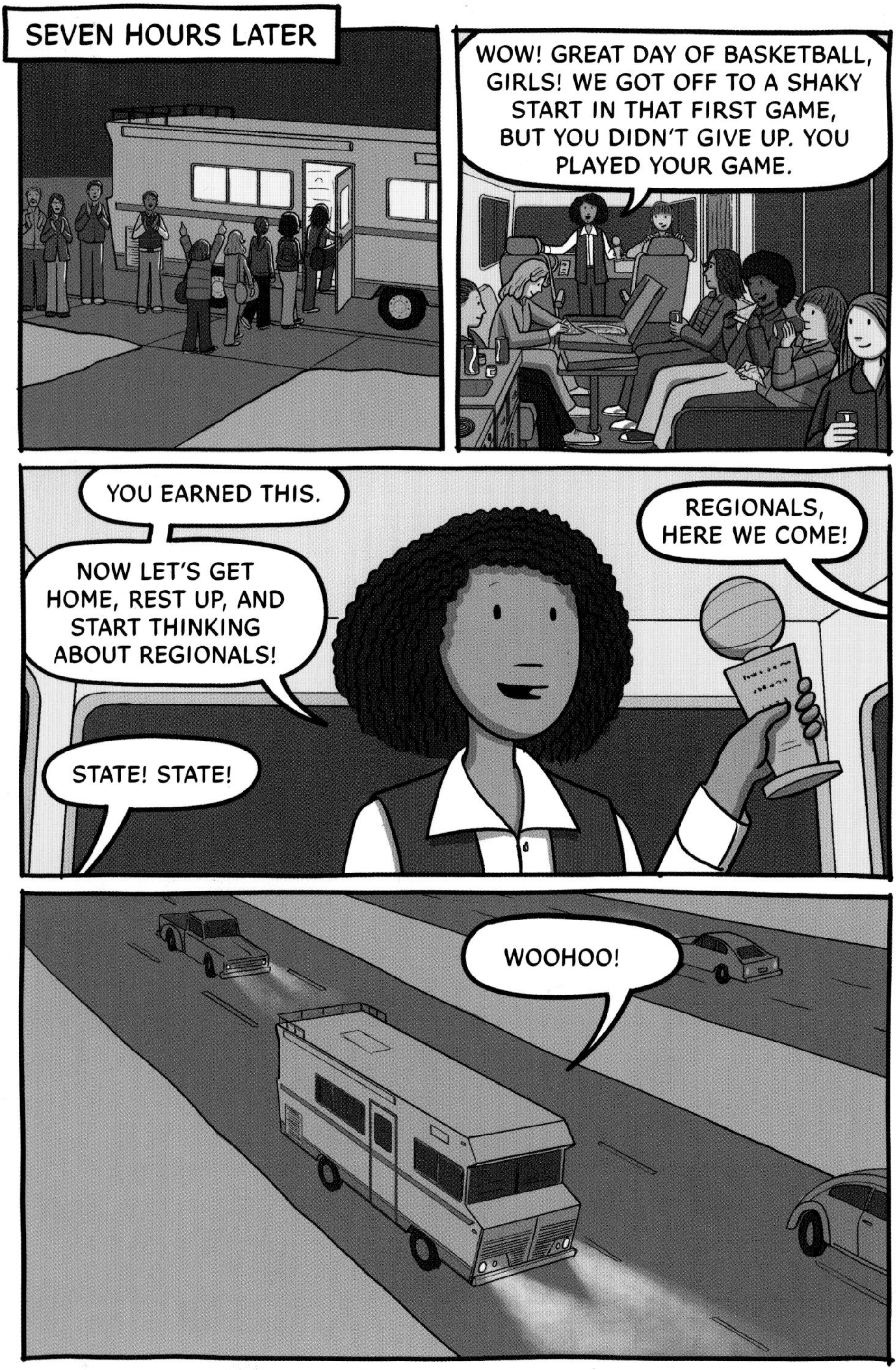
SEVEN HOURS LATER
WOW! GREAT DAY OF BASKETBALL, GIRLS! WE GOT OFF TO A SHAKY START IN THAT FIRST GAME, BUT YOU DIDN'T GIVE UP. YOU PLAYED YOUR GAME.
YOU EARNED THIS.
NOW LET'S GET HOME, REST UP, AND START THINKING ABOUT REGIONALS!
REGIONALS, HERE WE COME!
STATE! STATE!
WOOHOO!

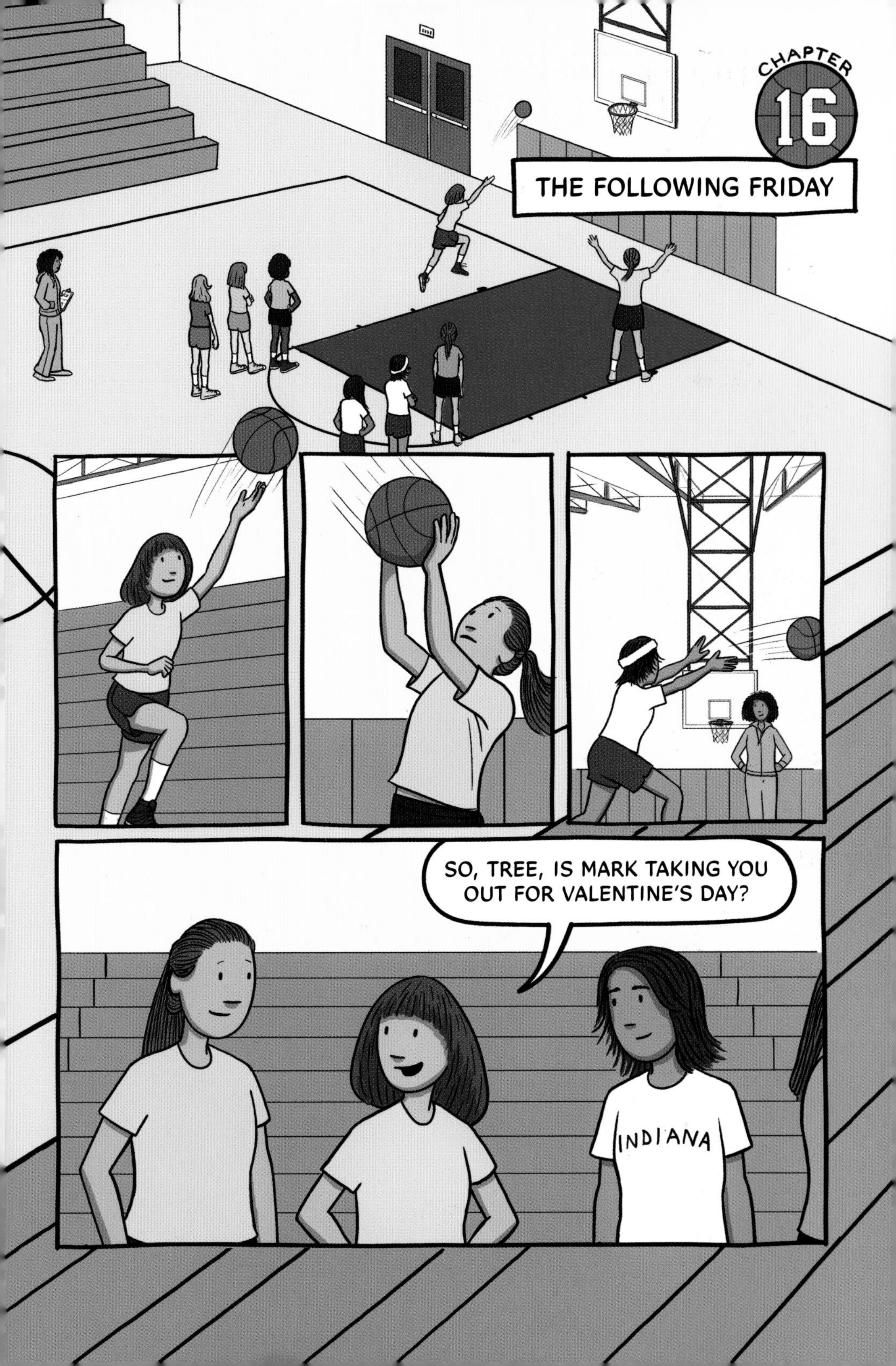
CHAPTER
16
THE FOLLOWING FRIDAY
SO, TREE, IS MARK TAKING YOU OUT FOR VALENTINE'S DAY?
INDIANA

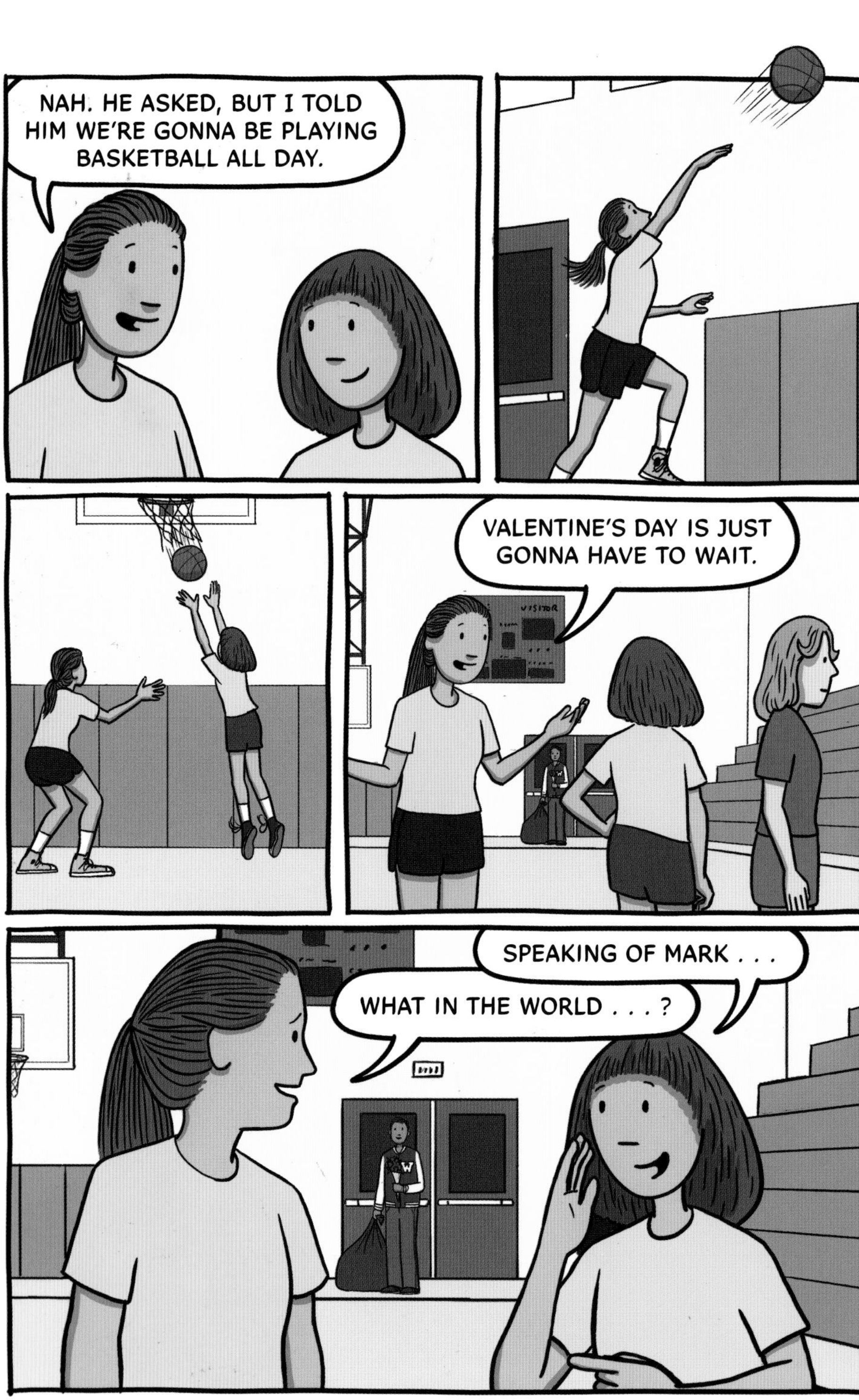
NAH. HE ASKED, BUT I TOLD HIM WE'RE GONNA BE PLAYING BASKETBALL ALL DAY.
VALENTINE'S DAY IS JUST GONNA HAVE TO WAIT.
VISITOR
SPEAKING OF MARK . . .
WHAT IN THE WORLD . . . ?

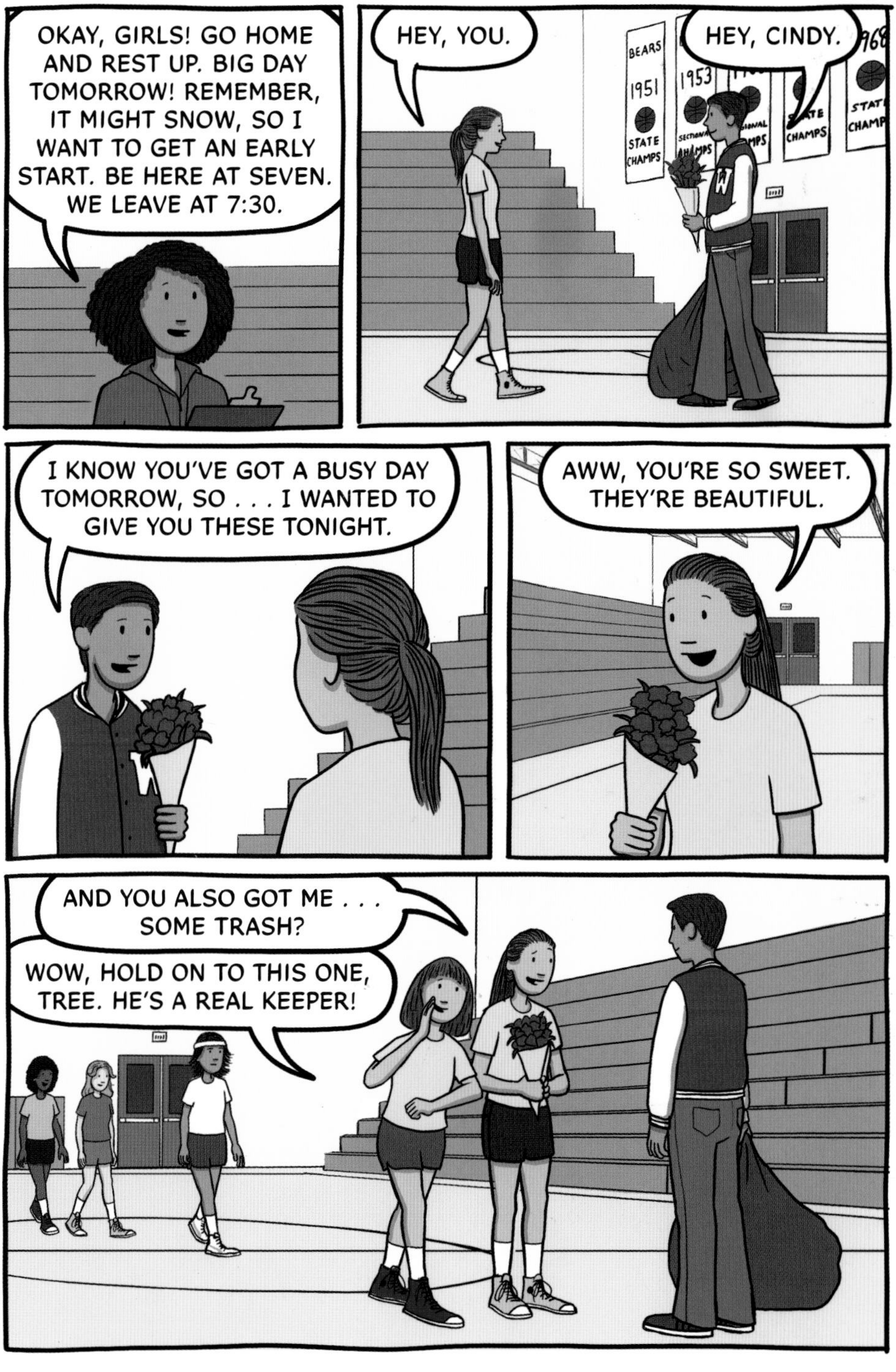
OKAY, GIRLS! GO HOME AND REST UP. BIG DAY TOMORROW! REMEMBER, IT MIGHT SNOW, SO I WANT TO GET AN EARLY START. BE HERE AT SEVEN. WE LEAVE AT 7:30.
HEY, YOU.
HEY, CINDY.
BEARS
1951
STATE CHAMPS
1953
I KNOW YOU'VE GOT A BUSY DAY TOMORROW, SO . . . I WANTED TO GIVE YOU THESE TONIGHT.
AWW, YOU'RE SO SWEET. THEY'RE BEAUTIFUL.
AND YOU ALSO GOT ME . . . SOME TRASH?
WOW, HOLD ON TO THIS ONE, TREE. HE'S A REAL KEEPER!

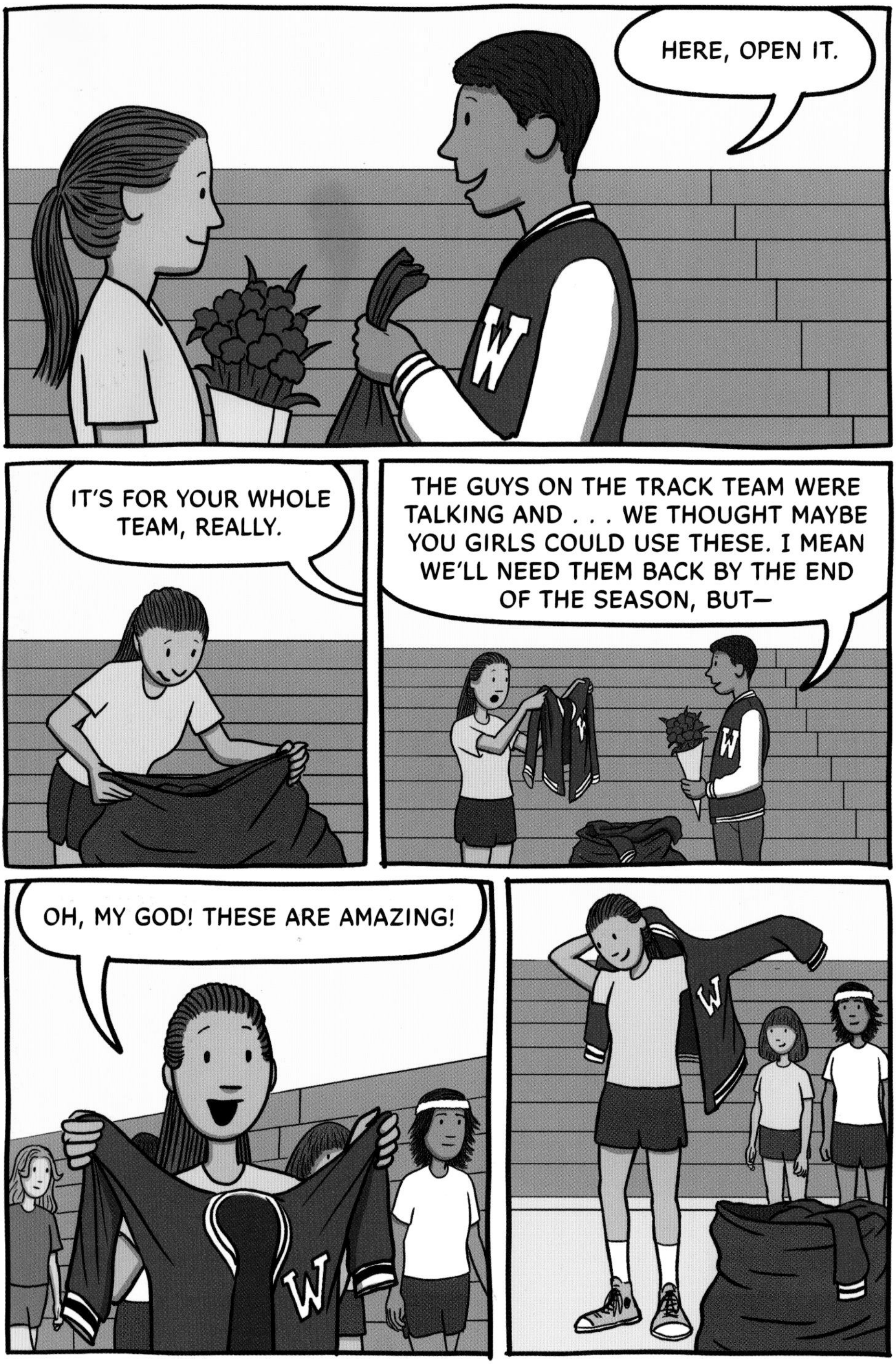
HERE, OPEN IT.
IT'S FOR YOUR WHOLE TEAM, REALLY.
THE GUYS ON THE TRACK TEAM WERE TALKING AND . . . WE THOUGHT MAYBE YOU GIRLS COULD USE THESE. I MEAN WE'LL NEED THEM BACK BY THE END OF THE SEASON, BUT—
OH, MY GOD! THESE ARE AMAZING!

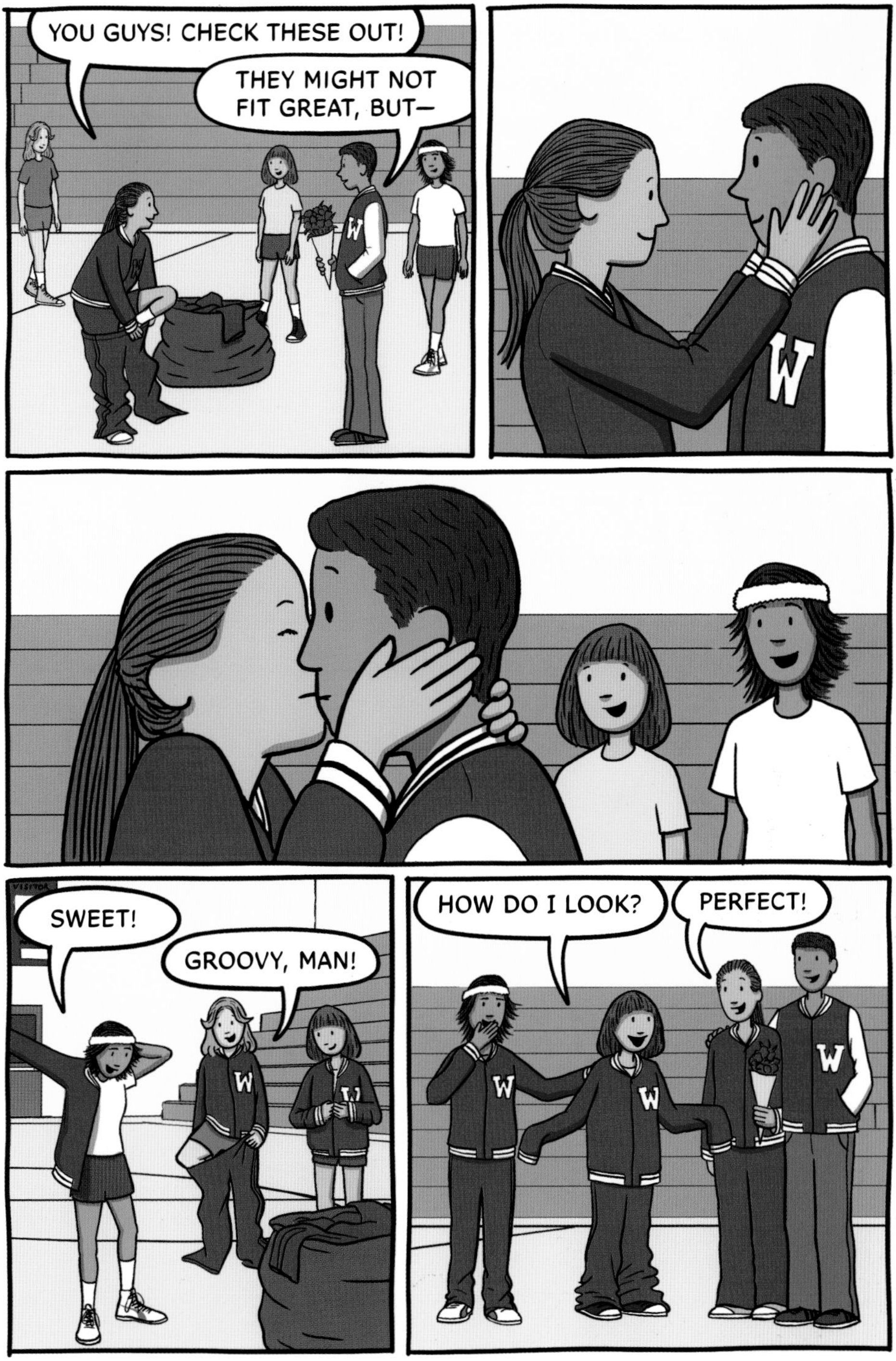
YOU GUYS! CHECK THESE OUT!
THEY MIGHT NOT FIT GREAT, BUT—
SWEET!
GROOVY, MAN!
HOW DO I LOOK?
PERFECT!

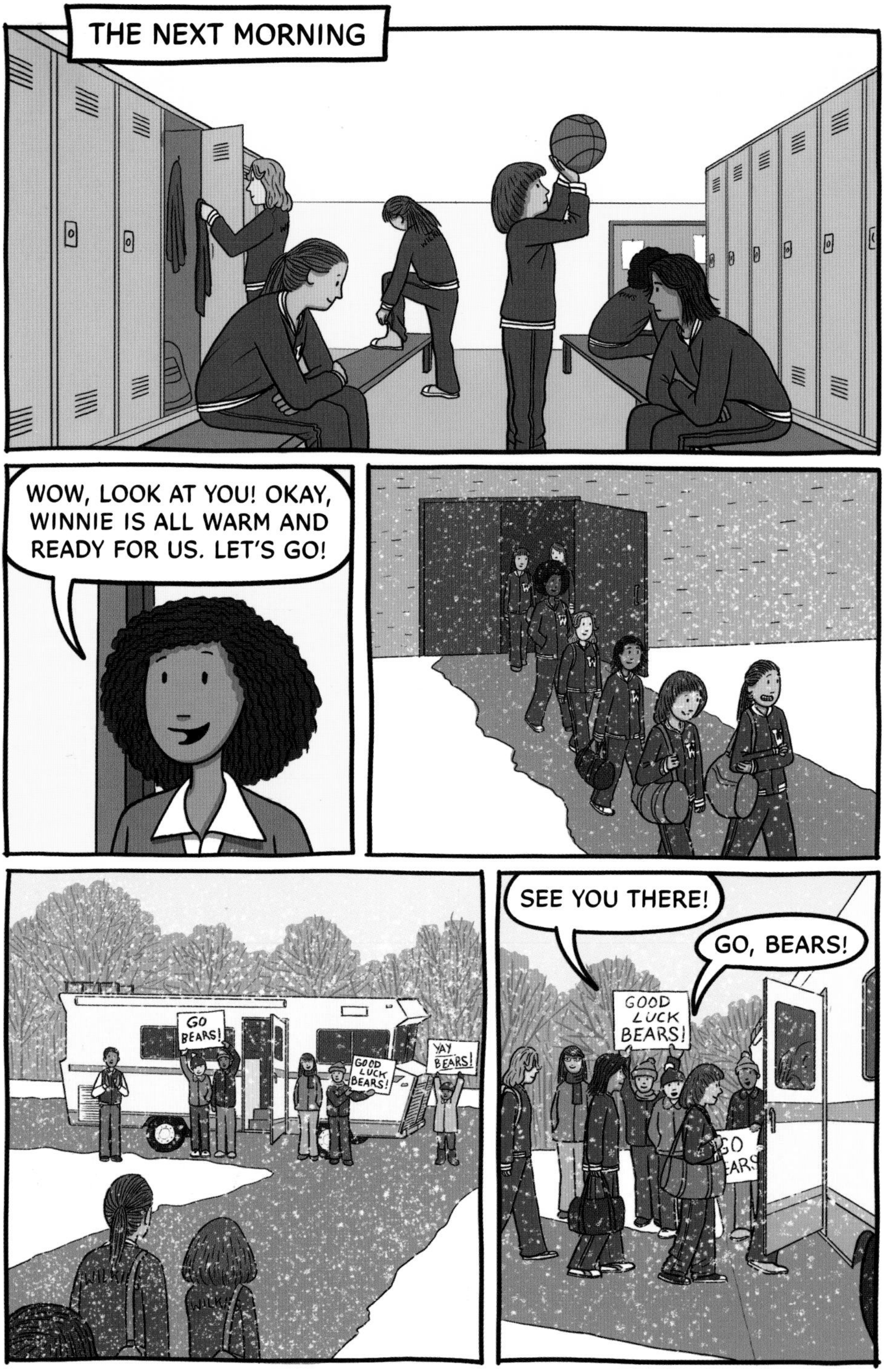
THE NEXT MORNING
WOW, LOOK AT YOU! OKAY, WINNIE IS ALL WARM AND READY FOR US. LET'S GO!
GO BEARS!
GOOD LUCK BEARS!
YAY BEARS!
SEE YOU THERE!
GO, BEARS!
GOOD LUCK BEARS!

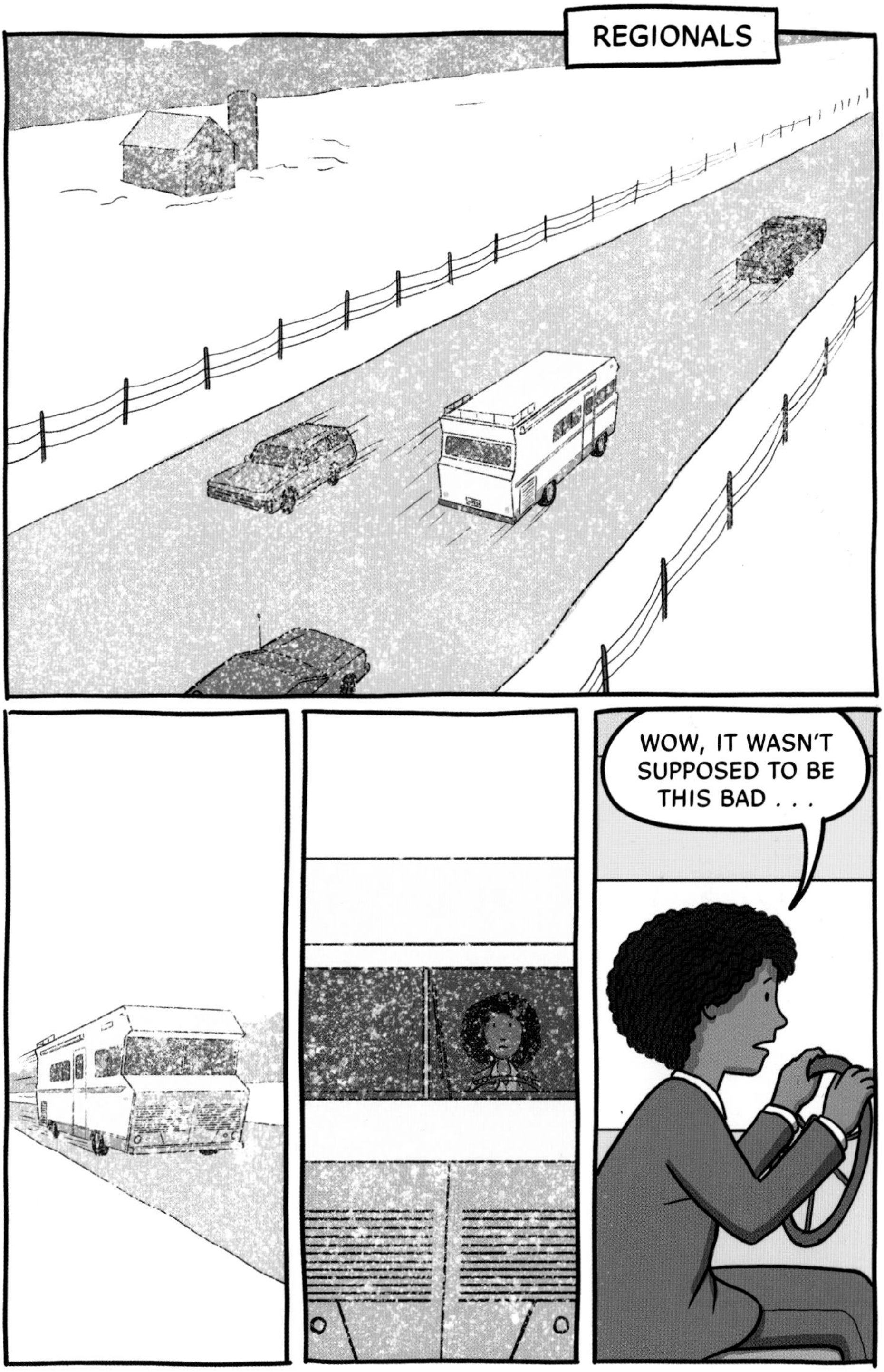
REGIONALS
WOW, IT WASN'T SUPPOSED TO BE THIS BAD . . .

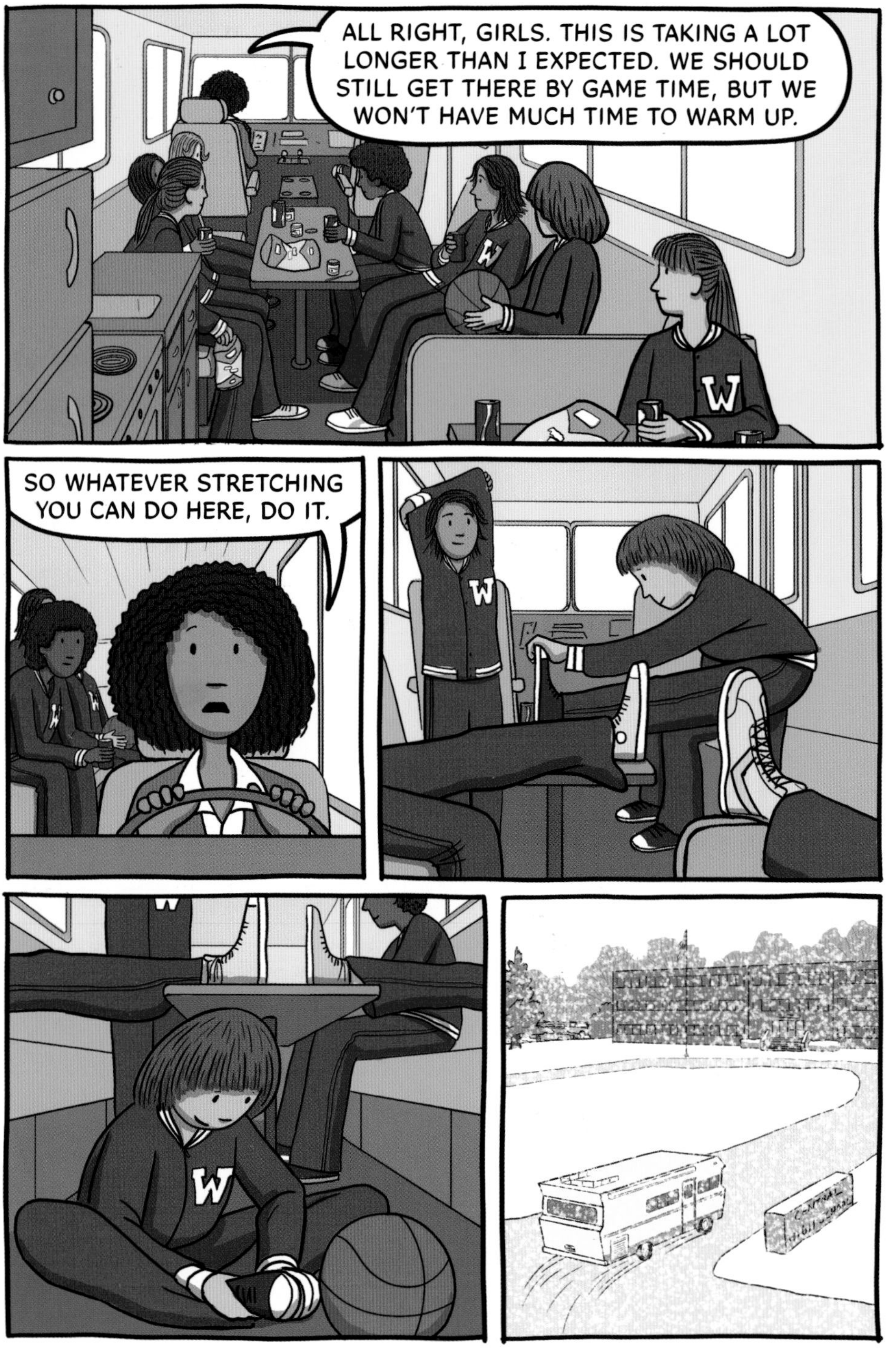
ALL RIGHT, GIRLS. THIS IS TAKING A LOT LONGER THAN I EXPECTED. WE SHOULD STILL GET THERE BY GAME TIME, BUT WE WON'T HAVE MUCH TIME TO WARM UP.
SO WHATEVER STRETCHING YOU CAN DO HERE, DO IT.

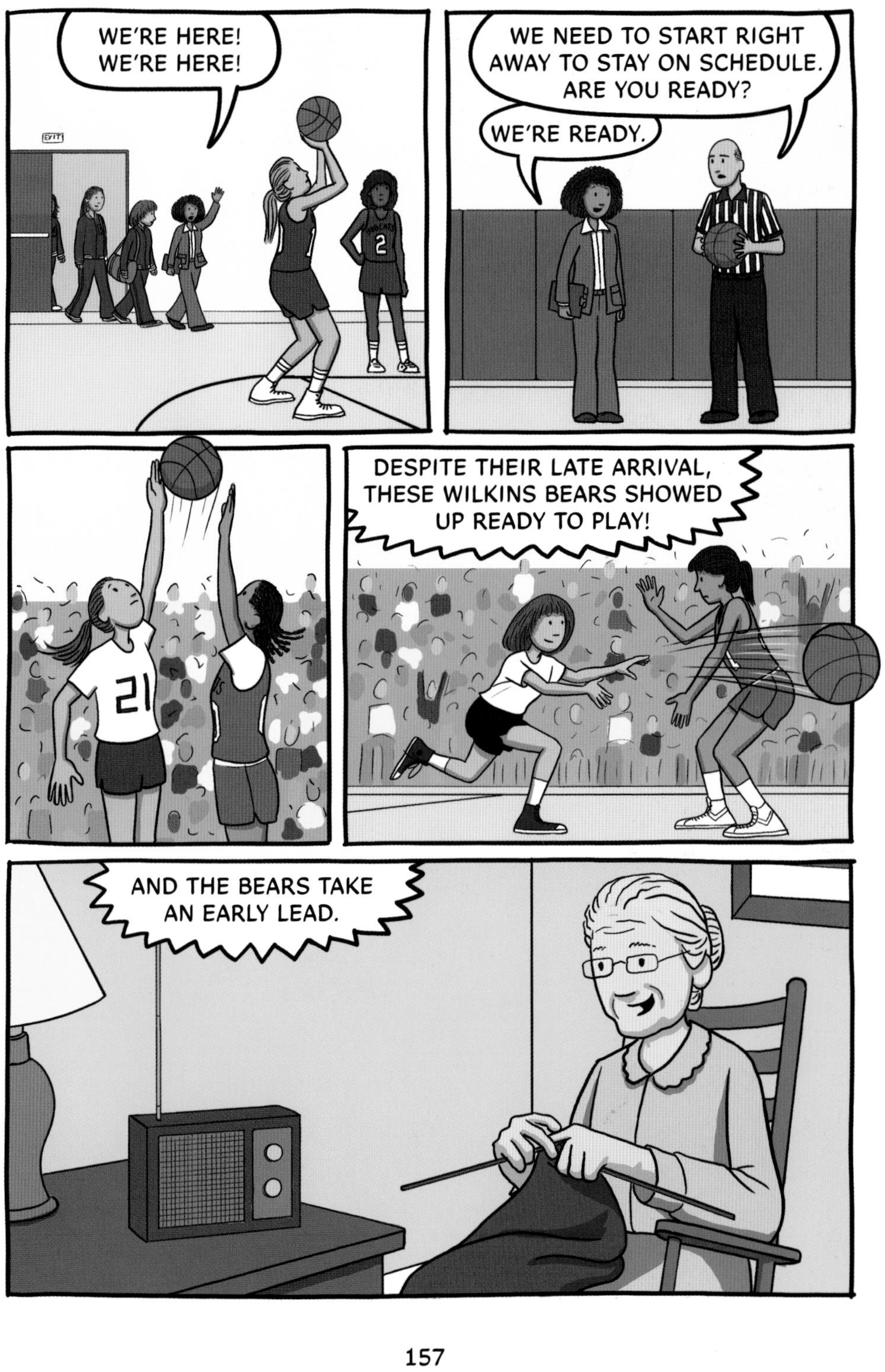

WE'RE HERE! WE'RE HERE!
EXIT
WE NEED TO START RIGHT AWAY TO STAY ON SCHEDULE. ARE YOU READY?
WE'RE READY.
21
DESPITE THEIR LATE ARRIVAL, THESE WILKINS BEARS SHOWED UP READY TO PLAY!
AND THE BEARS TAKE AN EARLY LEAD.

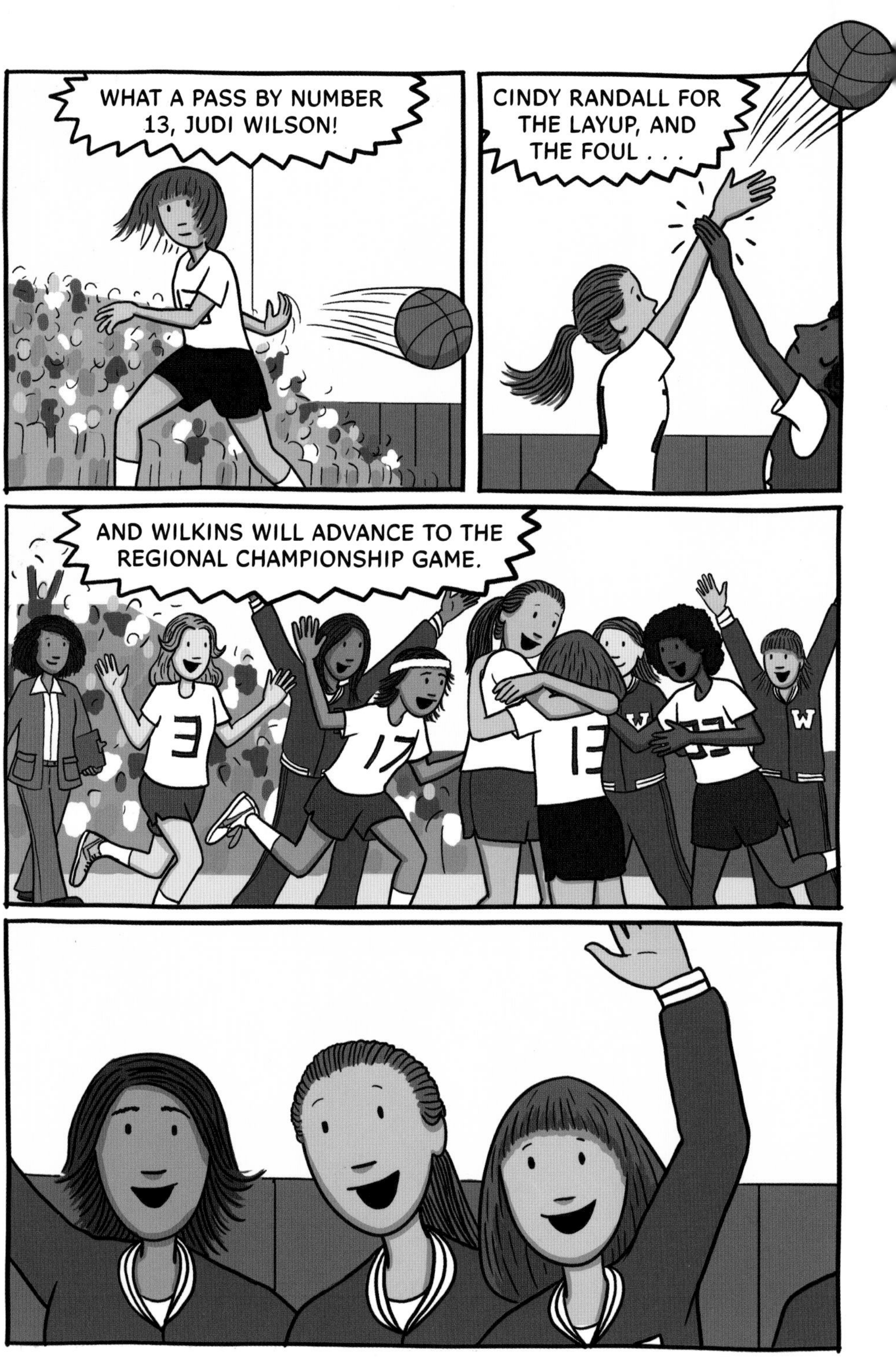
WHAT A PASS BY NUMBER 13, JUDI WILSON!
CINDY RANDALL FOR THE LAYUP, AND THE FOUL . . .
AND WILKINS WILL ADVANCE TO THE REGIONAL CHAMPIONSHIP GAME.

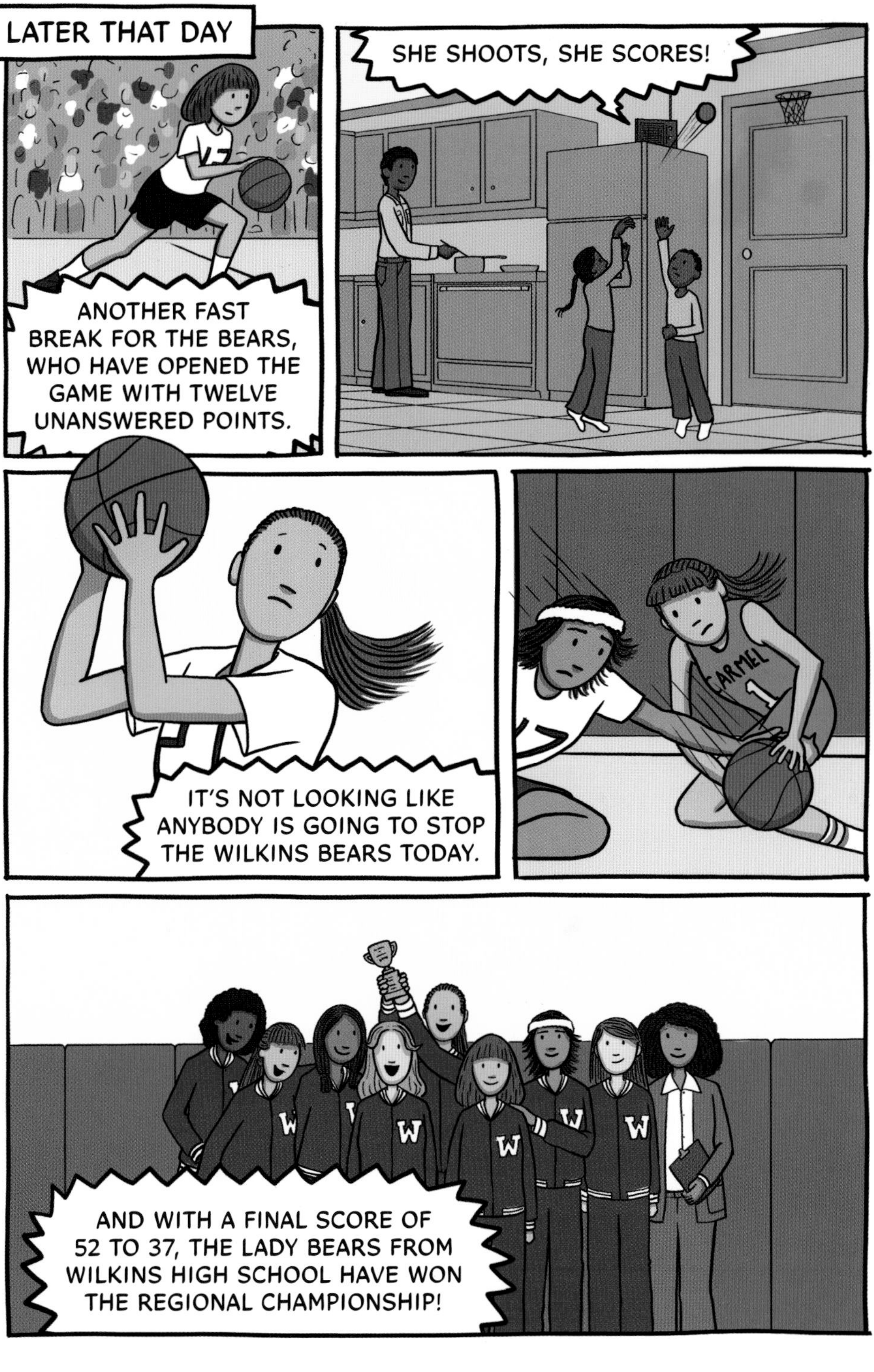
LATER THAT DAY
ANOTHER FAST BREAK FOR THE BEARS, WHO HAVE OPENED THE GAME WITH TWELVE UNANSWERED POINTS.
SHE SHOOTS, SHE SCORES!
IT'S NOT LOOKING LIKE ANYBODY IS GOING TO STOP THE WILKINS BEARS TODAY.
CARMEL 1
AND WITH A FINAL SCORE OF 52 TO 37, THE LADY BEARS FROM WILKINS HIGH SCHOOL HAVE WON THE REGIONAL CHAMPIONSHIP!

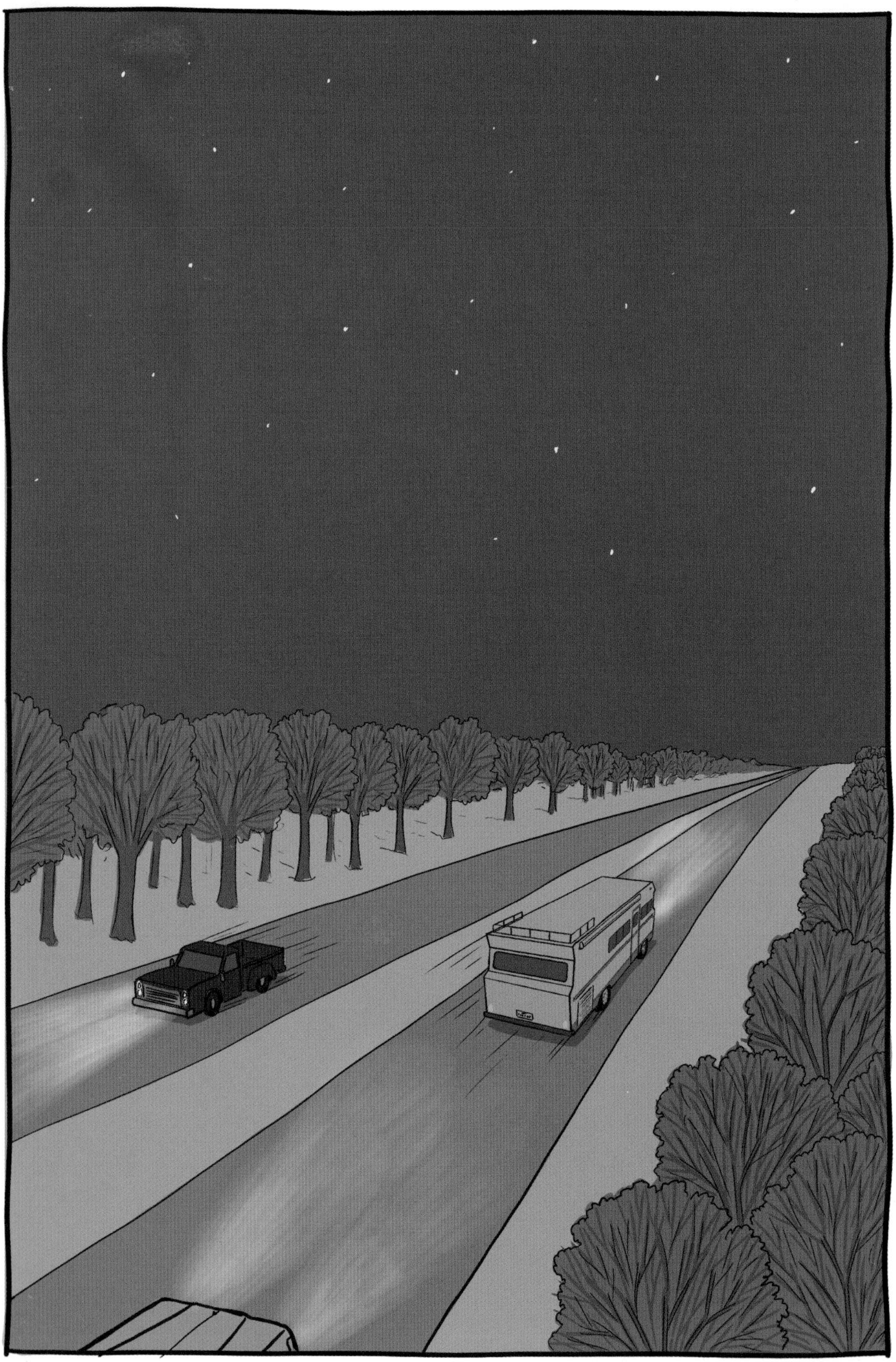

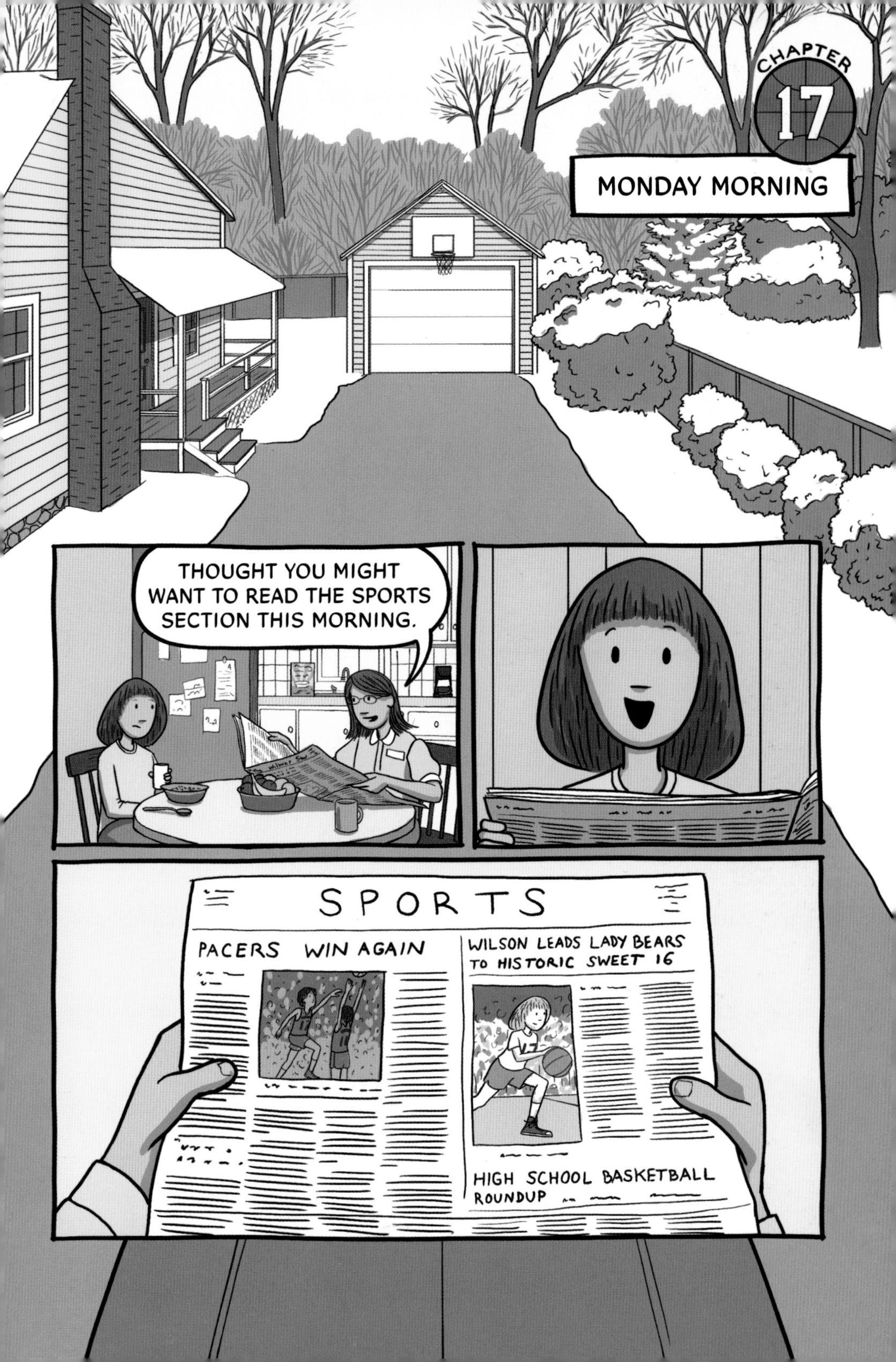
CHAPTER 17
MONDAY MORNING
THOUGHT YOU MIGHT WANT TO READ THE SPORTS SECTION THIS MORNING.
SPORTS
PACERS WIN AGAIN
WILSON LEADS LADY BEARS TO HISTORIC SWEET 16
HIGH SCHOOL BASKETBALL ROUNDUP

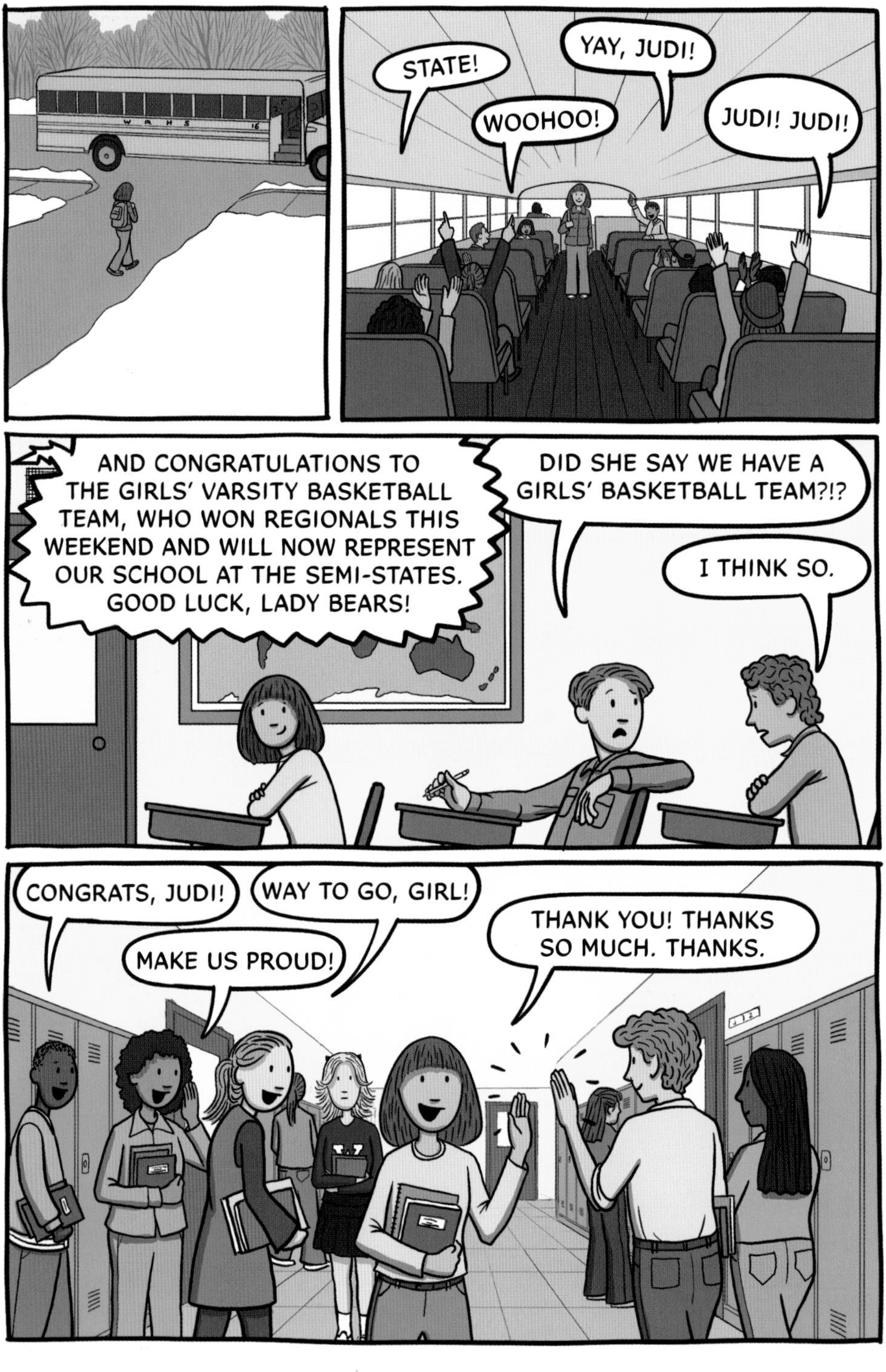
STATE!
WOOHOO!
YAY, JUDI!
JUDI! JUDI!
AND CONGRATULATIONS TO THE GIRLS' VARSITY BASKETBALL TEAM, WHO WON REGIONALS THIS WEEKEND AND WILL NOW REPRESENT OUR SCHOOL AT THE SEMI-STATES. GOOD LUCK, LADY BEARS!
DID SHE SAY WE HAVE A GIRLS' BASKETBALL TEAM?!?
I THINK SO.
CONGRATS, JUDI!
WAY TO GO, GIRL!
MAKE US PROUD!
THANK YOU! THANKS SO MUCH. THANKS.

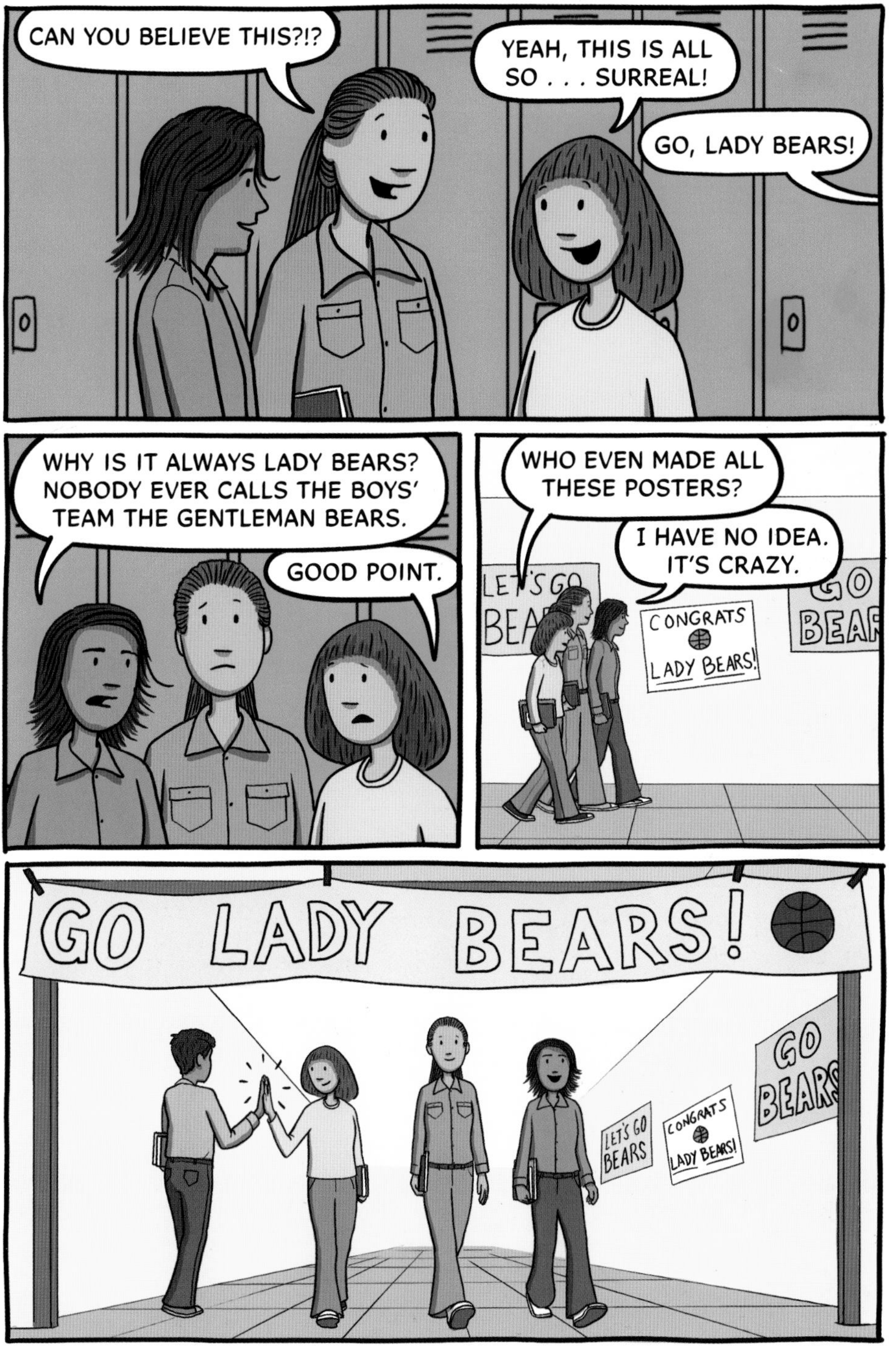
CAN YOU BELIEVE THIS?!?
YEAH, THIS IS ALL SO . . . SURREAL!
GO, LADY BEARS!
WHY IS IT ALWAYS LADY BEARS? NOBODY EVER CALLS THE BOYS' TEAM THE GENTLEMAN BEARS.
GOOD POINT.
WHO EVEN MADE ALL THESE POSTERS?
I HAVE NO IDEA. IT'S CRAZY.
CONGRATS LADY BEARS!
GO BEAR
GO LADY BEARS!
LET'S GO BEARS
CONGRATS LADY BEARS!
GO BEARS

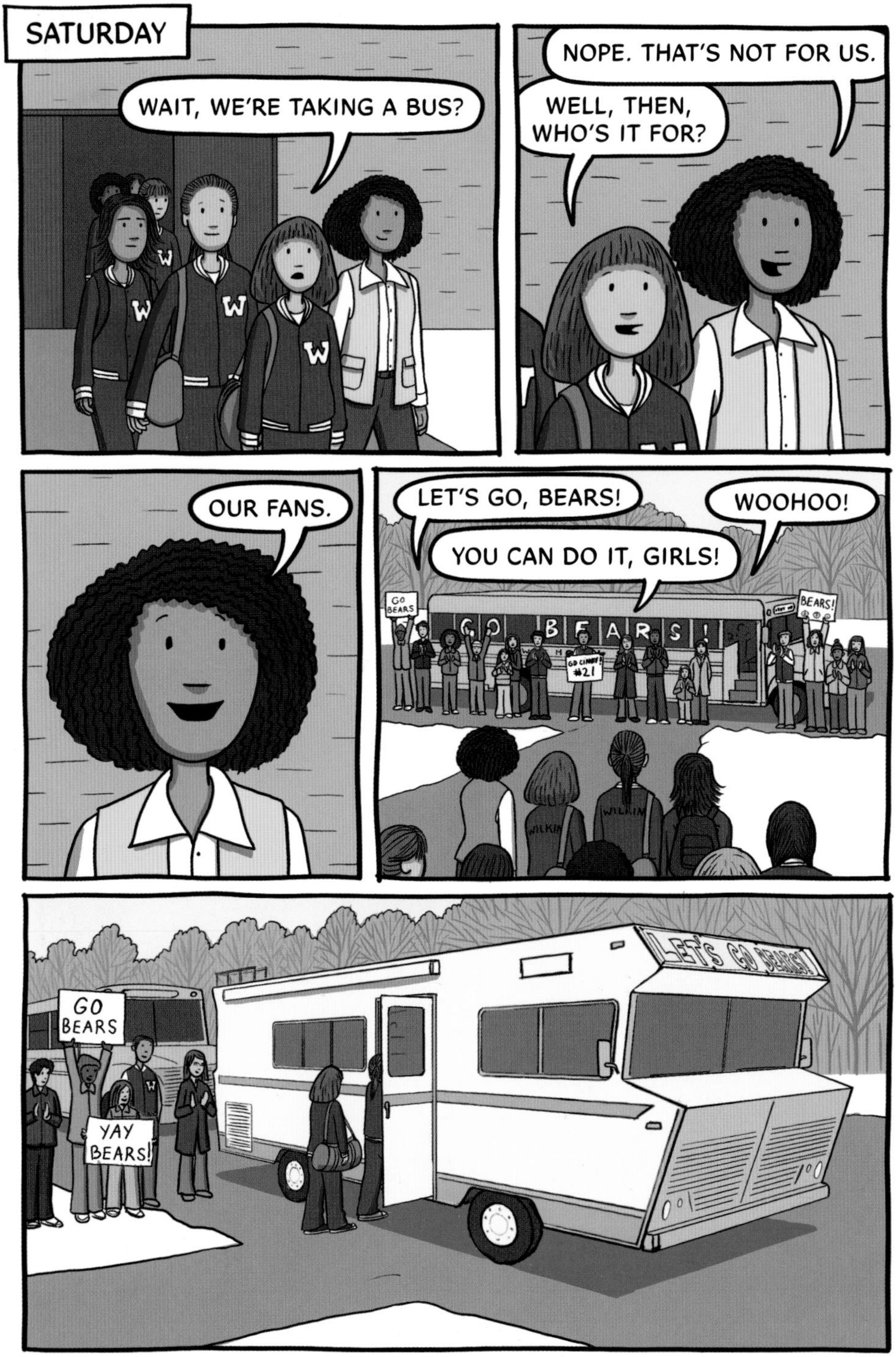
SATURDAY
WAIT, WE'RE TAKING A BUS?
NOPE. THAT'S NOT FOR US.
WELL, THEN, WHO'S IT FOR?
OUR FANS.
LET'S GO, BEARS!
WOOHOO!
YOU CAN DO IT, GIRLS!
GO BEARS
BEARS!
GO BEARS!
LET'S GO BEARS!
GO BEARS
YAY BEARS!

CHAPTER 18
SEMI-STATES

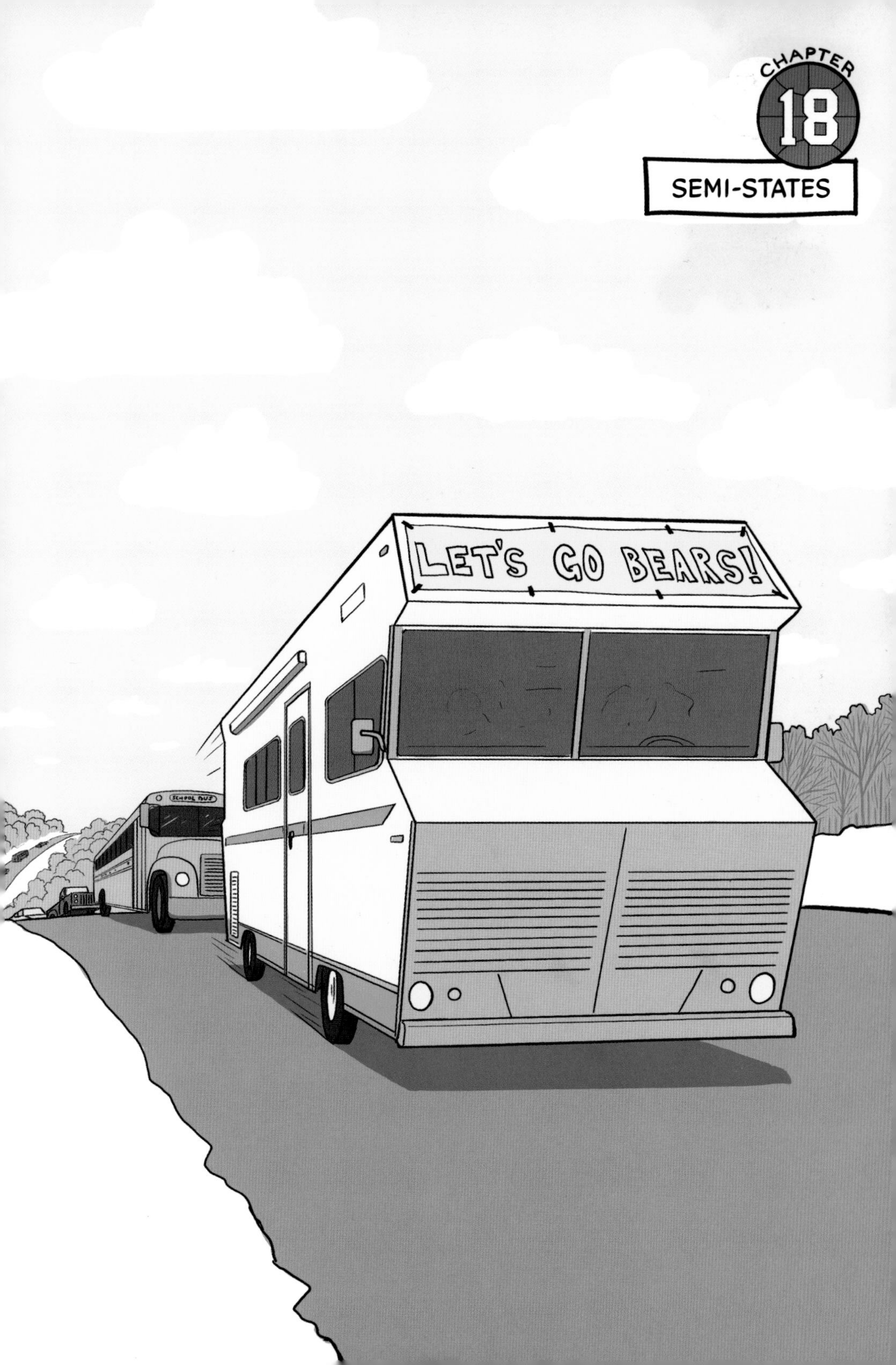
LET'S GO BEARS!
SCHOOL BUS

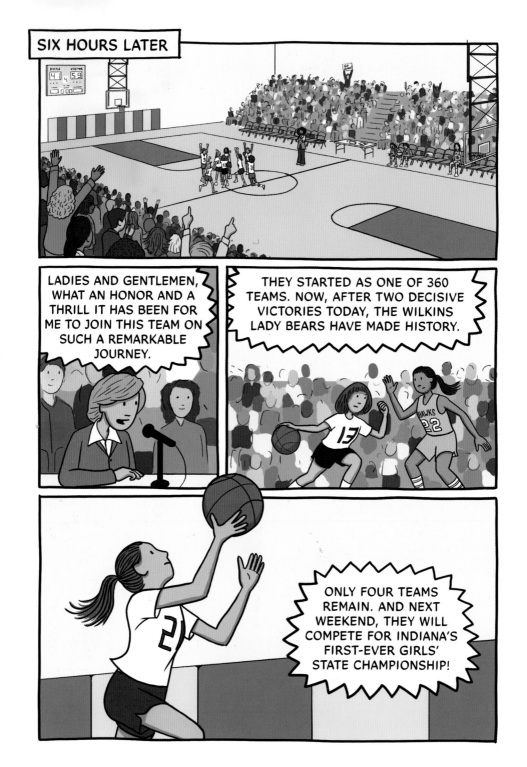

SIX HOURS LATER

LADIES AND GENTLEMEN, WHAT AN HONOR AND A THRILL IT HAS BEEN FOR ME TO JOIN THIS TEAM ON SUCH A REMARKABLE JOURNEY.

THEY STARTED AS ONE OF 360 TEAMS. NOW, AFTER TWO DECISIVE VICTORIES TODAY, THE WILKINS LADY BEARS HAVE MADE HISTORY.

ONLY FOUR TEAMS REMAIN. AND NEXT WEEKEND, THEY WILL COMPETE FOR INDIANA'S FIRST-EVER GIRLS' STATE CHAMPIONSHIP!

166

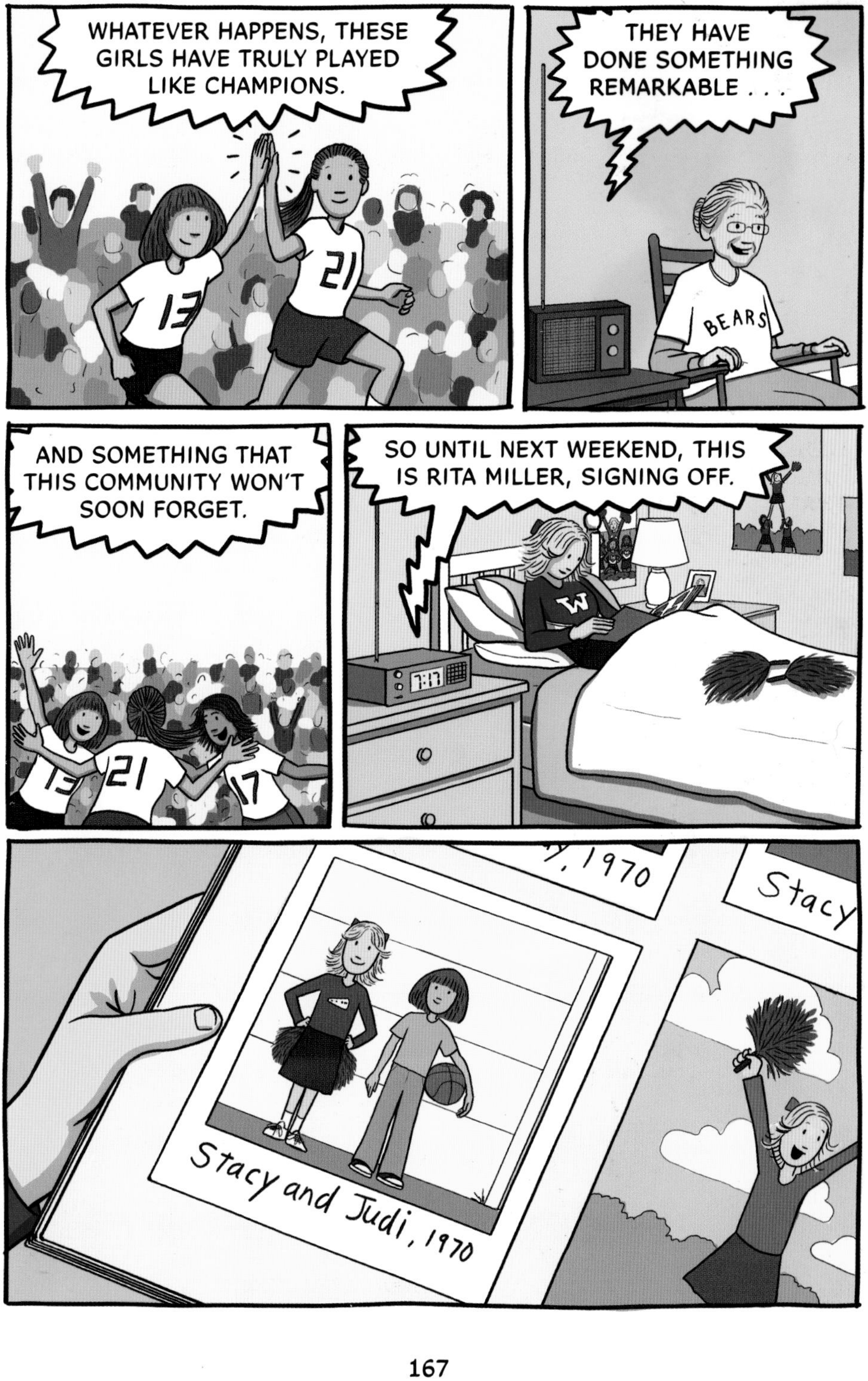
WHATEVER HAPPENS, THESE GIRLS HAVE TRULY PLAYED LIKE CHAMPIONS.
13
21
THEY HAVE DONE SOMETHING REMARKABLE . . .
BEARS
AND SOMETHING THAT THIS COMMUNITY WON'T SOON FORGET.
13
21
17
SO UNTIL NEXT WEEKEND, THIS IS RITA MILLER, SIGNING OFF.
W
7:17
, 1970
Stacy
Stacy and Judi, 1970

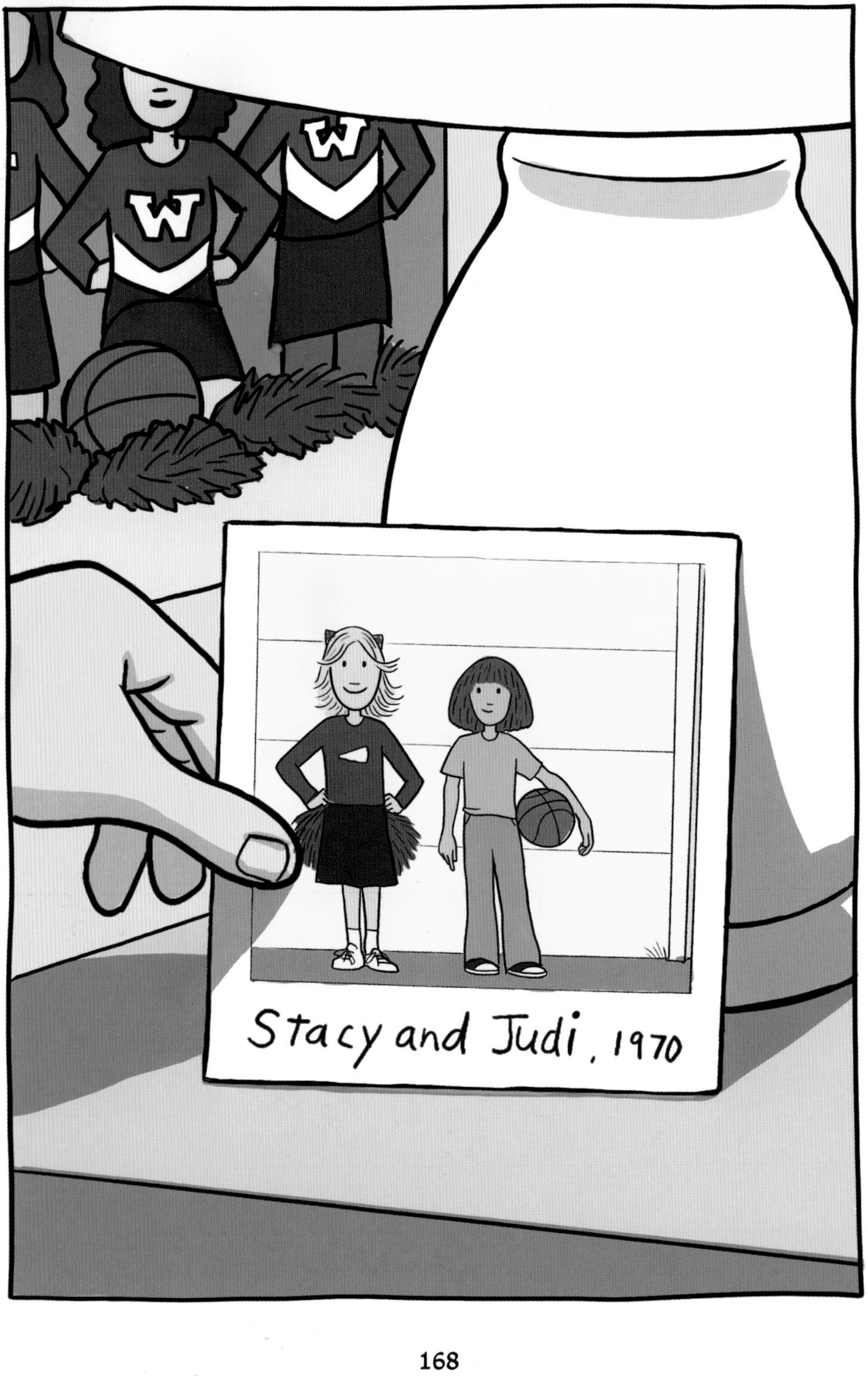
W
W
W
Stacy and Judi, 1970

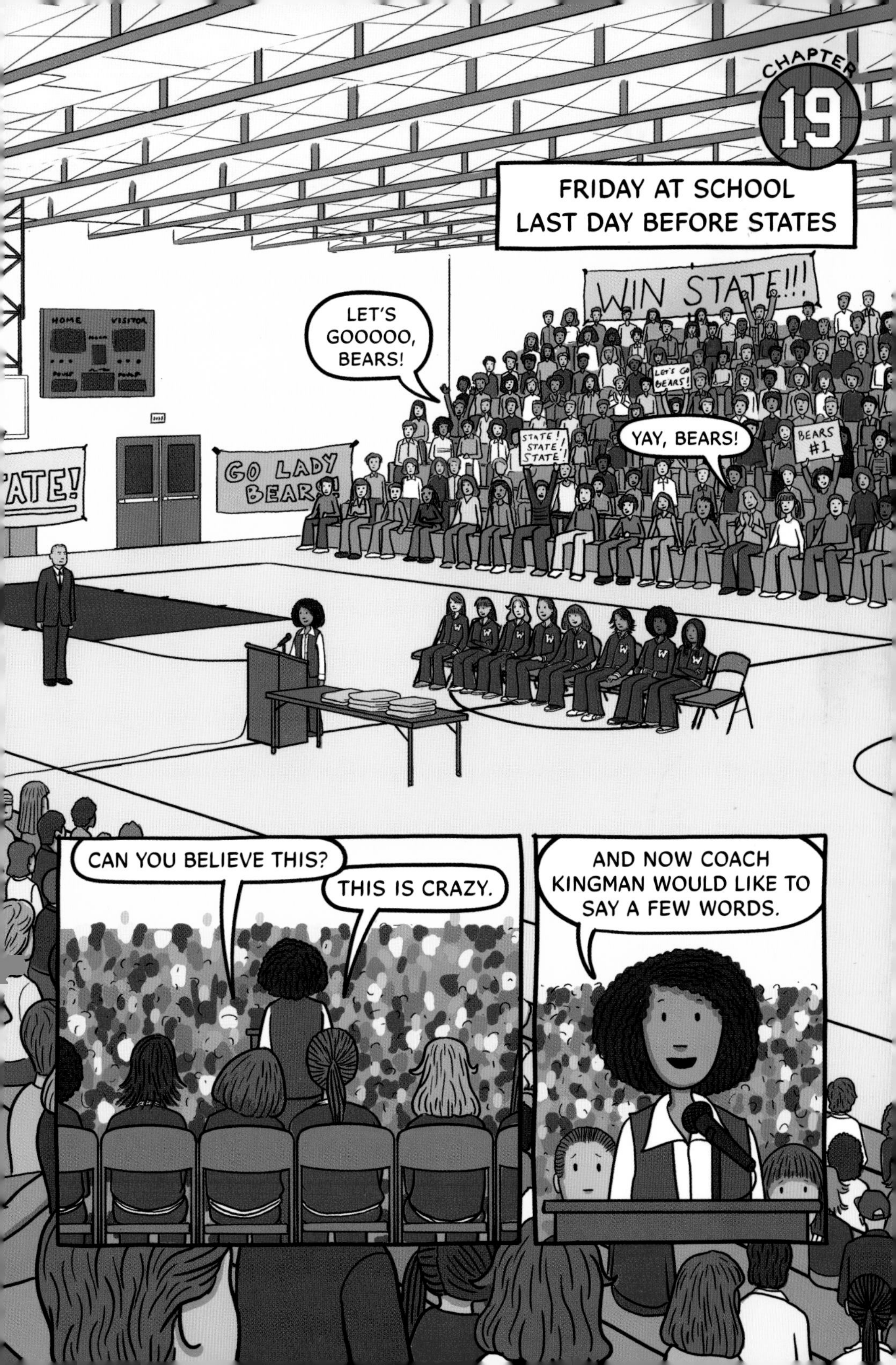
CHAPTER
19
FRIDAY AT SCHOOL
LAST DAY BEFORE STATES
WIN STATE!!!
LET'S GOOOOO, BEARS!
LET'S GO BEARS!
STATE! STATE! STATE!
YAY, BEARS!
BEARS #1
GO LADY BEARS!
CAN YOU BELIEVE THIS?
THIS IS CRAZY.
AND NOW COACH KINGMAN WOULD LIKE TO SAY A FEW WORDS.

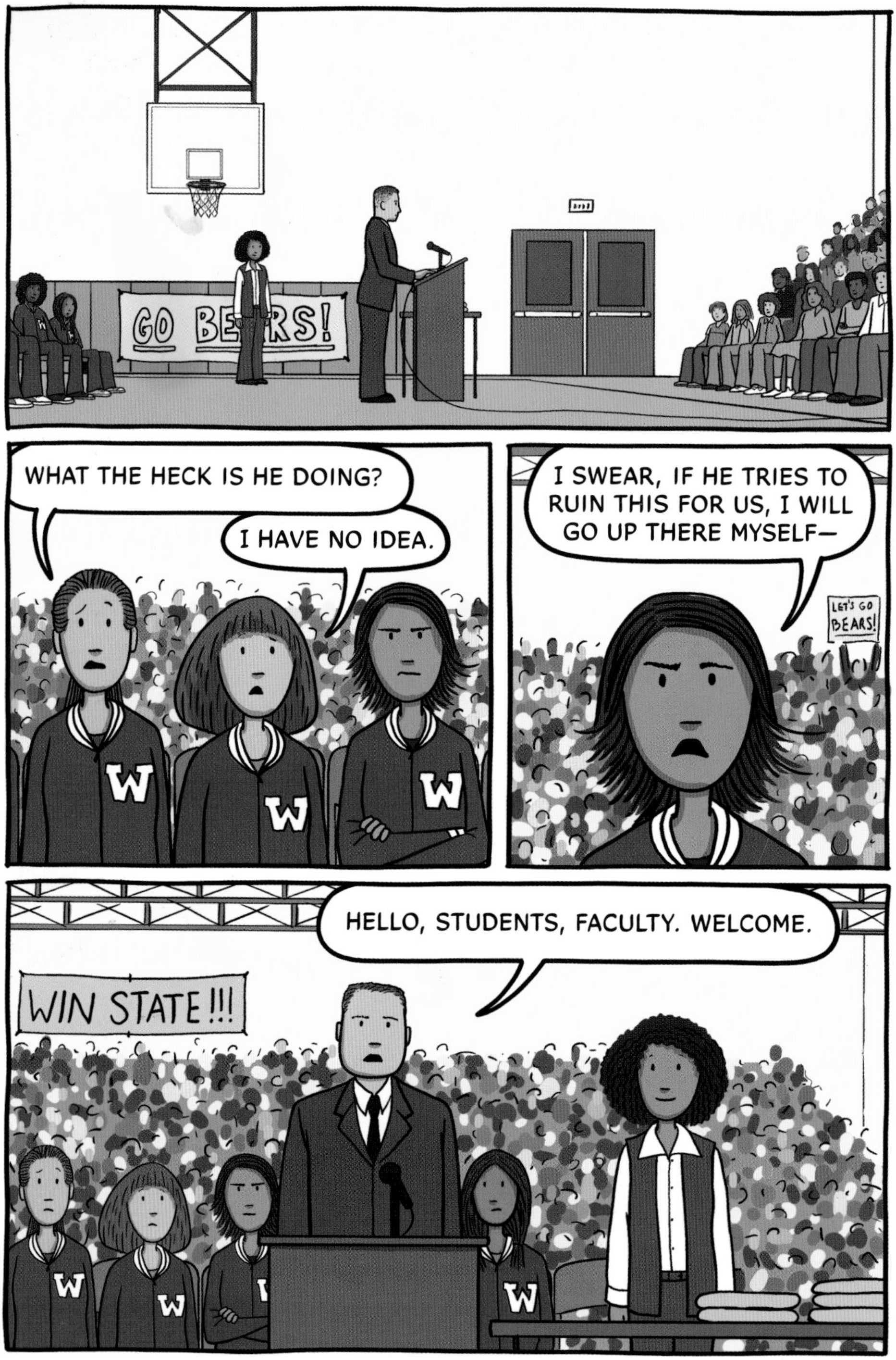
GO BEARS!
WHAT THE HECK IS HE DOING?
I HAVE NO IDEA.
I SWEAR, IF HE TRIES TO RUIN THIS FOR US, I WILL GO UP THERE MYSELF—
LET'S GO BEARS!
HELLO, STUDENTS, FACULTY. WELCOME.
WIN STATE!!!

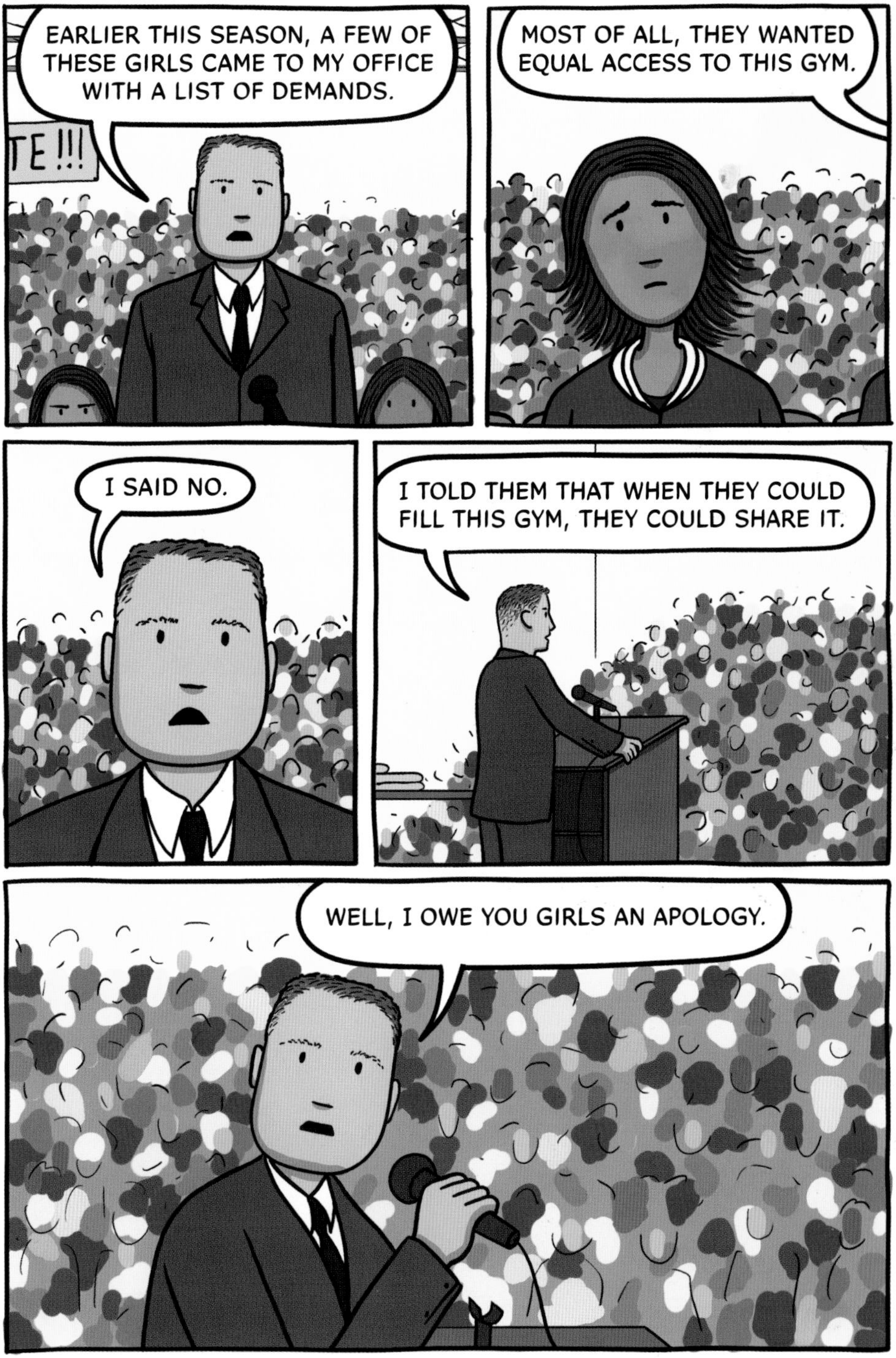
EARLIER THIS SEASON, A FEW OF THESE GIRLS CAME TO MY OFFICE WITH A LIST OF DEMANDS.
MOST OF ALL, THEY WANTED EQUAL ACCESS TO THIS GYM.
I SAID NO.
I TOLD THEM THAT WHEN THEY COULD FILL THIS GYM, THEY COULD SHARE IT.
WELL, I OWE YOU GIRLS AN APOLOGY.

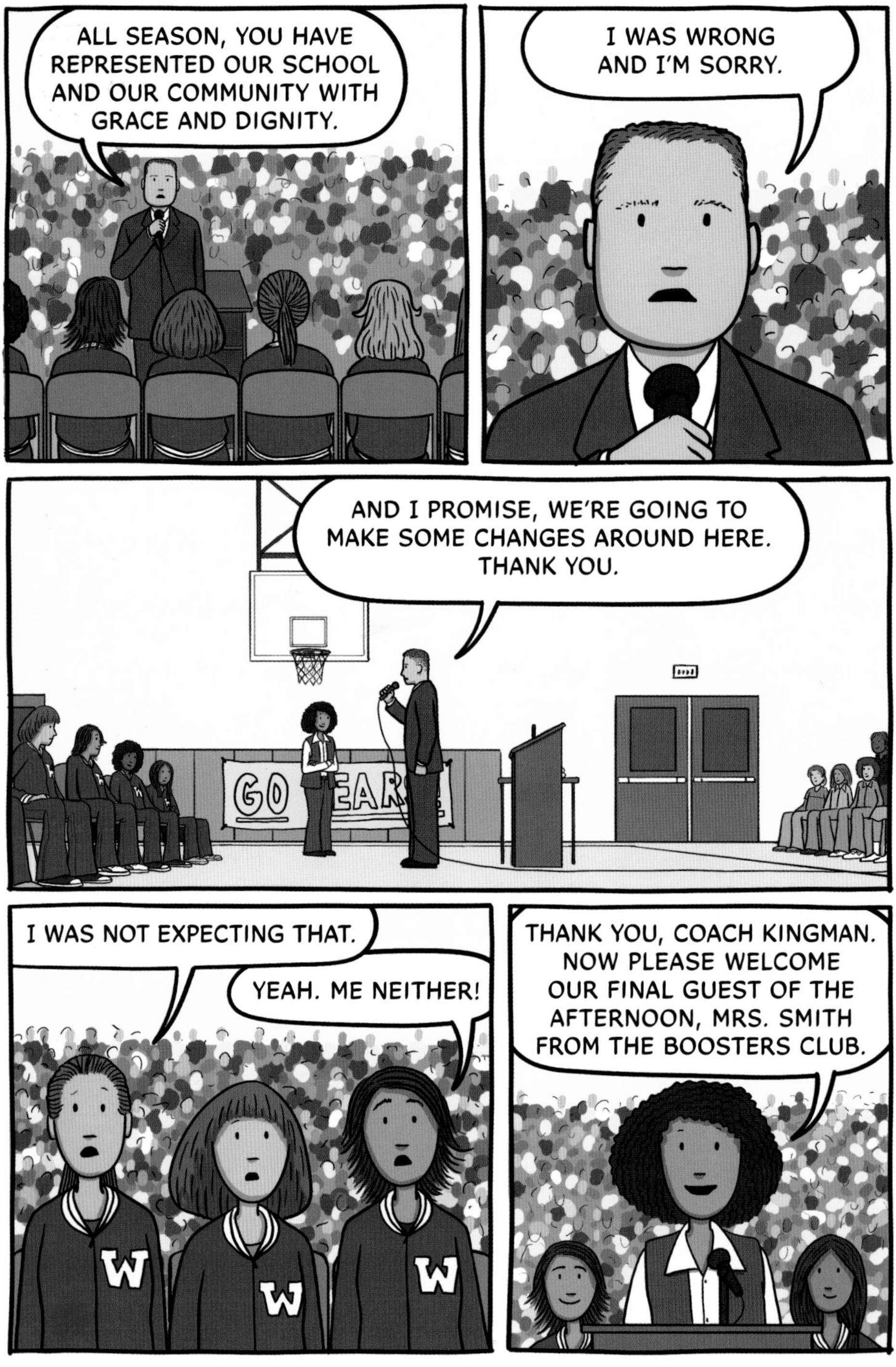

ALL SEASON, YOU HAVE REPRESENTED OUR SCHOOL AND OUR COMMUNITY WITH GRACE AND DIGNITY.
I WAS WRONG AND I'M SORRY.
AND I PROMISE, WE'RE GOING TO MAKE SOME CHANGES AROUND HERE. THANK YOU.
GO
I WAS NOT EXPECTING THAT.
YEAH. ME NEITHER!
THANK YOU, COACH KINGMAN. NOW PLEASE WELCOME OUR FINAL GUEST OF THE AFTERNOON, MRS. SMITH FROM THE BOOSTERS CLUB.

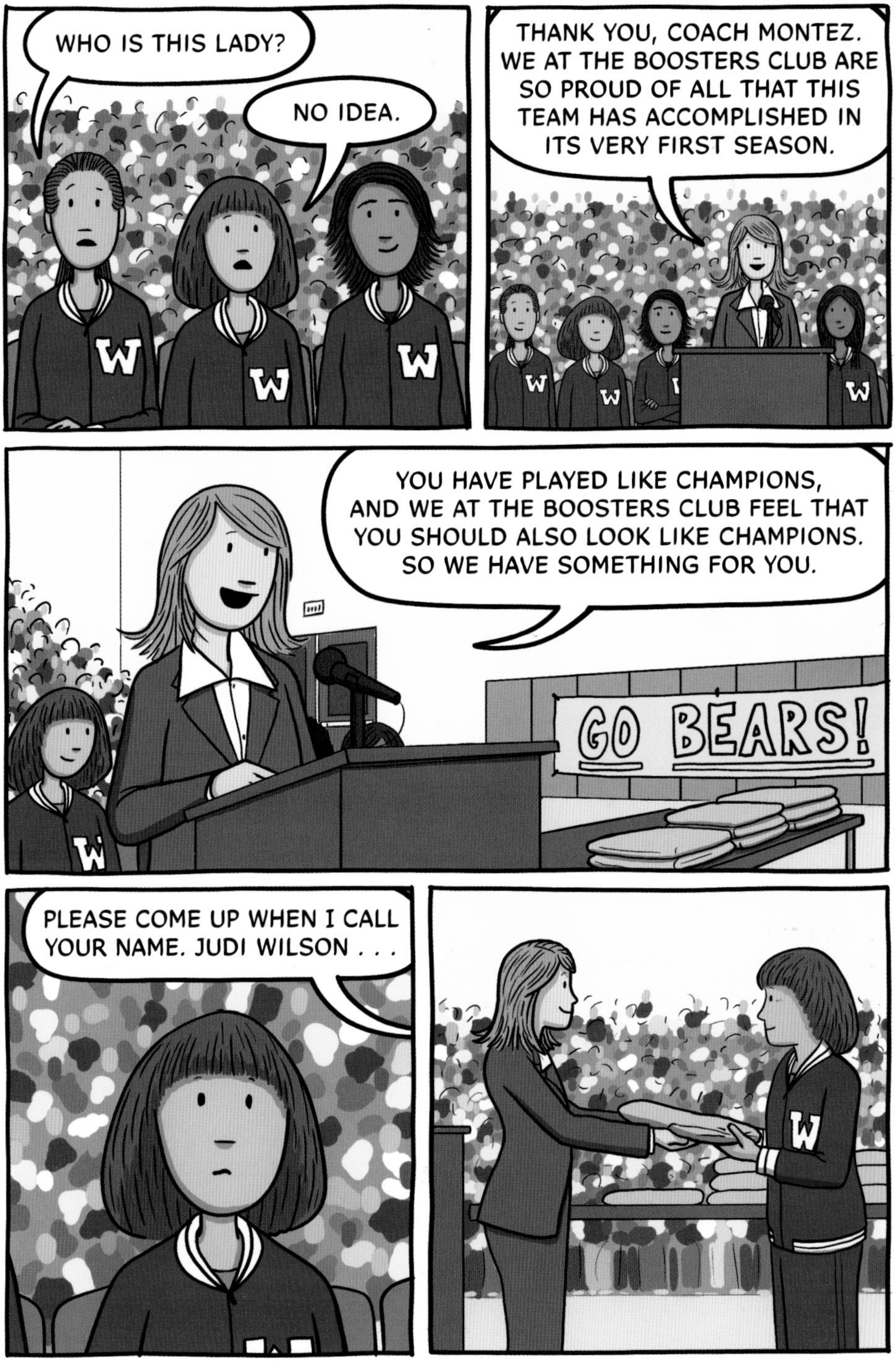
WHO IS THIS LADY?
NO IDEA.
THANK YOU, COACH MONTEZ. WE AT THE BOOSTERS CLUB ARE SO PROUD OF ALL THAT THIS TEAM HAS ACCOMPLISHED IN ITS VERY FIRST SEASON.
YOU HAVE PLAYED LIKE CHAMPIONS, AND WE AT THE BOOSTERS CLUB FEEL THAT YOU SHOULD ALSO LOOK LIKE CHAMPIONS. SO WE HAVE SOMETHING FOR YOU.
GO BEARS!
PLEASE COME UP WHEN I CALL YOUR NAME. JUDI WILSON . . .

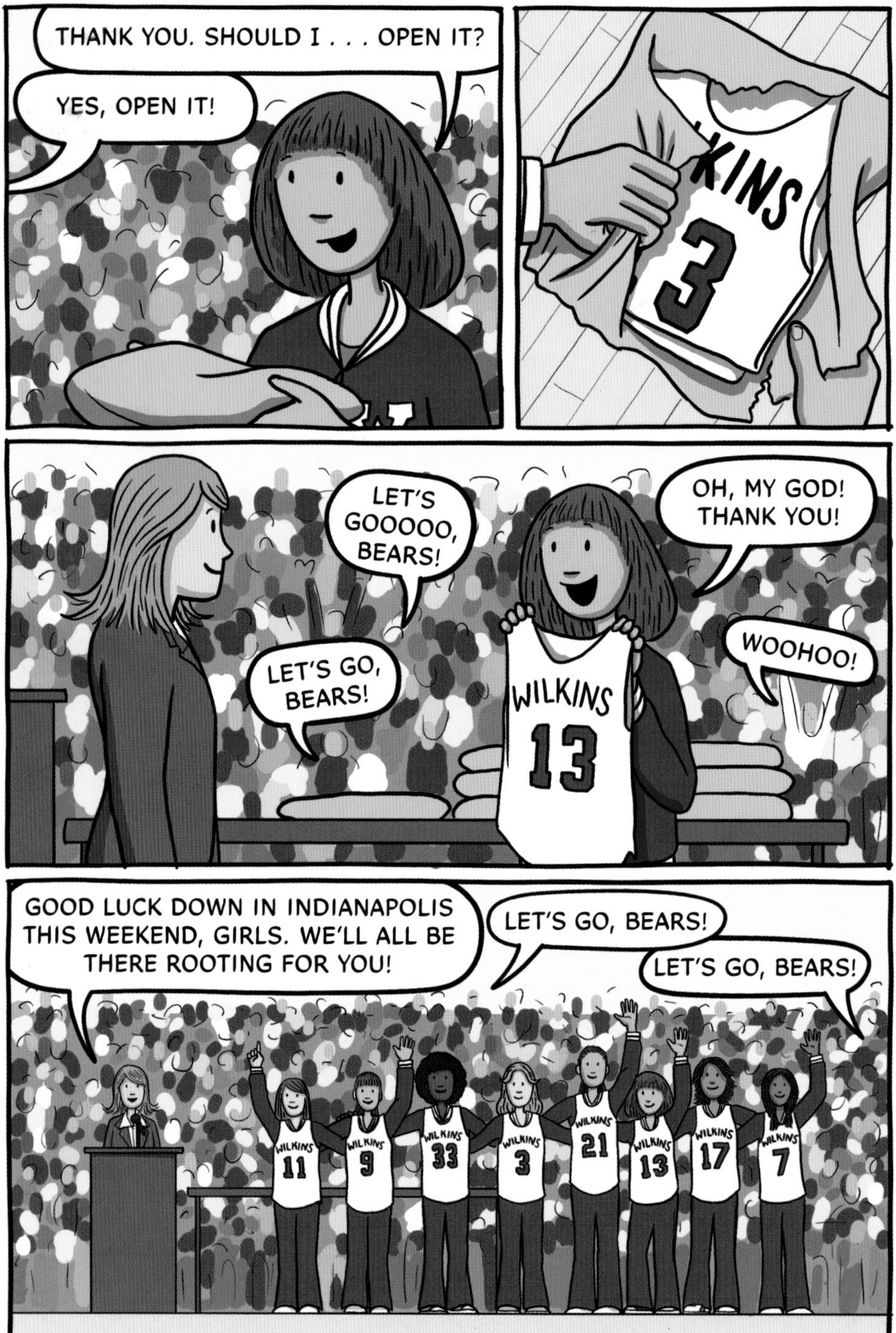
THANK YOU. SHOULD I . . . OPEN IT?
YES, OPEN IT!
KINS
3
LET'S GOOOOO, BEARS!
OH, MY GOD! THANK YOU!
WOOHOO!
LET'S GO, BEARS!
WILKINS
13
GOOD LUCK DOWN IN INDIANAPOLIS THIS WEEKEND, GIRLS. WE'LL ALL BE THERE ROOTING FOR YOU!
LET'S GO, BEARS!
LET'S GO, BEARS!

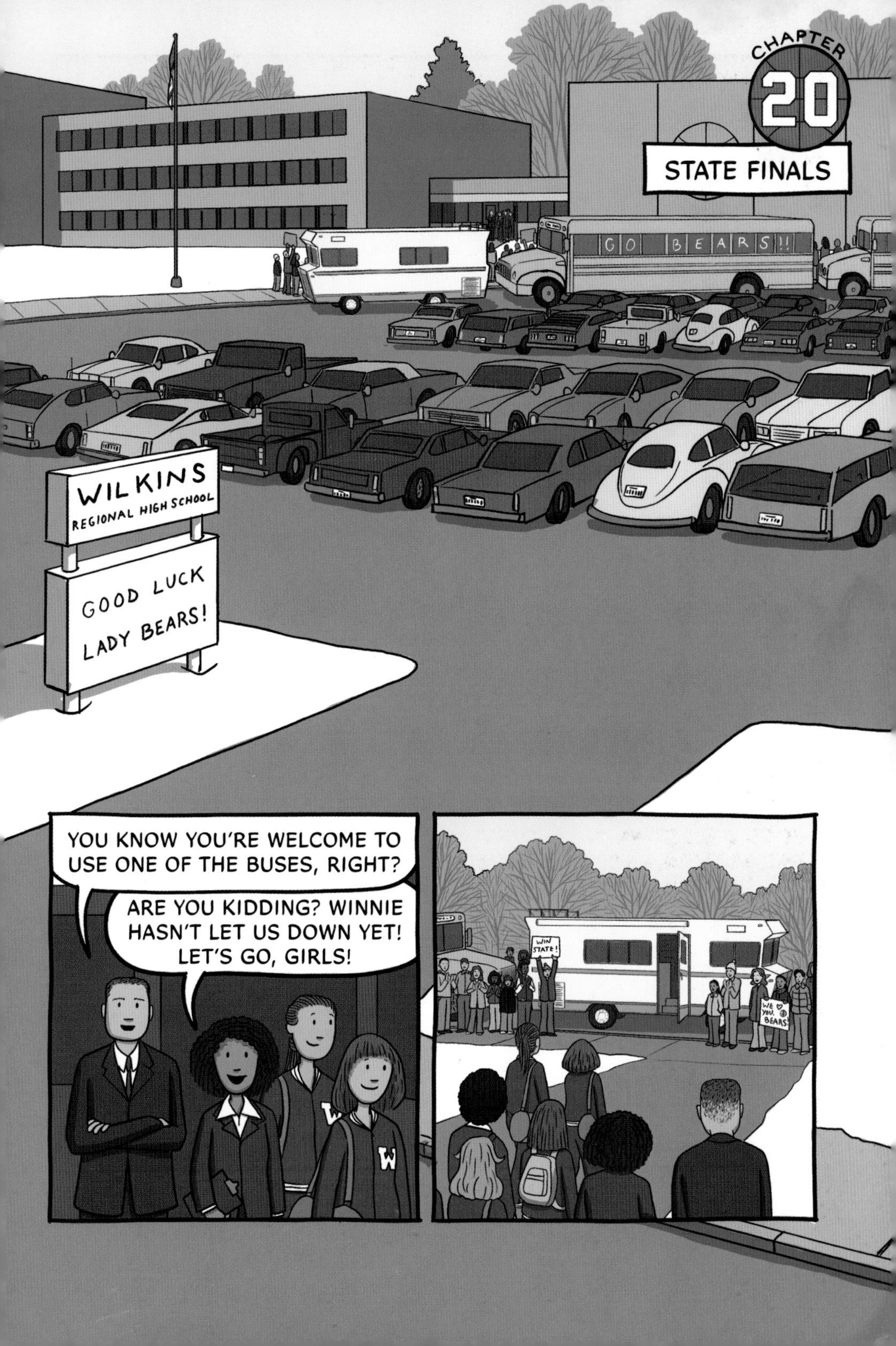
CHAPTER
20
STATE FINALS
GO BEARS!!
WILKINS REGIONAL HIGH SCHOOL
GOOD LUCK LADY BEARS!
YOU KNOW YOU'RE WELCOME TO USE ONE OF THE BUSES, RIGHT?
ARE YOU KIDDING? WINNIE HASN'T LET US DOWN YET! LET'S GO, GIRLS!
WIN STATE!
WE ♥ YOU, BEARS!

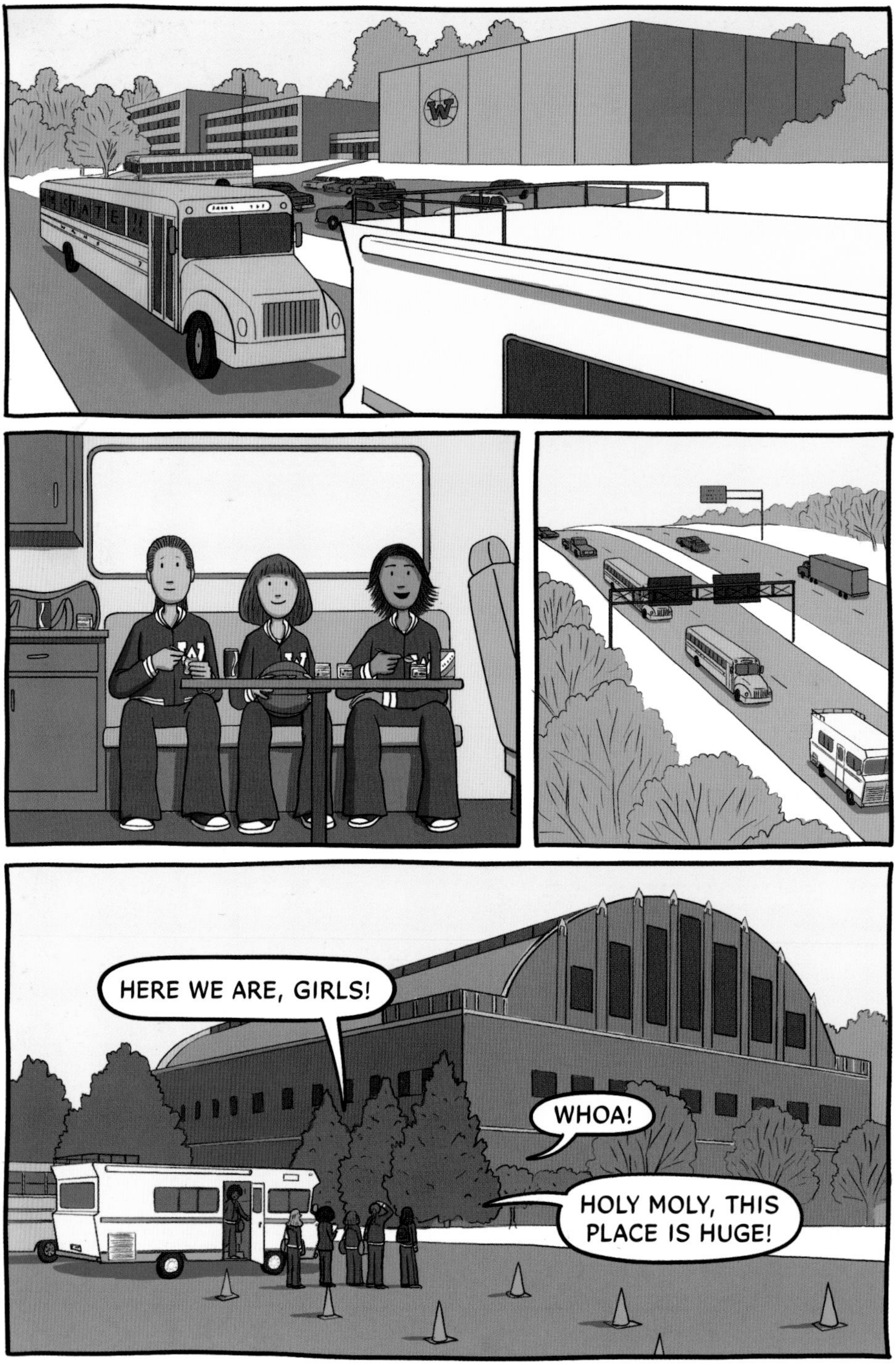
HERE WE ARE, GIRLS!
WHOA!
HOLY MOLY, THIS PLACE IS HUGE!

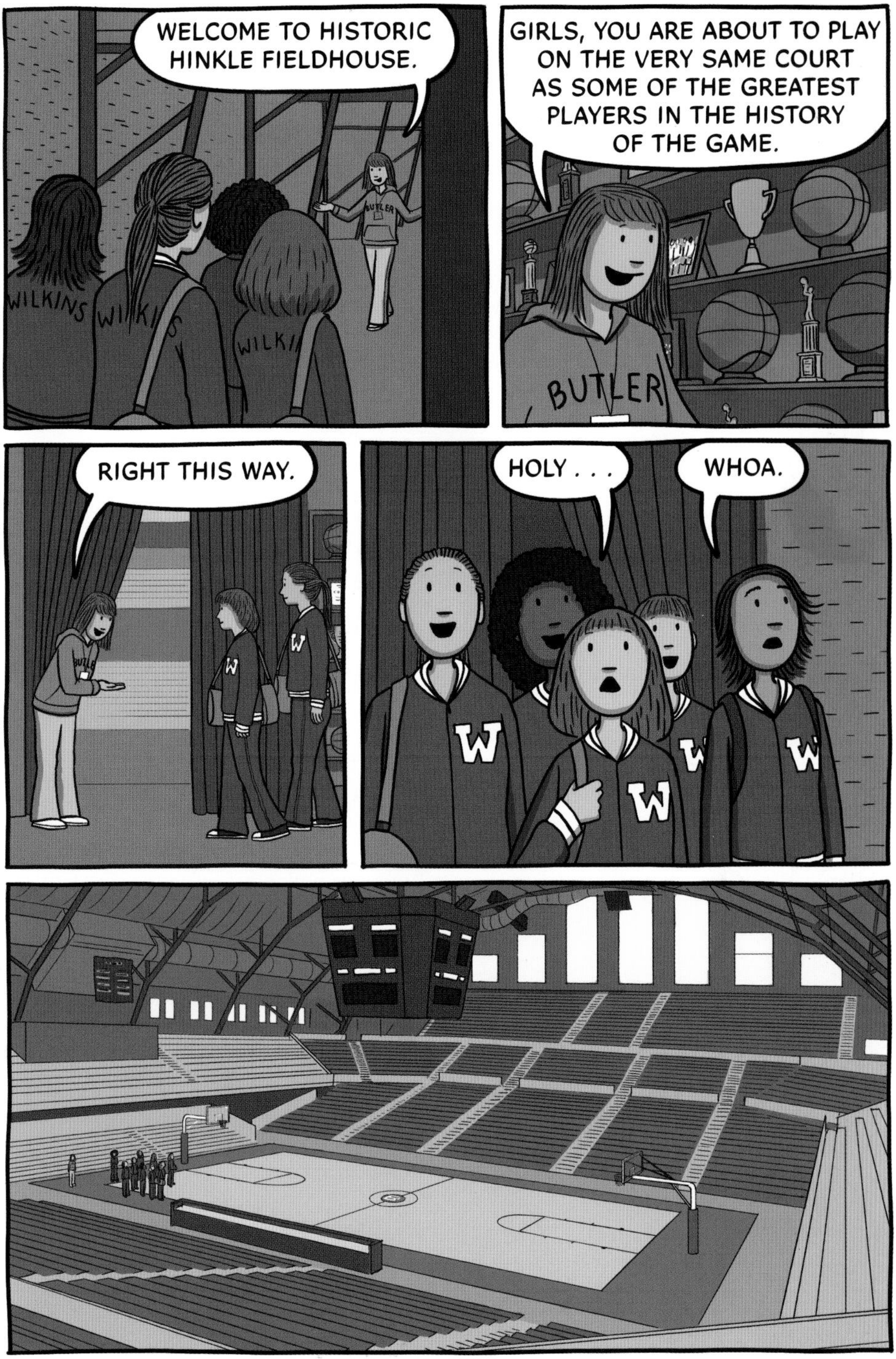
WELCOME TO HISTORIC HINKLE FIELDHOUSE.
GIRLS, YOU ARE ABOUT TO PLAY ON THE VERY SAME COURT AS SOME OF THE GREATEST PLAYERS IN THE HISTORY OF THE GAME.
BUTLER
RIGHT THIS WAY.
HOLY . . .
WHOA.

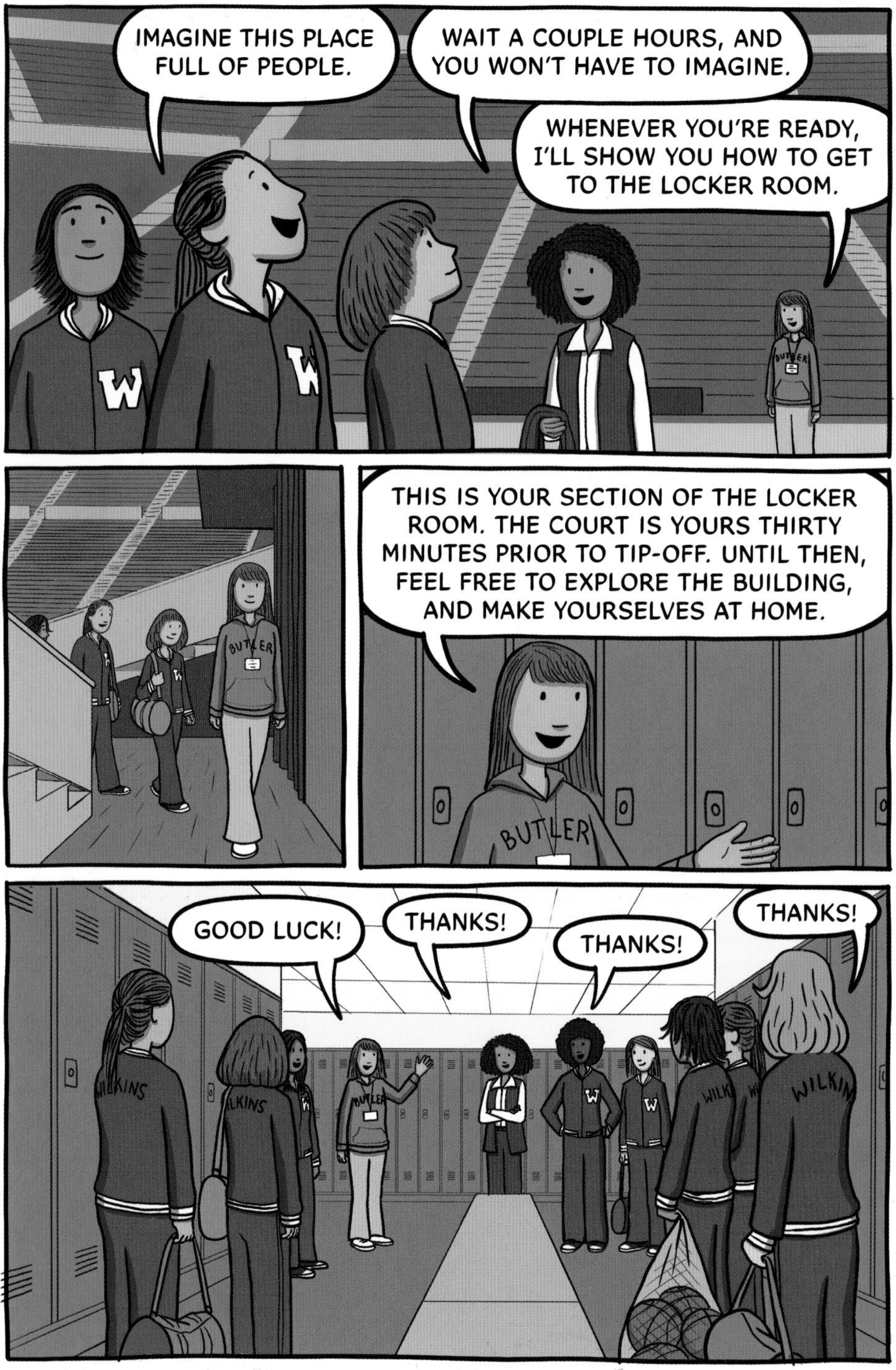
IMAGINE THIS PLACE FULL OF PEOPLE.
WAIT A COUPLE HOURS, AND YOU WON'T HAVE TO IMAGINE.
WHENEVER YOU'RE READY, I'LL SHOW YOU HOW TO GET TO THE LOCKER ROOM.
BUTLER
BUTLER
THIS IS YOUR SECTION OF THE LOCKER ROOM. THE COURT IS YOURS THIRTY MINUTES PRIOR TO TIP-OFF. UNTIL THEN, FEEL FREE TO EXPLORE THE BUILDING, AND MAKE YOURSELVES AT HOME.
BUTLER
GOOD LUCK!
THANKS!
THANKS!
THANKS!

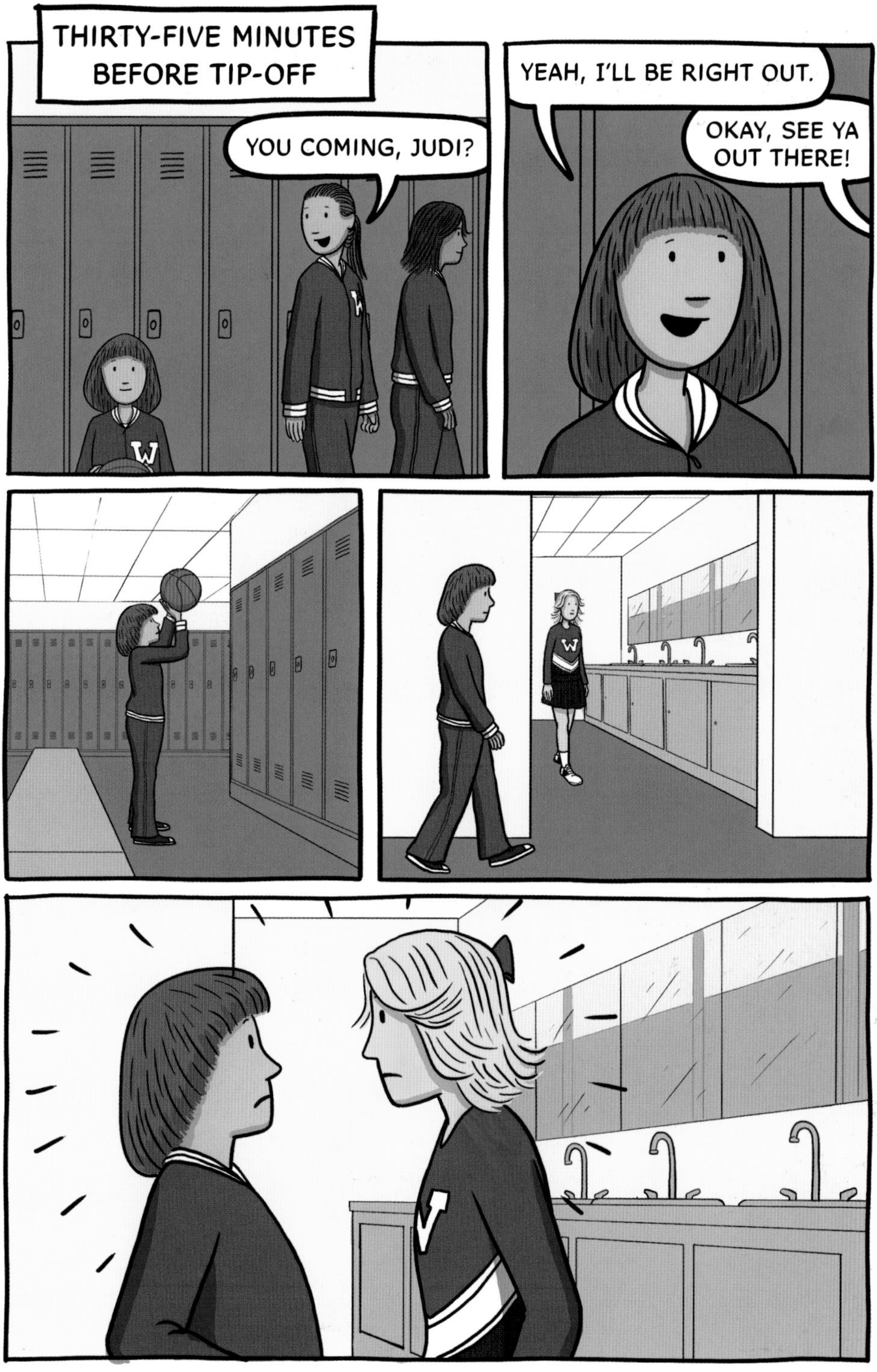
THIRTY-FIVE MINUTES BEFORE TIP-OFF
YOU COMING, JUDI?
YEAH, I'LL BE RIGHT OUT.
OKAY, SEE YA OUT THERE!

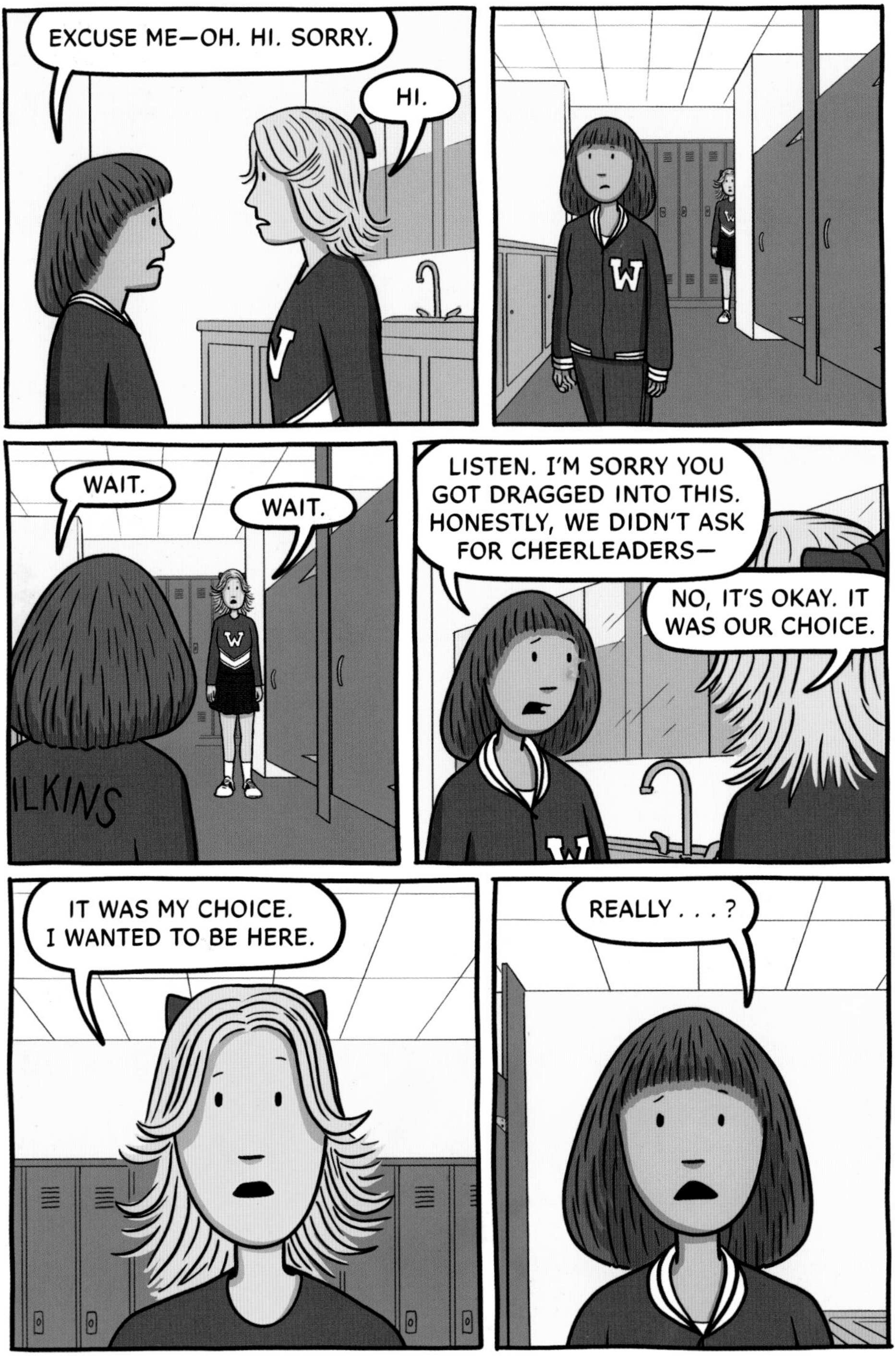
EXCUSE ME—OH. HI. SORRY.
HI.
WAIT.
WAIT.
LISTEN. I'M SORRY YOU GOT DRAGGED INTO THIS. HONESTLY, WE DIDN'T ASK FOR CHEERLEADERS—
NO, IT'S OKAY. IT WAS OUR CHOICE.
IT WAS MY CHOICE. I WANTED TO BE HERE.
REALLY . . . ?

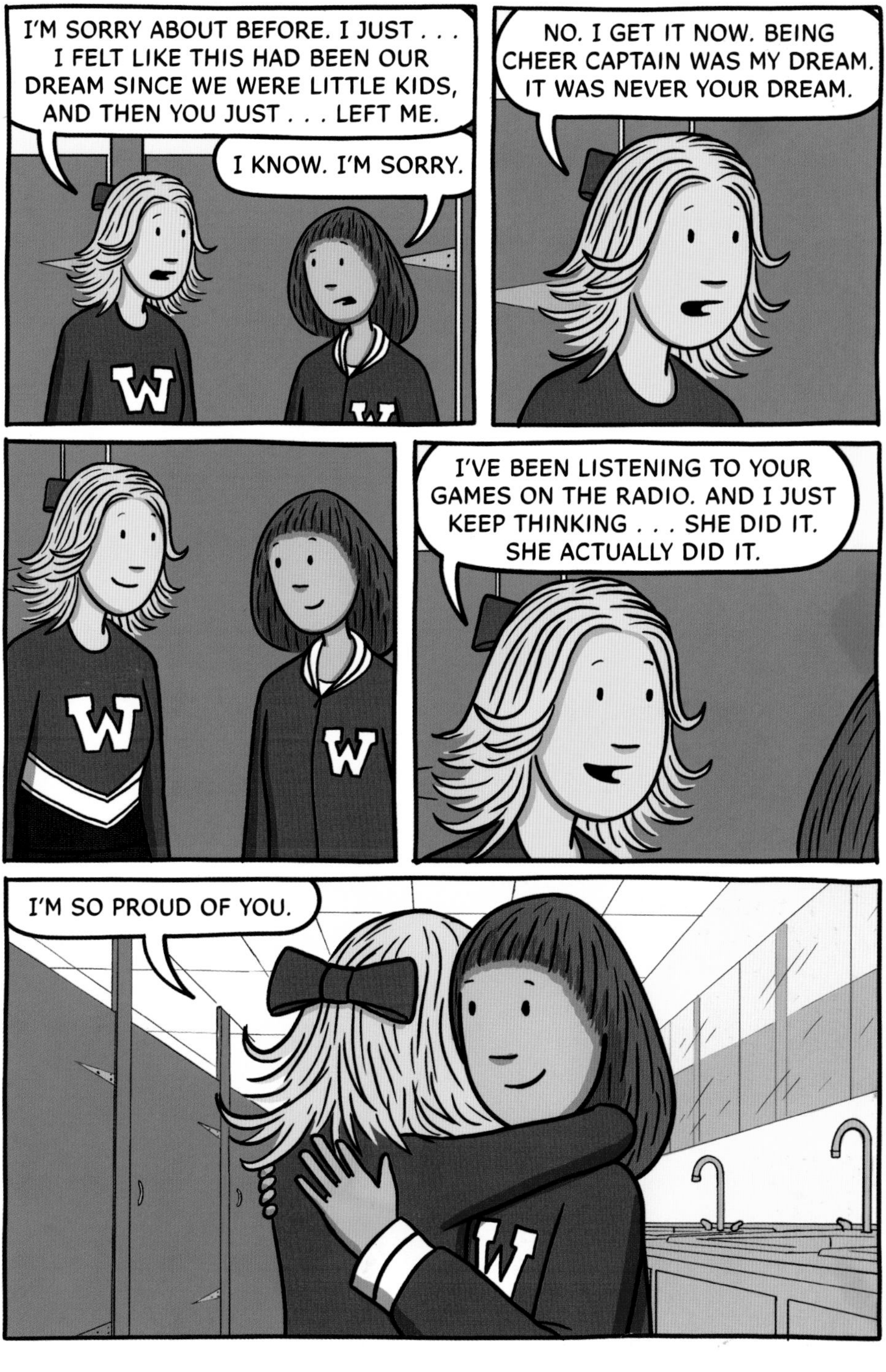
I'M SORRY ABOUT BEFORE. I JUST . . . I FELT LIKE THIS HAD BEEN OUR DREAM SINCE WE WERE LITTLE KIDS, AND THEN YOU JUST . . . LEFT ME.
I KNOW. I'M SORRY.
NO. I GET IT NOW. BEING CHEER CAPTAIN WAS MY DREAM. IT WAS NEVER YOUR DREAM.
I'VE BEEN LISTENING TO YOUR GAMES ON THE RADIO. AND I JUST KEEP THINKING . . . SHE DID IT. SHE ACTUALLY DID IT.
I'M SO PROUD OF YOU.

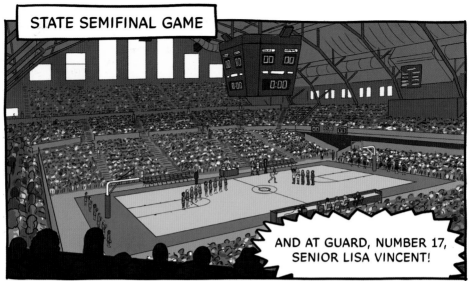

STATE SEMIFINAL GAME

AND AT GUARD, NUMBER 17, SENIOR LISA VINCENT!

ALSO AT GUARD, NUMBER 13, SENIOR JUDI WILSON!

AT CENTER, NUMBER 21, SENIOR CINDY RANDALL!

AND COACHING THE LADY BEARS, COACH MONTEZ!

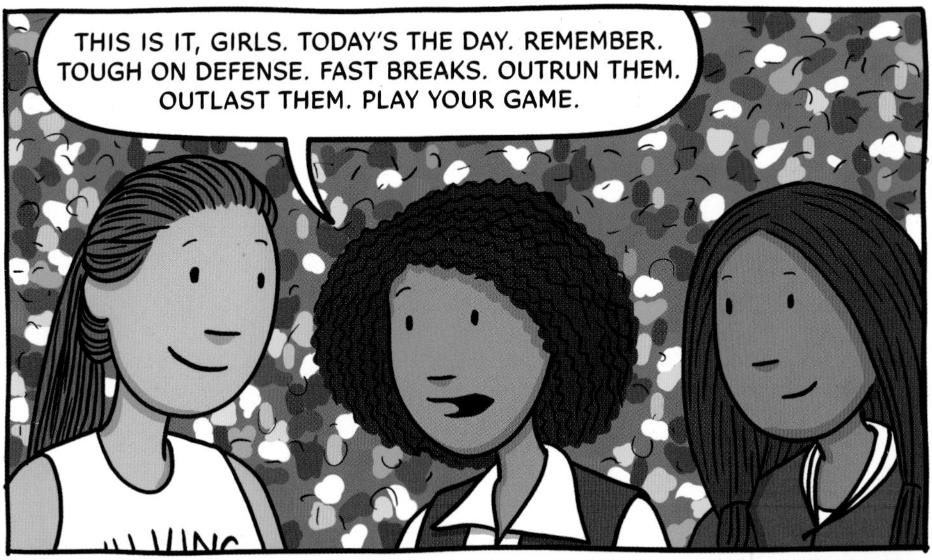
THIS IS IT, GIRLS. TODAY'S THE DAY. REMEMBER. TOUGH ON DEFENSE. FAST BREAKS. OUTRUN THEM. OUTLAST THEM. PLAY YOUR GAME.

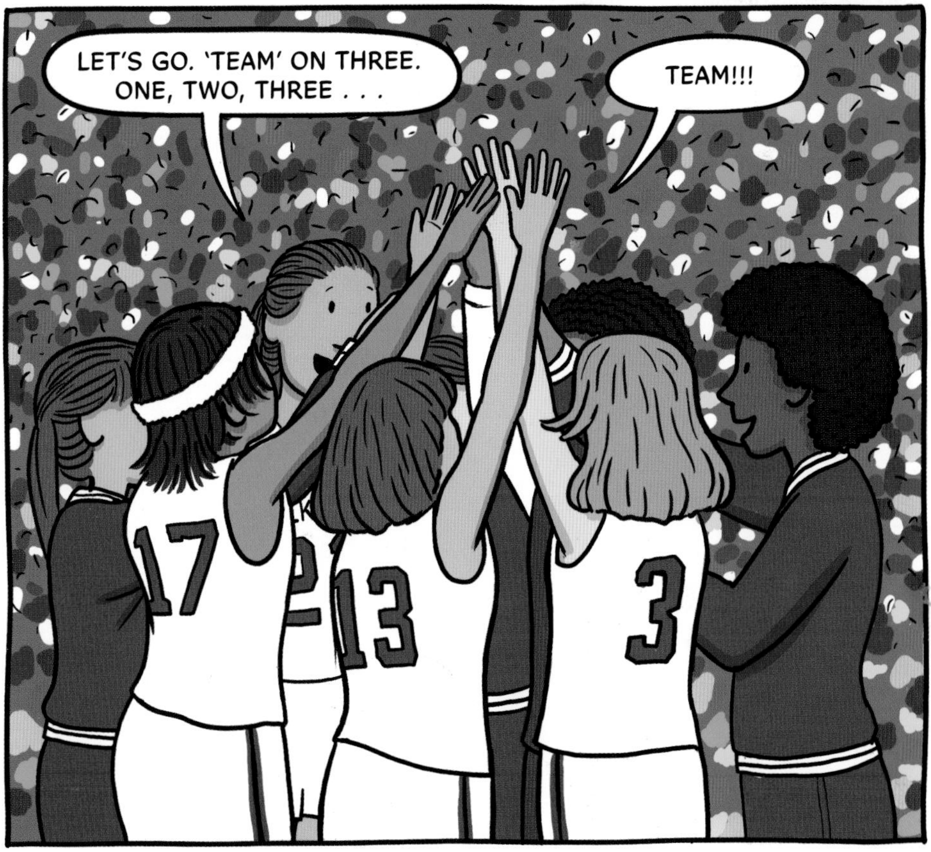
LET'S GO. 'TEAM' ON THREE. ONE, TWO, THREE . . .
TEAM!!!
17
13
3

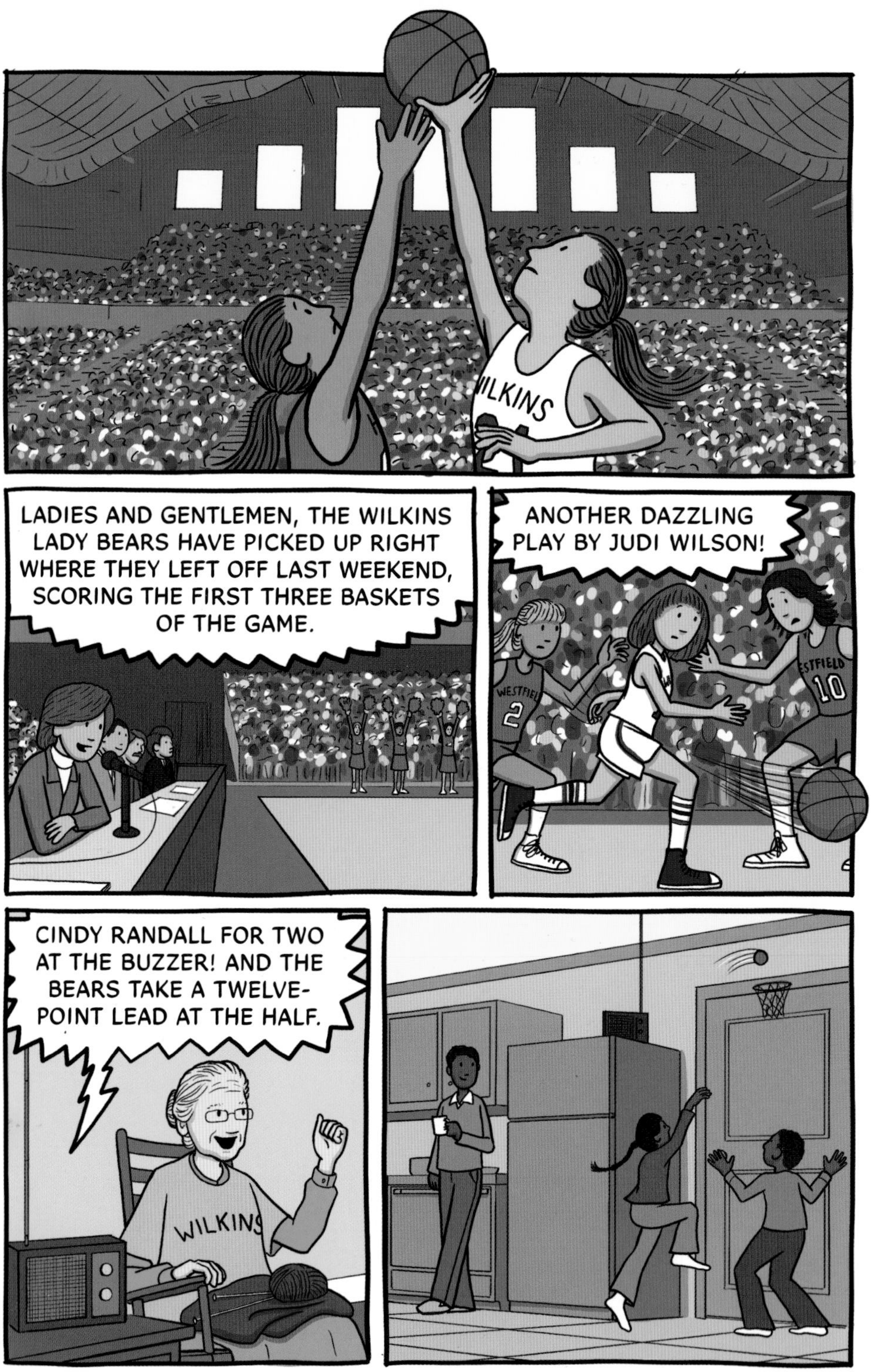
WILKINS
LADIES AND GENTLEMEN, THE WILKINS LADY BEARS HAVE PICKED UP RIGHT WHERE THEY LEFT OFF LAST WEEKEND, SCORING THE FIRST THREE BASKETS OF THE GAME.
ANOTHER DAZZLING PLAY BY JUDI WILSON!
WESTFIELD 2
ESTFIELD 10
CINDY RANDALL FOR TWO AT THE BUZZER! AND THE BEARS TAKE A TWELVE-POINT LEAD AT THE HALF.
WILKINS

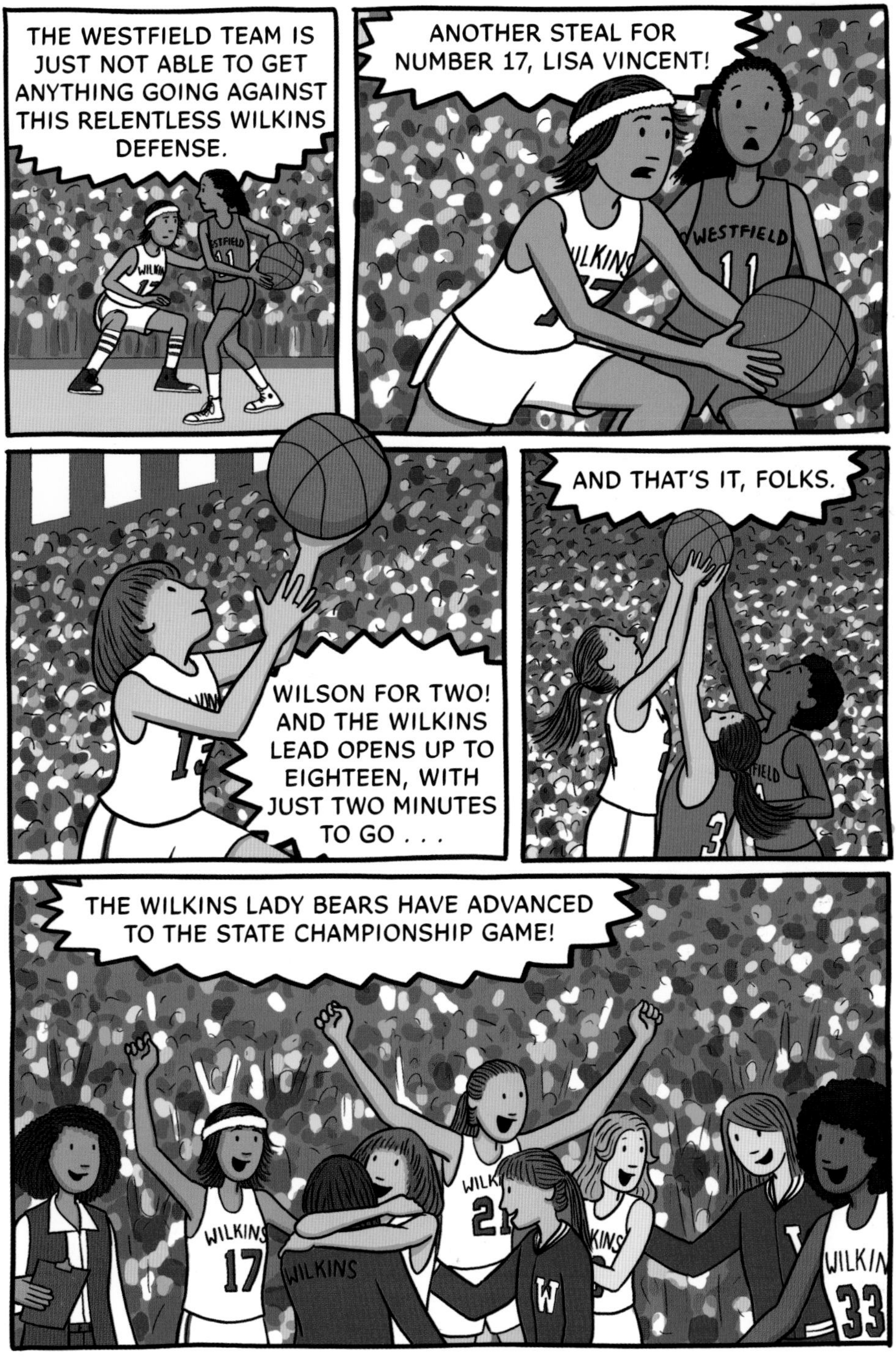
THE WESTFIELD TEAM IS JUST NOT ABLE TO GET ANYTHING GOING AGAINST THIS RELENTLESS WILKINS DEFENSE.
ANOTHER STEAL FOR NUMBER 17, LISA VINCENT!
WESTFIELD
WILSON FOR TWO! AND THE WILKINS LEAD OPENS UP TO EIGHTEEN, WITH JUST TWO MINUTES TO GO . . .
AND THAT'S IT, FOLKS.
THE WILKINS LADY BEARS HAVE ADVANCED TO THE STATE CHAMPIONSHIP GAME!
WILKINS
17
WILKINS
33

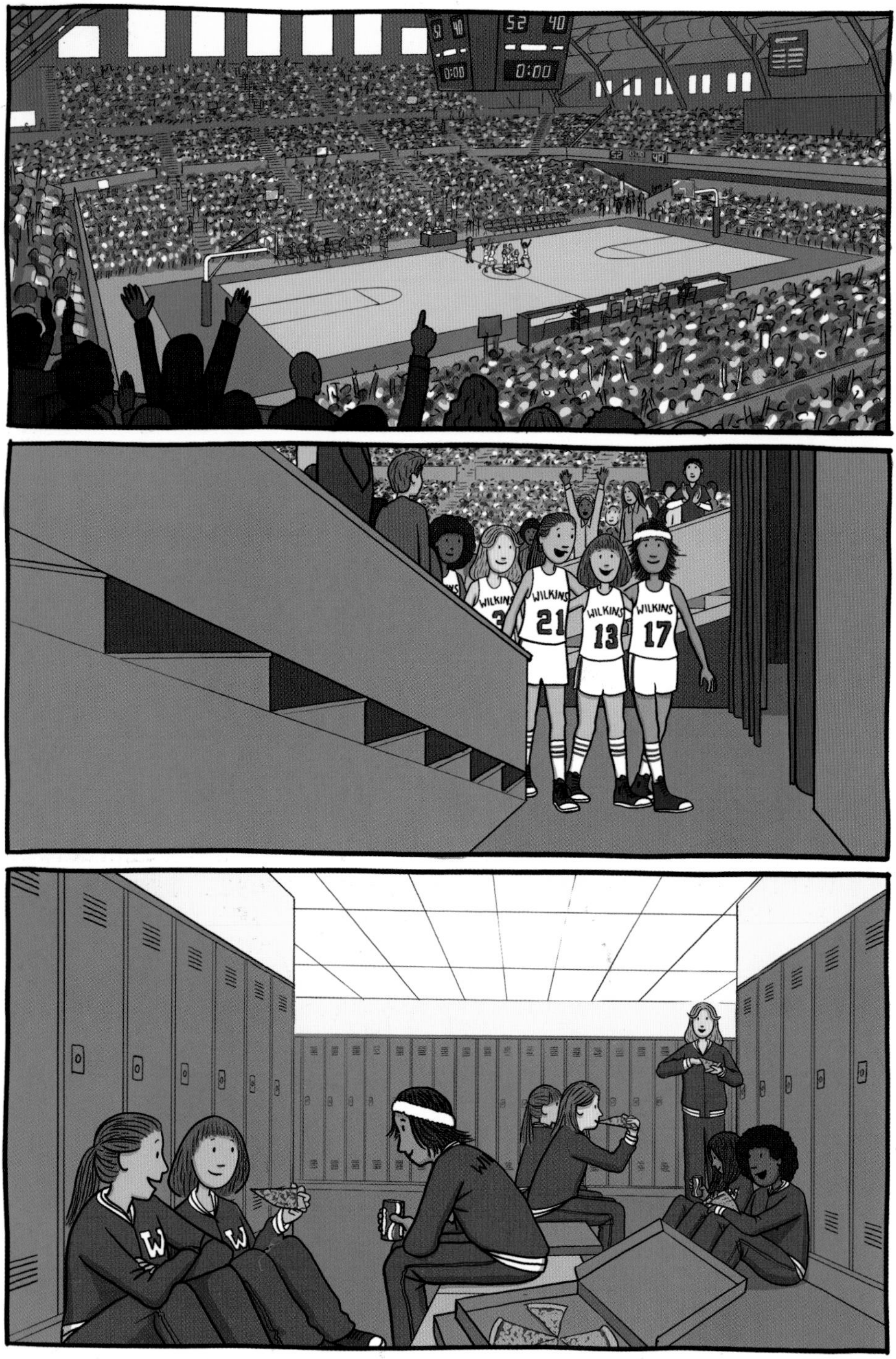
52 40
0:00
WILKINS
21
WILKINS
13
WILKINS
17

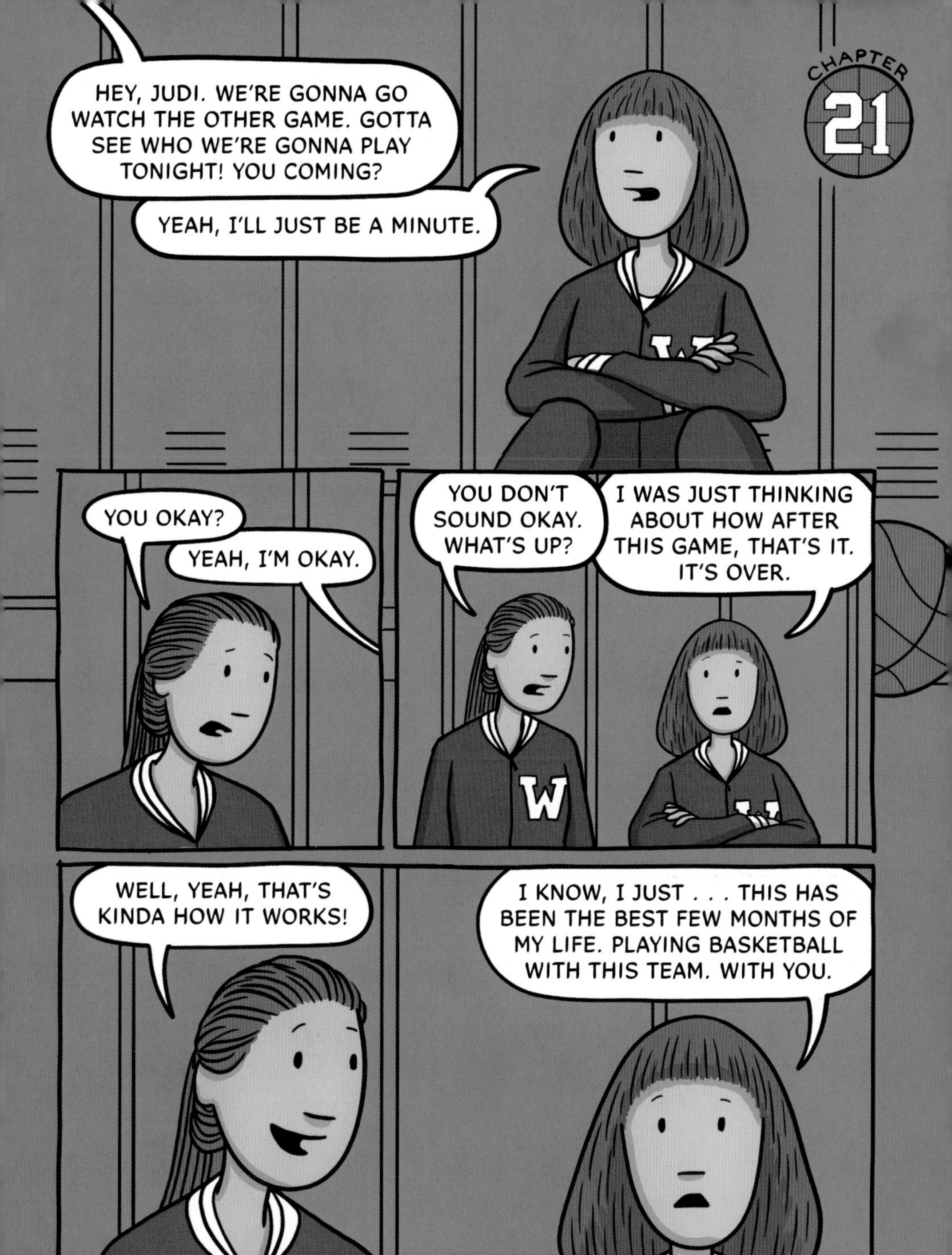
CHAPTER
21
HEY, JUDI. WE'RE GONNA GO WATCH THE OTHER GAME. GOTTA SEE WHO WE'RE GONNA PLAY TONIGHT! YOU COMING?
YEAH, I'LL JUST BE A MINUTE.
YOU OKAY?
YEAH, I'M OKAY.
YOU DON'T SOUND OKAY. WHAT'S UP?
I WAS JUST THINKING ABOUT HOW AFTER THIS GAME, THAT'S IT. IT'S OVER.
WELL, YEAH, THAT'S KINDA HOW IT WORKS!
I KNOW, I JUST . . . THIS HAS BEEN THE BEST FEW MONTHS OF MY LIFE. PLAYING BASKETBALL WITH THIS TEAM. WITH YOU.

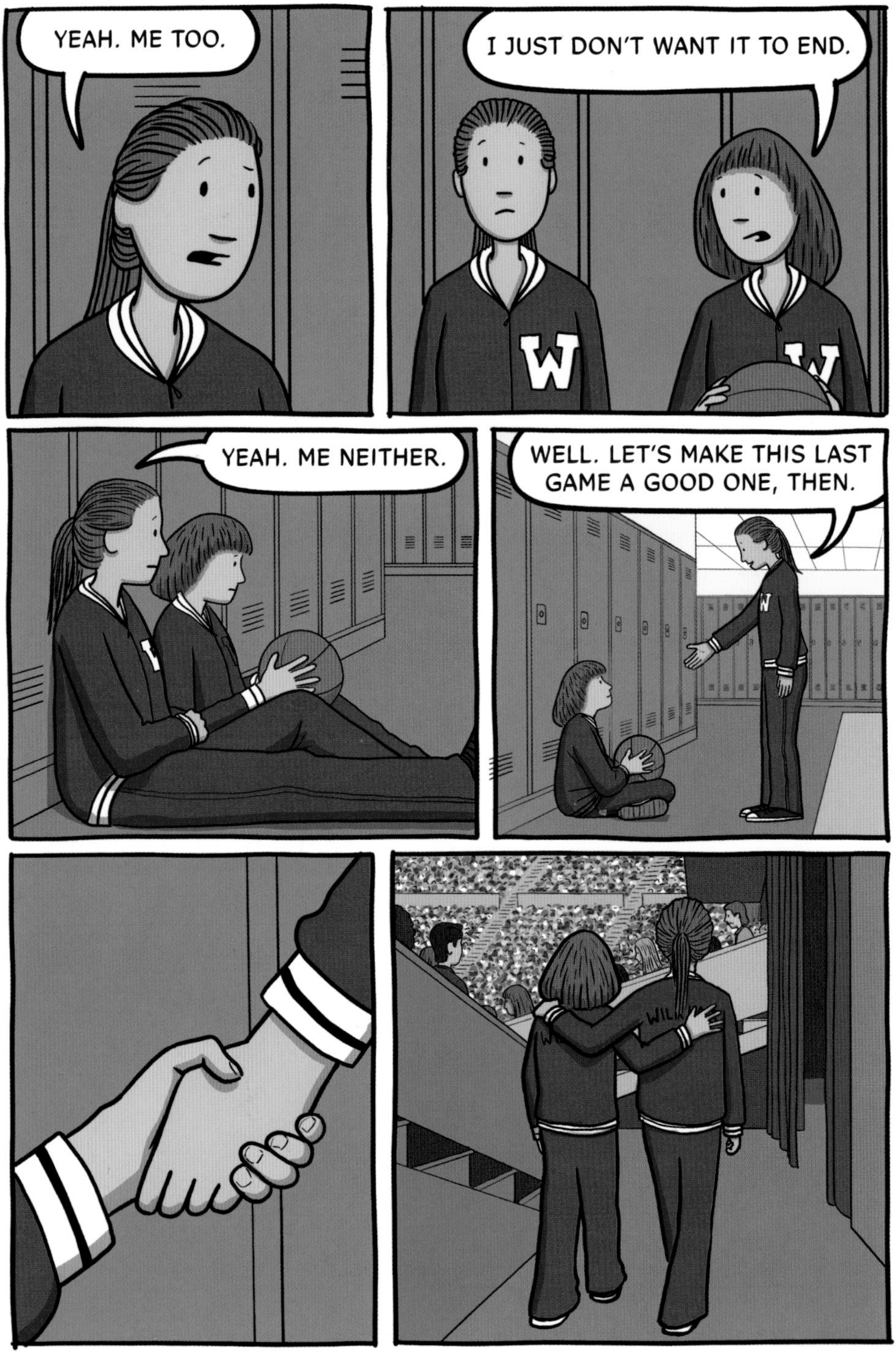
YEAH. ME TOO.
I JUST DON'T WANT IT TO END.
YEAH. ME NEITHER.
WELL. LET'S MAKE THIS LAST GAME A GOOD ONE, THEN.

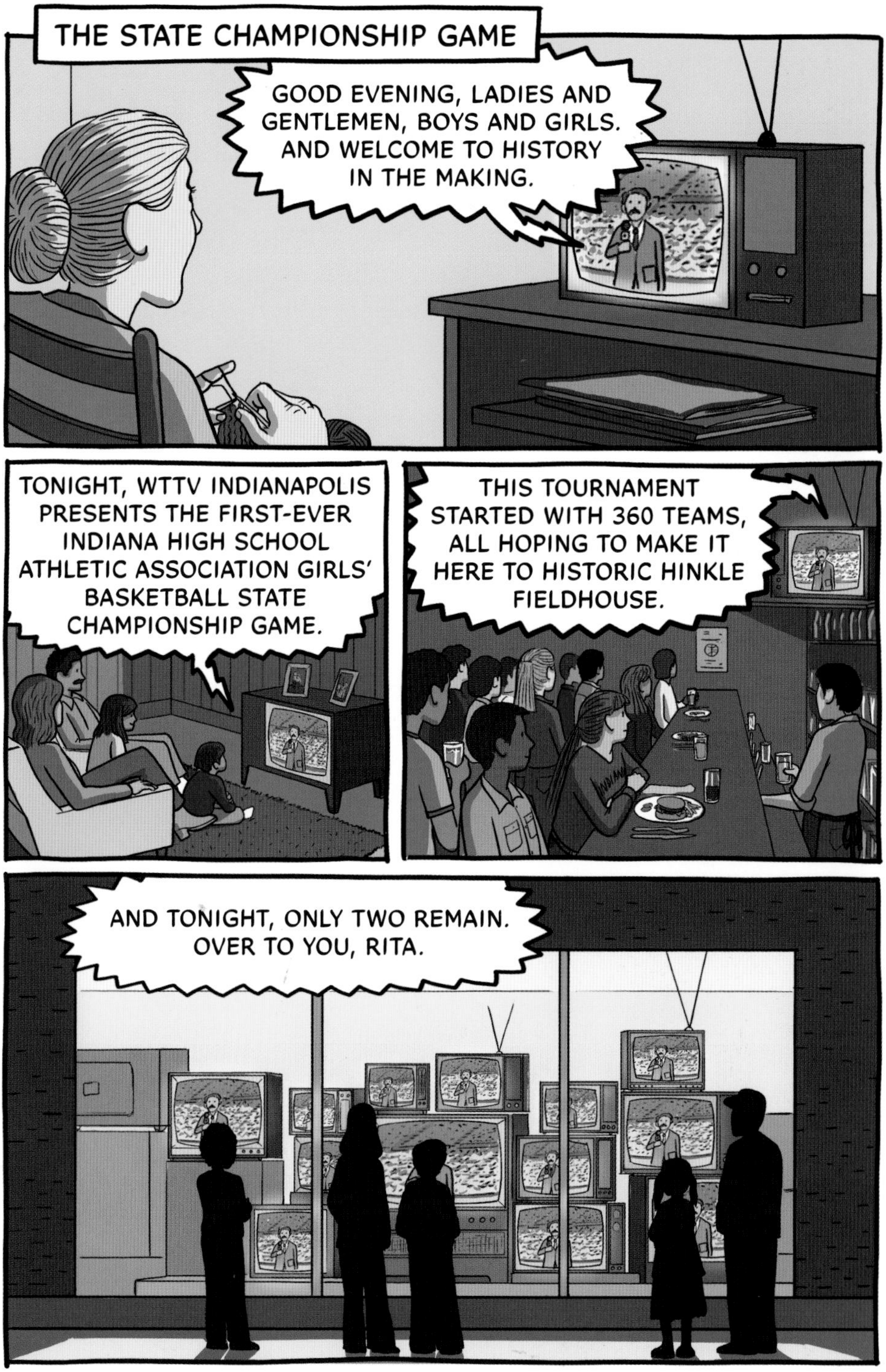
THE STATE CHAMPIONSHIP GAME
GOOD EVENING, LADIES AND GENTLEMEN, BOYS AND GIRLS. AND WELCOME TO HISTORY IN THE MAKING.
TONIGHT, WTTV INDIANAPOLIS PRESENTS THE FIRST-EVER INDIANA HIGH SCHOOL ATHLETIC ASSOCIATION GIRLS' BASKETBALL STATE CHAMPIONSHIP GAME.
THIS TOURNAMENT STARTED WITH 360 TEAMS, ALL HOPING TO MAKE IT HERE TO HISTORIC HINKLE FIELDHOUSE.
AND TONIGHT, ONLY TWO REMAIN. OVER TO YOU, RITA.

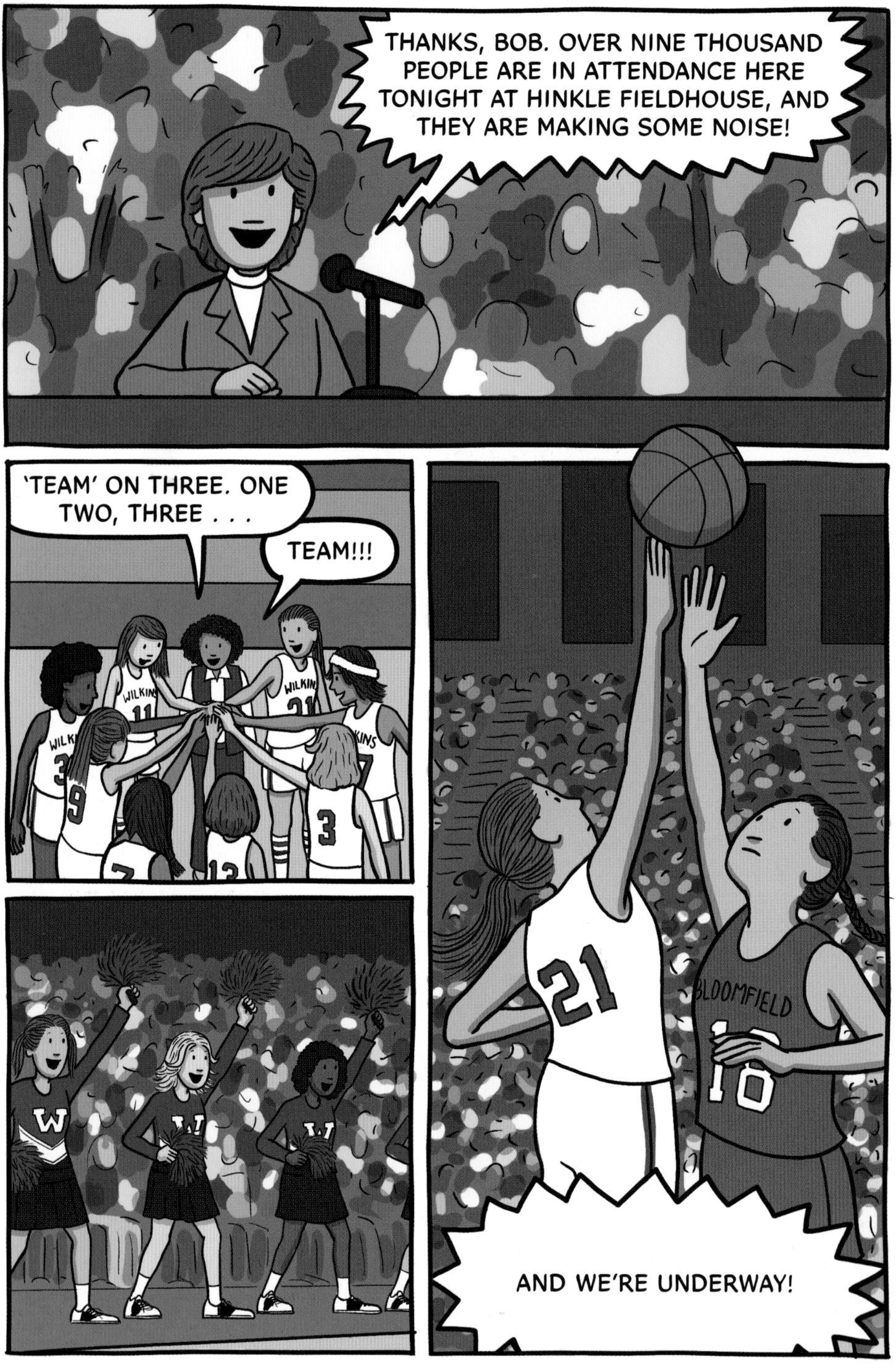
THANKS, BOB. OVER NINE THOUSAND PEOPLE ARE IN ATTENDANCE HERE TONIGHT AT HINKLE FIELDHOUSE, AND THEY ARE MAKING SOME NOISE!
'TEAM' ON THREE. ONE TWO, THREE . . .
TEAM!!!
AND WE'RE UNDERWAY!

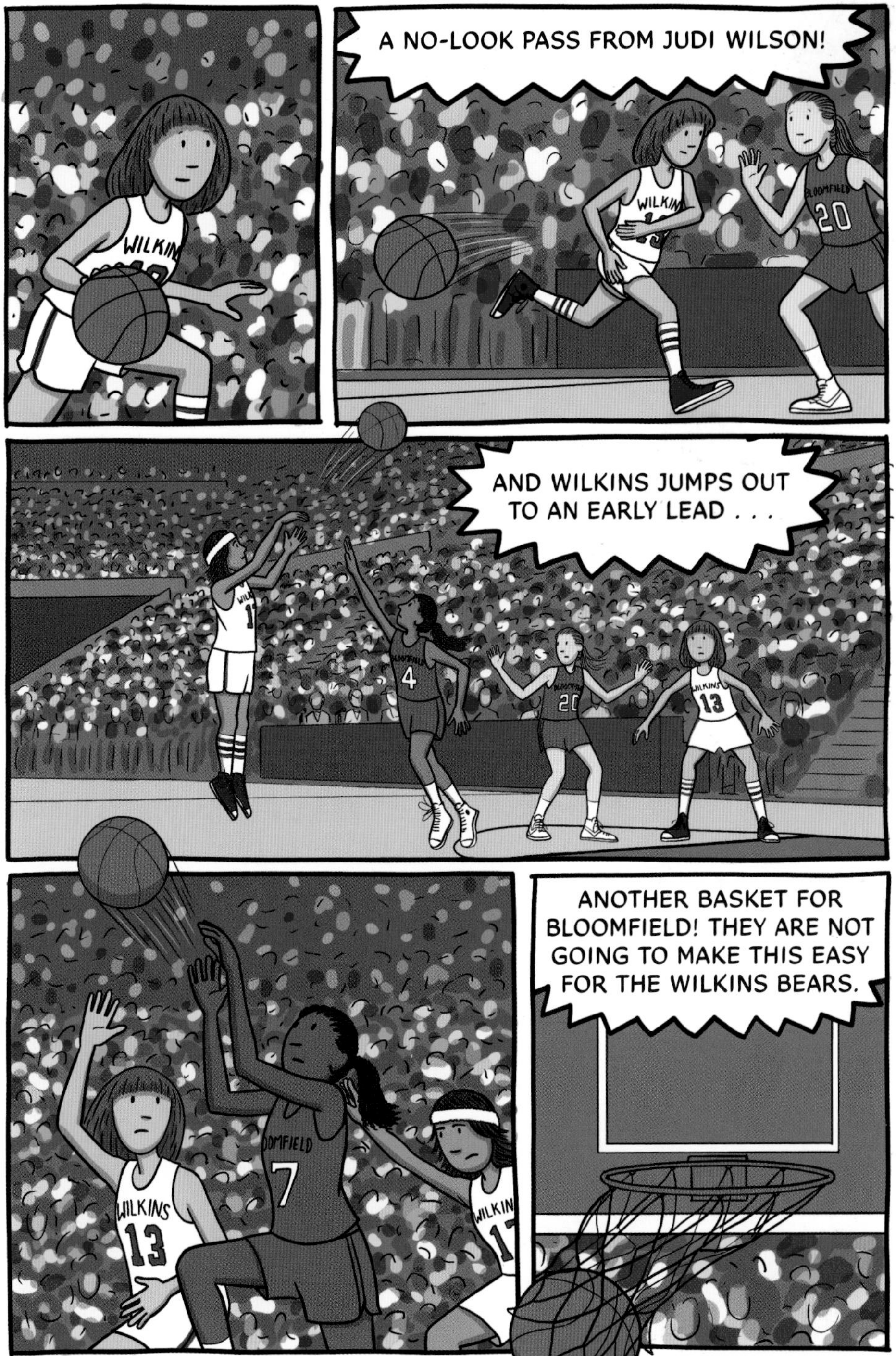
A NO-LOOK PASS FROM JUDI WILSON!
AND WILKINS JUMPS OUT TO AN EARLY LEAD . . .
ANOTHER BASKET FOR BLOOMFIELD! THEY ARE NOT GOING TO MAKE THIS EASY FOR THE WILKINS BEARS.

BUT NOW THE BEARS HAVE COME *ROARING* BACK!
AND THIS CROWD IS GOING WILD!
LET'S GO, BEARS!!!
WOOHOO!!!
MAN, THESE GIRLS CAN REALLY PLAY!
YOU'RE DARN RIGHT THEY CAN!

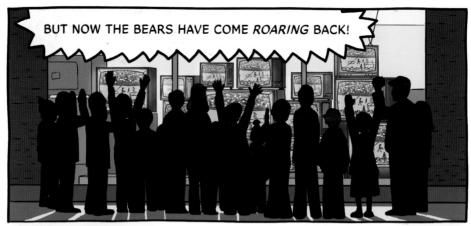

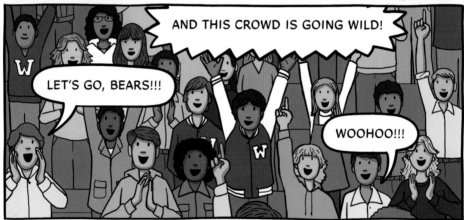

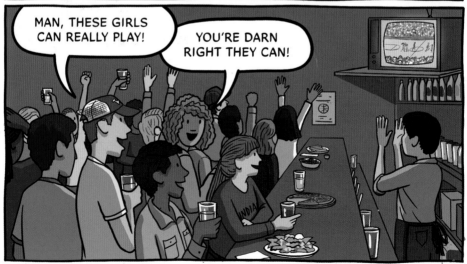

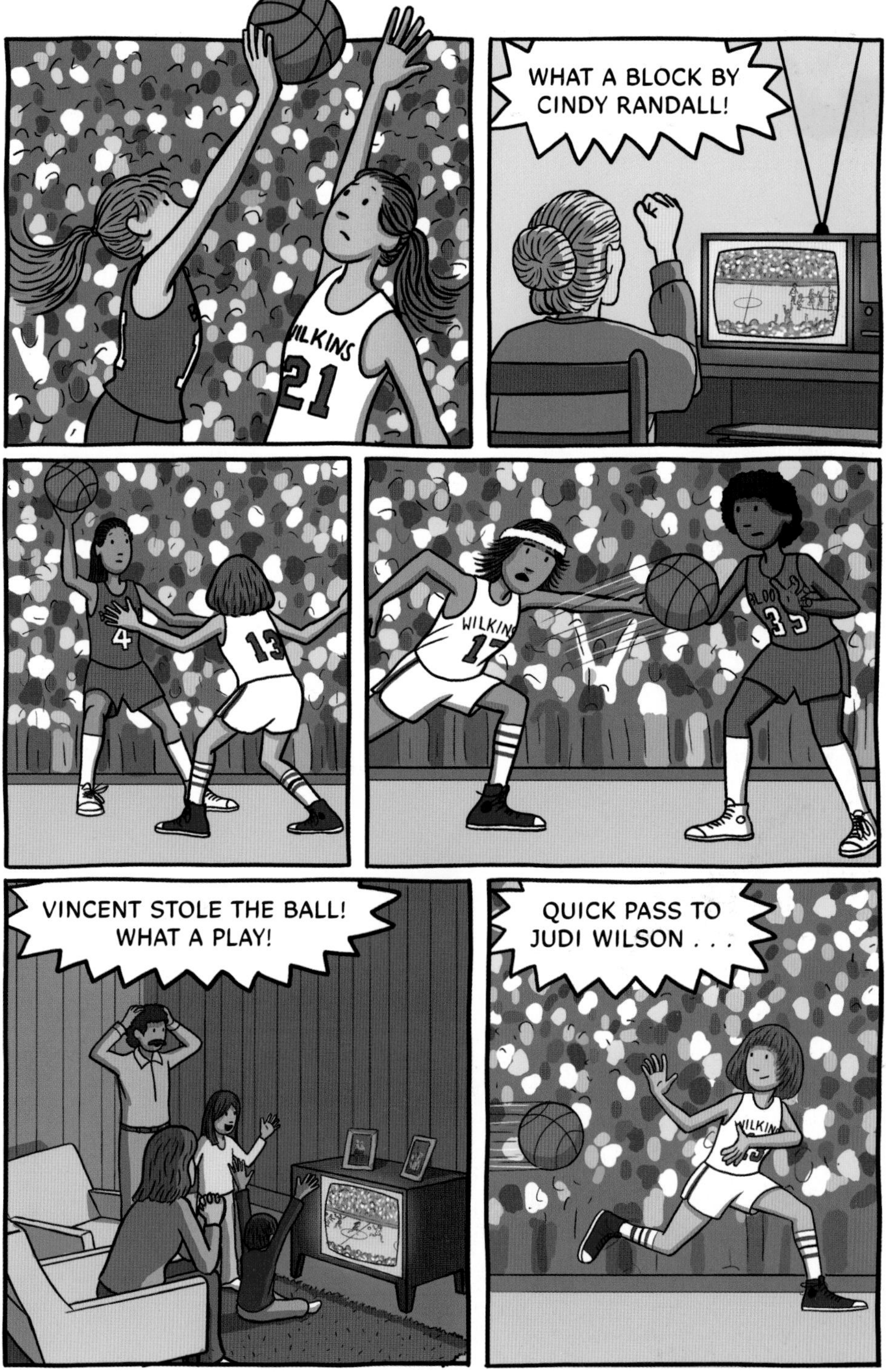

WHAT A BLOCK BY CINDY RANDALL!
WILKINS 21
WILKINS 13
WILKINS 17
VINCENT STOLE THE BALL! WHAT A PLAY!
QUICK PASS TO JUDI WILSON . . .

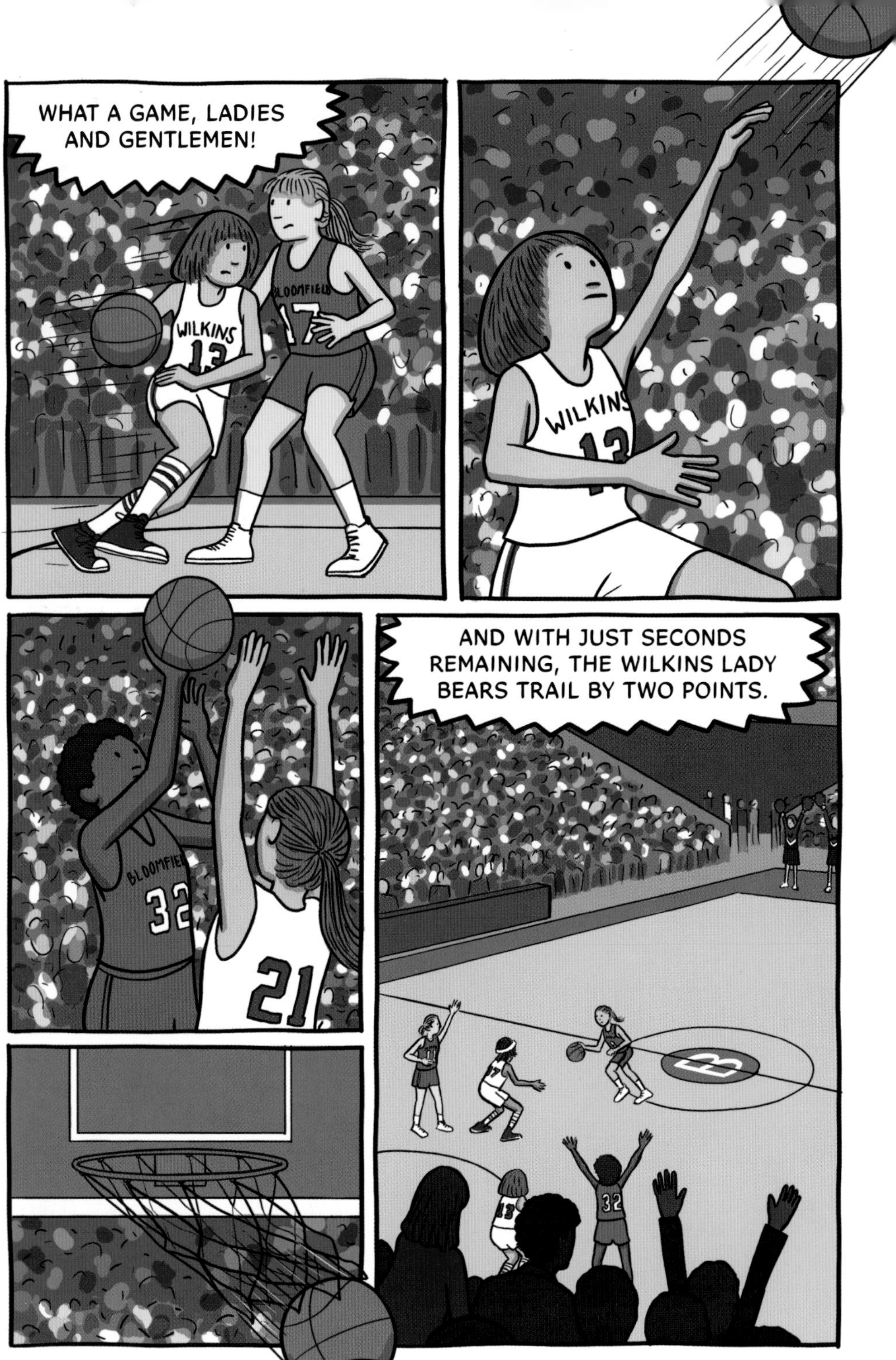
WHAT A GAME, LADIES AND GENTLEMEN!
WILKINS 13
BLOOMFIELD 17
WILKINS 13
BLOOMFIELD 32
21
AND WITH JUST SECONDS REMAINING, THE WILKINS LADY BEARS TRAIL BY TWO POINTS.
32

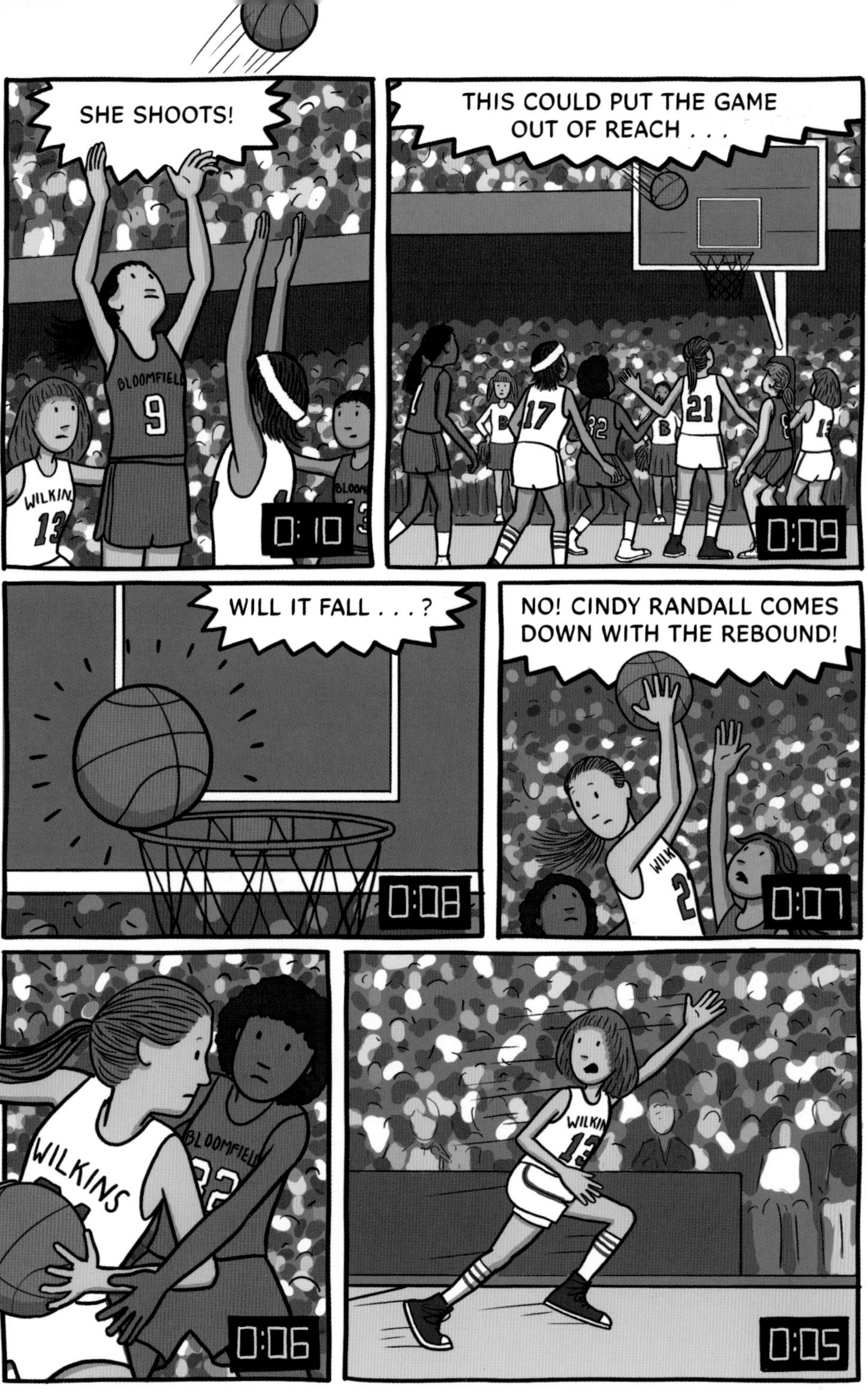
SHE SHOOTS!
0:10
THIS COULD PUT THE GAME OUT OF REACH . . .
0:09
WILL IT FALL . . . ?
0:08
NO! CINDY RANDALL COMES DOWN WITH THE REBOUND!
0:07
WILKINS
BLOOMFIELD
0:06
0:05

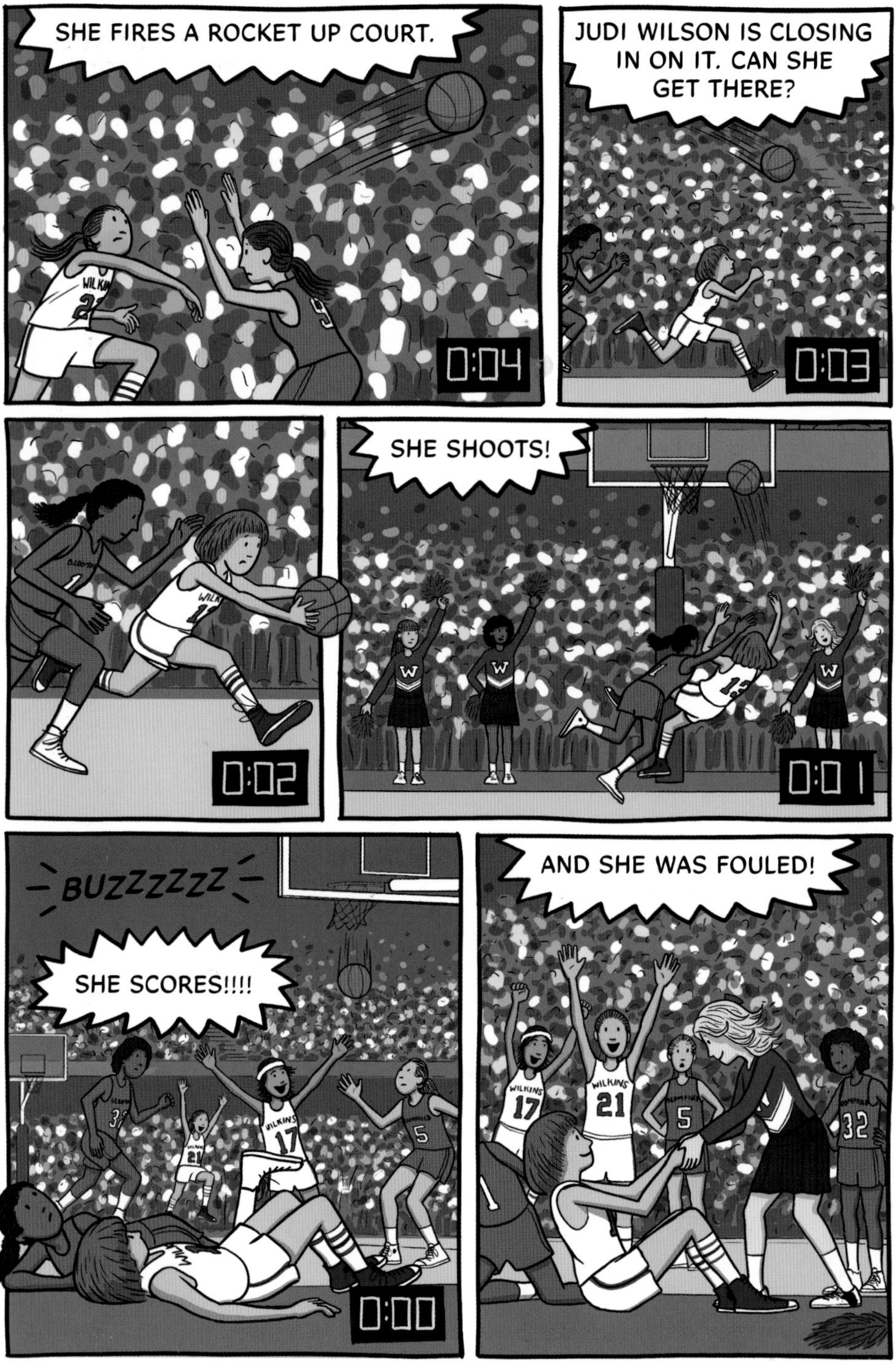
SHE FIRES A ROCKET UP COURT.
0:04
JUDI WILSON IS CLOSING IN ON IT. CAN SHE GET THERE?
0:03
0:02
SHE SHOOTS!
0:01
BUZZZZZZ
SHE SCORES!!!!
0:00
AND SHE WAS FOULED!

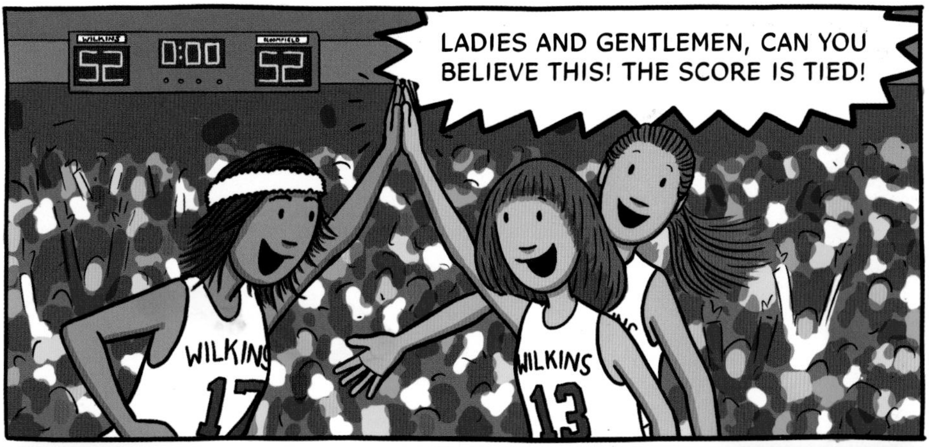
WILKINS
52
0:00
BLOOMFIELD
52
LADIES AND GENTLEMEN, CAN YOU BELIEVE THIS! THE SCORE IS TIED!
WILKINS
17
WILKINS
13

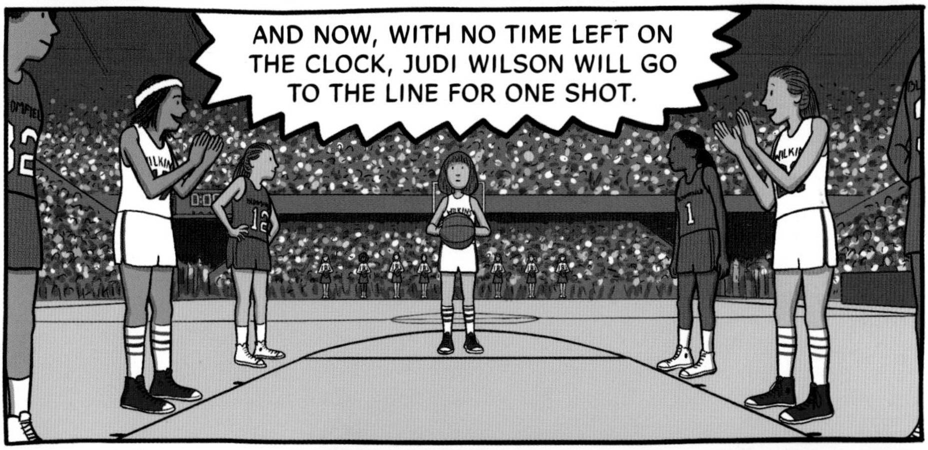
AND NOW, WITH NO TIME LEFT ON THE CLOCK, JUDI WILSON WILL GO TO THE LINE FOR ONE SHOT.

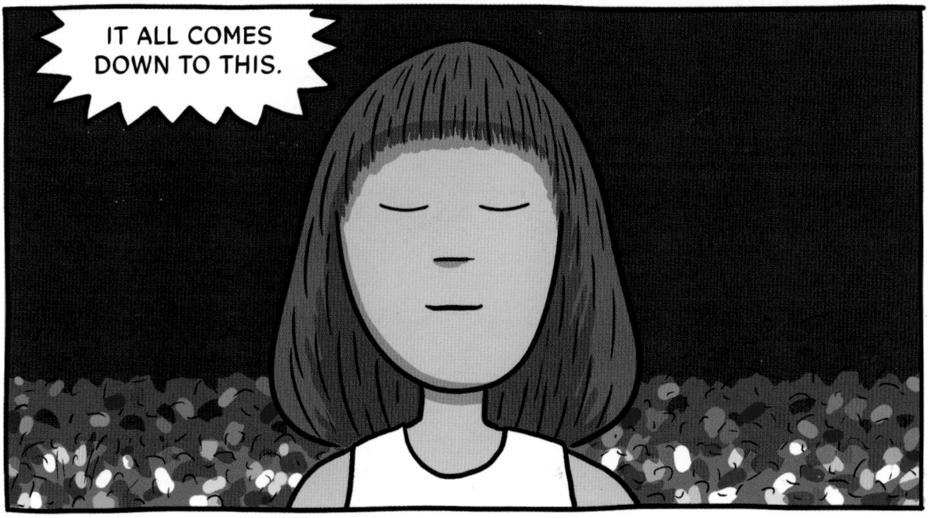
IT ALL COMES DOWN TO THIS.

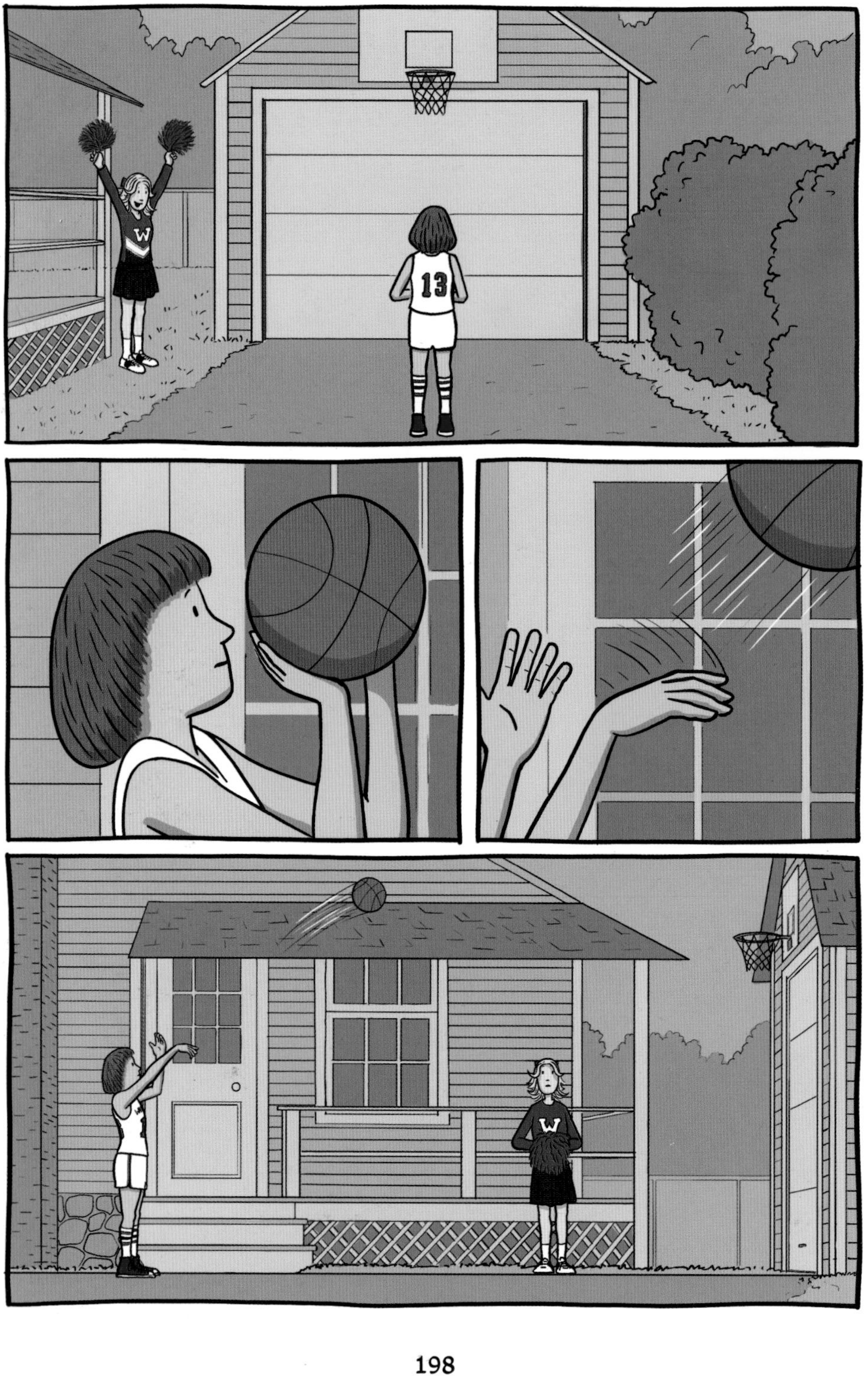
W
13

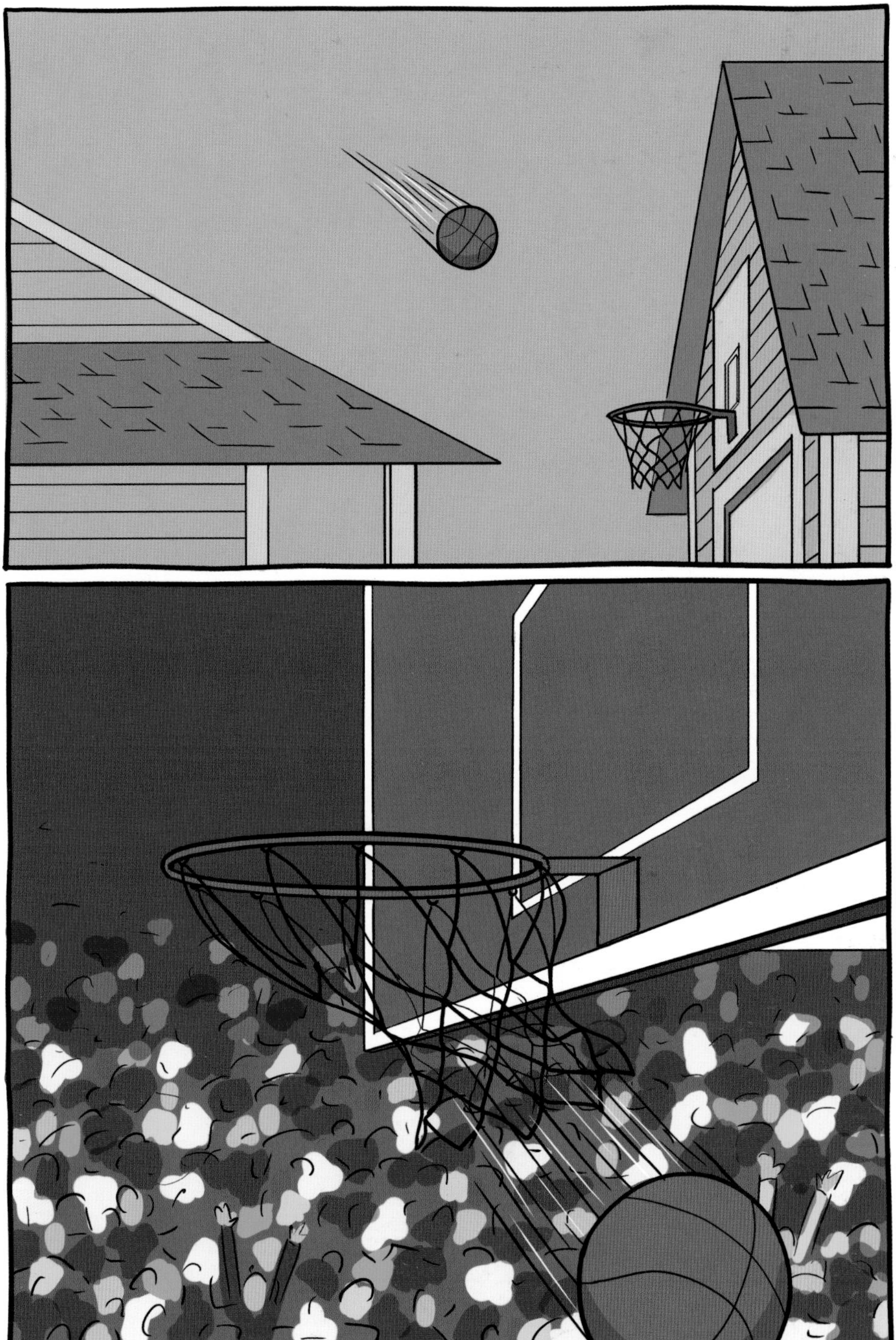

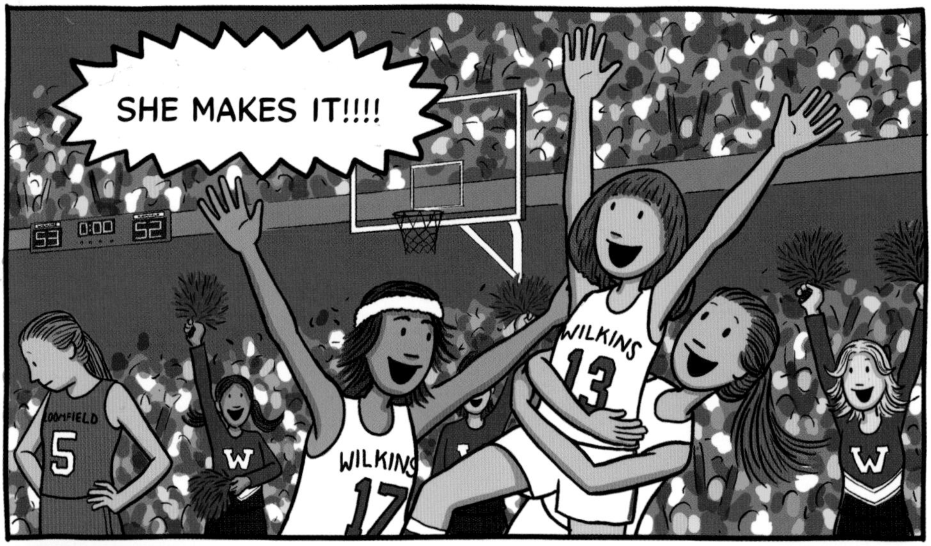
SHE MAKES IT!!!!
WILKINS 13
WILKINS 17
LOOMFIELD 5
W
53 0:00 52

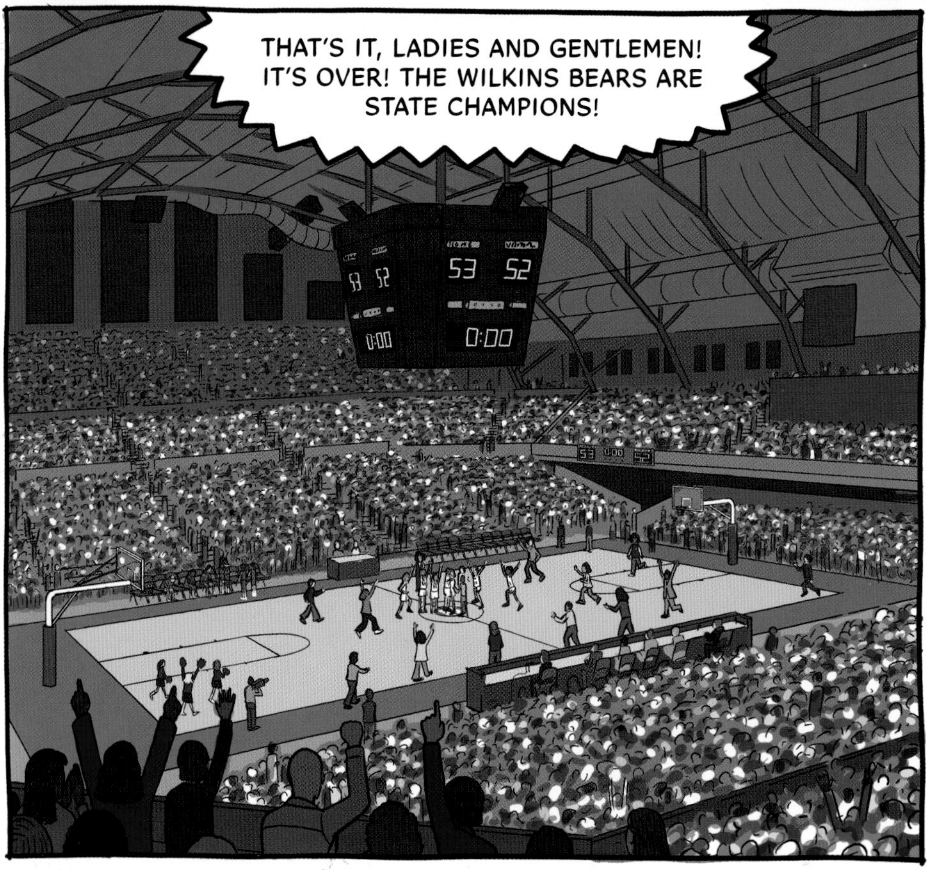
THAT'S IT, LADIES AND GENTLEMEN! IT'S OVER! THE WILKINS BEARS ARE STATE CHAMPIONS!
53 52
0:00

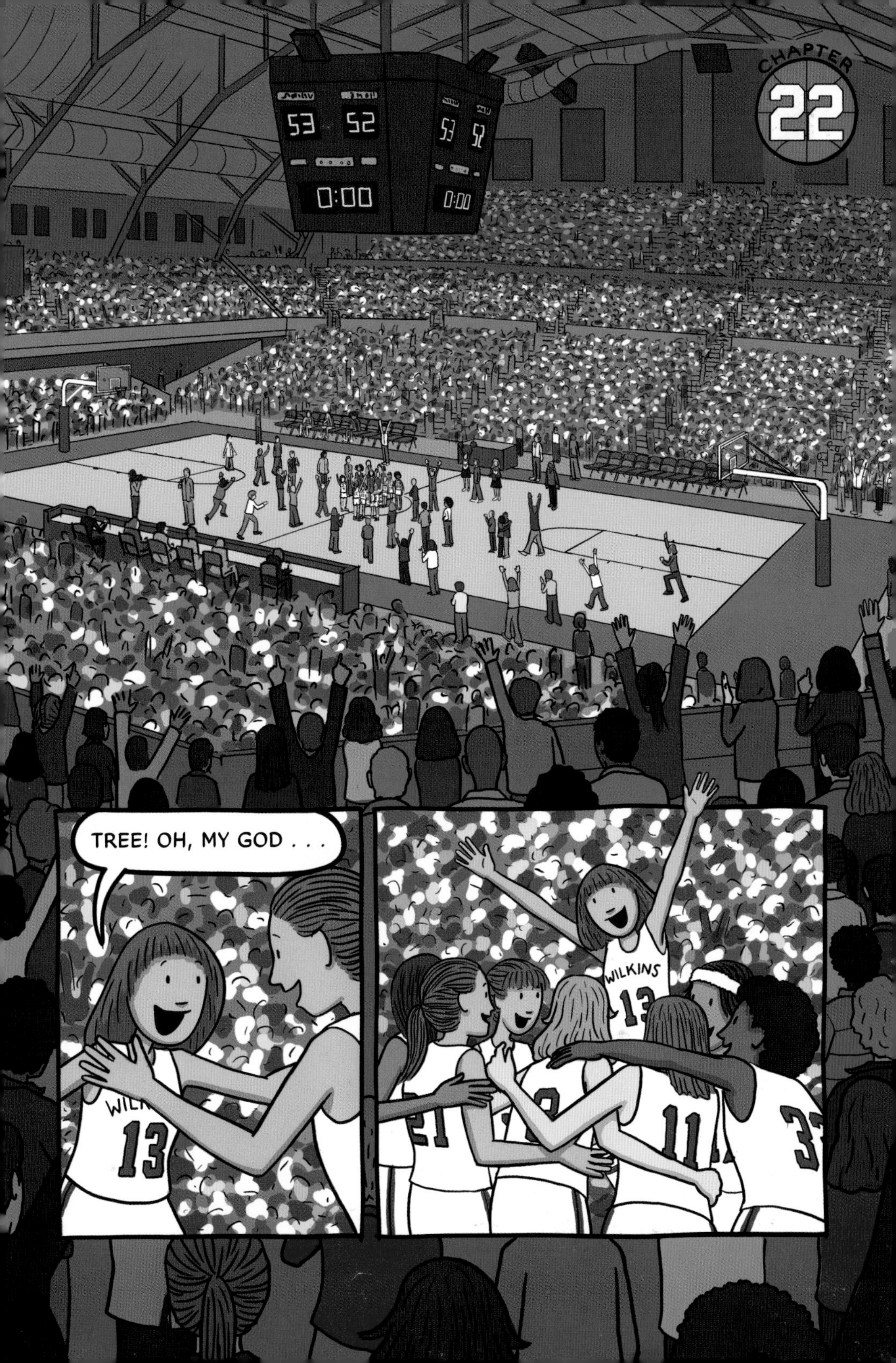
CHAPTER
22
53
52
0:00
TREE! OH, MY GOD . . .
WILKINS
13
WILKINS
13
21
11
37

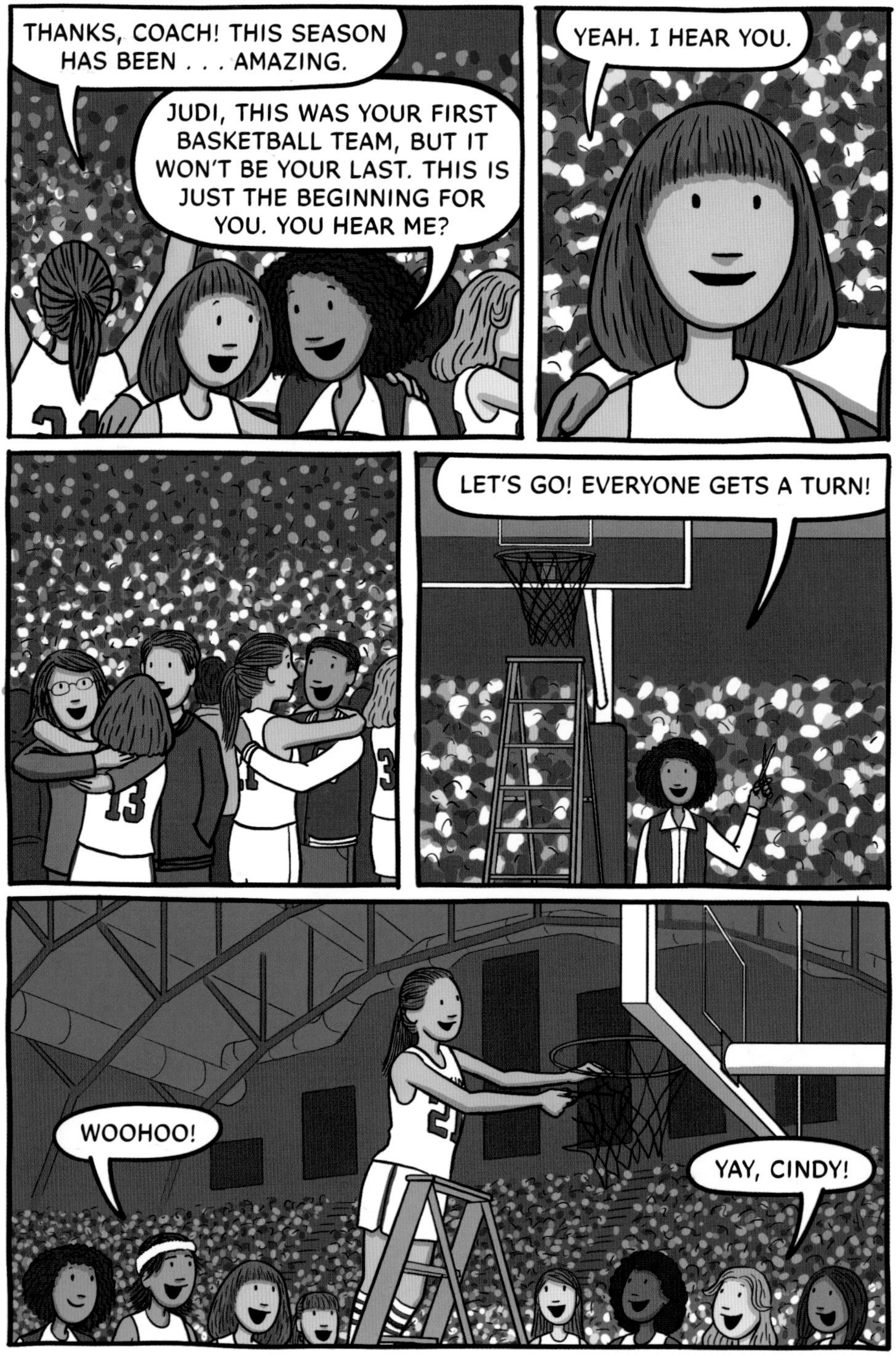
THANKS, COACH! THIS SEASON HAS BEEN . . . AMAZING.
JUDI, THIS WAS YOUR FIRST BASKETBALL TEAM, BUT IT WON'T BE YOUR LAST. THIS IS JUST THE BEGINNING FOR YOU. YOU HEAR ME?
YEAH. I HEAR YOU.
LET'S GO! EVERYONE GETS A TURN!
WOOHOO!
YAY, CINDY!

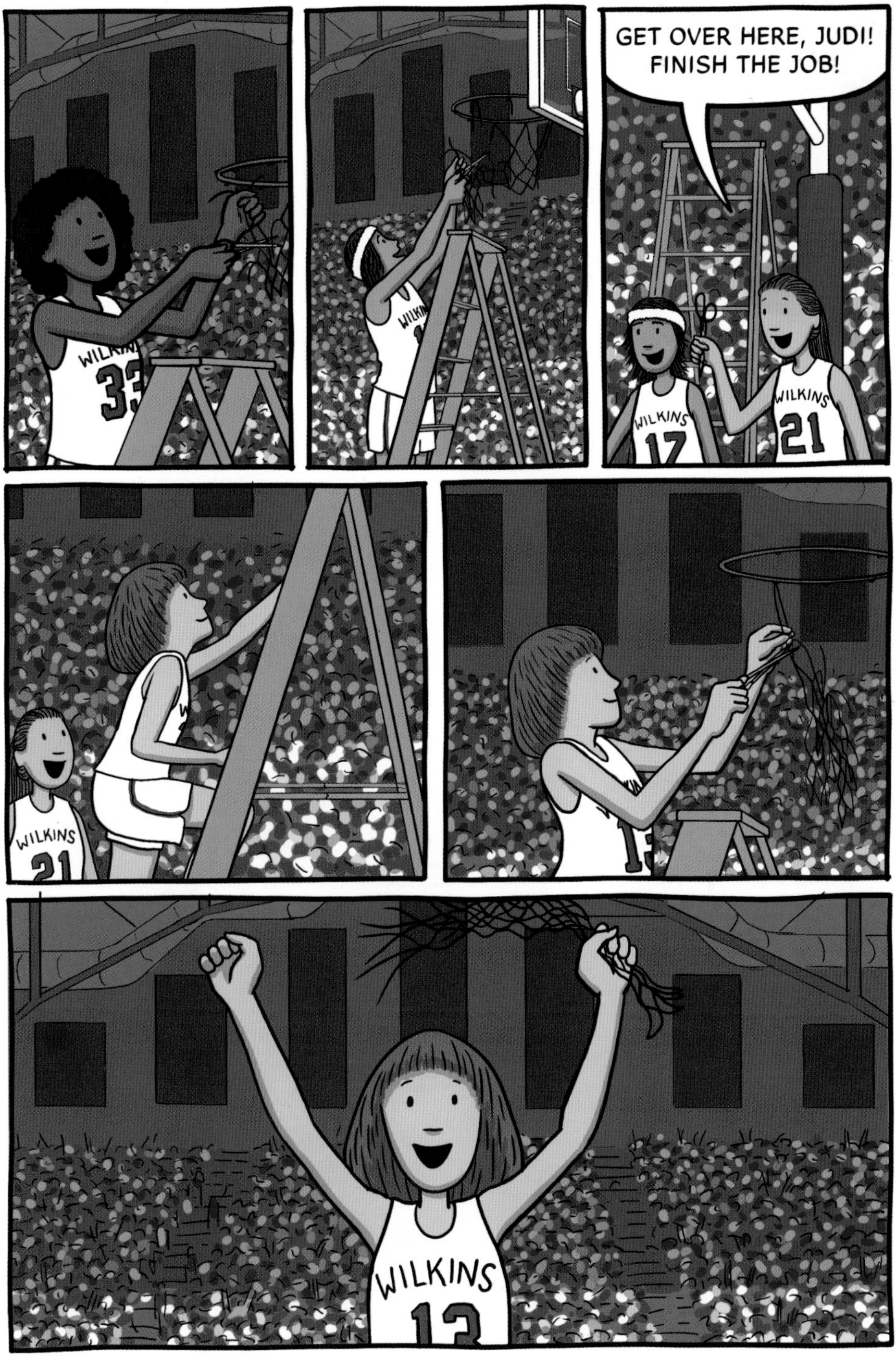
WILKINS
33
WILKINS
GET OVER HERE, JUDI!
FINISH THE JOB!
WILKINS
17
WILKINS
21
WILKINS
21
WILKINS
13

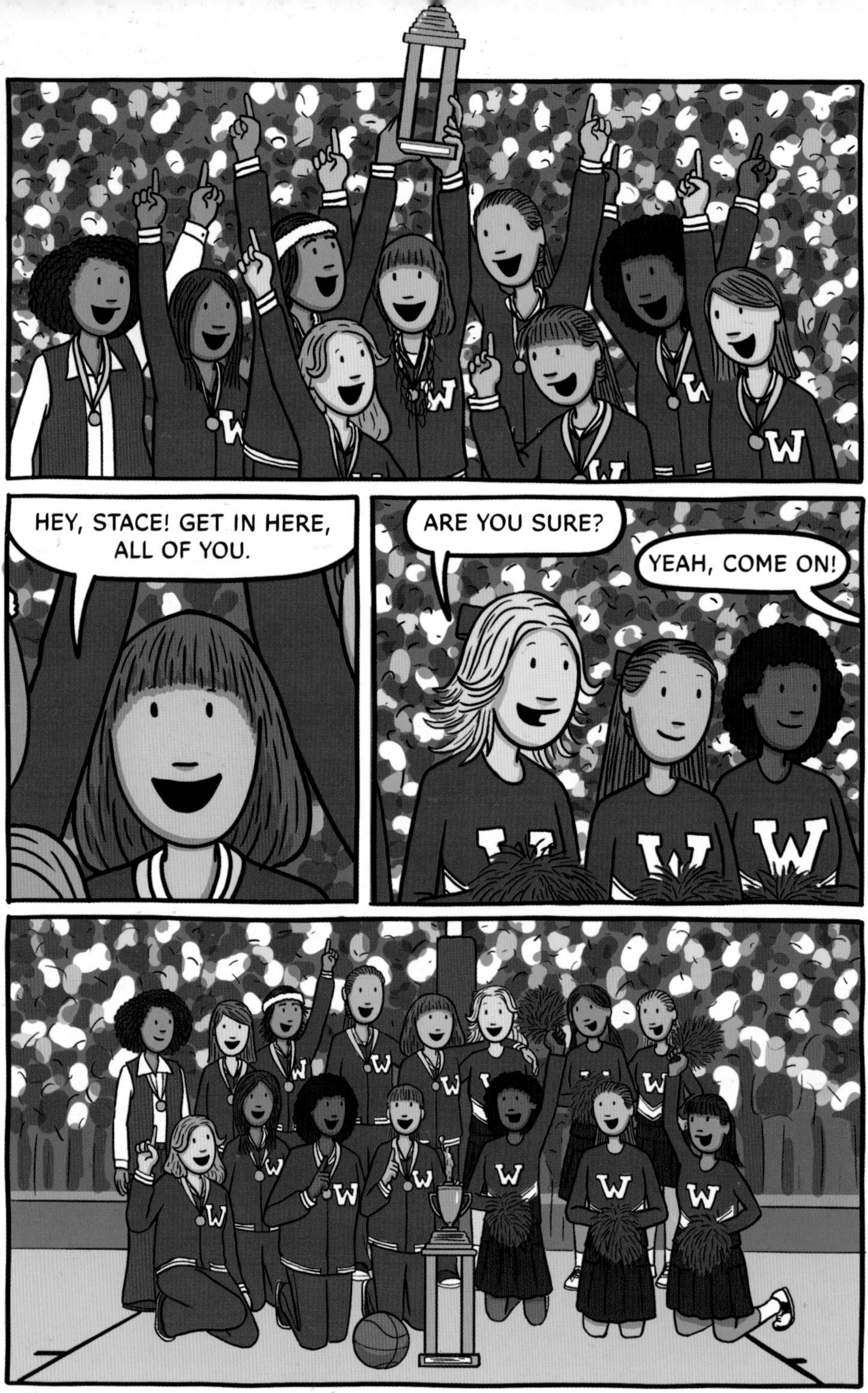

HEY, STACE! GET IN HERE, ALL OF YOU.
ARE YOU SURE?
YEAH, COME ON!

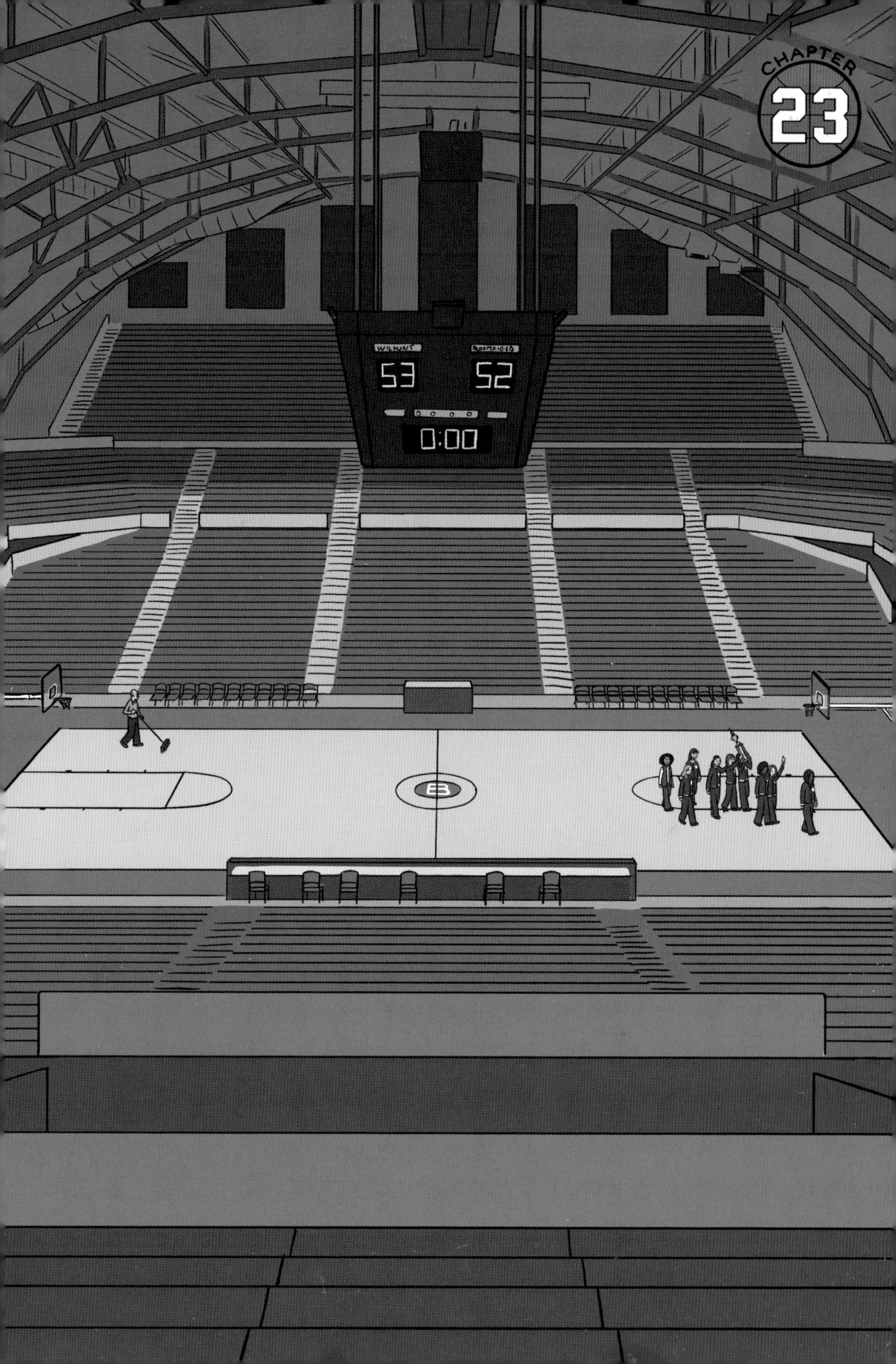
CHAPTER
23
WILKINS
53
52
0:00

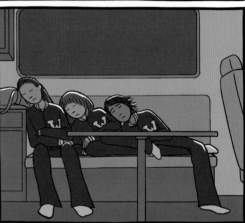

KNOCK, KNOCK!

ARE WE THERE?

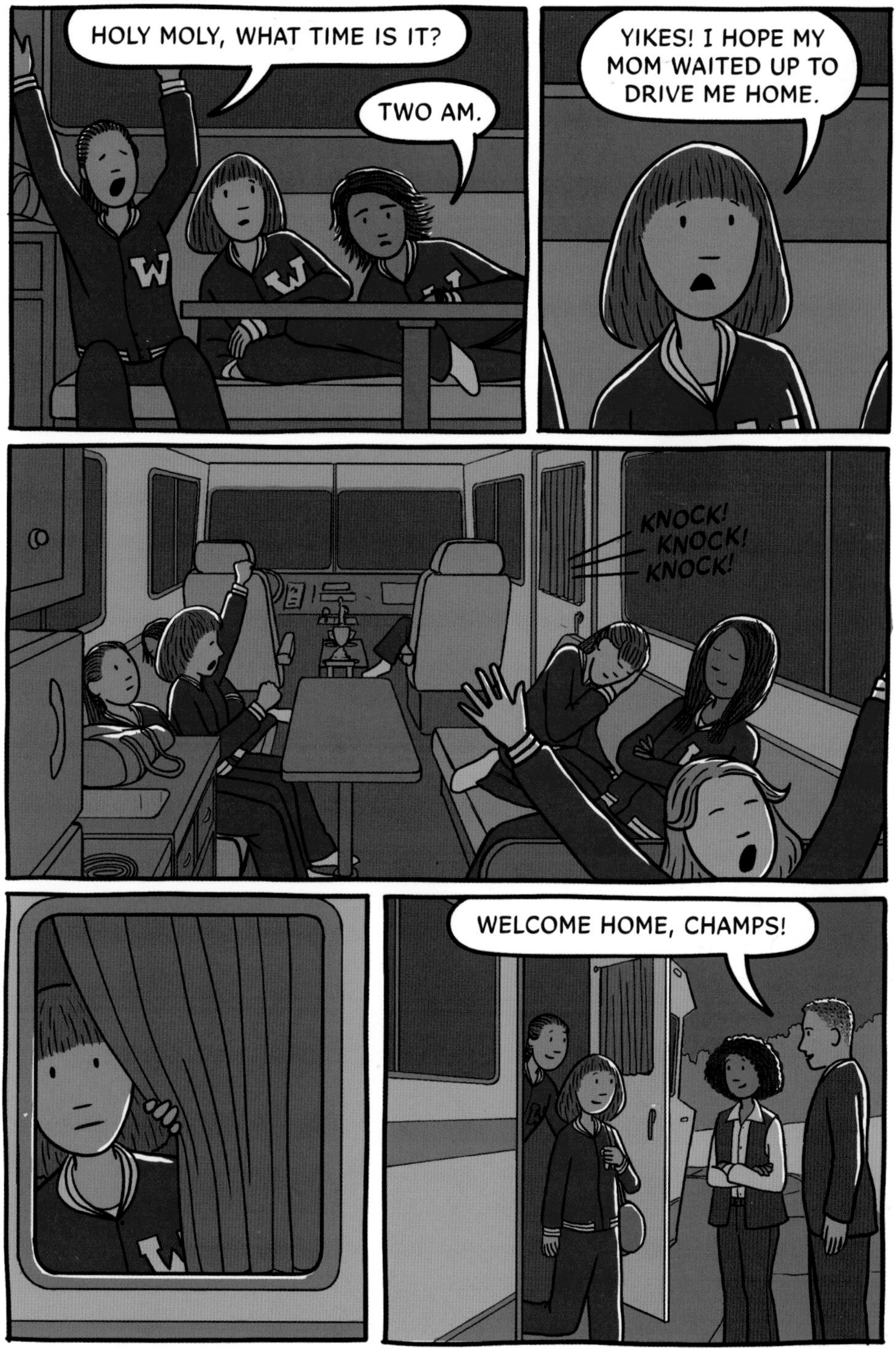
HOLY MOLY, WHAT TIME IS IT?
TWO AM.
YIKES! I HOPE MY MOM WAITED UP TO DRIVE ME HOME.
KNOCK! KNOCK! KNOCK!
WELCOME HOME, CHAMPS!

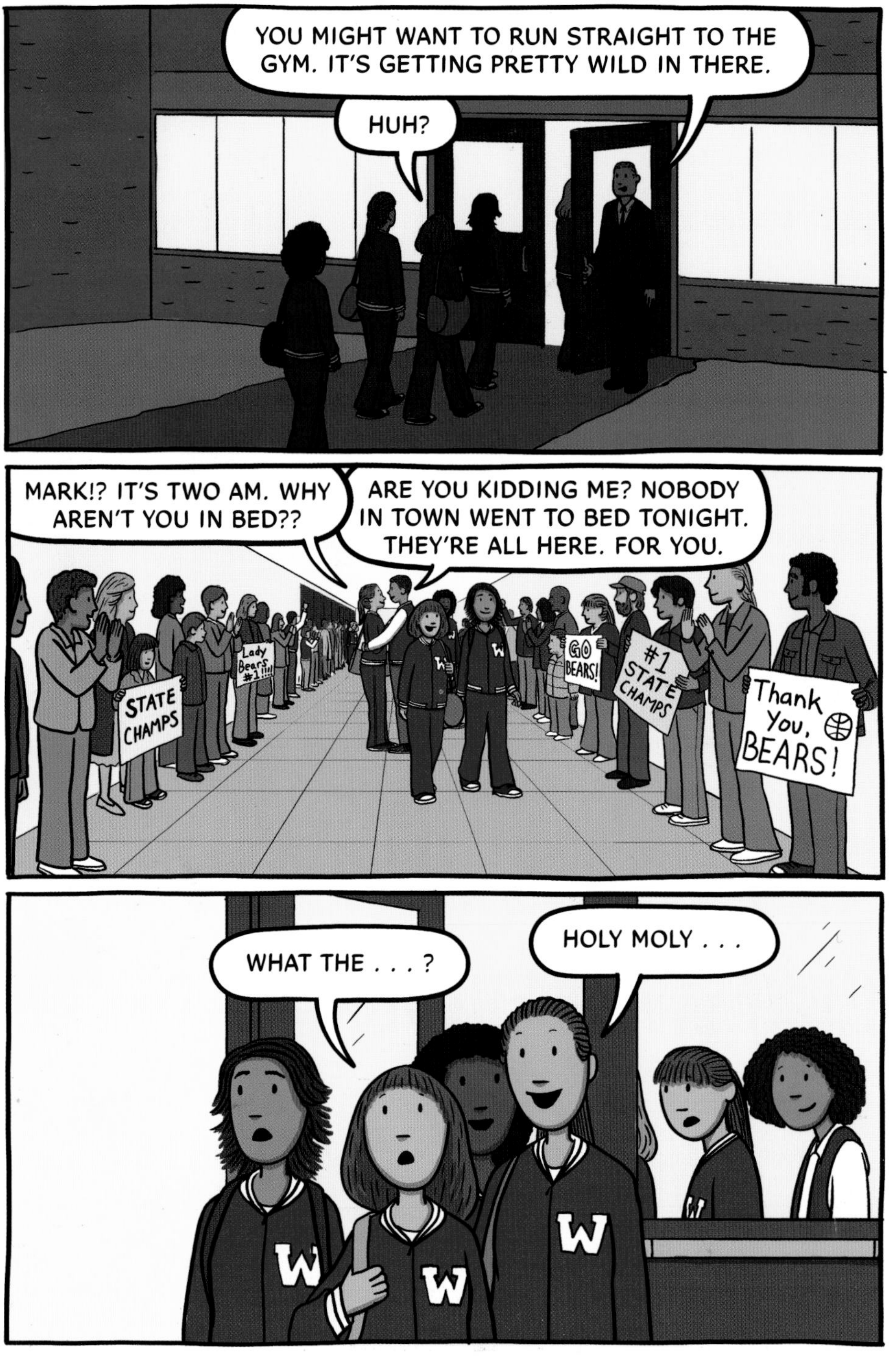
YOU MIGHT WANT TO RUN STRAIGHT TO THE GYM. IT'S GETTING PRETTY WILD IN THERE.
HUH?
MARK!? IT'S TWO AM. WHY AREN'T YOU IN BED??
ARE YOU KIDDING ME? NOBODY IN TOWN WENT TO BED TONIGHT. THEY'RE ALL HERE. FOR YOU.
STATE CHAMPS
Lady Bears #1!!!
GO BEARS!
#1 STATE CHAMPS
Thank You, BEARS!
WHAT THE . . . ?
HOLY MOLY . . .

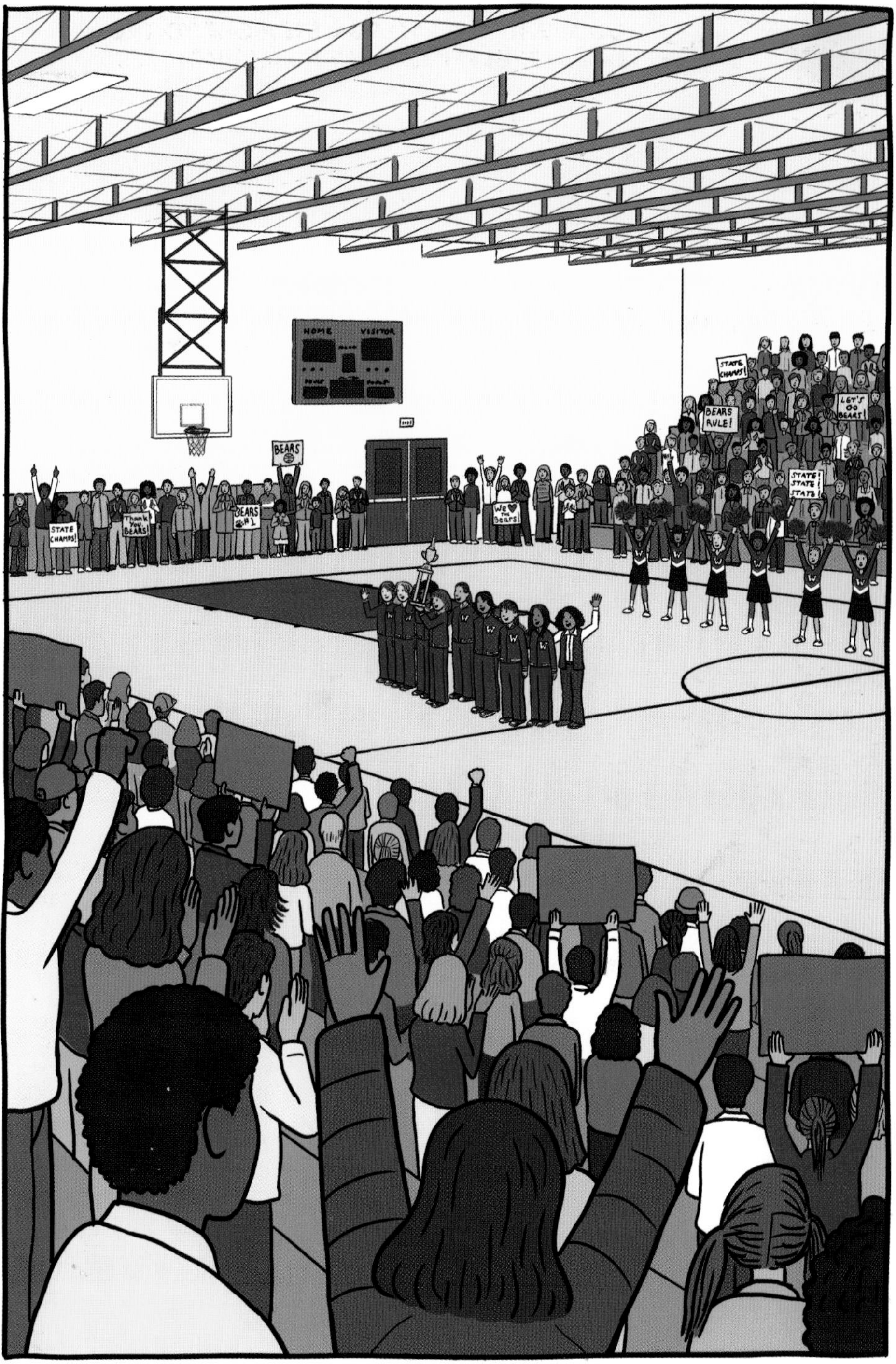
HOME
VISITOR
STATE CHAMPS!
Thank You BEARS!
BEARS #1
BEARS
We ♥ the Bears!
STATE CHAMPS!
BEARS RULE!
LET'S GO BEARS!
STATE! STATE! STATE!

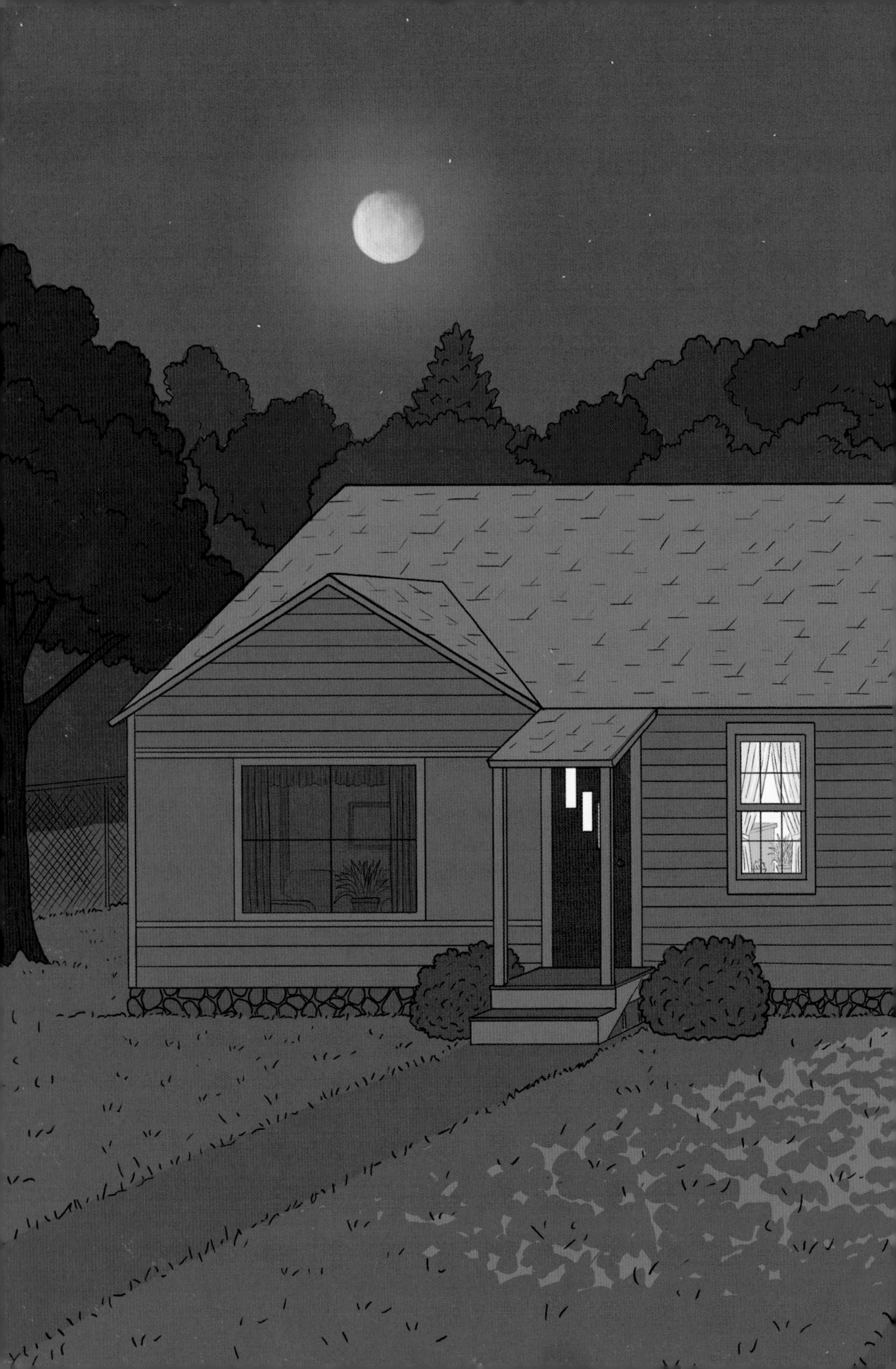

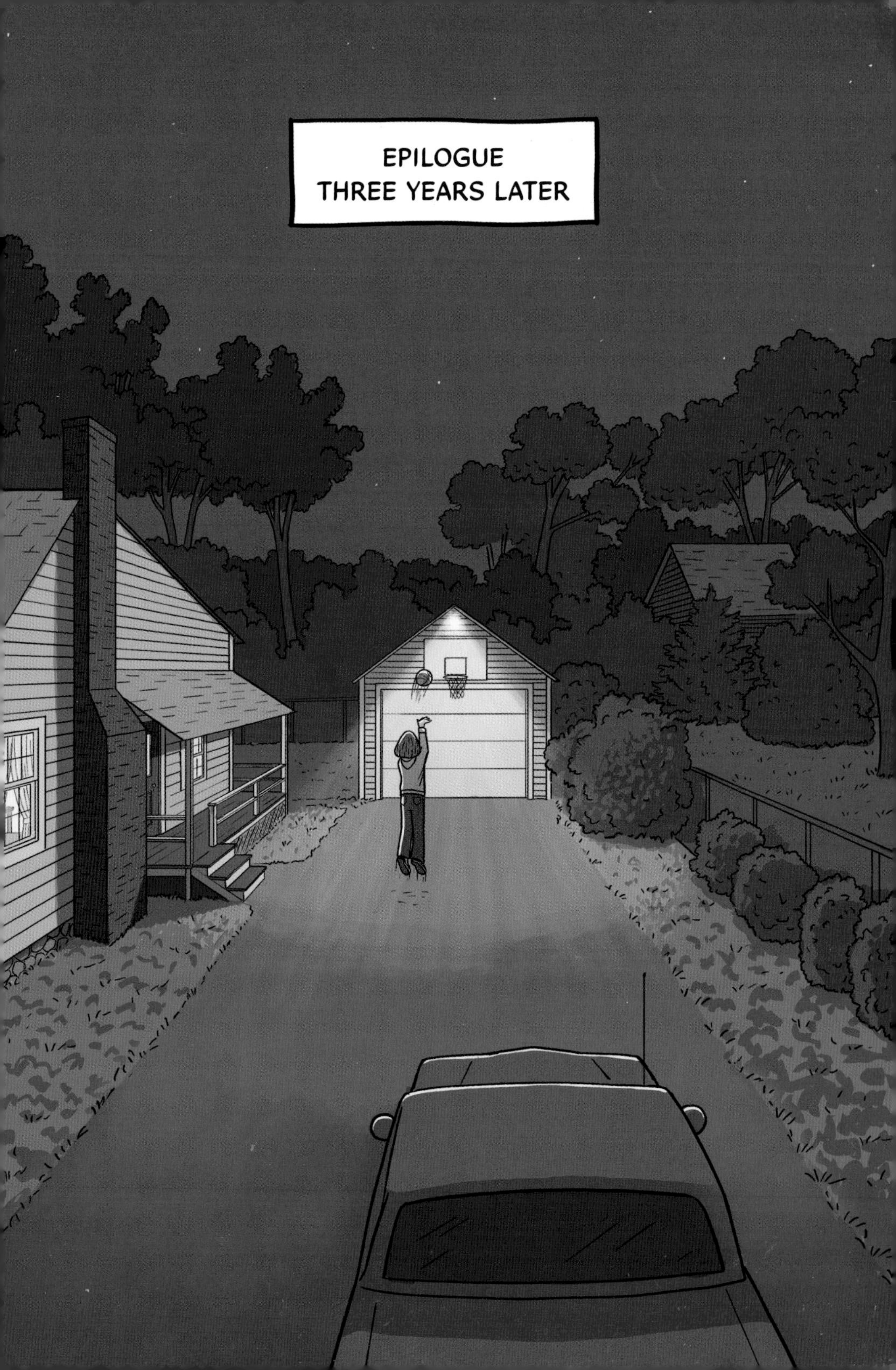
EPILOGUE
THREE YEARS LATER

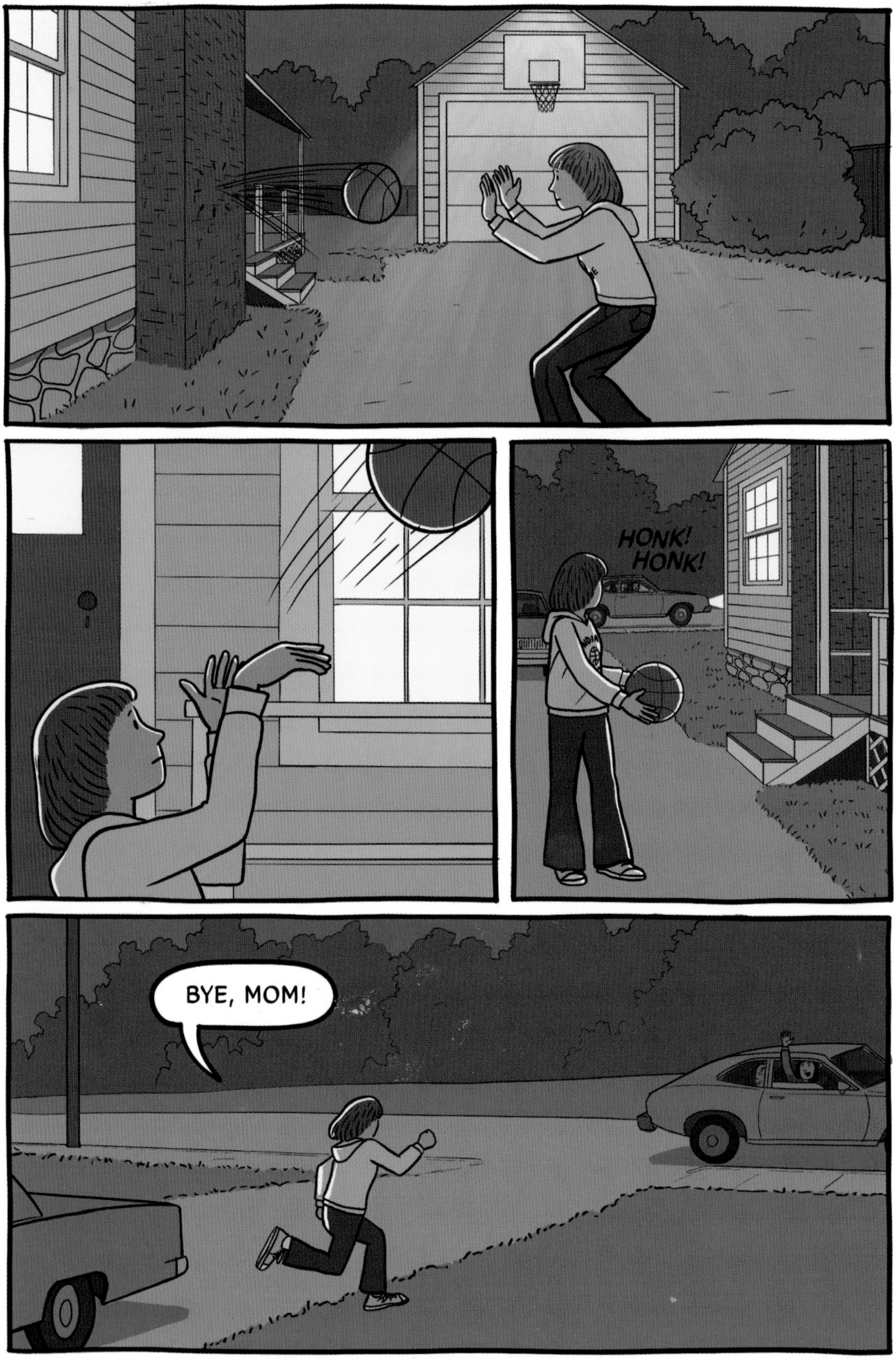
HONK! HONK!
BYE, MOM!

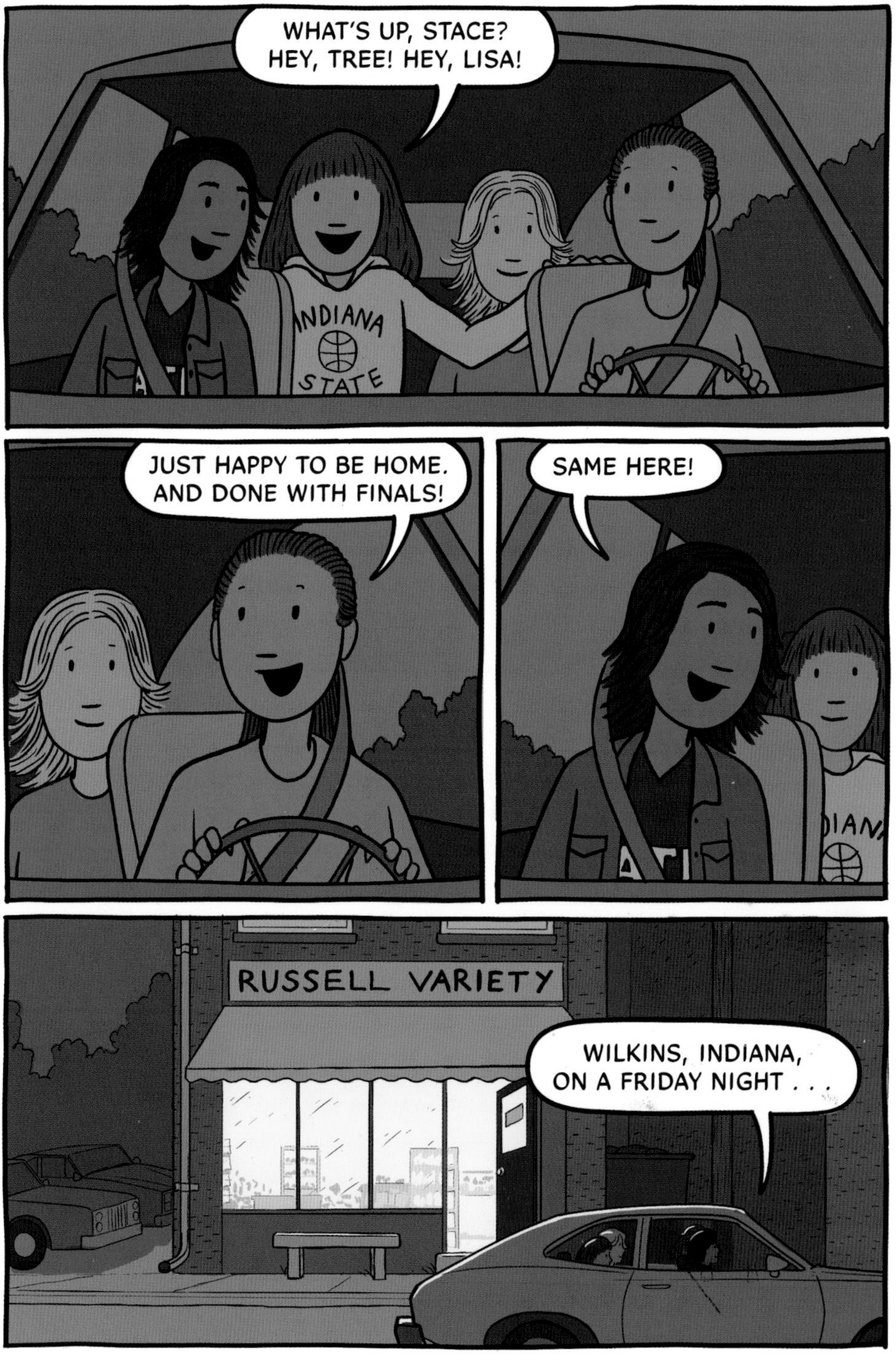

WHAT'S UP, STACE? HEY, TREE! HEY, LISA!
INDIANA STATE
JUST HAPPY TO BE HOME. AND DONE WITH FINALS!
SAME HERE!
RUSSELL VARIETY
WILKINS, INDIANA, ON A FRIDAY NIGHT . . .

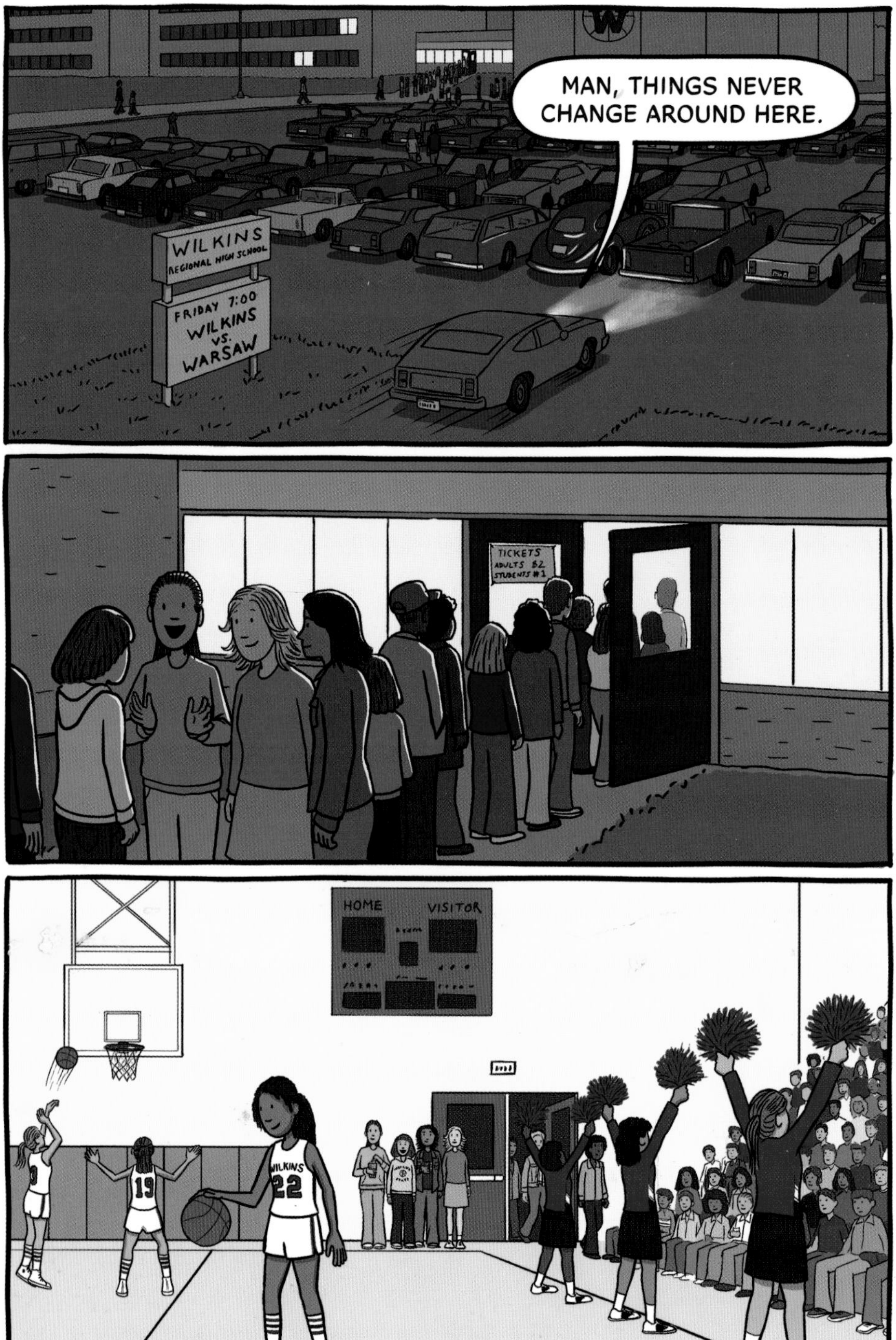
WILKINS
REGIONAL HIGH SCHOOL
FRIDAY 7:00
WILKINS
VS.
WARSAW
MAN, THINGS NEVER CHANGE AROUND HERE.
TICKETS
HOME
VISITOR
WILKINS
22
19

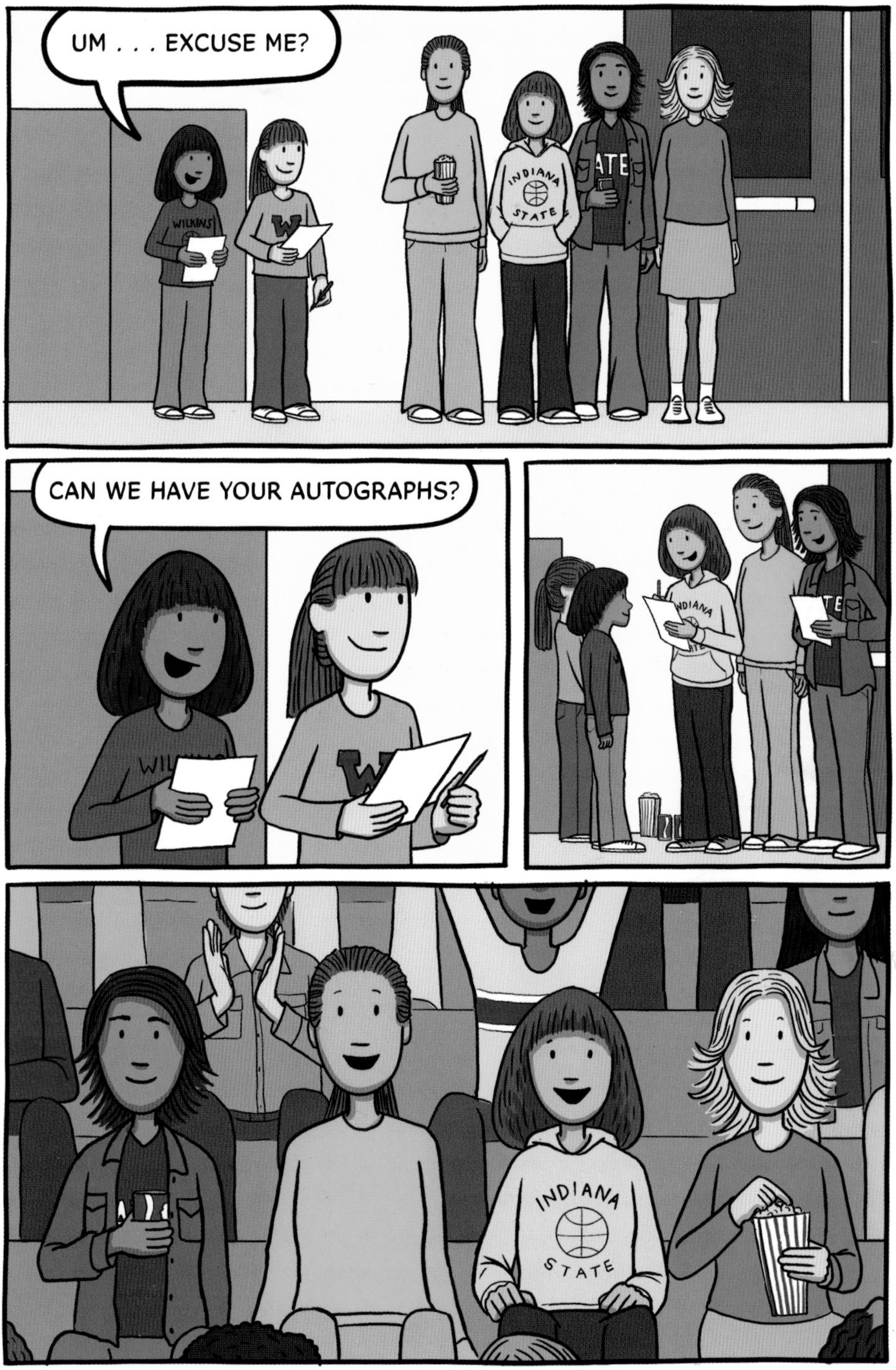
UM . . . EXCUSE ME?
WILKINS
INDIANA STATE
CAN WE HAVE YOUR AUTOGRAPHS?
INDIANA STATE

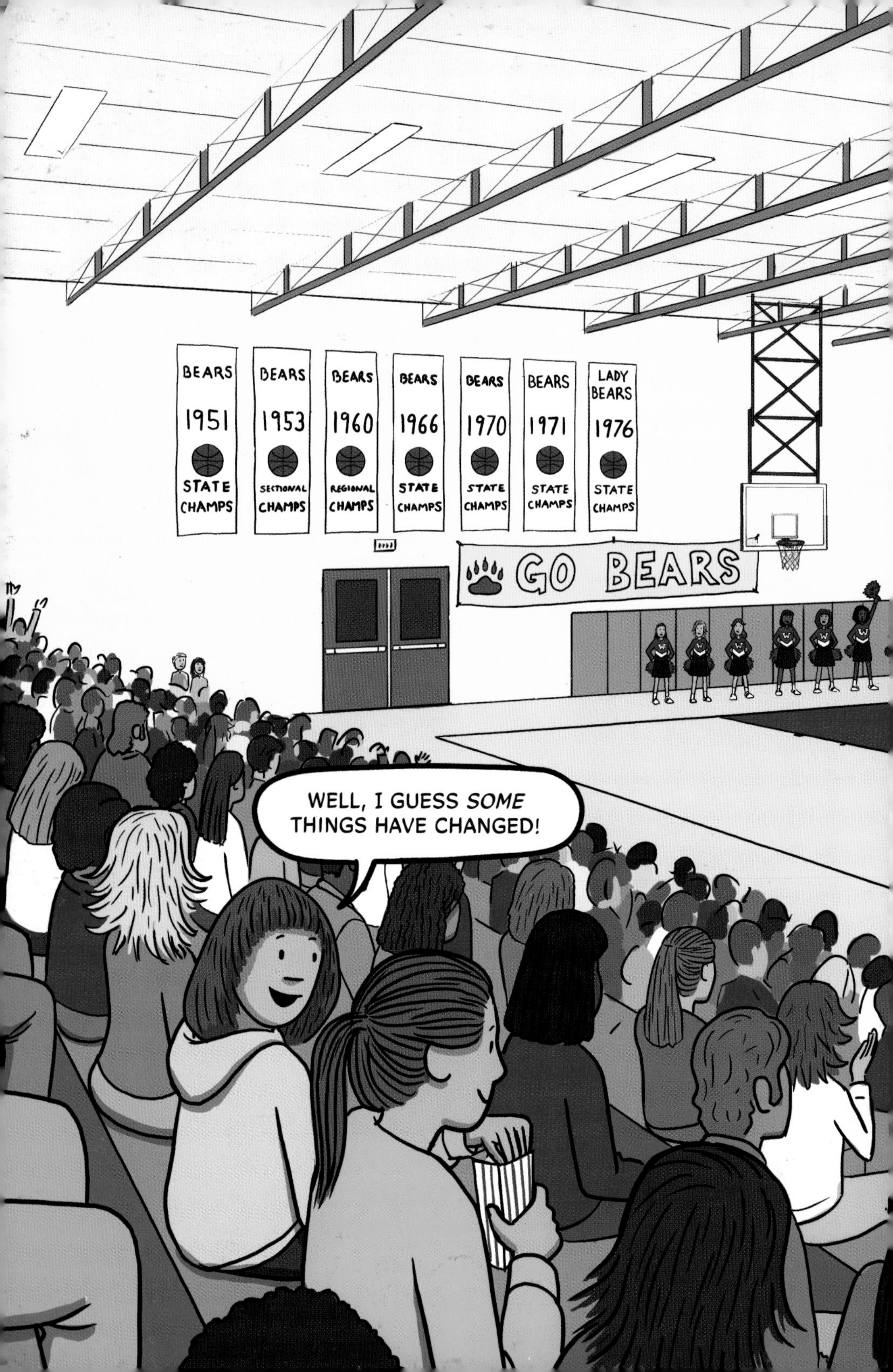
BEARS 1951 STATE CHAMPS
BEARS 1953 SECTIONAL CHAMPS
BEARS 1960 REGIONAL CHAMPS
BEARS 1966 STATE CHAMPS
BEARS 1970 STATE CHAMPS
BEARS 1971 STATE CHAMPS
LADY BEARS 1976 STATE CHAMPS
GO BEARS
WELL, I GUESS *SOME* THINGS HAVE CHANGED!

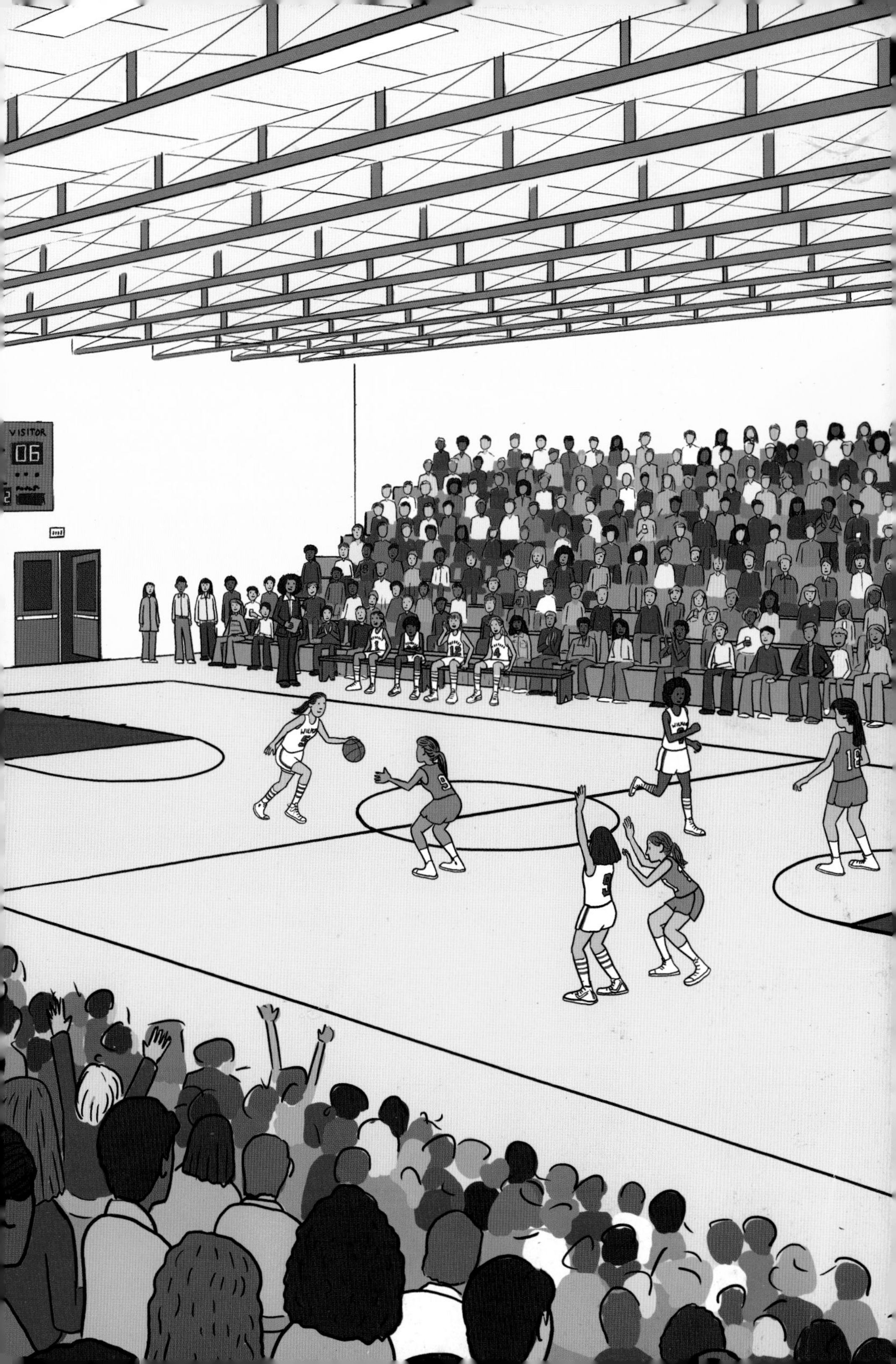
VISITOR
06

Hoops is a work of fiction, but it was inspired by the true story of Judi Warren and the 1976 Warsaw High School girls' basketball team. I first learned about this story back in early 2016, when I read Phillip Hoose's remarkable, eye-opening book, *We Were There, Too! Young People in U.S. History*. In this book, Hoose tells the history of the United States through dozens of fascinating stories about young people who made a difference in the world.

From the moment I first read the chapter about Judi Warren and her teammates, I felt like their story deserved its own book. I had written a few nonfiction picture books about professional athletes, and I loved the idea of creating a book that would show kids that sports heroes aren't always famous superstars making millions of dollars. Sometimes they're regular kids who play hard and stand up for what they believe is right.

I got in touch with Phillip Hoose to make sure I had his blessing before I ran with the idea. He kindly offered his full support and even helped me get in touch with the team's star player, Judi Warren. My plan, at first, was to tell this story as a nonfiction picture book, a format with which I was very familiar. I pitched the idea to the folks at Candlewick, and they were on board right away.

I started reading every article I could find about the team, and about Indiana high school basketball. I visited Hinkle Fieldhouse, in Indianapolis, where the Warsaw Tigers girls' basketball team had made history nearly a half century earlier. I spoke with three of the starting players—Judi Warren, Lisa Vandermark, and Cindy Ross Knepper, each of whom was incredibly generous with her time and shared such wonderful stories.

As I learned more about this team and dug deeper into the story, something unexpected happened: I stopped envisioning it as a picture book. I imagined something bigger, for an older audience. At the time, my daughters were thirteen and ten. I watched the way they devoured graphic novels like *Roller Girl*, by Victoria Jamieson, and *Smile*, by Raina Telgemeier, reading them over and over again. I felt like if I did it right, this could be that kind of story. I wanted to make a book that kids would want to read over and over again. Finally, I got up the nerve to tell my editor.

I wanted to make a graphic novel.

Of course, I had never made a graphic novel before. But my editor and art director at Candlewick trusted me to give it a try, for which I remain extremely grateful. The process seemed daunting at first. I didn't even know where to start. There were times when I got so stuck that I convinced myself that maybe doing a graphic novel just didn't make sense and maybe a picture book was actually the right way to go after all.

Perhaps the biggest roadblock I faced early on was figuring out how to tell a true story in graphic novel format. In most of the graphic novels I had read, the story was told primarily through pictures and dialogue. And since there was really no way for me to know exactly what these people said to one another several decades ago, that meant that I either needed to invent dialogue or somehow tell the story with no dialogue. Neither option appealed to me. I wanted my characters to be able to talk to one another, but not if it meant putting words in people's mouths that were never actually spoken.

Around that time, for inspiration, I rewatched the movie *Hoosiers*. One of the all-time great sports movies, *Hoosiers* tells the story of a fictional high school basketball team, inspired by the true story of a real high school basketball team. That got me thinking: maybe that was the solution. I started thinking of this book as a fictional story inspired by a true story. Suddenly my characters were free to talk to one another. They could joke around after practice. By writing the story as fiction, I could tell a great story that kids would (hopefully) want to read again and again while still honoring the legacy of what the 1976 Warsaw High School girls' basketball team accomplished.

Some of the characters in *Hoops* are loosely based on real people. Most obviously, the characters of Judi, Lisa, and Cindy are based largely on my conversations with their real-life counterparts, Judi Warren, Lisa Vandermark, and Cindy Ross Knepper. Other characters, like Stacy, are completely made up.

Much of the story in *Hoops* was inspired by real-life events. The 1976 Warsaw High School girls' basketball team really didn't have uniforms, or buses to games, or laundry service, or equal access to their own high school gym. A group of seniors, led by Lisa Vandermark, really did write a list of demands and take it to the athletic director. And the team really did go from playing games in front of a few loyal friends and family members early in the season to playing in front of an audience of tens of thousands of people on live prime-time television. The athletic director really did apologize to them in front of the entire school.

Before 1976, most people in Indiana had never watched a girls' basketball game. But for the tens of thousands of people who watched the girls' high school state championship game that year, either in person or on television, there was no denying that these girls could play. Judi Warren wasn't just a good basketball player "for a girl," as people at that time might have put it. She was a great basketball player, period. The 1976 Warsaw High School girls' basketball team not only changed the way that girls' sports teams were treated at their school; they also changed the way a lot of people thought about girls' sports in general, and they paved the way for countless girls who came after them.

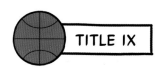

TITLE IX

Back when Judi and her teammates were in junior high, girls made up only 7 percent of high school athletes in the United States. But then Congress passed the 1972 Education Amendments, which included a section called Title IX. Title IX prohibited schools from discriminating based on sex and required schools to offer equal access and opportunities to girls, in education and extracurricular activities such as sports.

By the time Judi and her teammates were seniors in high school, four years later, 29 percent of high school athletes in the United States were girls. So while there was still plenty of room for improvement, Title IX had already had a huge impact.

In March 2021, as I was working on this book, University of Oregon basketball player Sedona Prince posted a video online, showing how the women's NCAA tournament workout facilities compared to the men's. All of the women's teams had to share one small rack of dumbbells, while the men's teams had access to a vast room filled with state-of-the-art exercise equipment. Her video went viral.

Soon after that, I got an email from Lisa Vandermark, the real-life inspiration for the character of Lisa in *Hoops*. "Reading about the NCAA's treatment of the women took me back forty-five years," she wrote. "Some things never change." However, because of the public backlash caused by the video, the NCAA apologized and set up a brand-new weight room for the women's teams.

As far as girls' and women's sports have come over the past half century, there is still a long way to go. And as frustrating as it is to know that athletes are still dealing with this type of inequality, I hope they can serve as inspiration to anyone reading this. History has shown that oftentimes change comes because of young people like Lisa Vandermark, Judi Warren, and Sedona Prince, who witness injustice and use their voice to take a stand for what they believe is right.

FOR AVA AND MOLLY, AND ALL THEIR TEAMMATES

ACKNOWLEDGMENTS

Thanks to Judi Warren, Lisa Vandermark, and Cindy Ross Knepper for answering all my questions and for taking the time to share their stories with me.

Phillip Hoose for introducing me to the story of the 1976 Warsaw High School girls' basketball team and for helping me get in touch with the players.

Katie Cunningham, Maryellen Hanley, Alex Robertson, and everyone at Candlewick Press for believing in me as I ventured way outside my comfort zone and for pushing me to make this book as good as it could possibly be.

My agent, Rosemary Stimola, for being a steady presence in my career, since the very beginning.

Scott Magoon, Ryan Higgins, Dan Santat, Mike Boldt, Renee Kurilla, Russ Cox, James Burks, and all my friends in the children's book community who offered encouragement and support, either online or in person, during the years I spent working on this book.

My nephew, Will Eastwood, who read and reread the first homemade copy of *Hoops* over and over again, back when it was just rough sketches printed on copy paper and held together in a three-ring binder, and compared it favorably to *Roller Girl*, which was pretty much the best compliment I could have hoped for.

Cece Bell, with whom I got to spend some time at an amazing conference called Nerd Camp in 2019, when I had almost given up on the idea of doing this book as a graphic novel, and whose infectious positive attitude helped convince me that I could do it and that it could be awesome.

The Eastwoods, the Woodwards, the Fogartys, the Bloodwells, the Smiths, and all my family and friends for their love and support.

My wife, Sarah, and my daughters, Ava and Molly, for everything.

My mother, Jane Tavares, for always being there for me.

And in loving memory of my father, Manuel J. Tavares.

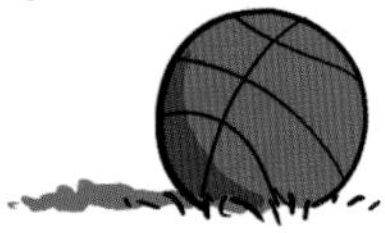

This is a work of fiction. Names, characters, places, and incidents are either products of the author's imagination or, if real, are used fictitiously. First edition 2023. Library of Congress Catalog Card Number 2022907002. ISBN 978-1-5362-0136-9 (hardcover). ISBN 978-1-5362-3195-3 (paperback). This book was typeset in Legendary Legerdemain and Gilroy. The illustrations were created digitally.
Candlewick Press, 99 Dover Street, Somerville, Massachusetts 02144. www.candlewick.com.
Printed in Shenzhen, Guangdong, China. 22 23 24 25 26 27 CCP 10 9 8 7 6 5 4 3 2 1